THEORETICALLY
PERFECT

AMY BAILEY
ALEXANDER C. EBERHART

THEORETICALLY PERFECT

Copyright © 2024 Amy Bailey & Alexander C. Eberhart

All rights reserved. No part of this publication may be reproduced, stored in a retrieval system, or transmitted, in any form or by any means (electronic, mechanical, photocopying, recording, or otherwise), without the prior written permission of the publisher.

This book is a work of fiction and does not represent any individual living or dead. Names, characters, places, and incidents either are products of the author's imagination or are used fictitiously.

FOR THOSE WHO SANG PRAISES TO A GOD
WHO ASKED FOR SILENCE.

ONE
CALEB

Saturday, December 16

"A church service? Like, with the preacher and the choir in robes and all that bullshit?"

Wren watches me from the edge of my bed, shreds of paper scattered around them in piles as they brandish a pair of scissors. They reach over to the nightstand, mashing the volume button on the side of my phone to quiet the Djo album I've got on loop.

"Yeah, I guess so," I reply, standing in front of my closet. "Theo didn't go into specifics." A pile of summer clothes I haven't touched in months covers the floorboards, a neglected assortment of bright colors and loose fabrics. Even my winter wardrobe–a conglomeration of hoodies and sweaters with holes worn in the sleeves–seems too bright for what I've dreamed up in my head. Aren't church services somber affairs? Or maybe that's only when there's a funeral.

"And you agreed to this?" Wren presses, brushing dark bangs from their eyes. "Without a gun pressed to your head?"

"It's Theo's family, Wren. I can't say no to the *only* thing they've ever invited me to. If Theo and I are going to work long-term, I've got to make an effort to connect with his family. I mean, Nate already loves me, but this could really help me score some points with his parents." I grab the cream-colored dress shirt from the hanger, holding it out in front of me as I turn to the mirror. "Oh good, I can look like a waiter. Perfect."

"I have a black button-down you can borrow," Wren says, gently pushing me out of the way as they help themselves to my closet. "You can wear it with this." They hold out a sparkly red bowtie my nana gave me for my birthday two years ago when I was going through a preppy phase.

I take the tie, running my fingers over the silky material. "You don't think it's too… loud?"

Wren cocks an eyebrow. "Are you sure you want to do this, Caleb? I know Theo would understand if you were uncomfortable. Hell, I'd be squirming out of my skin."

"It's fine," I say quickly, a heat prickling at the back of my neck. "Theo has been doing so well these last few weeks, and I want to do this for him. So what if I'm a little uncomfortable?"

Wren may not say anything outright, but you could fill a textbook with all the warnings coming from their face. And I know they're just looking out for me, but their knowing look makes me want to scream.

It's fine. Just one morning spent in a church. What's the worst that could happen?

"I'll go with the tie," I say, hoping at least it appeases them enough to drop the silent treatment. "Can I grab the shirt from you tomorrow?"

"Sure," Wren replies, their voice tight as they pick up their backpack from the bed, set aside the scissors, then check their phone. "I should get going anyway. My dad is landing at the airport in a couple of hours, and I promised Mom I'd ride down with her to pick him up."

"Your dad?" I repeat, my brain trying to wrap around the words. "I thought he was in Australia?"

Wren slings their bag over their shoulder. "He was, which explains the whole plane and airport thing."

"Sorry, I just–I didn't know he was coming into town."

"I told you last week," Wren says, hovering by the door. "Just a little holiday surprise. Nothing like some awkward family interactions to get you in the mood. Mama is already on edge because Mom agreed to let him stay at the house, so she'll probably have a nervous breakdown by Christmas Eve. Oh what fun. Wish me luck."

"Good luck," I call after them, but they're already down the hallway. I lean a shoulder into the wall, deflating with a sigh.

Man, I can't believe I missed that. How could I forget something so important in Wren's life? And here they were, helping me with my own silly problems, cutting pictures out for Theo's Christmas gift, and worrying about how I'm going to feel setting foot in a church for the first time. At least, a church that isn't haunted, that is.

My phone buzzes on the nightstand, pulling me out of my introspection. I open Theo's message, a smile growing across my face.

> **THEO**: gingerbread house is looking a little sketchy this year. We let Nate handle the frosting, and it's… well, I'll let you be the judge.

The picture comes through, and I can't stop laughing. Every joint of the gingerbread house oozes with a milky, wet goo that looks far too sus. Another buzz and a second picture arrives, Theo giving his brother a concerned look as he holds the door of the gingerbread house, the edges glistening with the questionable icing.

> **CALEB**: Incredible. Tell Nate that he's a legend, and he's in charge of all gingerbread construction from this day forward. Those gingerbread men have been having the time of their lives.

Heat lingers in my cheeks as I head downstairs, past the giant tree in the living room that's surrounded by open plastic bins because Mom is still decorating even though we're a week from Christmas, and into the kitchen, where I find Lola glued to the breakfast table same as when I got home three hours ago. Flames flicker from a candle on the countertop, filling the room with the scent of freshly baked cookies, even though I'm pretty sure the oven hasn't been turned on since Thanksgiving.

"Mom still at the office?" I ask, opening the fridge and grabbing a soda from the drawer.

Lola doesn't even look up from her laptop, the glowing white square reflected in her glasses a constant presence in the room. "Settlement negotiations. You know how people get around the holidays. All that generosity and peace on earth bullshit never extends to our line of work, unfortunately. I literally saw someone put in their settlement request that his wife not tell their kid that Santa isn't real if they share custody. Can you imagine making it to fourteen years old and still believing in jolly ol' Saint Nick?"

"People believe wilder things."

Lola finally looks up from her computer screen, her brow furrowed. "Yeah, I guess so."

"And it's fine," I say, running with the train of thought that starts picking up steam through my head. "Because, much like Santa Claus, people need to be able to believe in something. Something that makes them feel good and like the world isn't an active dumpster fire."

"Uh-huh." Lola watches me, the screen on her laptop dimming enough that I can see the whites of her eyes again through the glare.

"And just because *I* don't believe in Santa doesn't mean that I have to go around and try and convince other people that Santa isn't real, right? I mean, it would be wild for me to walk into a Santa convention and start spouting off facts about how outrageous it is to believe one festively plump holiday deity breaks into billions of people's homes while streaking through the sky faster than the speed of light, being pulled by magical cryptids that can fly but also have enough self-awareness to bully each other for their physical differences, right?"

Lola blinks. "You lost me. Let's skip to the part where you tell me what that was really about."

I take a long sip from my soda, the bubbles tickling my nose. Should I explain that I'm having second thoughts about going to Theo's church thing? It's not like I've intended to keep it a secret from my family. It's just been a busy week. Or at least that's the story I keep telling myself.

To be honest, I'm afraid they're going to try and talk me out of it. And if that happens, how am I supposed to be able to face Theo? I told him that I'd be there when he needed me. And that includes church functions, I guess.

"Theo invited me to his church tomorrow."

"And?" Lola coaxes me.

"I'm nervous," I admit for the first time out loud. "This is a huge step for our relationship–not just the two of us, but with me and his family. I mean, his mom is cool with us hanging out and whatever, but his dad literally won't even look at me when I'm at their house. It's like I'm invisible. So, if this will help him see that I'm making an effort to connect with his son, maybe it will go a long way into him coming around?"

Lola's expression softens. "Yeah, maybe."

"What is it?" I ask, sinking into the chair across from her.

She shakes her head. "Nothing. It's nothing."

Now I *know* she's lying. "You think it's a bad idea?"

"No," she says through a sigh. "I'm just worried about you, Caleb."

I swallow loudly. "Why?"

"Because you're my brother. And because I know people like Theo's dad don't change their minds very often. I just don't want to see you get hurt if things don't turn out the way you planned."

"So, I'll just make sure they do," I argue, my cheeks burning hot. "I'll do everything right, so his dad has to accept us. He'll see how happy I make

Theo, and he'll change his mind. He has to."

Lola looks down at her hands, her nose scrunching like it does when she's holding back tears. "Yeah, totally. If anyone can do it, you can."

I tug at the collar of my sweater, heat pooling at the nape of my neck. Lola doesn't say anything else; she just gives me a brief smile before returning to her laptop. The kitchen falls quiet, but my head is filled with noise. I wish Dad were here. He would know how to make me feel better. How to make sense of the swelling chaos that's hijacked my brain. But he won't be back in town till Christmas Eve, and there's no guarantee he'd pick up if I called him right now.

So, I do the next best thing, pulling out my earbuds and drowning out the noise with another round of Djo.

I can do this. I can keep us together.

I have to.

For Theo.

Sunday, December 17

The auditorium—or what did Theo call it? A sanctuary?—is nearly full when we walk in, a countdown clock displayed on either side of the stage reminding me how late I've made us. Theo scans the rows of finely dressed people, looking for the seats his mom saved for us. He finally spots her and leads us up the side aisle just as the band onstage begins to play, and the clock flashes zeros across the screen. Theo slides in first, mumbling excuses to the people already seated, and I follow along, my cheeks burning from embarrassment.

Theo's mom—Kora, she's asked me to call her—leans over and whispers something in his ear that makes the edges of his mouth twitch, but then he turns to me and gives a weak smile. I don't want to know what she said, but it's not hard to guess. I've already messed things up.

A guy with perfectly quaffed hair and a spray tan to rival reality TV royalty greets the congregation, inviting everyone to stand as they sing a song I've never heard of.

It's kind of like being at a concert, I guess. That's not so weird.

Theo keeps glancing over like he's afraid I'll bolt. I grip the back of the chair in front of me and glue my eyes to the screen displaying lyrics, doing my best to mumble along with everyone else.

To call the morning so far a disaster would be an understatement. My nerves kept me up far too late, worrying over the fit of the shirt I borrowed from Wren and whether or not I should wear the sparkly bow tie. Theo stayed on the phone with me till midnight, and after he had to go, I couldn't settle down, so I ended up mindlessly scrolling on my phone and fell asleep without setting an alarm, which meant being rudely awakened by Lola banging on my bedroom door because Theo was waiting in the driveway and scrambling to look even halfway presentable while Theo waited patiently downstairs. He'd never want to make me feel bad, but I know I stressed him out.

So, operation "Make Theo's Parents Like Me" hasn't gotten off on the right foot, but I'm determined not to make any more mistakes.

The song ends, and everyone returns to their seats as Spray Tan Guy starts talking with his eyes closed and it takes me a second to catch on that he's praying. Theo gives me a nudge, tucking his chin to his chest, and I quickly do the same.

"Father God, we thank You for each and every one of us who are here to celebrate the reason for the season, Your son, Jesus Christ."

A flurry of "Amens" ripple through the crowd around me.

Shit. Was I supposed to say it, too? I quickly mutter my own, "Amen."

Theo gives me a quizzical look, and I elbow him.

"Father, there are so many out there today who have lost focus this holiday season. They're hung up on things that don't really matter. Presents. Traveling. Watching all of those awful Hallmark Movies."

A gray-haired man on the row in front of us bursts out laughing, and Spray Tan Guy grins, his eyes still closed as the band begins to play softly under his words.

"Please bless Pastor Sheppard as he comes to bring us the good word. We ask these things in the name of Your Son, Jesus Christ. Amen."

Another round of "Amens" from the crowd, and Spray Tan Guy abandons his spot center stage as the lights dim and a group of people–dressed in white draping fabrics–start to stream across the stage, lining up along the back on risers in three distinct rows. The lights above us dim, candles lighting along the front of the stage as a guy dressed in all black lugs a huge wooden podium to the center, setting it down gently before hauling ass offstage.

The choir begins to vocalize along with the band, some ethereal tune that I'm sure sounds beautiful in the right context, but someone in the alto section is really off-key, and it's very distracting.

"God sent an angel to Nazareth, a town in Galilee."

A light illuminates that weird wooden podium and a man with salt-and-pepper hair stands at it now, leaning into the tiny microphone sticking out of the top. He's not dressed in strange robes like the rest of the people onstage, but in the most boring beige suit I've ever seen, complete with a brown tie. He pulls on a pair of glasses before he continues, "In Nazareth, there was a virgin named Mary. She was betrothed to a man named Joseph, from the family of David. The angel appeared to her and said…"

"Greetings!"

One of the white-robed people steps away from the choir, the spotlight hitting them and illuminating their pale, washed-out face. A woman enters the light beside them, dressed in drab-looking cuts of fabric. She reminds me of the town beggars they have at the Renaissance Fair every year, although they put on silly shows about washing clothes and performing sexual favors, so I get the feeling appearances are where the similarities will end.

"The Lord has blessed you and is with you, Mary."

The man at the podium picks up, "But Mary was very startled by what the angel said," he pauses long enough for the woman to react, clutching her chest like she's about to keel over. "And she wondered what this greeting might mean."

"What does this greeting mean?" the woman says in a voice that borders on robotic. She makes a sweeping gesture and steps half out of the spotlight.

Move over, Emma Stone. There's a new Oscar contender in the house.

I bite down on my tongue to keep from laughing.

"Don't be afraid, Mary," says the angel, grabbing her by the arm and pulling her back into the light. "God has shown you grace. You will become pregnant and give birth to a son, and you will name him Jesus. The Lord will give him a throne, and he will rule over the house of Jacob forever!"

"But how will this happen, since I am a virgin?" the theatrically-challenged Mary asks.

"The Holy Spirit will come upon you—"

A snorting laugh escapes the back of my throat, and I slap a hand over my mouth. Theo tenses in his seat beside me, and from two seats down, Kora leans over to look at me. I fake cough into my hand, giving her a shaky thumbs up with the other, and sink lower in my seat.

Keep it together, Caleb.

The choir is singing now, some joyous proclamation about Mary being knocked up by a ghost or something. I kinda missed a few lines there in the middle. Theo leans over ever-so-slightly closer, whispering, "You don't have to laugh every time someone says the word 'come.'"

At first, I'm worried he's mad at me, but then I catch the playful smirk on his lips, so I whisper back, "You could have warned me. I wasn't prepared for an impregnation by spirit spunk."

Theo's shoulders shake as he holds back his laughter, and the coiled tightness in my chest lessens. Maybe I'm not screwing up so badly. Or maybe he just doesn't care. Either way, it's a relief.

The wild story continues, acted out by what I can only assume are the most "creative" members of the congregation. Mary sports a swollen belly under the dirty clothes, and the guy playing Joseph looks like he's a good thirty years older than her. They cross from one side of the stage to the other as the choir sings song after song about angels and how brave Mary is, and honestly, it's kind of hard to keep up. But about half an hour into the program, they bring in an actual fucking donkey for Mary to ride on, and to be honest, I spent the rest of the time trying to figure out how the hell they got it on the stage.

Can donkeys climb stairs? Do they have an elevator backstage specifically for barnyard animals? What kind of budget are they working with here at Specter Christian Church?

Before I know it, there's a crying baby in Mary's arms and a bunch of people standing around her in a hay-filled hovel as the music swells for a final time and the lights return to normal in the auditorium.

The crowd applauds as the cast takes a bow, and I have to shove my fist in my mouth to keep from laughing as Mary's baby bump (a big red kickball with the word "Pow!" in bold letters) hits the ground and rolls across the stage.

"We hope you'll remember the reason for this season," the beige-suited man says, closing the large leather-bound book on his podium. "And as we invite those of you who are feeling the calling of Christ to come forward, we encourage those who are led toward generosity to please drop those tithes and gifts into the baskets located at the foot of the stage."

The band starts up as Spray Tan Guy appears from the wings, leading yet another song. The woman beside me taps me on the shoulder, and I step forward enough that she can squeeze by, joining the line of people now forming in the aisle. Some kneel down on the stairs to the stage. Others drop off envelopes into wicker baskets. And still more wait in line to speak with the man in the beige suit as he prays over them, one at a time, with hands raised up.

It's... a lot to take in. But since everyone is distracted by what's going on, I take the opportunity to watch Theo. His lips move along to the words of the song, but his voice is so soft I can barely hear it. Which is odd because I'm used to him shout-singing along to *Come On Eileen* in the car on our way to school. But here, he hides his hands in his pockets, and when the song comes to an end, his lips pull tight.

He just seems so… muted. But maybe that's how everyone is at church?

"Thank you all for joining us," Spray Tan Guy says, flashing a blindingly white smile. "We hope you enjoyed the story of our savior, and wish you all a merry Christmas from our family to yours."

With that, the lights come up full strength, and the auditorium comes alive around us as people weave through the aisles, shaking hands, hugging shoulders, and wiping tears away from misty eyes. I cling to Theo like a life raft, not wanting to be separated from him in these uncharted waters.

He gets quiet as we make our way through the crowds, focusing on the space where his feet fall instead of how many people are around, but then we're clear of the cluster of bodies, and Theo pulls me into a quiet corner, perking up again.

"What did you think?" he asks, grinning. He seems to realize he's standing really close, so he takes a half step back.

"Uh, It was… kinda camp."

Theo laughs, running a hand through his dark curls. "Yeah, it's not always like this. I told them to pull out all the stops to impress my–" he glances over his shoulder then leans in closer to say, "boyfriend."

"Shut up, you're so corny." I give him a playful shove, my cheeks burning. "I'm definitely going to need you to fill in some gaps in the storyline for me. I kinda zoned out in the middle, and I want to make sure I have everything straight."

Theo raises an eyebrow at me. "Seriously? It's the Christmas story. Haven't you heard it before?"

I shake my head. "The only Christmas stories my family is interested in involve stop-motion reindeer and Tim Allen dressed as Santa Claus."

"Oh man, I just threw you into all this, didn't I?" Theo reaches for me, then stops himself, shoving his hand into his pocket. "Yeah, sure. I can fill you in on all the craziness. We can talk on the way back home. Mom invited some people over for lunch, and she said that you're welcome to join us."

"Are you sure?" I ask, suddenly aware of just how much I want to touch him. An older woman catches my eye a couple of feet away, her eyes lingering on my sparkly bowtie. "I understand if it's easier that I'm not around."

Theo looks like I've slapped him. "Never say that again. I'll always want you around, Caleb."

My pulse thrums, the tips of my fingers tingling as he brushes his hand against my arm. "Cool. So, uh, what's for lunch?"

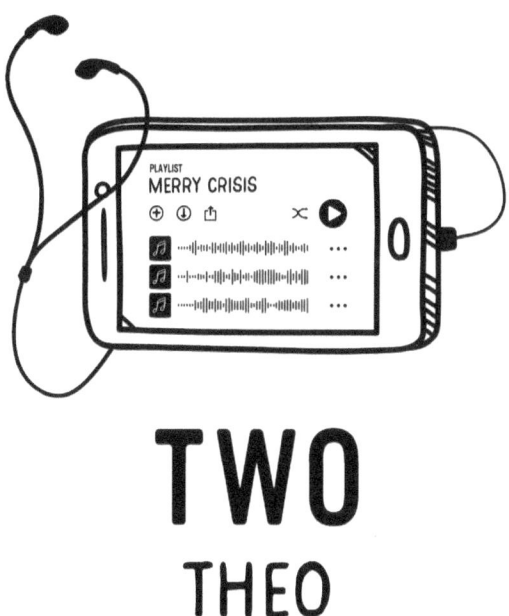

TWO
THEO

"So, you're saying Mary was a literal virgin?"

"Yep."

"Like...by ancient history standards, or like–"

I chuckle. "I don't know. Just a virgin. That's all the Bible says, and that's what makes Jesus's birth a miracle."

Caleb doesn't reply right away, so I quickly cast a glance at him in the passenger seat. His nose is scrunched in that adorable way I love, but there's a furrow between his brows that I wish I could smooth with my fingers. I'd do it in a heartbeat if I weren't driving.

"But, like," he starts again, just as confused as before. "How could they prove that? Back then?"

I shrug. "They probably couldn't. That's just what the Bible says about it. It's kind of part of the whole thing. There was a prophecy from like a thousand years before that said that Jesus would be born of a virgin, so...that's how people knew he was going to be the Savior."

"But that's not..." he trails off, then shakes his head. "Sorry. I shouldn't—I don't know. I'm just trying to understand."

"It's okay," I reply, squeezing his hand. "Don't apologize. I grew up on this story, and you didn't. I totally understand that it's all new to you."

Caleb hesitates a moment. "Yeah. It's…different."

I frown. Something about his tone is off, but I'm not sure if I should pry. Especially since–

"Yeah, Ian said the same thing," Nathaniel pipes up from the backseat, startling both Caleb and me. "He's never been to a church before. I think his parents are agey-ists."

I snort. "Do you mean 'atheists?'"

"Isn't that what I said?"

Caleb huffs a laugh out of his nose as I roll my eyes. "Sure," I say with a smirk, glancing at Nate in the rearview mirror. "Anyway, so yeah. That's the story."

Caleb nods. "Huh. Cool."

I want to press Caleb for more than just a 'huh, cool,' but we're already out of time. I pull into the driveway and park Eileen—my beloved red Honda Fit—in my usual spot, recognizing the Sheppards' silver SUV parked directly behind my dad's truck. All thoughts of the Christmas story and the desire to answer Caleb's questions are quickly replaced with anxiety again. Post-church lunches with my parents' friends can be…tricky. Especially throwing Caleb into the mix.

When it comes to acknowledging my newfound bisexuality, my parents are in two very different camps. Mom is trying her best to be accepting of my and Caleb's relationship. She almost always refers to Caleb as my boyfriend and extends the same house rules to us as she did with Sienna and me when it comes to being alone: no closed doors and no excessive physical touching. All things considered, I should be ecstatic about it. Dad, however, exists in a state of denial about the whole thing and has chosen to ignore our relationship altogether. He's cordial to Caleb for the most part, but he pretends that Caleb is just another one of my friends. It frustrates me sometimes—especially because I can tell it bothers Caleb—but honestly, it's far better than him barring Caleb from visiting, so I don't push back. It's not worth fighting over.

Unfortunately, though, when it comes to church and engaging with people from church, my parents are a united front: Caleb is a new friend from school. Period. Mom says it's to avoid unwanted attention, but I know shame and embarrassment when I see it.

I try not to think about it too much.

Fortunately, I also spot Harrison's white Toyota Corolla parked on the curb, and it eases some of the fear. At least we'll have Harrison and Elise to lessen the pressure on Caleb and me.

"Whose car is that?" Caleb asks as we step out of my car, pointing at the SUV.

"The Sheppards," I say quietly. "The, um—the pastor and his wife. And maybe their kids, I'm not sure."

Caleb's eyes go wide. "Like, the main guy from today?"

I nod, biting my lower lip. "He's pretty cool. You know, for a pastor."

Caleb goes quiet again, which triggers another spike of anxiety. I wish more than anything I could wrap him in my arms and kiss the worry from his face, but I can't risk the Sheppards seeing us being affectionate.

This sucks.

"Ugh, I hope Miriam's not here," Nathaniel grumbles as he shuts the backseat door. "I think Mom and Mrs. Sarah are trying to set us up."

I snicker. Miriam is the oldest of Mark and Sarah Sheppard's five daughters, and one year younger than Nathaniel. "That doesn't surprise me."

Nate makes a face. "I mean, she's nice and everything, but…" he trails off, scrunching his nose. "Not my type."

Before I can press Nate further or try to fill Caleb in on who Miriam is, Harrison's large hand claps me on the shoulder, nearly giving me a heart attack. "Hey, guys."

"Shit, Harry," I reply breathlessly, turning around to greet him and Elise. "I thought y'all were already inside."

Harrison shakes his head. "There's no way we're going in there without you guys. Talk about awkward."

He has a point. "Fair. Thank you both again for coming today. It means a lot."

"What are friends for?" Elise replies with a nervous smile. "Besides, it's one lunch. How bad could it possibly be?"

Just as I open my mouth to chastise Elise for saying the one phrase you're never supposed to say in times like this, a smaller blue SUV pulls into the driveway and parks directly behind Eileen. From behind the wheel, an eager, spiky-haired, Ray-ban-wearing Chase waves at us excitedly. His petite wife, Megan, offers us a kind, timid smile from the passenger seat.

"Shit," I whisper through clenched teeth, smiling and waving back.

"Who is that, again?" Caleb asks, matching my quiet volume.

"Chase. He's the youth pastor."

"So, like...another pastor, but just for the teenagers?"

Man, Caleb really is clueless about all of this. "Something like that."

"Theo, my man!" Chase calls out as he steps out of his car. "How are you, brother?"

I force a smile. "I'm good. How are you?"

"Better than I deserve," Chase replies with a wink. "Harry! Elise! Good to see y'all!"

"Good to see you too, Chase," Harrison says politely. Elise just smiles.

Chase takes off his sunglasses and flashes Caleb a curious grin. "Hey, man, I don't believe we've met! I'm Chase, the youth pastor at SCC!" He shoots a hand out to Caleb.

Caleb takes it and shakes his hand. "Caleb."

"Are you a friend of Theo's from school?"

Caleb nods. "Yep. A good friend."

"Well, welcome to the family, brother!" Chase bellows, promptly pulling Caleb in for a hug. Caleb stiffens but takes it, glancing at me nervously. All I can do is mouth an apology. As Chase lets go, he immediately wraps an arm around Megan, who is carrying some kind of casserole dish. "This is Megan—my smokin' hot wife and the love of my life."

Caleb blinks, and I can almost feel how hard he's trying not to visibly cringe. "Nice to meet you both."

"Nice to meet you, too, Caleb," Megan says brightly, then smiles at the rest of us. "Are y'all staying for lunch?"

I nod. "Yes, ma'am."

"Epic!" Chase says. "Let's get in there and eat!"

Chase and Megan lead the way to the front door, allowing the rest of us to exchange awkward glances as we file in behind them. I linger as close to Caleb as possible, brushing our pinkies together and offering a small smile that Caleb returns.

The moment we cross the threshold, I can already feel sweat permeating my thick layers. It's sweltering inside—an overcompensation of central heat to combat the cold outside, combined with the warmth radiating from the kitchen and the body heat of far too many people gathered in one place. To add to the sensory assault, a wild array of food smells hit my nose at once—ham, deviled eggs, cinnamon, garlic, and probably an excessive number of casseroles—and my stomach churns. From somewhere in the living room, I can hear an old Michael W. Smith Christmas album from the 90s playing, and while the music feels nostalgic in a vacuum, its presence amidst this specific kind of chaos fills me with a unique sense of dread.

"Oh, boy," Harrison mutters under his breath. I couldn't agree more.

"There you are, Theo," Dad says, descending the stairs as our eyes meet. His tone is stern but masked by his trademark politeness around company. "Go help your mother in the kitchen with drinks, please."

"I'm on it," I reply, compliance overtaking me immediately.

"Cal, come with us," Elise says in a rather uncharacteristically soft tone, looping her arm through Caleb's and leading him away from the mayhem with Harrison in tow.

With Caleb safe, I focus on the task at hand and try not to stress too much about how many people are in the kitchen. Granted, it's only Mom, Megan, Sarah, and two of the Sheppard daughters, but the energy and heat are already draining me.

"Oh, hi, Theo!" Sarah says excitedly. "My goodness, you get more handsome every time I see you!"

I force a smile. "Hi, Mrs. Sarah."

Mom flashes me a huge smile. "He really does, doesn't he?"

I turn back to the plastic cups, trying to hide my burning embarrassment. "Hey, Mom, how many people are we going to have?"

"Um, probably around twenty, I think. Right, Sarah?"

"Yes, we're just waiting for the Taylors and Miss Cynthia."

My stomach drops. Fuck. *More* people are coming?

"You and your friends are welcome to go downstairs after lunch, though, *aroha*," Mom adds with a wink. "Nate and the girls will help clean up."

I want to hug her, but it's too hot and weird. "Thank you."

"About time you showed up."

I nearly yelp with surprise at Grace's teasing voice behind me. "Jeez, Grace," I say, whipping around to face her. She's sporting a surprisingly festive sweater and wide-leg jeans, cuffed just enough to show off her beloved Doc Marten boots. "I thought you were working today."

Grace grins, her new lip piercing catching the light. "And miss the annual Briggs' Sunday Christmas lunch? Not a chance!"

I furrow my brow at her. I know her better than that. Grace hates these things almost as much as I do.

Her smile falters, and she leans in a little closer. "Mom begged," she mutters. "Apparently it can be a little…much in here with *them*." She nods towards the other women bustling around the kitchen. Now that she mentions it, Mom does look uncomfortable. "Plus, I figured you could use someone else in the ring with you if Dad decides to start anything."

I shake my head. "He wouldn't do that," I counter. "Never in front of company."

"I wouldn't put it past him," Grace insists, tearing open another roll of plastic cups next to me. "I mean, you've seen how worked up he gets about stuff sometimes."

A fresh wave of anxiety makes its way through my gut. She's not wrong. In early November, Grace and some of her schoolmates put together an incredibly detailed dossier for my parents to prove that homosexuality is not the abominable sin that the church has historically painted it to be after all. Unsurprisingly, Dad completely blew it off, claiming that everything Grace was presenting was nothing more than secular propaganda. Mom, on the other hand, vowed to keep an open mind, and I've seen her reading it from time to time. It gives Grace and I hope that Mom cares about us, but I can tell it upsets Dad that she's even entertaining it at all.

My parents rarely fight, but over the past few weeks, I've walked in on several heated arguments about all of it—Grace's dossier, Mom's open-mindedness, my relationship with Caleb—and it fills me with a special kind of dread and guilt I've never experienced before. I try not to think about it.

"Well," I finally reply, keeping my voice low. "I still don't think he'd make a scene in front of church people. Or anyone outside of family, really."

Grace sighs. "I hope you're right."

"Grace, honey, can you come help me with these platters?" Mom calls out from the other side of the kitchen.

"Heard, chef," Grace answers. She turns to me and gives my hair a gentle ruffle. "Hang in there, bud."

"You, too."

It feels like ages, but it only takes a few more minutes to set up everything for drinks. When I'm finally done, I escape the kitchen to find Caleb, Harrison, and Elise. As predicted, they're huddled on the deck outside, so I make a beeline for the back door.

"Hey, Theo?"

I freeze in place. Shit. "Yeah, Dad?"

Dad glances past me towards the crew outside. "Tell your friends to come inside, okay? We're about to eat."

"Okay," I say with a nod, then quickly slip out the door and shut it behind me. As the cold air hits my sweat-covered face, I release a contented sigh and lean against the door, finally able to breathe again.

"There he is!" Elise declares. "I was about to send Harrison in there to rescue you."

"Here I am," I mumble, my eyes falling shut as I take in the peace out here.

"You okay?" Caleb asks, suddenly closer than I expected.

I reluctantly force my eyes open to meet Caleb's soft brown eyes and nod. "Yeah, it's just…a lot in there. I'm supposed to tell y'all to come inside to eat, but…" I lean my head against the wall and let my eyes fall closed again. "I just need a second."

"I'm genuinely surprised your parents are making you deal with this crowd," Elise grumbles.

"I am, too," Harrison adds, his tone clearly irritated. "Seems unnecessary for you to be here."

I shrug. "It's church people."

There are a few seconds of silence before Caleb speaks up. "Why is that different?"

I open my mouth to answer, but for some reason, I come up empty. Why *is* it different?

Suddenly, there's a tapping on the window, and I jump.

"That's Nate," Harrison says before I can turn around. He pats me gently on the shoulder. "Come on, let's get in there before your dad gets hangry."

Harrison takes Elise's hand in his before leading the way inside, fanning a jealous flame in my gut. Of course *they* get to hold hands in front of these people. No one blinks an eye at Harrison and Elise for such a simple expression of love. But any display of affection between Caleb and me will "draw unwanted attention" or "make some people uncomfortable."

"Theo?"

I angrily shove my hands into my pockets to resist temptation. "Yeah?"

Caleb's eyes flicker between my hands and my face with concern. "Ready to go back in?"

I scoff, focusing my gaze on a point on the ground beside us. "Don't have much of a choice, do I?"

Caleb is quiet, hesitating for a moment or two before he speaks again. "Look, I can just—should I ask Lola to come pick me up?"

My stomach drops, and I glance back up at him. He looks like I've struck him. "What? No. No, why would you–"

"I don't know, I just…" he trails off, refusing to meet my gaze. "I feel like I'm just making things worse, and things are bad enough already without…me." He shrugs. "You've got enough on your plate, and I'm just making it harder."

I shake my head aggressively. "No, no, you're–" I sigh. "Please. Don't go. It's…it's going to be fine, right? We just have to make it through lunch, and then my mom said we can go downstairs for the rest of the afternoon."

Caleb stares back at the ground and doesn't answer.

"I'm sorry. Please stay. We can get through–"

There's a loud banging on the window, and I look up to see Elise motioning us to hurry. Shit.

"Okay," Caleb says softly. "You're right. I'll stay."

Relief washes over me like a tidal wave, and it takes every ounce of strength I have not to wrap my arms around him. "Okay! Okay, cool. Thank you, Caleb."

"Now, let's get in there before we get in trouble."

I make sure to keep a platonic distance from Caleb as we follow Harrison and Elise into the dining room, where everyone continues to carry on their separate conversations. Scanning the room, my eyes eventually land on Grace, who gives me a wink and Caleb an excited wave. I also spot Nathaniel doing his best to hide his annoyance as an awkward Miriam Shepphard inches further into his space, twirling her stringy brown hair and watching him fondly through her thick glasses.

Poor girl. The teenage desperation reeks off of her, and she likely doesn't even realize it. Was I that bad at fourteen? Hell, I was probably worse.

Dad abruptly clears his throat, and the room goes quiet. "Let us pray."

Caleb shoots me a panicked expression, so as everyone closes their eyes, I smile and lean into his shoulder. He relaxes into my touch, sending electricity up and down my arm.

"Dear Heavenly Father," Dad prays aloud. "Thank You for this beautiful day You have given to us, and thank You for the wonderful fellowship we've shared today."

Caleb's finger grazes against the back of my palm, and my heart thumps erratically in my chest.

"We thank You for this joyful holiday to celebrate the birth of Your Son, the true reason for the season. Please guide us as we navigate through this hectic time of year, and help us to remember to put You first in all we do."

I carefully caress Caleb's finger with my own, and I can't help the grin that takes over my face as our eyes meet.

"Father, thank You for an amazing service today. Thank You for Pastor Sheppard and for blessing him with the gift of preaching Your love to so many people. Please continue to bless him and his beautiful growing family."

Caleb smiles at me—the tips of his cheeks still pink from the chilly outside air—and a surge of warmth goes straight to my sternum, emanating out across my chest.

"Lord, we pray that You continue to guide us through the season and give us the courage to share Your love and Your message to those around us every chance that we get."

Our fingers are barely touching, and yet my heart is ablaze, sparks flying at every point of contact. I move to interlock our fingers—I know I shouldn't, but Caleb is a magnet, and I'm helpless to his pull.

"Thank You, Father God, for this incredible Christmas meal now set before us and for the wonderful people who've prepared it."

Caleb follows my lead, and everything else fades into the background. Only Caleb and I exist, and all I have to do is lean up a couple of inches and press my lips into his and—

"Forgive us our sins, and nourish this food to our bodies, and our bodies to your service. In Jesus' precious name, we pray, Amen."

The words out of my father's mouth jerk me out of my stupor, and I squeeze my eyes shut and rip my hand away from Caleb's. It's probably a bit more aggressive than necessary, but it's my own stupid fault for getting carried away. That was too close.

A chorus of "amens" echo around us, prompting everyone to begin lining up for food and drinks. I keep my hands in my pockets and my gaze fixed on Dad. Thankfully, he doesn't seem notice my slip up, and no one else is looking at me, either. Well, except for Nathaniel, who quirks up an eyebrow at me. After what seems like a safe amount of time, I turn back to Caleb, only to find that he's shuffled several feet away from me towards Harrison and Elise.

Good. That's safer. No more temptation.

I take a deep breath and head towards the food. Maybe eating something will ease some of the anxiety gnawing at my chest.

THREE
CALEB

"Lunch was great, Mom! We'll be downstairs!"

Theo shuts the door at the top of the staircase behind him, muffling the boisterous laughter coming from the dining room. His shoulders sink with a heavy sigh as he slowly descends, fiddling with the cuffs of his button-down.

I wait at the base of the stairs, watching him. I've been watching him all afternoon. And not just because I think he looks hot in his Sunday best.

He's just so… different around his family. Usually, whenever we spend time at the Briggs' house, the change in him is subtle. But today, with all of the people from his church and his dad hovering like a helicopter, it's like he's someone else entirely.

If I'm honest, it sort of freaks me out.

Theo wraps his arms around me when he reaches the bottom stair, the reverse in our height difference letting him rest his elbows on my shoulders. I catch him at the waist, holding him on that last step as I tuck my head under his chin, burying my face into his chest.

A chuckle rumbles through him as he squeezes my neck. "God, I needed that."

I try to reply, but my words get muffled against his sweater.

"I'm sure whatever you said was very cute," Theo says, letting his hold on me go slack.

Pulling away, I stick my tongue out at him, which just makes him laugh more. Good. He's spent most of the afternoon with a furrowed brow. No more of that.

"Does your family do this every Christmas?" I ask, stepping back into the hallway.

Theo nods, his dark curls bouncing. "Yeah, it's a lot. Pastor Sheppard and my dad have been friends forever, so it's like a thing every year with them. This is the first year Chase has shown up, though. Sorry, he's a bit cringe, but he means well."

"He was nice," I say, selecting my words carefully.

Theo pauses outside of the theater room, his hand on the knob. "And I'm sorry about the whole 'friend from school' thing. Again. It feels shit–*crappy*–I know, but it's only temporary. Once my dad comes around, we won't have to say it anymore."

"It's okay," I mutter, even though it feels like a lie the second it leaves my mouth. He's right, it is shitty, but I also know that it's what has to happen if I'm going to be with Theo. So, I have to accept it.

He throws a quick glance over his shoulder, then he looks at me again, this shining twinkle in his umber eyes that makes my stomach twist into a tangle of knots. "I love you," he says, his voice low. And before I can say it back, he's kissing me, warm lips and fingers sunk into my waist, washing away all of the things I'm holding back from him.

Because here, in these moments where Theo is mine, and there's no one else around, I know that he speaks the truth. He loves me, and I love him, and at the end of the day, all the little things standing in our way don't matter.

He pulls away sooner than I would like, his cheeks and the tip of his nose tinged red like he's been standing outside in the cold. "How much do you want to bet Harry and Elise are making out in there?" he asks, nodding his head toward the door.

I snort a laugh, my own face glowing with heat. "It's either that or they're arguing about something. I'd say it's a fifty-fifty toss-up."

"Only one way to find out."

With a quiet creak, the door to the theater room swings open.

"—know he's union-busting the elves. They have no rights!"

Harrison looks up from the back row of recliners, giving us a wave and Elise pauses her ranting long enough to say, "Finally. Back me up here, Caleb. Harry is trying to make the argument that Santa isn't the figurehead of Capitalism."

"Um, okay? Context?"

"How can that be?" Harrison cuts in, "He doesn't make a profit! If he was a capitalist, then he wouldn't be caught dead giving the toys away for free."

Theo shakes his head, moving over to the bar area where he powers on the projector. "Y'all are too much."

"Hear me out, Caleb," Elise continues, getting up from her spot beside Harrison and grabbing my hand. She drags me over to the row of seats where her boyfriend is sprawled out, his paisley tie pulled loose around his neck and his phone resting on his stomach. "Santa sells the personification of charity during the holidays, which then encourages us, the consumer base, to overspend and stretch ourselves thin to perpetuate the same illusion of charity, but really, we're just throwing our hard-earned money at the same three corporations who rake in billions of dollars in profits while exploiting the working class and fueling the dumpster fire that is consumerism. Are you following me?"

I nod along. "Barely."

"But you're talking about the *concept* of Santa," Harrison interjects. "My argument comes from the assumption that the magical legend known as Santa Claus is a real person. If that's the case, then he's obviously not some corporate shill."

"Not necessarily," I say, catching both of their attentions. "If we assume Santa is real, then he'd obviously be in support of making his holiday more popular. We already know he exploits the free labor of his indentured slaves, the elves. Would it be so hard to believe he'd sign an exclusive deal with a toy manufacturer to distribute his creations throughout the world? He'd make billions. Then he can continue doing his little charity show once a year bringing toys to everyone, when the rest of the year he's selling his wares at top dollar and using the profits to funnel money into the Christmas machine. Let's be honest, he's probably producing all those movies on the Hallmark channel my Nana is obsessed with.

"Oh, and don't get me started on the whole 'naughty or nice' thing because if we're letting some white-haired minor deity with a penchant for little kids start trying to sell us his own twisted sense of morality, then maybe it's a good thing climate change is melting his home."

They both stare at me, Elise grinning like a madwoman and Harrison honestly looking a little afraid.

"I love him," Elise says, looking at Theo.

"Get in line," Theo quips, crossing in front of us and nestling himself into the other half of my recliner. It's a bit snug, but I'm not complaining.

"You two can never break up." Elise takes my hand again, pulling it into her lap. "Where did you learn how to argue like that?"

"My mom's a lawyer," I explain, my cheeks flushing. "And my sister will be soon. I have to stay sharp if I want to keep up with them."

"Good luck, Theo," Harrison adds, pushing the button to bring his recliner up. "You're never going to win an argument."

"It's cool. We don't really argue anyways," Theo says, reaching for my other hand.

"Really?" Elise asks, looking bewildered. "Like, never?"

I shake my head, suddenly feeling self-conscious. Are we supposed to argue with each other? Is that what couples do? Elise and Harrison bicker all the time, but I just thought that was because Elise is who she is as a person.

"No. There have been misunderstandings, sure. But nothing that's blown up to a full-on argument."

Theo raises an eyebrow at me. "That's a good thing, right?"

"I'm not sure," I admit. "Did you have arguments with Sienna—"

He raises his free hand, cutting me off. "I don't want to talk about her."

"Sorry," I mutter, heat prickling at the nape of my neck.

An awkward silence falls over the group, but Theo exhales again, sinking deeper into the recliner, and says, "I didn't mean to say it like that."

"I get it," I assure him, giving his hand a squeeze. It's not much, but it's all I can do at the moment. His ex-girlfriend is still a sore spot for multiple reasons.

"Enough debating over Santa politics," Elise says, letting go of my hand and pulling her legs underneath her. "What movie are we watching?"

The conversation devolves into a list of options until, finally, Elise and Harrison agree on one. Theo starts the movie—I'm too distracted to catch the title—and I stare at the seams on the back of the recliner in front of me, lost in my head.

I shouldn't have brought up Sienna. Theo's definitely still upset about her outing him to his parents. And rightfully so. I would be upset, too, if I were in his shoes. Just thinking about it makes me angry on his behalf. The fact that I was in the same room as her earlier today makes me want to scream.

But what good would that do? I can't add any more stress to his life. I need to be the one supporting him, especially when it comes to his parents. To make them understand my relationship with Theo isn't some curse damning him to an eternity of suffering.

God, I can't believe people think that way.

Theo squeezes my hand, pulling my attention. His wide, dark eyes are practically drowning with concern. He must feel the anxiety radiating off me. I manage the most convincing smile I can, shaking my head.

His attention lingers, but eventually returns to the movie. He doesn't let go of my hand, even when the credits roll and conversation resumes. But I know he'll drop it again, just like he did after the prayer. And I can't get the thought out of my head.

The brisk December breeze chases away the lingering heat in my cheeks as I climb into Theo's red Honda. With some slick maneuvering on his part, Theo convinced his mom to let him drive me home sans a chaperone since Nate was tasked with entertaining the Sheppard girls for the evening.

He starts up the playlist we made together last week before shifting into reverse and resting a hand on my seat as he looks through the back windshield. It's only a little past five, and already the sun is low in the sky, streaking thin, wispy clouds with brilliant orange and reds. This close to Christmas, the roads are slammed with last-minute shoppers and folks from out of town getting ready for the holiday, so it takes us longer than usual to get back to my place. A tan RV sits in front of the house–evidence that Nana has arrived for her annual holiday visit–but my parent's cars are both missing from the driveway.

"Is your family going camping?" Theo asks, turning down the music.

I snort a laugh. "Oh, hell no. The Raynards are strictly indoor people. That's my Nana's RV. She drives it down from Maine every year to spend the holidays with us. She wasn't supposed to be here till tonight, though. I should let Mom know."

I pull out my phone, firing a quick message off before I see the notification in the muted "Family" chat–

> NANA: **WHERE THE HELL IS EVERYONE?**
> **Shit, sorry, my caps lock was on.**

> MATERNAL UNIT: **Still out shopping, Mom. The lines are CRAZY. We'll be home in a bit. Caleb, if you beat me home, let Nana in.**

> NANA: **Not to worry, I can get inside. Haven't met a door my library**

card can't open.

MATERNAL UNIT: Mother, please don't set off the alarm again. We'll be there soon.

NANA: How'd I raise such a killjoy?

SISTER: Nana, you're my hero.

DAD JOKE MASTER: Lynn, there's a key out back under the flower pot. Please don't break another window.

"There's a good chance Nana's already committed a B&E, so I should probably get in there and make sure she didn't hurt herself."

"Hang on," Theo says, unfastening his seatbelt. He reaches into the floorboard behind my seat and pulls out a red and green striped gift bag with tissue paper sticking out of the top. "I know we're both busy with family stuff, so I wanted to make sure you got this before Christmas."

The glittering bag sparkles in the fading sunlight.

"It's not much," Theo continues, averting his eyes as he offers the bag. "But it seemed weird not to get you something." I take the bag, and it's heavier than it looks as it falls in my lap. "And don't feel like you need to get me anything–I mean, it's okay if you did, but it's also cool if you didn't because, like, I wasn't expecting anything in return, so don't think that you have to–"

I interrupt his rambling by leaning over the center console and planting a kiss on his cheek. "Thank you, Theo. I've actually got something for you, too, but it's upstairs. Did you want to come up and get it?"

Theo's eyes brighten with a grin, the red tinge in his cheeks spreading. "Yeah, I mean, I can't stay long, but yeah, I can do that."

We exit the car, a burst of cold wind coaxing us quickly to the door which I unlock, ushering him inside. Jolly Christmas music booms through the house at a deafening level, and Theo plugs his ears as I shout, "Nana?!"

A familiar head of bleached-blond and gray hair peeks around the corner. "Caleb! Merry Christmas, sweetheart!"

Nana bulldozes her way through the foyer, wrapping me up into a peppermint-scented, bone-crushing hug.

"When did you get here?" I ask, but Nana scrunches her face and holds up a finger.

"Siri! Pause!"

The deafening music stops, leaving a ringing in my ears.

"What did you say, sweetheart?"

"Never mind," I reply, stepping beside Theo and grabbing his hand. "I want you to meet someone, Nana. This is my boyfriend, Theo. Theo, this is my Nana, Lynn."

Theo holds out his free hand, putting on a wavering smile. "Nice to meet you."

Nana knocks his hand away, pulling him into another hug, but he's still holding onto me, so it becomes one of those weird three-way hugs, but Nana doesn't seem to mind. "Aren't you the cutest thing? Caleb, you have good taste. It runs in the family."

Theo stumbles back from the embrace, looking at me with a bewildered expression. "Um, thank you?"

"I've been decorating," Nana continues, pulling a stray strand of tinsel out of the knit of her Christmas tree sweater. "Your mother always was a procrastinator, so it's a good thing I got here early. Why don't you two come help me put the star on top of the tree?"

"Theo can't stay long," I tell her, "we're going to go grab his gift from upstairs, then I'm all yours."

"Well, piddle," Nana huffs. "Not that I find you boring or anything, Caleb, but I was looking forward to getting to know Theo. Guess we'll have to take a rain check."

"He's not going anywhere, Nana," I assure her, steering Theo toward the stairs. "There will be plenty of time for that later."

"Till next time, Theo!" She calls after us, then from the living room she yells, "Siri, play!"

The music resumes its ear-splitting volume, but soon enough, we're behind the closed door of my bedroom.

"She seems… spirited," Theo says, hovering by the foot of my bed.

"That's a good word for her," I agree, setting my gift bag down on my desk. "Apparently, she's always been like that. Mom has a thousand stories of growing up when it was just the two of them, and Nana was working for the DA's office in Atlanta. She used to bring Mom along to trials sometimes."

"She's a lawyer, too?"

"Runs in the family," I say, opening the door to my closet. Wren and I have been working on Theo's gift for a couple of weeks, but keep it tucked away, just in case he might spot it when he's over. "Though, I think it may just be the women. I can't say I have the calling." I carefully extract the gift from its hiding place but hesitate before turning around.

What if he thinks it's dumb? Or what if he says he likes it but is just trying not to hurt my feelings? Maybe I should put it back and tell him his gift got lost in the mail.

"I made you something," I say before I can chicken out. "Crafting isn't really my thing, so I had Wren come help me with a couple of parts. And I didn't really know how to wrap it, so you'll have to close your eyes!"

"Okay, they're closed."

"I mean it, no peeking!"

"My eyes can't be any more closed."

I move quickly over to the bed, carefully positioning the posterboard so that it faces Theo. The glue has dried nicely, so it doesn't look like I lost any photos in the transition.

"Okay, you can look."

Theo's eyes flutter open, catching on me before they move to the collage on the bed. My magnum opus. It took me forever to collect pictures from everyone's social media accounts and figure out the best layout.

"My mom got me a photo printer for my birthday back in March," I say as Theo looks over my creation. "I've been looking for a reason to use it. The pictures on the outer edge are of the whole friend group. I even threw in a couple of Nate and Grace that I stole from your Insta. Then, as you get closer to the center–"

"It's us," Theo says, a smile creeping over his lips.

I nod, watching him take it all in. The pictures of the two of us frame the center of the collage, making the rough outline of what I hope looks like a heart.

"I left the center empty," I explain, pointing to the void space in the middle of the heart. "I figured we could put a really special picture there."

Theo nods, swallowing. His finger traces the edge of the posterboard.

"Do you like it?" I ask, unable to contain the question any longer.

"I love it," he says, his voice husky. "Really, I love it, Caleb. I just… I got you sour gummy worms and the new *I Love You Seymour Shura* manga. But this is a whole other level."

"You got me the new one?!" I tear into the gift bag, finding the wrapped manga under a massive bag of gummies. "I've been avoiding spoilers for weeks!"

Theo laughs. "Don't even pretend it's the same. I'm going to get you back, I swear!"

"I really do like it," I tell him, clutching the paperback to my chest. "And I can blame my next cavity on you, so there's that."

He laughs again, bouncing off the edge of the bed and wrapping me up in a hug. "You're the best, you know?"

"I do. But you can still tell me as much as you want."

He kisses me, lips gentle against mine. "The best," he whispers, then kisses me again, and again and again, till my head is swimming and the room is stifling, and there's nothing left to do but say goodbye.

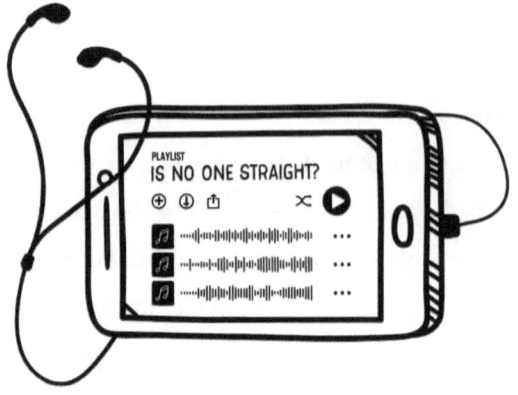

FOUR
THEO

Wednesday, January 3

THEO: wish me luck tonight. Sienna is back from Christmas vacation *eye roll*

CALEB: You could always skip, you know... :P

THEO: haha. I wish.

CALEB: I won't tell ;)

"You coming?" Nathaniel asks from the passenger seat.

I sigh, my fingers hovering over my keyboard as I try to think of a response to Caleb. "Yeah. You go on ahead."

"Not if you're gonna bail," Nate replies, settling back into the seat. "I want to bail, too."

I shake my head. "You know Dad would kill both of us."

Nate snorts. "Nah, just you."

Rolling my eyes, I stow my phone into my pocket and reluctantly step out into the chilly January air, joining Nate as we make our way toward the Foundation building.

Wednesdays are my second least favorite day of the week—second only to Sundays, of course. I used to feel guilty about it, but now, not so much. Unlike Sundays, Wednesday nights' service only lasts about ninety minutes, and most of that time is spent in our small groups. Small groups are just an arbitrary way of dividing the youth group into classes based on grade level and gender, so my small group consists of about ten guys who are also in eleventh grade and two adult leaders who lead the discussions and take prayer requests. It's not too bad, if I'm honest. I can mostly space out or just enjoy time with Harrison. And best of all, it's very easy to avoid Sienna.

I spot Sienna as soon as I walk in—her hair is impossible to miss and even harder to ignore given how similar its shade is to Caleb's—so I linger on the opposite end of the room from her and wait for Harrison. I pull my phone out of my pocket to finish my text to Caleb, but before I can unlock it, there's a tap on my shoulder.

"Hey, Theo."

I turn around to find a familiar face—Jake Buchanon, one of the guys from my small group. We've known each other since elementary school, but only from church, as he attends a private Christian school. His shaggy brown hair hangs down in his gray eyes, but there's an expression on his face I can't decipher.

"Oh, hey, Jake," I reply with a casual smile. "What's going on, man?"

Jake eyes me up and down, then glances behind me. "Can I talk to you for a second? Like…alone?"

Alarm bells ring in my head immediately, but I'm too stunned to think of a reason to say no. I quickly scan the room for Harrison, but there's no sign of him. "Um…sure?"

Jake nods once, turning towards the hallway that leads to the bathrooms. He angles himself in the corner, and I join him, standing a few safe feet away.

From here, Jake has visibility from all directions, which makes my heart rate spike impossibly higher. What could he possibly want to tell me in private? Does he know about Caleb? Did Sienna tell him? Who all has he told now? Am I about to be hate crimed?

After what feels like his fourth time making sure the coast is clear, his focus zeroes in on me. "So, uh, I started watching *Hudson's Haunted Habitats* over the Christmas break."

My stomach drops. There it is—all my worst fears confirmed. *He knows.* "Oh, yeah?" I finally say, determined to be casual. "It's great, right?"

"Yeah. I heard they did an episode on that old creepy bologna church over on Holly Street, so I had to check it out." He studies me as he speaks, and I genuinely wish he would just spit it out. What does he want?

"I know, right?" I reply with a chuckle, rubbing my hand against the back of my head. "It's crazy."

His eyes narrow. "So…do your parents know you have a boyfriend?"

Panic claws its way to the surface, and I have to resist the urge to clamp a hand over his mouth. "Do—um—what?" I sputter.

Jake looks around again, then leans closer. "Sorry, I should have said that quieter," he says in a hushed voice this time. "My bad. But, um…do they?"

My mouth hangs open. "I…I don't know what you're talking about."

Jake hesitates, then reaches out to touch my shoulder. "Look, Theo–"

"I don't want to have this conversation," I blurt, flinching away from his hand. "I have to go find—"

"I'm gay, too."

I freeze. "W–What?"

Jake inhales sharply before taking a step forward. "I'm…yeah. I'm also—" his eyes scan the area again before he continues. "—into guys. Like. Very much so."

Instead of answering, I simply stare at him. Jake Buchanon? *Gay?* Is he serious? Or is this a trap? I've never picked up any vibes from him before, but…is that really a thing? Do people pick up vibes from me? Are gay vibes different than bisexual vibes? What even are "vibes," anyway? Is there actual science behind that, or is it just more of a—

"How did you tell people?" Jake continues, seemingly unaware of my inner turmoil. "I've known I was…like this for most of my life, but I'm so scared of what people will say or what my parents will do. But then I watched that interview with you and Hudson, and just… The way you just said it on camera like that? It was crazy, man. Like you had no fear at all."

I finally blink out of my stupor, only to shake my head at him. "Oh, believe me, I had fear. Lots of it. Too much of it, even."

Jake shrugs. "Didn't seem that way to me."

My gaze lowers to a fixed point on the ground past Jake's feet as I let his words sink in. Is that how Jake sees me? As someone brave? *Am* I brave? I mean, I did one brave thing one time, but does that make me a brave person?

"So, who all knows about it?"

That grabs my attention. I take a sharp breath. "Not many people. It's a long story, but I don't want to talk about it here–"

Jake snorts. "I mean, that interview has millions of views, so a lot of people *know*, but I just meant of the people we know."

I shake my head aggressively, squeezing my eyes shut to block out the fresh wave of panic. "Look, Jake, I said I don't want to talk about it here. We can talk after church or something."

Jake frowns. "Theo, I'm not trying to–"

"Theo, everything okay?"

Relief washes over me at the sound of Harrison's voice echoing from the entryway. He's eyeing Jake suspiciously, and Jake takes a considerable step back from me.

"Hey, Harry," I exhale. "Yeah, everything's fine."

Harrison's eyes stay fixed on Jake. "Cool. Jake. How's it going?"

Jake nods. "Good," he blurts nervously. "I was just talking to Theo about

Triple H, but I just remembered I have to pee before service starts, so, um, I guess I'll see y'all in there." And with that, Jake disappears into the men's bathroom without another word.

"What was that about?" Harrison demands, still glaring at the bathroom door.

I let out a shaky laugh. "I guess all those months of pestering our small group to watch Triple H is finally coming back to bite me."

Harrison furrows his brow for only a moment, but then his eyes widen. "Oh, shit."

"Yep."

"Has he told—"

"I don't know."

"Is he going to—"

"I don't know."

Harrison tenses beside me. "I'll talk to him."

I shake my head. "No, I can take care of it myself. He just…caught me off guard, that's all."

Just as Harrison opens his mouth to respond, Chase's energetic voice booms into the microphone, beckoning everyone to gather for worship.

Harrison glances back at the bathroom door, but I clap his shoulder. "It's fine, Harry. I'm fine."

This seems to satisfy him, and the two of us make our way into the main room, where the band and Sienna are starting their set. I can feel Sienna's eyes on me, but I ignore her completely, keeping my eyes fixed on the television screen above the stage where the lyrics are displayed. At some point, I notice Jake sneaking back into the room. Our eyes meet for barely a fraction of a second, but I quickly look away.

As worship wraps up, Chase is back at the front of the stage, wearing his trademark eager grin as he scans the crowd. "Let us pray."

I close my eyes and bow my head, but I don't pick up on much of the prayer after that. I can't stop thinking about Jake. Not just the fact that he knows about Caleb and me, but I also can't seem to wrap my head around the fact that he's gay. How did I miss it? Is my gaydar really that bad? He says he's known for years, but shouldn't I have noticed? It also begs the question—are there others? I sneak a peek during the prayer, glancing around the room and wondering who else in the youth group might also be gay, bisexual, lesbian, or…any of the other letters in the not-straight community. I guess I should learn those at some point.

"We know we are all selfish, sinful beings that desperately need Your grace. Keep us humble, Lord. Show us how to put You first in everything we do. In Jesus' name, we pray, Amen."

Selfish, sinful beings.

I squeeze my eyes shut again, guilt swelling in my gut for thinking about my own problems right now. The Jake thing can wait.

"So let's jump right into it!" Chase begins as everyone makes their way back to their seats. "We've been talking about the book of Romans for the past couple of weeks, but today, let's really unpack and discuss original sin and how it still affects us today. Now, for those who want to follow along, turn to Romans chapter three in your Bibles…"

My focus continues to wane as the night continues, and it completely plummets once we're in our small group. I can't avoid Jake here. Jake sits just across the circle from me, two seats away from Brandon, our small group leader. I'm mostly successful at evading Jake's gaze, but I still end up wondering how many other guys have already watched the Saint Catherine's episode of Triple H, too, and they're just waiting to bring it up. Would they come to me first? Would they tell other people? Is my love life part of the youth group gossip now? Has Sienna brought it up to her small group, perhaps as a prayer request? Sienna used to gush about how close she is to her small group all the time, so it wouldn't surprise me if all the junior girls knew about Caleb and me by now.

Once small group is over, Harrison and I make a beeline for the backdoor to head toward our cars in the parking lot. Just the sight of Eileen's glossy red paint is enough to bring my anxiety down again. Freedom is only a few hundred feet away.

"Hey guys, wait up!"

My chest tightens again. Harrison and I turn around to see Jake jogging up behind us. Harrison tosses me a look, and I shrug.

"Hey, Jake," Harrison greets him flatly, barely slowing his pace to the cars. "What's up?"

"I just wanted to talk to you—both of you," Jake replies, then looks at me. "Did you tell him?"

I frown. "Tell him what?"

"That I'm gay?"

Harrison nearly trips over his own feet. "Wait, what?"

We finally reach Eileen and Harrison's white Toyota Corolla parked beside her, and I try to act casual. "That wasn't really my news to share," I say with another shrug. "Trust me, it's not cool to be outed when you're not ready."

Jake's brows furrow at that. "Oh, yikes. That's messed up. Who outed you?"

I shake my head and shove my hands in my pockets. "I'd rather not talk about it."

"Wait, wait, hang on," Harrison says, holding his hands up. "I feel like I need a second to catch up. When did this happen?"

Jake scoffs. "When did I become gay? Great question. So technically, I'm pretty sure I was born this way, as are most gay people, but I probably first started to suspect it when I watched *How To Train Your Dragon* when I was maybe five or six? There was something about Hiccup that made me feel–"

"You know that's not what I meant," Harrison interrupts. "I mean, when did you come out? Is it still a secret?"

"Oh, yeah," Jake replies. "I mean, my best friend from school knows. Y'all remember Shauna? I've brought her to SCC a couple of times, but she goes to a different church across town. Other than her, it's just you two."

Harrison's eyebrows shoot up as he looks back and forth between Jake and me. "Wow. Okay. And I assume you told Theo because…" he trails off.

I nod. "Yeah, he watched the Triple H interview."

Harrison sighs. "Got it. Okay. Thank you, now I'm up to speed."

I turn to Jake and manage a smile. "So, Hiccup was your gay awakening, huh? Not bad."

Jake chuckles. "Thanks. I definitely could have done worse, so I'm pretty happy with that." His smile fades at the sound of a family loading up in their SUV a few yards away, and he steps a little closer to me. "Hey, listen—um—is it okay if I text you sometime?"

I blink at him, a tiny bit of panic threatening to surface. "Oh, uhh—Jake, I'm flattered, really, but, um—no, I'm still with—"

"No, no, no, shit, sorry—" Jake blurts out, shaking his head wildly. "Not like that. I mean, you are cute, don't get me wrong, but—shit, that's not—look, I respect that you have a boyfriend, and I'm super happy for you guys. I just—" he stops himself and takes a breath. "I really just want a friend. Someone who's going through the same shit that I am. No one else is really out at my school, and I just—I don't know, I feel like maybe having someone to talk to who's been through it will make it feel less…lonely, you know?"

As I absorb Jake's words, I take him in as well. His gray eyes are glossy with the threat of tears, and I can hear the sadness in his voice. He's alone in this. From almost the very start, even when I was in denial of my feelings for Caleb, I have always been surrounded by support. Not only do I have Harrison, Oliver, Elise, Grace, Nathaniel, Mom, Freddy, and Wren in my corner, but I also have Caleb, the best boyfriend in the world—someone who loves me, believes in me, advocates for me, and knows exactly the kinds of things I'm going through. Jake doesn't have a Caleb. He has his friend Shauna, which isn't nothing, but I know it's something else entirely to have another not-straight person to confide in and talk to.

Finally, I smile at Jake and pat his shoulder. "Yeah, man. Of course, you can text me anytime. Let me give you my number."

Jake releases a breath with a relieved grin as he digs his phone from his pocket. "Thanks, Theo. I really appreciate it."

I type my number in his phone and hand it back to him. "Don't mention it. You shouldn't have to go through this alone. We've got to stick together, you know?"

Jake nods, swiping his sleeve against his face. "Yeah. We really do." He flashes a mischievous grin. "And I promise to be on my best behavior so you can tell Caleb he has nothing to worry about."

I laugh. "That's probably the last thing Caleb's got to worry about. We've already had to go through hell just to be together at all, so I don't think jealousy is even on our radar. Besides–" I gesture vaguely at myself. "Not much here worth being jealous over."

"I wouldn't be so sure," Jake replies, crossing his arms over his chest. "I'm calling it now—when you get to college and really start living your life as a gay man, you're going to be drowning in interested guys."

"Bi, actually," Harrison mutters quietly, clearing his throat as Jake and I look at him. "He's bi, not gay."

Jake's eyes widen. "Oh, shit, then you'll have girls *and* guys coming out of the woodwork before long. Caleb better watch out!" Jake winks and elbows my arm.

"*Psh*, yeah, right," I scoff. The idea of anyone—male, female, or otherwise—pursuing me romantically has always been preposterous to me. With my messy dark hair, sharp features, and five-foot-six stature, I'm a far cry from the most attractive guy in Specter. Add to that my severe social anxiety, average intelligence, and a general lack of any interesting skills or hobbies, and let's just say I'm surprised I have any friends at all. I honestly don't know what Caleb sees in me, but whatever it is, I'm thankful for it.

"Whatever you say, dude," Jake says, clapping his hands together. "Anyway, I'm starving. Do you guys want to grab some food?"

Harrison looks at me, and I nod. "Definitely. Let's get out of here!"

Dinner with Jake and Harrison almost has me miss my curfew, but fortunately, I'm able to shoot my parents a quick text explaining I was out with a friend from church, and I'm just barely able to pull into the driveway about five minutes late. Dad initially eyes me with suspicion as I rush in the door, but as soon as I explain that it was Jake Buchanon—son of one of the elders, Jim Buchanon—he looks visibly relieved.

I try not to dwell on the fact that Dad's trust in me has only diminished after he found out I was dating Caleb. I've always been "the good kid," the rule follower, and I've always been able to fly under the radar because of my parents' unwavering certainty in my compliance. Not anymore. Now my father looks at me with suspicion and concern, and I know it's because he's worried that I'm out kissing a boy again. Or worse—more than kissing.

I try not to let it get to me. There's no point in fighting. I just have to grin and bear it until I can move out and live my own life. It's the only way.

I retreat to my bedroom for the night, finish a bit of homework, and text Caleb and the crew a bit for about an hour or so before bed. Just as I'm about to go to the bathroom to brush my teeth—

"I can't believe you're still entertaining this phase of his."

I freeze at the top of the stairs at the sound of my father's frustrated voice.

"Oh, Michael, come on," Mom replies dismissively. "You and I both know this isn't a phase–"

"It's a phase, Kora. This is textbook teenage rebellion. Times have just changed, that's all. Instead of doing drugs or joining gangs, the cool thing to do now is experiment with sexuality and gender."

My stomach twists as I realize that they're talking about me. I remain perfectly still, a marble statue at the top of the stairs. I don't dare move a muscle—I hardly even breathe as I listen as hard as I can.

"I don't think so, Mike. I really don't. Theo's not rebellious. That's not who he is—"

"Every teenager is rebellious at some point," Dad argues. "It would be naive of us to think Theo is any different."

"And you really think this would be how Theo would rebel? To what end?"

"There is no end—kids don't think that far ahead. This is just a cry for attention. Just like Grace's tattoos and piercings, this is Theo's way of acting out." Dad pauses, then lets out a dry laugh. "I'm just praying that Nate's rebellion is more predictable."

Mom is quiet for a moment. "Michael, I really think you should look at some of the material Grace—"

"No."

"—she just put so much work into it—"

"Kora, you know I'm not going—"

"—and I think it would mean a lot to both of them—"

"Kora, that's *enough*."

I shudder at Dad's commanding tone. The entire house goes completely quiet—all I can hear is the sound of my own heart pounding in my ears.

Finally, Dad sighs. "I know you're just trying to be a good mother to your son. I know that, and I don't want to stand in your way. But as his father, I have a job to do, too—to put my son on the right path. As long as he's under my roof, I can't put up with blatant immoral behavior."

Blatant immoral behavior. The phrase burns my ears, branding the inside of my skull.

"Come on, Michael, he's never exhibited—"

"French kissing a boy at a public event and declaring his sexuality on an internet show? That's pretty blatant in my book. It's unacceptable, and you know it."

Unacceptable. That's how my dad sees me. That's how he sees my behavior. My relationship with Caleb. *Blatant, immoral, and unacceptable.*

Mom releases a shaky, defeated sigh. "You're going to push him away. You know that, right?"

"I have faith, Kora. God will give me the words to say to get through to him. I know my son, and I know he's going to come around."

"And if he doesn't?"

A long silence drapes over the house. "He will," Dad states firmly with finality. "He'll do the right thing. He has to."

He has to.

Without making a sound, I slip back into my bedroom and silently shut the door. Tears burning behind my eyes, I turn out my lights, sink to the floor, and wrap my arms around my legs.

Unacceptable.

He's going to come around. He'll do the right thing. He has to.

FIVE
CALEB

Saturday, January 6

"Caleb! Over here!"

Freddy sails across the ice with ease, skidding to a stop before he collides with the wall surrounding the makeshift rink. Andrew follows close behind but isn't nearly as graceful as his boyfriend and sort of crashes into the wall to stop himself.

"Sorry," Andrew mutters, gripping the wall with one hand while fixing his glasses with the other.

"No one watching would know it's your first time," Freddy assures him, wrapping an arm around Andrew's waist and pulling himself closer. "You're doing great!"

Andrew gives a sheepish grin. "And you're a terrible liar."

The Specter fairground still has remnants of the Christmas town they build every year leading up to the holidays. Half-dead trees that didn't get taken home wait in rows to be piled up and burned. Booths made to look like gingerbread houses sit abandoned with hand-painted signs still advertising holiday treats that are long gone. At the center of the makeshift town is a huge ice skating rink, which stays open through the winter season.

A bitter breeze blows, and I shiver in place, pulling my hat down over my ears.

"Where's Theo?" Freddy asks, tearing himself away from his shameless flirting.

"He's getting our skates," I say, pointing back towards the makeshift shed where they store the rentals.

"Such a gentleman," Freddy coos, scooting over to the gap in the wall and stepping out onto the faux grass that surrounds the rink.

"I'm going to take another lap," Andrew tells us, gingerly releasing his death grip on the wall. "If you see me fall, no, you didn't."

"Just don't take out a kid on your way down!" Freddy calls after him before returning his attention to me. "Ugh, I think I'm falling for that clumsy idiot."

"Seriously?" I balk, shoving my hands deeper into my jacket pockets. "I never thought I'd live to see the day Freddy Desoto actually admits he's falling in love."

"Rude!" Freddy knocks his shoulder into mine. "But accurate. I can't help myself, Caleb. He makes me feel things. Stupid things."

"Like emotions?"

Freddy's face crumples. "Yeah, those. Yuck, I can't believe I'm admitting this."

"Oh my god, you *are* a human being. I just lost a bet with Wren."

"Shut up," Freddy says with a chuckle. "I'm being serious. I've never felt this way about someone before."

He says it with a smile, but there's something underneath that–an anxiety in his eyes that makes my stomach clench. Freddy has been my best friend for long enough that I know when something is amiss.

"Then what's wrong?" I ask.

"Nothing," he says, quickly averting his eyes.

"Andrew's right, you're a terrible liar."

"That's not fair," Freddy scoffs. "You two can't gang up on me like that."

"Seriously, though. Is everything okay?"

Freddy watches Andrew out on the ice, the edges of his mouth curling into a smile. "Yes. And that's the problem, I think. It's all too good. It can't last–"

"Sorry that took so long," Theo announces himself, holding out a pair of scuffed skates. It takes a second for him to register the look on my face, and he quickly adds, "My bad, is something up?"

Freddy shakes his head, gingerly moving to the opening again and stepping out on the ice. "Hurry up and get out here. I want to see how many times Caleb falls on his ass."

I take the skates from Theo, backstepping to a wooden bench where I untie my shoes. Theo settles in beside me. "Is everything okay with Freddy?"

I don't really know how to answer that or if I should even be talking about this with Theo. Freddy wouldn't want anyone to worry over him. He keeps things close to his chest. At least things that matter to him. To most, Freddy appears to be an open book. He's quick to give you his opinion, even if you didn't ask, and doesn't shy away from many topics. But when it comes to personal matters, he's got things locked down tighter than security at a Taylor Swift concert.

"I think so," I answer, convincing myself it's not quite a lie. I try not to lie to Theo. But it's not always possible. "Thanks for getting these," I say, wanting to change the subject. "I'm not as terrible a skater as Freddy makes me out to be."

"I might be," Theo says with a grimace. "I should have brought Nate's skateboard pads. I have a feeling I'll go home covered in bruises."

"Just hold on tight to me," I tell him, lacing up my skates. "I won't let you fall."

Theo gives me a crooked smile. "What happens if I pull you down with me?"

I ponder that for a moment, then slide closer and lower my voice. "If you want me on top of you, Theo Briggs, you don't have to fake clumsiness. You could just ask."

Theo's cheeks–already pink from the frigid air–flush scarlet as he directs his attention to the laces of his skates, clearing his throat.

My own face burns as I nudge him with my shoulder. "All joking aside, I'm glad we're doing this. We haven't been able to have a proper date in forever. How did you manage to convince your parents to let you out unchaperoned?"

He pulls the strings on his skates tight, taking time to chew on his words before he says, "I may not have been a hundred percent honest with my mom about who is in attendance tonight. But don't worry, I've got Harry covering for us if she decides to check in, so we've got all the time in the world. I just–I wanted us to have a night to ourselves."

"Oh," I say, my pulse suddenly thrumming in my ears.

Did he mean…? No, that can't be it. We haven't talked about taking things to the next level physically, so I shouldn't think that's what he meant. But maybe that's why he seems so distracted. Is he worried about bringing it up with me? Sure, he's confessed his feelings for me on a multi-million subscriber YouTube channel, but this is sex we're talking about. He's bound to have hang-ups from all of the religious mumbo-jumbo he's got bouncing around in his head.

Maybe I should bring it up first. Just to break the tension.

"Got it," he announces as he finishes lacing. Kicking his feet out, he stands, wobbling like an unsteady toddler on the blades of his skates. I grab him by the elbow to keep him upright. "Thanks. I think I'll be okay once I'm on the ice."

"You have done this before, right?" I ask as he braces himself against me.

"Um, yeah, once. Oliver invited me along with his stepmom a few years back, but I don't remember much about how it went. Hopefully, that wasn't due to head trauma."

We reach the wall surrounding the rink, and I help him up onto the ice. His foot slides out from under him, and he spins to grip the railing. "Piece of cake," he huffs, holding himself up.

I follow him onto the ice, slowly circling around to his other side. I offer my hand. "Here, just hold onto me."

Theo looks at my hand, and I pretend not to notice the hesitation or the way he looks over his shoulder to see if anyone is watching.

That has nothing to do with me, I remind myself.

He takes my hand, gingerly letting go of the railing, and I pull him toward me, catching him at the waist with my other hand and turning him in the right direction. Other skaters circle the rink at staggered paces, the faster towards the center of the circle, while those less sure on their feet stay to the outer edges. Freddy races by with a holler, quickly followed by Andrew, who weaves around a family with a newfound grace.

Guess he's a fast learner. Next to me and Theo, the two of them look like an Olympic figure skating team. All they're missing are the sequined leotards.

"I'm going to get us both killed," Theo says, his face twisted with concentration as he stares down at his feet.

"Relax," I coach him, pushing off the tip of my skate and propelling us forward. "No one is watching you. No one will care if you fall."

The tension in his muscles seems to slack, at least a little, and he eases into our first turn, rounding the end of the oval rink and starting back in the opposite direction. Another couple passes us on the left, the man and woman holding hands as they sail along the ice. I can't help but grin because even though I'm practically holding him upright at the moment, I know that one day, that will be me and Theo. Just the two of us, skimming along, reminiscing about the day spent picking each other off the ice and laughing, and not remembering the stares from nosy strangers or the anxiety of someone else finding out something that Theo still wants to keep hidden—

I stop myself before the train of thought takes a dark turn. I know it's not fair of me to dwell on the fact that Theo is still uncomfortable with us being open about our relationship. I know it's not his fault, but it's still something that he has to come to terms with. He tells me that he's working on it and that he knows there's a happy medium between his feelings for me and his faith, but what happens if he never gets to that place?

And how long do I wait for him?

The question makes me recoil, like I've bit into a sour apple.

"I think I'm starting to get the hang of it," Theo says, tearing his eyes away from his feet long enough to glance over at me. But then his foot slips out from under him, and before I can get a better grip on him, he's on his butt, wincing.

I skid to stop, quickly circling behind him to make sure he doesn't get run over. "Upsie daisy," I say, grabbing him under the arms and helping him up. Ice shavings stick to the back of his gray peacoat, and I brush them off, then hesitate, realizing I'm practically slapping his rear end.

"I jinxed myself, didn't I?"

"Maybe a little," I tease, taking his hand in mine and pulling him into motion once more. "How's your butt?"

Theo's cheeks are inflamed with embarrassment, but he manages to clap back, "You tell me. You were the one getting acquainted with it."

We both laugh as Freddy appears at our side, slowing his pace to match our snail speed. "Nice wipeout," he says, turning around to face us while still skating backward. "Did you hurt anything?"

"Just my self-respect," Theo mutters, his grip tightening on my hand.

Andrew joins our group as well, skirting beside Freddy and placing a hand across his stomach to steer him away from any collision courses as he shows off. "Freddy makes all of us look like amateurs."

"How did you get so good at this?" Theo asks.

"My *abuela* would bring me and my brother here every weekend during the winter when Mom was in flight school. It was a nice way to get out of the house, and she had a crush on the old man that ran the hot chocolate stand, so it was a win-win."

I wince at the mention of Gabriel–Freddy's brother–even though he doesn't seem fazed. Gabriel passed away when Freddy was eleven, and it's not something we usually bring up in conversation.

"Pretty soon, I was living my Adam Rippon fantasy and trying to convince my *abuela* to sew sparkles onto my winter coat." He laughs, lost in the memory for a moment, before addressing Theo, "I'm guessing your family didn't come here often?"

Theo shakes his head. "There's always so much going on around the holidays at church, and we never had a free weekend."

"Tell me about it," Andrew commiserates. "There's the children's programs, and the cantatas, and the Angel Tree toy drives, not to mention the week leading up to Christmas, where I practically live in a choir robe. I'm surprised I had time to wrap anything!"

"What church do you go to again, Andrew?" Theo asks.

"Specter First Methodist," he answers, brushing a sandy bang from his eyes. "My mom is one of the Elders of the church, so I get roped into pretty much everything around there."

Theo nods, and he looks like he wants to ask another question, but he never does.

"Not to change topics," Freddy says, spinning back the right way and addressing us over his shoulder, "but all of this amazing grace and poise makes a boy hungry. We're thinking Pizzapalooza after this. Are y'all in?"

"That sounds dope," Theo answers, then turns to check with me. "Is that okay?"

"Sounds heavenly," I answer, snorting at my own joke.

"Awesome," answers Freddy. "Now, no offense, but I'm about to leave you all in the dust. Catch me if you can!"

He breaks away from Andrew, digging his skates in and rocketing around an older couple as we come around the turn. Andrew takes off after him, and Theo and I decide it's best to keep to our snail's pace.

But Theo doesn't let go of my hand–except the times he falls down–so I celebrate the small victories.

"I don't want to head home yet."

Theo and I are sitting in Eileen outside of Pizzapalooza. A cardboard box of our leftovers sits in my lap, and Freddy and Andrew already hugged us goodbye before they pulled off in Andrew's car.

I check the clock. It's only eight fifteen.

"Okay, then we won't."

He's been quiet today. Quieter than usual, I should say. Let's be honest, it's hard to get a word in between Freddy and Andrew, but even in the moments it's been the two of us, there's a delay in his response, like his thoughts are buffering.

I reach over the armrest, taking his hand in mine. "Did something happen at home? With your parents?"

Theo shakes his head, his gaze fixed out the windshield. "It's a church thing. I'm not going to bother you with it."

Oh. That's not what I was expecting at all.

"You could if you wanted to. If you need someone to listen, I mean. Not sure I'd be much help beyond that."

He looks at me now, dark eyes nearly black in the dimness of the street lamps. Then he's smiling, an exhale escaping his lips. "Thank you, but it's just something I have to work through on my own." He squeezes my hand, then pulls away to start the car. "Now then, where to?"

"Did you want to catch a late movie?" I suggest, pulling my phone out to search for times. "Shit, the last one started at eight. Um… we could always go back to my place and hang out?"

"Sold," Theo announces, pulling his seatbelt on. "I owe you a walloping in Mario Kart."

"Yeah, right," I snort. "If I remember correctly, you fell off Rainbow Road so many times I lapped you."

"Well, I've been practicing," Theo argues, flashing a grin. "And I think that the turtle shells are going to turn in my favor."

"We'll see about that."

The drive back home isn't as eventful as a lap around the Mario Kart track, but we make it one piece. Lola's car is in the driveway, but Mom's is missing, which isn't that odd for a Friday night.

"I'm home," I call from the front door, kicking off my sneakers and hanging my coat. The sounds of the television and a grunt from the living room draw me close enough to find Lola sprawled out on the couch in her usual spot, files stacked in neat rows along the coffee table.

She looks up from her work long enough to give a half-nod. "Can't talk," she says, her fingers flying across the keyboard. "I have to finish this deposition report in the next hour so I can catch up with some friends at Patty's."

"Where's Mom?" I ask, ignoring her request not to talk.

"With Dad on a date night," she answers, not skipping a beat in her typing. "They left about half an hour ago."

"Ew."

Lola snorts a laugh. "And once again, I'm the only one in this house who doesn't have a date. It's fine, everything is fine..." she trails off, getting absorbed back into her work.

"We'll be upstairs," I say, not waiting for her response as I return to Theo, waiting at the base of the stairs. He's shed his jacket as well, showing off a long-sleeved t-shirt with a band name I don't recognize. There's a constant rotation of those in his wardrobe.

"Ready to lose?" he asks.

"Keep telling yourself that. Maybe it'll come true."

Upstairs in my room, the Mario Kart-nage rages on for about an hour before I hear Lola call up the stairs, "I'm heading out!"

Theo frowns, setting down his controller. "I should probably get going."

"You don't have to rush off."

He's sitting on the floor, leaning back against my bed, while I've made a nest for myself of pillows and blankets on top.

"You've already proved your kart-driving superiority," Theo says, wincing as he pushes himself off the floor. He rolls his shoulder, grimacing.

"What's wrong?"

"I think my falls on the ice are starting to catch up with me," he explains. "Something tells me I'm going to have some serious bruises tomorrow."

I scoot to the edge of the bed. "Come here, let me see."

Theo hesitates. "It's fine, really."

"Trust me, I've spent years patching up Freddy's various sports injuries. I'm practically a doctor." I pat the space beside me on the bed expectantly.

He sighs but gives me a smile as he flops down beside me, then hisses through his teeth. "I should have worn thicker pants. Jeez."

"Okay, let's see the damage." Theo's leg presses against mine as I turn to him, placing a gentle hand on his shoulder and applying pressure. "Does that hurt?"

"A little," he says, looking down at the floor.

I move my hand, fingers trailing to the collar of his shirt. I pull the fabric away from his skin, trying to get a better look. "Take your shirt off."

"W-What?" stammers Theo.

"It's not a big deal," I say, fighting a grin. "I've seen you shirtless."

"Well, yeah, but not in your bed."

True. And we're home alone, I realize. This wasn't exactly planned out, but *if* there were any intentions from either party for something to happen tonight, I have to say the pieces are falling into place nicely. I can see why he's so nervous.

I hold up a hand in front of him. "I swear, my intentions are pure. I just want to make sure I'm not sending you home looking like you've been attending fight club. I'm already in deep enough shit with your parents for turning you bi."

Theo grimaces again, but it's not from his injuries.

"Sorry," I add softly. "That was a bad joke. You know that's not how this works."

"I know." He stands up suddenly, reaching for the hem of his shirt and pulling it off in one swift motion. "There, at least I'm not in your bed anymore."

In the light from my bedside lamp, Theo's skin is warm honey. The tan from long summer days by the pool hasn't faded much in the winter months, and the trail of freckles that line his collarbone is particularly distracting as I join him in standing, inspecting the shoulder in question. Sure enough, on the outer part of his left shoulder blade, a dark, discolored patch looms under the skin. I trail a finger over the smooth surface, and Theo shivers at the touch, his eyes closed.

"That's going to look worse tomorrow," I say, suddenly feeling the slightest bit of guilt for dragging him onto the ice this afternoon. "But I think you'll live."

"Is that your professional medical opinion, doctor?"

There's a playfulness in his voice that spurs me on.

"I'd like to try a quick treatment if you'd be willing?"

Theo throws me a questioning look, then nods slowly.

My pulse hammers in my ears as I step closer to him, my hands grabbing him gently at the waist as I lower my lips to his shoulder and plant a soft kiss along the bruised skin.

Theo sucks in a breath.

And now that I'm here, with the taste of Theo's skin on my lips, I can't help but push a little further. I kiss farther up his shoulder, my hands pulling him closer to me. He exhales at that, his eyes still closed. Then I'm moving again, leaving a trail of kisses along the curve leading up to the crook of his neck, where I pause.

"Is this okay?" I whisper.

He nods, his breath coming in short gasps.

I return to my work, kissing him just below the ear, and Theo's body goes rigid. He steps out of my hold, his back to me for a split second before he turns around and practically tackles me with a kiss, both of us stumbling back and landing on the edge of the bed once more.

Theo's hands grasp at my shirt, unfastening the buttons till his warm fingers trail down my chest, and it's my turn to let out a gasp as his lips trail down my neck, and I feel teeth scraping against my skin.

My brain is on fire, and I can't think as Theo pushes me gently backward. My back hits the bed as he crawls on top of me, both of us panting. But just as he leans down for another kiss, he stops, a moment of clarity flashing in his dark eyes.

Vibration. His hand reaches for his pocket, and the screen of his phone illuminates the sharp angles of his face. He straightens, quickly untangling himself from me and standing.

"Theo? What's wrong?"

He shakes his head, scooping his shirt from the floor and pulling it over his head. "I have to go," he says as if it's an answer to my question.

"Are you okay? Did I do something–"

"No." He turns back to me, eyes locking with mine. His features twist like he's in pain. "I just have to go. Sorry."

Without another word, he storms out of my room, leaving me half-dressed and wholly confused.

SIX
THEO

Unacceptable. Unacceptable. Unacceptable.

Dad's voice bounces around my skull as I practically sprint to Eileen. It's loud, clear, and undeniable.

Blatant immoral behavior. Unacceptable.

My hands are shaking as I buckle my seatbelt and start the engine. I retrieve my phone from my pocket to stare once again at the text notification on my screen, only to toss my phone onto the passenger seat and grip the steering wheel.

Not here. I can't read it here.

I pull out of Caleb's driveway and start driving. I don't even really think about where I'm going yet. I just drive.

My phone buzzes again, but it's a text from Caleb this time. I grimace, guilt twisting in my gut as I remember Caleb's look of hurt and confusion as I fled from his room.

I should have said something to him. I should have explained why I was suddenly leaving—why I couldn't risk even another second in Caleb's presence. Surely he would understand, right?

But… *would* he understand?

As far as Caleb knows, I'm over feeling guilty and ashamed of our physical relationship. I've moved past it. I no longer care what other people think, and the only reason I'm still hesitant about public displays of affection is my parents' insistence.

But we weren't in public tonight. We were alone in Caleb's room. Alone in Caleb's *house* even. If there were ever an opportunity to finally take that next step in our relationship, tonight would have been it.

We could have had *sex* tonight.

If I hadn't gotten that text, Caleb and I could have—

The thought alone sends a wave of heat down my body, which only causes more panic and guilt to take its place.

Fuck, fuck, fuck.

I drive as carefully as possible to the nearest gas station and park. With a shaking breath, I unlock my phone to finally read the text from my dad.

> **DAD:** Hey Theo. I just wanted to let you know that I've been praying for you every single day. I love you and I'm proud of you. You are smart, kind, compassionate, and brave. If I didn't care deeply about you and your salvation, I wouldn't say anything, but my faith compels me to speak the truth, and I simply ask that you prayerfully consider some Bible passages I've put together. Your mom told me that you are with Harrison tonight, but is there a night this week that you and I can talk? Let me know. Thank you.

I feel like I'm going to throw up.

Of all the times for my dad to send me a text like this, *of course* it had to be tonight. At that moment. Right when Caleb and I were about to–

Immoral. Unacceptable.

I press my forehead against the cool texture of the steering wheel as I focus on breathing.

It's just a text, I remind myself. Dad doesn't know where I was or what we were doing when he sent it. There's no way. He even mentioned me being at Harrison's place. I'm not in any trouble. Everything is okay. Everything is fine.

It takes a few more minutes for the panic to subside, but once it does, I carefully navigate back home.

I shoot Caleb a text as soon as I park Eileen in my driveway, apologizing for leaving so abruptly. It's admittedly pretty vague, but I don't want to burden Caleb with the stuff about my dad. I don't want to worry him again. As far as he knows, my dad is slowly coming around to the idea of his son having a boyfriend, and it's only a matter of time before he accepts Caleb into the family.

What a fucking fairy tale. But that's kind of how Mom acts, too, waiting for Dad to have some kind of breakthrough that probably isn't coming. I honestly wish she wouldn't. It just makes it worse.

"You're going to push him away. You know that, right?"

"I have faith, Kora. God will give me the words to say to get through to him. I know my son, and I know he's going to come around."

The conversation has been playing on repeat all the way home.

My heart sinks again as I pull up to the house. I don't see Grace's car in the driveway, so she's either still at work or out with friends tonight. It's probably for the best, honestly. Grace has had enough fights with Dad lately—I don't want to be the cause of another one.

The house is quiet as I cross the threshold, and I say a silent prayer that my dad is busy as I sneak up to my room and flop onto my bed. My thoughts are racing, and my stomach is in knots. I can't keep this bottled up, but it's not like I can talk to Caleb about it. He wouldn't understand. This is all so foreign to him.

Who can I even talk to about this?

After a few moments of debate, I decide that maybe the old group chat might have some helpful advice for me. Or at least they'll make me feel better with a funny meme…

THEO: I have a bit of a serious question

> if you guys can handle that

OLIVER: uh oh

HARRISON: Sure, man. What's up? Elise: of course, Theo! <3

OLIVER: i'll try my best

My fingers hover over the keys as I consider how to phrase what I'm about to ask. These are my closest friends. Surely, they'll have at least some sort of advice.

> THEO: my dad sent me a text tonight, and it really has been messing with my head. I won't go through the whole thing, but it pretty much said that he thinks that me and Caleb being together is screwing up my faith.
>
> and I know that it's not true—Grace has been helping me with this stuff since I told her about me and Caleb—but it's still my dad saying all this stuff and it's really making me second guess myself.
>
> that makes no sense. sorry, this is all over the place.

OLIVER: it's okay, man. don't be sorry.

HARRISON: Your dad is just old school. Give him time. I think he'll come around eventually.

ELISE: Fuck him! (sorry, I know it's your dad) :(

OLIVER: did he actually say that he has a problem with you and Caleb?

THEO: not directly. he never says anything directly. just passive-aggressive comments till you do what he wants.

ELISE: Just ignore him. He's the one with the problem, not you.

HARRISON: You should talk to him. Be honest about how he's making you feel.

OLIVER: maybe have Grace in on the conversation? she likes to put your dad in his place lol

THEO: yeah, those are good ideas, guys. thank you.

I lock my screen, tossing my phone to the opposite end of the bed. I should have known there wasn't some magical answer to my problem. And I know they're just trying to be helpful, but they don't know what it's like in my head right now. Hell, even *I* don't know what's going on in here half the time.

My phone buzzes against the comforter, and I roll over to it, swiping open to view the new text.

Huh, it's an unknown number.

[UNKNOWN]: Hey Theo, it's Jake from small group
I know this is weird and random, so it's okay if you say no, but... can I ask you something?

My eyes widen. That's some weird timing.

THEO: hey Jake. sure, what did you want to ask?

The three dots pop up in our conversation, then disappear, cycling through a few times before his next message comes through.

JAKE: I've been thinking about maybe coming out to my parents. But, I'm not sure how my dad is going to react. He's not exactly the most open-minded person. He's not like, a bigot or anything. Honestly, I don't think I've ever heard him say a single thing about Queer people, but I'm still afraid.

THEO: I may not be the best person to talk to about this... my own family situation is all kinds of messed up right now.

JAKE: Sorry, I'm not trying to pry or anything. I just... I guess I just thought talking to another queer person might help me make up my mind.

I pause, staring at the word "queer" till it's burned into my vision. I guess I've never really considered that a label for myself. "Bisexual" was big enough to wrap my head around. But "queer" brings on a heap of new implications that I have no idea how to approach.

THEO: I'm not sure how much help I can be, but I'm here if you need to talk.

JAKE: Thank you, Theo. And sorry for cornering you at church the other day. I really wasn't trying to make a scene or anything. Honestly, I was just excited that there was someone else like me in the youth group.

THEO: it's no big deal. I was a little thrown off, but I appreciate you being discreet. I may have told the world about Caleb on HHH, but I'm not quite ready for it to be all over church, you know?

JAKE: I totally get that. I can't tell you how much that meant to me, by the way. Seeing you talk about Caleb during the interview. He's really lucky to have such a great guy like you as a boyfriend.

My cheeks flood with heat. Yeah, some great guy I am. I practically ran away from Caleb earlier. God, I have to fix this stuff in my head before it makes me do something even more stupid.

THEO: thanks. I'm lucky too. he's been so great.

JAKE: Was that him sitting with your family during the Christmas service?

THEO: yeah, that was him. took some convincing on my end to get him to agree to come. he had a lot of questions lol

JAKE: That bowtie he had was AMAZING. Tell him I want to know where he got it from.

THEO: haha, I'll be sure to ask.

JAKE: Okay, I won't take up any more of your night.

THEO: feel free to text me again if you need to talk.

JAKE: Thank you, Theo. <3

I switch back over to my text thread with Caleb, rereading his response to my bullshit excuse.

CALEB: It's completely fine <3. I'm sorry if I made you uncomfortable earlier. I didn't plan on us having the house to ourselves, and I may

have gotten carried away. It won't happen again, I promise.

A grunt of frustration escapes my chest as I roll over, planting my face into the coolness of my pillowcase. And suddenly, all I can think about is Caleb's lips on my neck and how smooth his chest felt.

Immoral. Unacceptable.

I cringe, squeezing my eyes shut.

This is really getting old.

Monday, January 8

"Oliver, you're such an idiot."

"No, I'm actually a genius. You just refuse to acknowledge it."

My face cracks into a smile as I approach our table, bracing myself for yet another ridiculous argument between Elise and Oliver that I'll surely be forced to pick a side on. It's absolutely worth it, though as I make my way to my usual seat between Oliver and Caleb, currently facing away from me.

"Hi, Theo," Harrison mutters from across the table from my seat. "Welcome back to the dysfunctional table."

Caleb twists around at the sound of my name, and my stomach flutters as his soft brown eyes meet mine. Before I set my tray on the table, I quickly check around the lunchroom for any church friends, and when I don't see them, I lean down to press a kiss into Caleb's copper curls. He smells like coconut and comfort, and for a split second, I want nothing more than to bury my face in him.

"Hey, you," Caleb says with a smile as I pull away, his cheeks tinted pink.

"Hey," I reply as I settle into my seat. "So, what did I miss?"

Caleb scoots a few inches closer. "Honestly, I can barely keep up myself."

"Oh, just the usual," Elise replies, clearly not hearing Caleb's response. "Oliver's being the himbo of the group."

From the other side of Caleb, Wren snorts as they drop their lunch tray on the table.

"Okay, rude," Oliver snaps. "Although I appreciate that you think I'm hot. I'll take it."

Elise rolls her eyes. "That would be what you'd take from that."

"Umm, excuse me," Freddy chimes in. "The position of Group Himbo is already taken, thank you very much."

"Aww," Andrew coos, leaning into Freddy. "No one is taking that away from you, babe. There can be multiple himbos in a friend group."

"Hang on, what qualifies someone as a himbo?" Harrison asks in his typical logical fashion.

"A himbo needs to be three things," Elise declares, holding up a hand to count. "Buff and pretty, a total sweetheart, and dumb as a rock."

Freddy gestures to himself. "Hello? That's obviously me." He glances over to Oliver. "Sorry, Ollie, but you're not quite there yet."

"You think he's too smart to be a himbo?" I ask, quirking an eyebrow.

Freddy scoffs. "No, I mean he's got no muscles!"

Oliver dramatically clutches his chest in feigned dismay. "What? No, I'm only missing the dumb part! I have muscles! I have oodles of muscles!"

"Oh, honey," Caleb says, reaching past me to pat Oliver's admittedly skinny forearm. "You're very pretty."

"And you're sweet," I add with a grin. "When you want to be."

Oliver yanks his lanky arms out of our reach, folding them across his chest in an exaggerated pout. "Y'all are unbelievable."

After a bit more giggling across the table, I finally turn my attention back to Oliver. "So what were you saying that got you called a himbo?"

"Well, I *was* going to set you up with your next big TikTok content, but *apparently* it's not good enough," Oliver replies defeatedly. "It seems that *some* people here don't even want me to try."

Elise sighs. "Oliver, you know that none of our parents are going to go for that."

"Go for what?" Caleb asks before I can get the words out.

Oliver wraps an arm around me and rests his hand on Caleb's shoulder, grinning ear to ear. "Picture it," he says, outstretching his right arm over the lunch table. "We all spend a night at The Kendling Hotel."

I inhale sharply. *Oh.*

"The what?" Freddy asks with a mouth full of sandwich.

"The Kendling Hotel," Oliver repeats excitedly. "It's a very old, very haunted hotel in downtown Atlanta, a few blocks away from Grady. Triple H did an episode on it like three years ago."

I know exactly which hotel Oliver is referring to. I'd completely forgotten about it. My mind races as I immediately start to consider the logistics.

Harrison snorts. "A hotel near Grady? No way, man. My parents would never—"

"Hold on, let me finish!" Oliver shouts. "Not just us! We'd have an adult chaperone."

"What adult in their right mind would chaperone this lot?" Wren asks.

"My stepmom!" Oliver replies, leaning over further to answer Wren. "She's been driving me crazy trying to plan something for me and my friends, and I think she'll probably just let us do whatever we want."

"What makes you think that?" Elise asks skeptically.

"Because she's desperate for me to like her," Oliver says, rolling his eyes. "She's only in her thirties, so adulthood hasn't completely smothered her lust for life yet. Honestly, she'd be pretty cool if she wasn't such a try-hard. It's kind of sad, really."

"And what makes you think our parents will be okay with her being the chaperone?" Harrison asks. "I don't even think she's met my parents."

He's right. Even if my parents have met Oliver's stepmom at some point,

I highly doubt they'd be willing to entrust her with us for an overnight excursion. Especially in downtown Atlanta, where my father believes I'll surely be murdered in cold blood the moment I enter the city limits. For someone who preaches about not living in fear, my dad certainly fears a lot of weird shit.

"I have a plan for that," Oliver says casually. "Trust me, once I hand the reins to Ashley, she'll win over all of your parents in a heartbeat."

Harrison and I exchange dubious glances. "Look, Oliver, it's a great idea on paper," I offer. "But you know my parents. They're not going to be that easy to convince."

"Yeah," Caleb adds. "Especially if *I'm* going to be there."

My heart sinks. He's right. I hate it, but he's right.

Oliver pats me supportively on my arm. "Oh, ye of little faith. Let me handle this, all right? You'll see!"

The table goes uncharacteristically quiet for a few moments, and I take the opportunity to reach for Caleb's hand. He immediately accepts it and begins rubbing reassuring circles against my thumb. Despite Oliver's optimism, I'm confident my parents will say no to this entire thing, so there's no need to get my hopes up. I'm just thankful for a distraction. My brain has been a nightmare all day, unable to stop thinking about Saturday night on Caleb's bed, my dad's horribly timed text, and Jake's casual use of the word "queer." I've been avoiding my dad ever since. Maybe if enough time goes by, he'll forget about it.

If only.

"So," Freddy breaks the silence. "What's so special about the Kendling Hotel? It sounds fancy."

"It used to be one of the fanciest hotels in the state," I answer, unable to stop myself from info-dumping. "It was constructed right at the turn of the century and was even one of the tallest buildings in Atlanta for a while. But in the thirties, there was a horrible fire. Like, really bad. One of the worst hotel fires in American history, I'm pretty sure."

"Oh wow," Andrew says with wide eyes. "Did a lot of people die?"

"Oh yeah. I think somewhere around one hundred and twenty people died, and dozens more were injured."

"Holy shit," Freddy mutters. "No wonder it's haunted! And you guys want to spend the night there?"

"Freddy, have you ever met us?" Wren says with a chuckle. "That's kind of our thing."

"Um, it's *y'all's* thing," Freddy replies. "I think I'll pass. How about you, Andrew?"

"Yeah, I don't mess with ghosts," Andrew agrees. "Sorry, it's a no for me, too."

"Your loss," Oliver says with a shrug.

Not long after, the lunch bell rings. As our group reluctantly parts ways to head to our respective classes, I stay close to Caleb's side for as long as possible.

"Hey," Caleb asks quietly. "I know I said it over text, but I really am sorry about the other night. I didn't mean to get so carried away—"

I shake my head to stop him. "Don't be sorry. It wasn't your fault." I squeeze his hand and wish more than anything I could explain more, but I don't want to upset him. I've put him through enough. I just want him to be happy. He deserves to be happy—he deserves so much more, but the least I can do is protect him from this. I smile reassuringly, hoping it's enough to convince him. "I'm fine now. Don't worry."

Caleb studies me for a moment but eventually relents. "Okay. I'll try not to."

"Good." I lift our clasped hands to my lips and kiss the back of his palm. "I love you, you know."

"I know. And I love you, too."

Warmth radiates in my chest. We love each other. And that's all that matters.

SEVEN
CALEB

Friday, January 12

"I can't believe this actually came together."

Wren sets their phone down on the armrest of the tattered couch. We've just finished watching the Triple H release, and Freddy looks up from his spot on the floor, pulling himself away from whatever ooey, gooey back and forth he and Andrew have been locked into all night. Every time I look over, he's got the biggest grin on his dumb face. It's adorable and super annoying.

"Huh?"

"At least pretend you're paying attention," I tease Freddy, tossing a popcorn kernel at him. It lands on the cushion of curls atop his head, but he doesn't seem to notice. "The group text has been blowing up all day."

Freddy's nose scrunches. "Ah, I muted that thing ages ago. You guys talk too much."

"Gee, thanks." Wren throws a pillow at Freddy, but it goes wide. "Glad to know your friends mean so much to you."

"I love you both dearly, but if I have to suffer through any more of Oliver's endless shitposting or another argument between Elise and Harrison in the group thread, I'm going to yeet my phone into the nearest chasm. Why do straight people always have to make everything about them?"

"Brave of you to assume Elise is straight," I chime in.

"Is she not?"

I shrug. "She hasn't told me otherwise. You're making assumptions, Freddy, darling."

"Whatever, just tell me what you're talking about."

"We're going to the Kendling Hotel next weekend," I say, resisting the urge to throw another object at him. He's just being Freddy. I don't know why it's getting to me today.

Freddy's eyes go wide. "Whoa, really? I thought y'all were joking."

"Apparently not," says Wren, rising from their seat. They wander over to the makeup station, pulling open a drawer and digging through it. "Oliver's stepmom must be some kind of logistics savant."

My phone buzzes, and I open the itinerary that Wren was referring to. "Wow, it's very detailed."

Freddy scrambles to his feet, then forces himself into the space next to me in the armchair. "So, you and Theo will be sharing a room, I take it?" He wiggles his eyebrows in this way I can only describe as obscene.

Warmth grips the back of my neck. "Yeah, and Harrison and Oliver will be there too, so it's not like we'll be alone or anything."

"But you'll be sharing a bed," Freddy continues. "And we all know what happens under the sheets when the lights go out." He drags a finger along my leg and I swat it away.

"Is sex all you ever think about?" I ask, the heat spreading to my face.

What I don't tell him is that I've been thinking the exact same thing all week.

Freddy quirks an eyebrow at me. "Pretty much. And you two never want to talk about it, so I'm always forced to be the one to bring it up. How did I become friends with such prudes?"

Wren returns with a basket of nail polish bottles and an exasperated sigh.

"Fine, Freddy. What act of depravity are you going to regale us with this evening?"

Freddy folds his arms across his chest. "Now I'm not so sure I want to share."

"Fine by me," I say, untangling his legs from mine and joining Wren on the couch. My nails are chipped to hell, and they could use a fresh coat. "I actually like Andrew, and I'm not sure I want to hear about whatever the two of you do behind closed doors. How can I look him in the eye after that?"

Wren snorts a laugh, unscrewing the cap off a bottle of black polish.

"Then give us an update on you and Theo," Freddy replies, sprawling out in the armchair with a grand flourish. "Have you convinced that sweet angel to do the Devil's tango yet?"

I purposefully avoid Freddy's leering stare, absorbed in choosing a new color for my nails. Maybe a green? Yeah, Theo would like that.

"Yeah, I'm curious too." Wren nudges me with their shoulder. "Not that you *have* to tell us anything. It's up to you."

"We haven't done anything," I say, my voice tight. I don't know why I haven't told them what happened last week. How the minute my shirt came unbuttoned, Theo freaked out and literally ran away. Maybe they could help me figure out why it happened or why I feel so fucking shitty every time I picture the look on his face before he left.

But I can't bring myself to tell them. It would make it all too real. In my head, I could at least hold onto the hope that Theo was telling me the truth. Once I say it out loud....

"I mean, we've kissed and stuff, but that's it. We're taking things slow."

Wren gives an exaggerated nod while Freddy stares at me with a look of incredulity.

"Well, you've got a whole weekend of haunted hotel fun ahead of you," Freddy says after a moment. "Just be sure to hang a sock on the door if you two decide to do more than 'kissing and stuff.' I'd hate for you to scar poor Oliver like that."

"I think Harrison may take it worse," Wren suggests. "Or maybe they'd both decide to stay with the ghosts forever and jump out the window."

Freddy and Wren laugh, and I manage to crack a smile. They never fail to lighten my mood. It's one of the many reasons I love them both.

"I guess I could stand to hear about you and Andrew," I say, uncapping the bottle of deep green polish–Theo's favorite shade. "The two of you have been chatting non-stop anyway. What's going on?"

"Funny enough, we're actually planning our date for next weekend. We'd go this weekend, but he's got some church trip to an apple orchard that sounds very boring. Anyway, he told me last night that he thinks he's ready to take our physical relationship to the next level, so we've been talking all day about what he wants to do and what each other's boundaries are. Is it weird to say I'm nervous? I've never cashed in someone's V-card before."

"Virginity is a patriarchal invention," Wren interjects.

Freddy rolls his eyes. "Even so, I want to make sure that it's a good experience for him. My first time was sort of terrible. Bad breath is such a mood killer. Andrew's first time should be perfect. He deserves it." Freddy pauses, scrunching his nose. "God, when did I become such a sap?"

"I was going to ask the same question."

Freddy cuts me a look that forces a giggle out of me. "Ugh. I hate this." He flops back against the cushion, burying his face in his hands. "Where did the badass Freddy who didn't give a shit about breaking hearts go?"

Wren sets down their polish brush, crossing over to wrap their arms around Freddy's neck. "He grew a heart, the poor bastard. Caleb, I think our little Freddy is actually in *love*."

"We never thought the day would come," I join in, careful not to smudge my wet nails as I rustle Freddy's hair. "I think I might cry."

Freddy squirms under our love. "Okay, okay, that's enough of the squishy stuff. You're starting to freak me out."

Wren releases their hold on him, squatting down so they're at eye level.

"Hey, Andrew's first time is going to be great because he'll be doing it with someone who cares enough about him to actually give a shit."

Freddy gives a small nod, the corners of his eyes shining with moisture. "Yeah, you're right. Thanks, Wren. That means a lot. You forgot to mention one little thing, though."

Wren rests a hand on his arm. "What's that, honey?"

"That I also give really great head."

"Get out of my house."

Freddy cackles as Wren pounces on him, shoving him further into the cushion.

"You. Are. The. Worst." Wren punctuates each word with a playful smack to Freddy's backside as he twists underneath them.

I'm laughing hard enough that I've got tears in my eyes when Wren finally climbs off him, straightening their band t-shirt and inspecting the ruined paint on their nails.

Freddy peels himself from the armchair, cocking an eyebrow at me. "You didn't want to get in on the physical violence?"

"Nah, Wren's got that part covered."

"Damn right." Wren pumps a fist in the air.

Freddy rights himself, running a hand through his hair and picking out the piece of popcorn that miraculously stayed in place. "All jokes aside, I guess we're all in for an eventful time next weekend. You guys will be getting haunted, and I'll be getting laid. Here's hoping they both go well!" He grabs one of the cans of Coke from the coffee table, raising it into the air.

"That one's mine."

Freddy shrugs, taking a long sip, then belching. "What's a little backwash between friends."

"Andrew is so lucky to have you," Wren mutters, rolling their eyes.

"Caleb, can you come in here for a minute?"

Mom's voice travels down the hall from the kitchen as I close the front door behind me. The rest of the night at Wren's devolved into us convincing Freddy to paint his toenails Andrew's favorite shade of orange and then sharing TikToks till it was already past nine, and Freddy offered to drop me off on his way home.

I set my backpack down by the door, kick off my shoes, then head for the kitchen.

To my surprise, both Mom and Dad are there to greet me, standing at the island counter, a pot of coffee resting between them. Dad looks tired–he just got back in town this morning, and probably hasn't caught up on his sleep–and Mom is still dressed from the office, so she probably hasn't been home long.

"What's up?" I ask, a sense of dread swelling in my stomach, even though I'm pretty sure I've got nothing for them to hold against me. My last report card? Straight A's. Curfew? Haven't missed a single cutoff. Pregnancy scare? Well, they don't have to worry about that.

"We wanted to talk to you about the trip," Dad starts, pulling over a stool and settling on top of it.

"Oh. Okay." My pulse spikes, my feet glued in place by the kitchen table. Are they having second thoughts? Maybe Mom's phone call with Ashley didn't go as well as I thought it did. No, that can't be it. The two of them were laughing over some nineties movie reference that Ashley made, and after she got off the phone, Mom mentioned wanting to go out for drinks with her. Maybe Dad read up on the hotel and got spooked? Nah, that can't be it. He doesn't even believe in ghosts, and he loves historical buildings. I'm surprised he's not tagging along, to be honest.

"This is going to be the first time you and Theo are staying overnight, away from home," Mom says, gripping her coffee mug and holding it in her hands like a comfort object. "And we wanted to know that we trust you to make good decisions while you're away."

"O-kay." I separate the syllables to show I'm not following.

"You're both approaching adulthood," Dad picks up, throwing a glance over to Mom. "And I know that boys of your age are going to… do things that boys of your age want to do."

Oh god. Please, no. This can't be happening.

Dad continues, rushing through the words like he's trying to get them all out in one breath. "Your mother and I want to make sure you know that we trust you to stay safe and that you and Theo won't rush into anything that you're not ready for."

I want to sink into the fucking ground. The earth needs to swallow me up right fucking now. Take me, dirt! I'm all yours!

"But that's your call to make," Mom jumps in. "We're not here to tell you what to do with your body, only that we're here to help you with any questions you might have. Plus, there's something we wanted you to have before you started packing. Go ahead, Bert."

Dad pulls out a small cardboard box from his jacket pocket and sets it on the counter. It takes me less than a second to recognize the logo, and my desire to spontaneously combust has never been greater.

"Oh my god, I don't need those."

"Condoms aren't just for preventing pregnancy," Mom counters, clutching her mug even tighter. "There's loads of STIs going around–"

Dad snorts a laugh, and Mom cuts a look at him.

"What? You said loads."

Mom rolls her eyes, and I see my chance to butt in.

"Okay, look," I say, steering this dumpster fire of a conversation before it gets any worse. "I appreciate this, really I do. But this is all totally unnecessary."

My parents share another look between them.

"I know this is uncomfortable, Caleb," Dad says, taking a serious tone. "But it's important to your mother and I that we know we've done everything to prepare you for the realities of life. This conversation may not be relevant to you right now, but if–and when–the time comes, we want you to be prepared with all the knowledge and tools you need to stay safe."

"Well, when you put it like that…"

"We love you, Caleb," Mom says, setting down her mug. "Trust me, this isn't our favorite topic either. But we're all mature enough to have this conversation. At least, you and I are." She cuts another look at Dad, who just shrugs.

"Okay, okay. I'll take them, I guess." I scurry over to the counter, grab the box, and shove it into my pocket as quickly as I can. "Was there anything else?"

"Ah, um, yeah," Dad fidgets on top of his stool, reaching into the bowl of fruit on the countertop and pulling out a single banana. "Just wanted to make sure you're clear on how those work." He reaches into his pocket once again and pulls out a single wrapped condom, setting it next to the phallic fruit.

"I've got it," I say quickly, backing away from the counter. "Thanks again. I love you guys too. I'm going to leave now."

I bolt out of the kitchen before they can argue, and a shared sigh follows me down the hall. Good to know they're just as relieved at my departure as I am.

At the base of the stairs, I take a second to let out a breath. Why the fuck is everyone in my life suddenly so caught up with talking about sex? It's like there's a huge sign on my forehead that says, "I tried to boink my boyfriend."

It wasn't like that, though. I really wasn't trying to push things with Theo. It just happened. And now I can't think about him without seeing that look on his face–the pain in his eyes. Was I the cause? What did I do to make him feel that way? It can't be a coincidence that it happened just as things were getting hot and heavy. But how can I ask him about it if he keeps assuring me everything is fine?

I blot the tears of frustration from my eyes.

This isn't something parents cover in their sex talks.

Hurrying up the stairs, I make a beeline for my room, wanting to get rid of the contents of my pocket as quickly as possible.

"Caleb?"

I stop outside Lola's door just as she opens it, leaning against the frame. She's in her PJ's even though it's barely nine-thirty. Her red, curly hair is pulled back off her face, and she's got her glasses on, which means she's probably spent her evening wrist-deep in a term paper.

"What's wrong?" she asks, quirking an eyebrow.

"It's nothing," I reply, taking another step toward my room.

Lola catches me at the elbow. "Beep, beep, beep. That's the bullshit detector going off, bro. I thought you realized you can't hide stuff from me by now. Come here." She drags me into her bedroom, closing the door behind her. She sits me down on the end of her bed, lifting my chin with a finger. "Honey, you've been crying. What's going on?"

"It's nothing," I repeat, shoving my hand in my pocket to try and cover the bulbous shape of the condom box.

Lola isn't convinced. She pulls over the chair from her desk, sinking into it. "Does this have anything to do with Mom and Dad cornering you in the kitchen?"

"Oh god, you knew about that?"

Lola laughs, nodding her head. "They asked me to clear the room when you sent the 'on my way home' message. How bad was it? Did Dad try to put a condom on a banana?"

"He did that to you, too?"

"Oh yeah, but the condoms he got were extra lubed, so it kept slipping out of his hands. Mom had to step it. It was mortifying."

"Yeah, I can imagine." I pull the box out of my pocket, putting my embarrassment on full display. "They wanted me to have these before I leave on the trip with Theo."

"Oh, you poor thing," Lola says through her snickering. "I know that sex talks can be traumatizing, but they're nothing to cry over."

I toss the box aside, looking down at my hands. "I wasn't crying about that."

"You can talk to me, Cal," Lola says, any laughter dropped from her tone.

"If you want."

Heat builds behind my eyes, and I have to blink a few times before the tears start spilling over.

"Hey." Lola's hands are on mine, her voice soft. "You're okay. Just let it out."

I take in a shuddered breath, trying to swallow the lump in my throat, but it doesn't go down, and the tears really start flowing, running down my cheeks.

"I think I fucked things up with Theo." I dab at my face with the end of my sleeve. "And I don't know what I did, and he keeps telling me everything's fine, but I know it's not–I can *feel it*–and I can't talk to him about it and–"

My breath hitches with a sob, cutting off my words.

"Take a second," Lola says, sliding from her chair onto the bed next to me and wrapping a gentle arm around my back.

I fold into her side, wrapping both arms around her as my chest heaves. The crying lasts a lot longer than I want it to, but eventually I'm able to reel myself back in, and only Lola's tear-stained shoulder is worse for wear.

"Tell me about it," Lola says after my breathing returns to a normal pace, her arm still holding me in place.

"Last week, when me and Theo came back after our date," I start, my voice hoarse and barely audible. "We were in my room. And things got… heated between us. I kept checking in with him, making sure he was okay with what we were doing. I didn't want him to freak because I know he's still figuring some stuff out. We got to this moment on my bed, and he just stopped, like he was coming out of a trance or something. When I asked if he was okay, he had this expression–" I shudder, the image of Theo popping into my mind. "It was like he was in pain. Like looking at me made him hurt."

Lola listens quietly, her hand now working small circles on my back.

"He sent me a text later that night apologizing, but he wouldn't tell me what happened. I tried to ask, but every time, he shut me down, saying that I didn't do anything wrong. But that can't be true. Things were going so well between us, but I think I pushed him too far."

Fresh tears well in my eyes, but I blink them away, taking a deep breath to steady myself.

"I can feel how much you love him," Lola says after a moment. "You wouldn't be this torn up if that wasn't the case."

"I do," I say through an exhale. "And he says that he loves me, and I haven't had any reason to doubt him. But this… I don't know what to do."

"Maybe he just needs a little time," Lola offers, brushing away more tears from my cheeks. "You said it before. He's still figuring things out. I remember a few months ago when you were crushing on him so badly, you told me that being with him was worth all of these big feelings it brought up. Well, now it sounds like you and Theo need to have a little heart-to-heart just to make sure you're on the same page."

She's right. As much as I hate to admit it, I've been dancing around the subject long enough. I need to tell Theo how it made me feel when he walked out. Maybe then he'll trust in me enough to talk about whatever is going on with him.

Maybe.

"You're right. I'm going to talk to him."

Lola pumps her fist in the air. "Woot woot! I love to hear it. Say it again."

"No chance in hell," I reply through a laugh.

"Well, look at it this way, Cal." She grabs the box of condoms from behind us, dangling them in front of my face. "If the two of you can clear the air, Dad's got you hooked up to bang a few out while you're at it."

"Oh my god, shut up!" I snatch the box from her, rocketing off the bed.

"Don't be silly, wrap your willy!" Lola calls after me as I flee her room.

I slam the door to my bedroom behind me, throwing the stupid box into the corner with my unpacked suitcase before falling face-first onto my bed.

Sometimes, I hate this family so much.

But I love them all the same.

EIGHT
THEO

Sunday, January 14

Slipping out of church today is easier than usual. Dad was quietly summoned away during worship for what I can only assume is someone from his Sunday school class wanting to get baptized. Mom is busy helping with the children's ministry, and Nathaniel's small group was roped into communion duty. Harrison is visiting Elise's church this week. So as soon as the final song begins, Jake and I make our escape to Eileen to wait for Nathaniel.

Just as we arrive, Jake swears under his breath. "Shit."

"What's wrong?"

"I forgot to tell my dad I was going with you," he replies, retrieving his phone from his pocket. "I'm just gonna call him real quick, probably leave him a voicemail."

"Sure, go ahead," I say, leaning against the door of Eileen. "We're still waiting for Nate, anyway."

As Jake steps away, I open the car door and settle in the front seat. There's no one else around yet, and I enjoy the chilly January weather, so there's no need to start Eileen's engine—I can simply sit with the door open, relaxing as

I wait. In fact, it's the first time I've felt any semblance of peace all day.

There was a time not very long ago when waking up every Sunday for church was nothing more than a simple routine. For the most part, going to church every week felt like a minor inconvenience—a small price to pay to avoid displeasing my parents. Some Sundays were worse than others. There were definitely days when dragging myself out of bed for church felt a lot like clocking into work or going to school—a necessary chore I couldn't get out of, so why bother fighting? The guilt of skipping church for my own selfish reasons far outweighed any possible benefits as far as I could tell, so I never really considered risking it.

Nowadays, it's not quite that simple.

Now when I go to church, I listen to the same old Bible lessons and recall all the things Grace and her school friends taught me about the church's deeply homophobic and misogynistic history. I smile and greet church members I've known my whole life and wonder how much their perceptions of me would change if they found out I had a boyfriend. I watch Sienna leading worship, and I relive that horrible moment on the Ferris wheel late last year, and the all-consuming terror and shame that followed. I sing along with hymns and praise music, and slowly realize that where I used to feel a connection with God, I feel…

I feel *nothing*.

"Hey, Theodore."

I'm so caught up in my own thoughts that I don't even recognize the syrupy sweet smell of vanilla until it's too late. "Sienna."

Sienna's piercing blue eyes are bright and wide when I finally meet her gaze. Her eyelids shimmer with an unfamiliar bronzy glow as she blinks, and her lashes flutter dramatically. She's wearing significantly more eye makeup than usual—which is to say, any makeup at all. It's honestly a bit unsettling.

"How—how are you? How've you been?" she asks eagerly, nervous energy radiating off her in waves.

I look past her for Jake or Nathaniel—anyone that can get me out of this conversation—but Jake is facing away from me, just out of earshot and still on his phone. "I'm fine," I answer. "How are you?"

"Good," she answers quickly. "I'm very blessed. Far more than I deserve."

I nod, still avoiding eye contact. "Good. That's, uh—I'm glad to hear it."

There's a moment of awkward silence, and I scramble to think of some kind of excuse to make her leave, but Sienna clears her throat before I get the chance. "Yeah, hey, um, Theo, I just wanted to—" she stammers. "—it's been good to see—well, I'm just really glad you're here."

"Of course," I answer, robotically at first, but something about her words doesn't sit right. I frown at her. "Why wouldn't I be?"

Sienna shakes her head dismissively, her orange curls swirling around her face. "Oh, no, yeah, of course, I was just—nevermind, it doesn't matter."

I narrow my eyes. "You were just what?"

She shifts her weight from one leg to the other, then tries to shrug it off. "It's silly. I was just a little worried for you—about you, I mean, spiritually, after—well, you know, after everything that happened."

My stomach twists, anger swelling in my gut as I stare at her. My mind races with responses, a flurry of well-deserved cruelty I want to throw back in her face, but all that comes out is a slow, deliberate echo of her own words. "After everything that happened?"

Sienna's face drains of color. "I'm—I'm sorry, I shouldn't have said—"

"And by 'everything that happened'," I interrupt, lifting myself up and out of Eileen and onto my feet where I only barely match her height. "Are you referring to when you outed me to my parents?"

Her mouth snaps shut and her grip on her purse tightens. "Theo, I'm sorry, I shouldn't—"

"No, I just want to make sure we're both talking about the same thing," I snap, my voice dripping with sarcasm. "Because when you say it like that, *'everything that happened,'* it almost makes it seem like it was just something that *happened* to me, like an accident." I take a step closer to her, and she takes a step back. "When, in fact, it was something done *to* me—intentionally, knowingly, and on purpose—by you. Do you know what I mean?"

Sienna nods, her panicked eyes darting around in search of someone to rescue her, which just makes me angrier. She knows I would never hurt her. Why is she trying to make people think that I'm a threat to her?

Shit, does *she* think I am a threat to her?

"Is there a problem over here?"

Chase suddenly appears beside us wearing an uncharacteristically serious expression. His eyes are fixed mostly on Sienna, and I'm immediately aware of how bad this looks.

Sienna gulps audibly. "N–No, everything is fine," she squeaks unconvincingly. "I was just leaving."

"Things don't seem fine to me," Chase says sternly. "In fact, I'd say it's pretty sus. Theo, do you have anything to say for yourself?"

"They were just talking, Chase," Jake calls out before I can answer, and all three of us whip our heads towards Jake as he approaches. "Theo was minding his own business in his car waiting for me to finish talking to my dad. I don't know what they're talking about, but whatever it is, I know she started it."

Chase furrows his brow as he turns back to Sienna and me. "Is there something the three of us need to discuss in private? Perhaps invite Joyce or Brandon, or maybe some parents in on the conversation?"

Sienna shakes her head. "No, sir."

"Theo?"

"No, sir."

Chase continues staring us both down for several more uncomfortable moments until he finally lets out a sigh and runs a frustrated hand through his spiky hair. "Look. I know at some point you two had some of kind of… *situation-ship*, and I don't know if that's still ongoing or what, but what I do know is that you don't need to bring that junk here, okay?"

I nod my understanding, casting my eyes to the ground. I can feel my neck and cheeks beginning to burn with embarrassment.

"Well, maybe Sienna needs to mind her own business for once," Jake mumbles.

"You say something, Jacob?" Chase asks pointedly.

I glance up to see Jake glaring at Sienna hatefully. I wince. "Jake, don't—"

"I said," Jake replies, turning his angry gaze back to Chase. "I think Sienna needs to mind her own business and leave Theo alone."

Sienna makes a pitiful sound—something between a gasp and a sniffle—and Chase's eyes narrow in on Jake. "Jake, that's enough. Apologize to Sienna, right now."

Jake's eye twitches, but he says nothing.

"Jacob Buchanon, I mean it. Apologize now."

Jake looks my way, and I silently plead with my eyes. *Please. Anything to end this conversation.*

Finally, he sighs. "Sorry, Sienna."

Sienna nods, averting her eyes to the ground and crossing her arms tightly across her chest.

"Thank you," Chase exhales. "Now, let's all go our separate ways, maybe pray about this, and get back together on Wednesday with better attitudes, alright?"

"Will do," I mutter.

"Sure thing," Jake grumbles.

"Amen," Sienna whispers, and it takes another bout of strength not to roll my eyes.

And just like that, Chase is all smiles again. "Dope! Good talk, everyone. Now, Sienna, I did have some things I wanted to talk to you about worship on Wednesday if you have a few minutes?"

"Of course," Sienna replies, her perky energy already returning as she and Chase turn and make their way toward The Foundation building.

Jake and I exchange a wordless stare just as Nathaniel approaches Eileen with wide eyes.

"Ready to go?" I ask.

"Yep," Jake says.

Nate groans. "Man, how do I miss all the good stuff?" he grumbles as he opens the rear door and climbs in.

The three of us end up going through the drive thru of a local burger joint, parking in the back of the lot, and eating in the car with the engine running. The last thing I want to do right now is interact with other people, especially if those other people are from church. Fortunately, Jake and Nate feel the same way.

To my dismay, however, it isn't long before the subject of Sienna comes up again.

"Man, Sienna really pisses me off," Jake seethes, crumpling up the foil that once held his greasy burger. "Like, I used to feel fairly neutral about her. She's always seemed pretty harmless—maybe a little annoying from time to time, but that's all. But now, knowing what she did to you? Outing you to your parents? I can never look at her the same way again. I mean, who does shit like that? What a bitch."

I can't help but flinch at his harsh words, despite how much I agree with them. Maybe it's because Nathaniel is in the car, but then again, I've definitely heard Nate use similar language about Sienna, so I keep my mouth occupied with a handful of fries.

"And the fact that she still has the gall to try and talk to you like nothing happened?" Jake continues. "Unbelievable. There's no way she doesn't know what she's doing. She gets to say whatever she wants to you, and if you engage at all, she can turn around and play the victim to everyone else and get away with it. It's disgusting. Chase has no idea who he's dealing with. Or what she's capable of."

"And he can't find out, Jake," I counter. "I can't just tell Chase that Sienna outed me without outing myself to him in the process."

"I know, and that makes it fucking worse!" Jake barks. "It's bullshit!"

"It really is," Nate chimes in from the backseat. "She shouldn't be able to get away with it."

I shake my head. "Look, guys, I appreciate that y'all have my back, but there's seriously nothing we can do, so I think we should just drop it and move on"

Jake scoffs, shifting aggressively in the passenger seat. "But what if she pulls that shit again? If she believes that reconciling with you is what God wants, she's never going to stop."

Shit. He's right. "I don't know. Maybe I just need to try harder to avoid her."

"But how?" Nathaniel asks. "Sienna is always at church. It's not like you can just stop going. Dad would lose his shit on you again."

"Unless," Jake says thoughtfully. "Unless you just stay away from the youth group. Do stuff at church that you know she's not involved in."

"Like what?" I ask bitterly.

"You could volunteer to help with the kids' ministry with Mom," Nate suggests.

"Or the tech team," Jake adds. "Or communion, or the worship band—hell, anywhere, really, as long as it's not the youth band."

Hmm. Helping out with the kids sounds like a lot of work, but the tech team could be something. "Do they let teenagers do that stuff?"

"Definitely," Jake answers. "Plus, think of how good it makes you look to your parents. You said it yourself—your dad has been all over you lately. But this? Willingly volunteering your time to serve in a ministry? That is a guaranteed way to get back on his good side."

Holy shit. I can't believe I haven't thought of this before. It's a win-win. I can put some distance between Sienna and me and get back in Dad's good graces. I glance back at Nate in the rearview mirror. "Do you think Dad will buy it?"

Nate raises an eyebrow. "I can't see why he wouldn't. It's very on-brand for you—always trying to suck up to adults."

Jake snorts beside me, and I roll my eyes. "Gee, thanks," I mutter sarcastically.

"Just saying," Nate adds with a shrug.

He's right, and we all know it. Which is exactly why I know it'll work. "Yeah, it's definitely worth a shot."

"You know," Jake adds. "I think I might tag along, too. I could definitely use a break from the endless redundancy of Sunday school every week. I mean, there's only so many ways we unpack stories from a two-thousand-year-old book, right? Isn't it time to move on?"

I let out a small laugh. "I think if my dad heard you say that, he'd have an aneurysm."

"I'm starting to think our dads might be the same person."

"I'm so sorry."

Jake smiles. He raises his paper cup half-full of soda towards mine. "To outsmarting our shitty dads until we're old enough to get the hell out of here."

There's a familiar twist of guilt in my stomach as I glance at Nate in the backseat, but I swallow it down and mirror Jake's grin. "Cheers," I say as I tap my cup to his.

"How was church for you today, Theo?"

I blink out of my thoughts when I realize Mom is talking to me at the dinner table. "It was fine," I answer with a casual shrug. "The usual."

"The usual, huh?" Dad says, a hint of sarcasm in his voice. "Church boring you these days, son?"

Shit. That's not how I wanted to bring this up. "No, nothing like that."

Dad watches me for a moment, then turns his attention back to his dinner.

I catch a glimpse of Nathaniel, and our eyes meet across the table. He gives me the subtlest of nods, encouraging me to press on.

I chew on the inside of my cheek. Maybe this is actually the perfect segue to bring this up. I straighten my posture to face them and clear my throat. "Actually, I've been thinking about changing things up a little."

Dad stiffens, and Mom's eyes go wide.

Nathaniel arches an eyebrow at me.

"How so?" Dad asks tensely.

"I was thinking about maybe joining the tech team on Sundays," I blurt. "Like, maybe help with the audio and visual stuff for Big Church? I don't know, I don't feel like I'm getting as much out of church as I used to, so I want to try to volunteer and see if serving helps me feel closer to God."

Mom and Dad exchange a glance, then Mom smiles at me. "Is that so?"

I nod. "Yeah. I think I could be pretty helpful when it comes to AV stuff."

Mom beams. "That's lovely, *aroha*. I'm sure your father can get you in touch with the right people at church to get you plugged in."

Dad is studying me closely, but he nods. "Yeah, I'll shoot Frank a text tomorrow and see if he can add you to the rotation." He narrows his eyes. "The tech team usually has to show up extra early on Sunday mornings—like around 7 AM. Are you sure you can manage that?"

"Yeah, I think I can handle it."

"And they don't get to sneak out early to beat the lunch crowd."

"I know."

"And you need to pay attention through the whole service."

"Michael, come on," Mom nudges him.

"I know, Dad," I insist confidently. "I can do it."

"All right, all right," Dad relents. "I'm just making sure you understand what's expected of you as a member of the team. I have no doubt you'll be great at the technical stuff."

"I understand," I say earnestly. "I'll take it seriously, I promise."

Dad's expression finally softens, and he smiles. "Good," he says, patting me firmly on the shoulder. "I'm proud of you, son."

My chest swells at his words, like the enormous sails of a ship after a huge gust of wind. "Thanks, Dad."

"You're very welcome."

I glance at Mom to see her grinning ear-to-ear.

Unsurprisingly, Nathaniel says nothing. But he doesn't need to.

For the first time in months, my dad is proud of me.

CALEB: Have your parents said yes to the Kendling Hotel thing yet? Theo: I'm working on it

THEO: haven't asked yet

CALEB: You should probably do that soon, silly! It's less than a week out now.

THEO: don't worry, I will <3

Thursday, January 18

"The Kendling Hotel?" Mom frowns, her face twisting with disgust. "Isn't that the old historic hotel near Grady Hospital?"

I shuffle my feet nervously. The ghost-hunting weekend trip—already fully booked and planned by Oliver's stepmom with a full itinerary and everything—is now only three days away. I've procrastinated it for as long as I could, far too anxious to bring it up to either parent all week, but today is my last chance. Dad isn't home from work yet, and Mom's furiously typing away on her laptop, clearly distracted by something going on at work. It's the perfect opportunity.

As long as I don't fuck it up, that is.

"I mean, yes, but Ms. Ashley Hammond will be there, too. Oliver's stepmom. She's paying for the rooms."

"Rooms? Plural?"

"Yeah, I think they're adjoining hotel rooms."

"How many people are going?"

I swallow, counting in my head but very carefully excluding Caleb. "Um, there's six of us, I think. Oliver, Harrison, Elise, and our friend Wren. Plus Ashley makes five, and I'd be six."

Mom furrows her brow. "Isn't Wren Caleb's friend?"

I shrug. "They're our friend now, too."

"What about Caleb? He's not going?"

I shove my hands into my pockets to keep from fidgeting. I didn't want it to come to this, but I have no choice. I have to lie. "No. He can't. He has a family thing."

Mom turns away from her laptop to study me with narrowed eyes. My heart is pounding violently against my ribcage, and I feel like I might puke. She's going to figure it out. She's going to know I'm lying. She's my mom, she's going to see right through—

"Okay."

I stare at her for several seconds before finally blinking. "Really?"

She nods. "Yes, really. You can go as long as you keep your phone's location on so we can check on you. If you're going anywhere else in the city, you text us. If we see you anywhere on the map that's not the hotel, your father and I will have to assume you've been kidnapped and we're coming to search for you. Understand?"

I nod eagerly. "Yeah, yeah, I understand. Thanks, Mom!"

"Be smart. Stay together. Don't go outside after dark."

"I know, we won't—"

"And keep your phone charged—"

"Mom—"

"And if a homeless person approaches you—"

"Mom," I say a little louder, reaching out to touch her shoulder gently. "I know. I'll be careful."

Mom sighs, her lips twitching up into a smile. "I know. I trust you. And I trust Ashley, too. Just be careful."

"I will. I promise."

"Good." Mom places her hand over mine and pulls me in to kiss my cheek. "I love you, *aroha*." "I love you, too, Mom."

Unacceptable. Blatant immoral behavior.

Guilt is already building up like bile in my stomach, churning and twisting as I hear Dad's words echoing in my head again. Maybe Dad's right. Maybe that's who I've become now. A liar. A rebellious teenager. Immoral. *Unacceptable.*

Before I let my thoughts spiral any further, I clear my throat. "Well, I'll leave you to your work stuff. I've got homework to finish, too."

Mom runs a hand through her hair, her dark eyes already glued back to her laptop screen. "Thanks, sweetie. Dad should be home with dinner in an hour or so."

I nod my understanding, turning to make my way upstairs. Once I'm in the safety of my bedroom, I shake myself out of it. There's no use dwelling on it. What's done is done. I've got other things to focus on.

THEO: okay guys, I'm officially in. mom said yes to this weekend

OLIVER: woooo! About time!

CALEB: Awesome!! <3<3

HARRISON: Nice!

ELISE: yay!! <3

OLIVER: I was getting worried there for a bit

they didn't care about you going overnight on a trip with your bf?

I stare at the text from Oliver for about a second or two before deciding to ignore it. Change the subject. We have a mission, after all. No room for distractions.

THEO: okay let's talk ghosts. if we're gonna capture something again, we need to try and replicate the conditions of St. Catherine's as best we can

OLIVER: YES! I have some plans!
    I was gonna wait until Saturday to tell you but Ashley is such a paranormal/true crime freak that she actually got us some ghost-hunting tech!!

ELISE: seriously?? That's so funny!

CALEB: Sounds fun!

HARRISON: *eye roll emoji*

THEO: holy shit that's awesome!! what specific things did she get?

OLIVER: shit I forgot, let me go ask her

WREN: Details, Oliver. You can't forget the details.

HARRISON: You guys know that paranormal investigation technology is a scam, right? Ashley didn't spend money on that stuff, did she?

ELISE: *gif of Michael Jackson eating popcorn*

THEO: lmao here we go

I chuckle softly to myself, then sigh with relief. Another crisis averted. Maybe I can do this after all.

Saturday, January 20

Despite my excitement, the guilt of lying to Mom continues to haunt me over the next several days leading up to our weekend trip to the Kendling Hotel.

When Saturday morning finally arrives, I quietly pack my overnight bag and creep out of the house while Dad is on his run and Mom is still asleep. I drive straight to Caleb's house to pick him up on the way to Oliver's, where we're all supposed to meet to carpool to Atlanta. Even though I haven't talked to God in a hot minute, I whisper a quick "thank You" that Caleb lives just two neighborhoods away from Oliver, and I doubt my parents will even notice the tiny detour if they're tracking my location.

I don't even need to text Caleb that I'm here—I already catch a glimpse of his auburn hair in the window of his living room just before he walks out the door. As soon as our eyes meet, Caleb flashes me an adorable smile, and my worries all but melt away.

What's done is done, I remind myself. Caleb and I are together, and everything is going to be fine.

After tossing his overnight bag into the backseat, Caleb plops into the passenger seat with a huff.

I lean across the console to plant a kiss on his cheek. "Morning, hot stuff," I say, pitching my voice lower in an attempt to sound sexy, but it definitely comes out more as a croak.

Caleb laughs, his cheeks already tinting pink. "Hot stuff? Really?"

I give him a playful shrug, pretending not to be mortified by my own bizarre behavior. "Just trying it out."

Before I can pull back, Caleb gently cups my face and leans in for a proper kiss. As soon as his lips are on mine, I'm a fucking goner. I sigh into the kiss, heat radiating across my chest and down my spine. My hand moves of its own accord into Caleb's hair, fingers carding through his soft curls, and my heart soars into overdrive.

Caleb is mine, and I am his, and nothing else in the world matters.

Eventually, Caleb gently pulls away, but not before pressing our foreheads together. "We better get going," he whispers breathlessly. "Don't want to keep them waiting, right?"

I nod, reluctantly twisting back into the driver's seat. "Yeah. That'd be a tragedy."

We share another sweet smile before I put Eileen in reverse and back onto the road, interlocking our hands across the console like we always do.

The drive from Caleb's house to Oliver's isn't long, so Caleb and I only have a few minutes to ourselves before we all pile into the Hammonds' minivan. I'm grateful that Ashley offered to drive so that I don't have to brave Atlanta traffic. I love driving Eileen in most places, but never in Atlanta.

"So," Caleb says after a minute or two. "You never mentioned how you convinced your parents to let you go on an overnight trip with me."

I grip the steering wheel a little tighter and keep my eyes focused on the road. "There's nothing really to tell," I say with a shrug. "We'll be sharing a room with Oliver and Harrison, so it's not like we're alone in a hotel room together, right? Plus, Oliver's stepmom is chaperoning. So I guess they figured it was fine."

I decide not to mention that I lied to Mom about Caleb coming. I probably shouldn't lie to Caleb, too, but is that what I'm doing? Am I lying to him? Am

I just a liar now?

"That makes sense," Caleb replies, stroking my thumb with his. "Is it weird that I'm still surprised?"

I manage a tight smile. "No, I'm surprised, too." I give his hand a light squeeze. "But, hey, I'm mostly just excited! I'm ready to capture some orbs again. Or maybe even something better, you know?"

"Maybe! Didn't you say Oliver was bringing like dowsing rods or something?"

I'm grinning ear-to-ear now, happy for a distraction. "Dowsing rods, an EMF meter, an EVP recorder, and an infrared thermometer."

"Holy shit, really?"

"Yeah!" I exclaim eagerly. "I told him it wasn't necessary, but apparently, his stepmom has friends who are super into ghost-hunting, so they just have this stuff lying around. So even though we only have one night, I'm really hoping we get something. Anything!"

"Nice!"

"It'll be like Saint Catherine's again, but way cooler this time."

Caleb goes quiet for a few moments, and an unmistakable tension fills the car. "Theo, can I—can we talk about something?"

My stomach flips, anxiety quickly consuming me. "Oh, um—I mean, yeah, sure, of course." I glance at my phone's GPS. We're four minutes away. "What's up?"

Caleb shifts nervously in his seat, his fingers still interlocked with mine on the console between us. After several agonizing seconds, he inhales sharply. "Look, about what happened in my bed—"

My shoulders slump. "Caleb—"

"I know you said you're fine and that I didn't do anything wrong, but—"

"You didn't," I insist, squeezing his hand. "It was a 'me' problem. Not your fault."

"Well, still, I feel like we should—"

I shake my head. "I'm fine, Caleb. I told you."

"But maybe—"

Suddenly, the soft ambient background vocals of Saint Motel are violently interrupted by my phone's loud ringtone, and we both jump. I peer at my phone, only for the blood to drain from my face.

"It's my dad," I say flatly.

Caleb releases his grip on my hand, straightening in his seat. "Are you gonna answer it? I'll be quiet."

"Yeah, I have to—I have to take it."

Caleb just nods, going completely silent and still.

After one more deep breath, I press the "answer" button. "H-Hey, Dad."

"Heya, kiddo! Have you gotten to Oliver's house yet?"

I clear my throat. "Almost there. What's up?"

"Do you have a minute? I was on my run when you left this morning, so I didn't get to tell you to have a good trip!"

"Oh," I breathe, attempting a light laugh. "Thanks, Dad. Hope you have a good weekend, too!"

"I'm sure Mom already told you all the usual stuff—be careful, keep your phone on you, stay together and all that stuff."

"Yeah, she did."

"Good, good. Glad to hear it. You'll text us if you need us, right?"

"Yeah, I will."

"Okay, good." He pauses, and I open my mouth to say goodbye, but he continues. "Hey, before I forget, I had a nice chat with Jim Buchanon yesterday, and I mentioned you coming home late that one Wednesday night when you and Jake had dinner. Sounds like Jim didn't realize you and Jake were getting close."

"Oh, okay," I reply, not really sure what else to say. Why is this important?

"He's thrilled to see Jake spending more time with friends from church, and I couldn't agree more. You should try to have Jake over sometime soon. I think you guys could be good influences on each other."

I roll my eyes. There it is. The ulterior motive behind Dad's call—trying to persuade me to hang out with more people from church instead of people from school. He automatically assumes that everyone from church is a good influence while everyone from school is a bad one. Maybe Dad thinks if I hang out with more people from church, I'll stop being bisexual. Which makes it even more amusing considering the real reason Jake and I are becoming friends in the first place.

"Did I lose you, Theo?"

"Oh, no, sorry," I answer quickly. "I'm almost to Oliver's house, but yeah, Jake's pretty cool. We'll see."

"All right, good to hear," Dad continues. "Well, I won't hold you up. Be safe, be good, and have fun!"

"Thanks, Dad. Will do."

"Love you, kiddo."

"Love you, too."

The line disconnects just as I'm pulling into Oliver's driveway. I sigh as I put the car into park. "Sorry about that," I grumble to Caleb. "He would've been weird if I didn't answer."

"It's fine," Caleb replies, an uneasy tone in his voice. "Who's Jake?"

"He's a guy from my small group at church, and he's the son of one of my dad's friends and one of the elders at church."

"Ah, that makes sense," Caleb says quietly. "You guys hang out a lot?"

Now that I'm parked, I turn to face Caleb and frown. Caleb's gaze is trained forward, staring at the Hammonds' open garage. "We didn't until recently, but it's a long story." I gently reach across the console to place my hand on his forearm. "You ready?"

Caleb blinks out of his daze but doesn't meet my eyes as he unbuckles his seatbelt and reaches for the door handle. "Yeah, let's get going."

Anxiety clutches my chest. Something's wrong. "Hey, are you okay?"

Before I get an answer, there's an abrupt knocking on my window that makes me jump. "Come on, slowpokes," Oliver taunts with a mischievous grin. "Y'all can make out when we get there. Let's get this show on the road! We've got a haunted hotel to get to!"

"Okay, okay, give us a second," I call out, turning back to Caleb—only to watch the passenger door shut with Caleb already out of the car.

Shit.

Everything happens rather quickly after that. I hear the distinct groan of the Hammonds' garage door opening right before the rest of the crew makes their way out to the navy blue Honda Odyssey parked beside me.

I remove my phone from the mount on my dashboard and scramble out of the driver's seat just as Ashley rounds the corner. Her sandy blonde hair is tied back in a messy bun, not unlike how Oliver usually styles his hair. She smiles broadly after gulping whatever liquid she has in her massive sticker-covered steel tumbler and waves. "Good morning, Theo! Hi Caleb!"

"Hey, Mrs. Hammond," I reply politely.

"Oh, please, none of that," she says, waving her hand. "I'm just Ashley this weekend."

"Is this everything you guys brought?" Oliver asks, pulling out both mine and Caleb's overnight bags from Eileen's backseat.

"Uh, yeah, I think so," I reply, trying to figure out where Caleb went.

"Look who finally decided to show up," Elise declares, punching me lightly in the shoulder.

"They're not late," Harrison clarifies. "We just showed up early."

Ignoring them, I finally spot Caleb standing by Wren in the garage, who eyes me warily. Oh, shit. Have I already fucked up this early?

"Okay, everyone," Ashley announces. "Last call for the bathroom!"

Oliver tosses my and Caleb's bags into the trunk with the rest of the luggage, then rolls his eyes. "It's only a forty-minute drive, Ashley. We're not little kids."

Ashley gives Oliver a pointed look as she pulls her keys out of her huge handbag. "You say that now, but I'm not stopping until we're in the parking deck of the hotel."

As soon as the doors are unlocked, Oliver yanks open the sliding back door and practically leaps inside, somehow contorting his tall, lanky body to crawl into the third row of seats.

"Dude, are you sure you want to be in the very back?" Harrison asks skeptically. "Will your legs even fit back there?"

"Shit, maybe not," Oliver mutters, his voice muffled. "Or wait, maybe I can—ow, *shit,* can you guys just—"

"Language, Oliver!" Ashley squeaks. "The girls may not be here, but I still don't want to hear you swearing every few seconds."

"My bad."

By "the girls," Ashley is referring to her younger daughters from a previous marriage, Bella and Charli. Yes, they are named after characters from the *Twilight* series. I distinctly remember the annoyance on Oliver's face the first time he told us about his new stepsisters. And Elise's high-pitched, uncontrollable laughter that followed.

"Oliver, why don't you and your freakazoid legs sit shotgun?" Wren suggests, suddenly right behind me with Caleb in tow. "I'll sit in the back with the lovebirds."

"I hope you're not referring to Elise and me," Harrison grumbles. "I'm not crawling back there."

"We will!" I volunteer eagerly, suddenly remembering that Ashley is pretty cool and doesn't care about two boys holding hands. I glance over at Caleb with pleading eyes. "Is that cool with you, Caleb?"

Caleb shrugs. "Sure."

I pretend his indifference doesn't feel like a gut punch.

"Ugh, fine," Oliver groans, climbing back out of the van with a grunt. "Guess that means I'm in charge of the music then!"

Ashley snorts. "We'll see about that."

With Oliver out of the way, Wren climbs into the back row first, followed by Caleb and me. Harrison and Elise take their seats in the middle row, and before I know it, we're pulling out of the driveway and heading towards the interstate. Oliver and Ashley bicker about the music only briefly before settling on some old-school Lady Gaga. Their dynamic feels more like a sibling relationship than a parent and child, which I guess makes sense considering their age gap.

I settle my hand in the space between our legs, and although it takes longer than usual, Caleb slowly moves to interlock our fingers. Relief washes over me at the gesture, and I relax against him. Something still doesn't feel right, though, and I know I have to do something.

"Hey, are you okay?" I whisper, just loud enough for him to hear.

"I'm fine," Caleb answers tersely.

Dread fills my stomach again. I have to fix this. "I'm sorry we didn't get to finish our conversation in the car," I say. "We can try again when we get there, okay?"

Caleb stiffens slightly beside me. "Promise?"

I nod, then extend the pinky of my other hand out to him. "Promise."

Caleb links his pinky with mine, and I can practically feel the tension melting away as I rest my head on his shoulder. He presses a quick kiss to the top of my head and holds my hand for the rest of the drive.

NINE
CALEB

"Ghost tours, this way! Check in on the left! Sir, if you're looking for the furry convention, you want the Marriott down the street."

The lobby of the Kendling Hotel is far busier than you'd expect a one-hundred-year-old haunted hotel to be. A crowd of people wearing matching lanyards moves past us, led by a bored-looking tour guide dressed in an old-timey bellhop's uniform.

He speaks with a monotone voice that can only be described as "boring enough to kill."

"Here, you have the lobby, a place where guests would come to check in for their luxurious retreats. No photos, please."

Ashley waits in the check-in queue lined with velvet covered stanchions, her phone out as she snaps pictures of the surrounding lobby, then quickly stows her phone before she's caught by Mr. Lively over there. The rest of us have taken over a seating area off to the side by a coffee table covered in pamphlets for all of the different ghost tours and special events the hotel puts on. Apparently, we're a week early for "Haunted hors d'oeuvres" in the dining room, which really does bring up a load of questions. Are the little quiches full of angry spirits? Do the serving trays float around the room? Is that really how you spell hors d'oeuvres?

"This place is nice. How many people died here, exactly?" Elise asks, propped up against Harrison on a tufted loveseat. They finally seemed to have gotten over whatever bickering was going on in the backseat on the trip down.

"A hundred and fifteen," Wren answers, half of their face obscured by one of the colorful pamphlets. "A fire broke out, and apparently, there was only one staircase. Only the people from the third floor down made it. Well, and those that survived the jump. But that wasn't very many…."

Elise blanches, and Harrison pats her leg gently.

"You watch way scarier stuff, babe."

"Yeah, but this is real people," she whispers back, still loud enough we all can hear.

"Ashley booked the full experience, too," Oliver chimes in, looking up from his phone. His long legs are draped over the armrest of the chair he's sitting sideways on. "We get to do the full tour tomorrow, but tonight, after dinner, we have two hours booked in one of the supposedly haunted suites on the thirteenth floor. I think it was the owners' suite."

"That's so dope," Theo says, squeezing my hand in an adorable display of excitement. He turns to me, flashing a goofy grin, and I can't help but return the smile. Even if it feels like he's been avoiding talking to me. "I call dibs on the dowsing rods first!"

Wren lowers the pamphlet, shooting Theo a baleful glance. "Over my dead body."

"Be nice," I fire back, sticking out my tongue at them for emphasis.

"What are we going to do in the meantime?" Harrison asks.

We all look to Oliver, who swipes on his phone and reads from the itinerary that Ashley made. "It says free time till dinner. I heard Ashley mention she was going to get a massage, so I think we're on our own."

Oh, good. Maybe I'll get a chance to talk to Theo before we get too busy tonight. I just need to get him away from the distractions of our friends long enough to clear the air. Then maybe I can just relax and stop worrying about messing things up.

"Rooms are ready," Ashley calls to the group, flashing a fistful of room keys. She hurries over excitedly, handing them out. "We're on the sixth floor, boys in six-oh-six and the rest of us in six-oh-eight. I'm so excited! I haven't had a sleepover since the times of Mary-Kate and Ashley."

Wren raises an eyebrow, looking at me for a translation, but I only shrug. I have no idea what she's talking about.

"Is Mary-Kate a friend of yours?" Oliver asks.

"Olsen?" Ashley runs a hand through her hair, looking down at the ground and muttering to herself, "And no one understands that because none of you were born yet, so I'm going to pretend I never said anything. Cool, cool."

The gang gathers up their luggage (Theo's bag has a Hudson's Haunted Habitats tag because of course it does), following Ashley to the elevator and piling inside. The walls are mirrored glass, so all I can see in every direction is an endless reflection of my friends. Elise and Harrison holding hands. Wren absorbed in a stack of pamphlets. Oliver and Theo chattering animatedly about ideas for recording tonight. And me, watching the boy I love nearly bubble over with excitement.

I wish I could share in it. But the weight of this unspoken thing between us is dragging me down.

With a dignified *ding*, the elevator spews us out onto the sixth floor, and we move in a huddled group, searching for our rooms. Once we find them, we split off, Ashley, Wren, and Elise heading into the first room while Oliver, Theo, Harrison, and I take the second. Oliver swipes the key on the door, letting us in. He lets out a huff. "Huh, for a haunted hotel, you'd think there'd be more spiderwebs."

The inside of the room looks much like any other hotel I've stayed in—with the exception of that time my dad accidentally booked the "clown suite" on one particularly cursed summer vacation—with bland colored walls, a floor of musty carpet, and two beds nestled between the bathroom and the windows, overlooking the city. Theo rushes over to the curtains, drawing them back to get a glimpse of the street below. Another brick building faces us from across the way, but if I crane my neck hard enough, I can spot the Ferris wheel at Centennial Olympic Park.

Oliver splays out on one of the beds, his gangly limbs stretching from one side to the other as he lets out a sigh. "This is comfy. Where are you going to sleep, Harrison?"

Harrison shoves Oliver's foot over, making room for him on the corner of the bed. "Next to you, Stretch. So keep your cold feet to yourself, and nobody will get hurt."

Right. Sleeping arrangements. Theo and I are sharing a bed, which is definitely cool and not at all nerve-wracking. What if he freaks out again? I don't know if I can stand another look like he gave me last week. It'll destroy me.

Theo throws his duffle bag onto the free bed, giving me a crooked smile. "This is us, then."

"Uh, yeah." I follow suit, setting my stuff down on the comforter and trying to shake the worry from my head. Everything will be fine. Theo's literally taken naps practically on top of me. We've been in the same bed before. This won't be any different.

Except the last time we were on the bed….

"Can we talk soon?" I ask in a low voice.

"Hey, they've got an indoor pool," Harrison says, looking up from his phone. "We should check it out!"

Oliver springs off the bed like a bullet, wrapping an arm around Theo's shoulder and pulling him away before he can answer me. "What do you think, Theo? Haunted hotel pool party? It does have a certain ring to it. You can make it the new TikTok trend."

Theo throws an apologetic look my way before saying, "Yeah, I mean, it sounds like fun. We can hang there till it's time for the spooky stuff tonight.

Harry, can you text the others and let them know the plan?"

"On it," Harrison replies, pushing his glasses back into place as he types one-handed. He reaches for his bag next, pulling out his camera, then digging around for a second before grumbling something under his breath. "Shit, I think my charging cable fell out in the van. I'm going to go down and see if I can find it."

Okay, cool. Maybe Oliver will go with him, and then Theo and I can get a second to clear the air–

"I'll come with," Theo says. "I wanted to go down to the lobby anyway and see if they have earplugs. Harry, I love you to death, man, but your snoring is going to keep me awake all night."

Harrison rolls his eyes. "It's not that bad."

"Grab me some too?" Oliver asks, falling back onto the bed. "Sorry, Harry, but you're a freaking freight train. I keep thinking you're going to swallow your tongue."

"At least I don't talk in my sleep," Harry fires back. "Theo over here will have a full-ass argument with himself."

I snort a laugh. I've only ever heard him mumble when he nods off. "Oh great, so what you're saying is that no one is going to be getting any sleep tonight?"

"If you're lucky," Oliver quips, flashing me a sly grin.

Theo opens the door to the room abruptly, calling over his shoulder, "We'll be back." Harrison scrambles after him, the heavy door shutting with a loud *thunk*.

There he goes again. Running away from me instead of talking. I sink onto the edge of the bed, a sigh of frustration escaping.

"That bad, huh?" Oliver is propped up on his side, looking over at me. "Something going on with you two?"

"What makes you say that?"

Oliver quirks an eyebrow. "You don't think I can tell when something is going on with one of my best friends and his boyfriend? Give me a little more credit, Caleb. We've been over this—I may be beautiful, but I'm not dumb."

Okay, so Theo obviously hasn't talked to his friends about what's going on. Which doesn't make me feel any better, honestly. It just means that whatever is happening in his head, he's going at it alone.

"We had a… misunderstanding, I guess. And he keeps telling me that he's fine, that *we're* fine, but we're not. And he won't talk to me about it. I'm just so frustrated."

I blink a few times to get rid of the moisture that builds in the corner of my eyes.

Oliver runs a hand through the ends of his ponytail. "Theo is a tough nut to crack. Trust me, he doesn't just do this to you." Oliver sits up, tucking his legs under him. "A few years back, when the panic attacks were getting really bad, he did the same thing to me and Elise. We knew something was going on, but he just kept telling us everything was fine. It wasn't till he had a full-on attack in the middle of school assembly that we got the whole story. You see, he's got this image of himself, this perfect picture in his head of the person that he aspires to be. And that's what he wants people to see. This illusion he's created. It's like he's scared to let anyone see him any differently. Even his friends. Even you, I guess."

"But he doesn't have to be that way with me," I argue, the heat behind my eyes building again. "After everything we went through just to be together, why would he keep something from me like that?"

"Look, I may not be dating him, but I know Theo. He's obviously in his head about something. What exactly was this misunderstanding about?"

"It's, uh… personal. Sorry."

Oliver's expression twists in confusion. "Now I'm even more curious. But, hey, I'm not trying to pry. Look, the point is, Theo is the way he is. He's always going to overanalyze everything, and he's going to bust his ass trying to make things perfect."

"But if he just told me what was going on, maybe I could help him."

"Maybe," Oliver says, giving a shrug. "And maybe he's not ready to share that part of himself with you."

I swallow the lump in my throat. "I hadn't thought about it like that."

Oliver leans back on his hands with a smug grin. "See? Told you I was too smart to be a himbo."

Could it be that Theo doesn't want to open up to me? That he's keeping secrets? Does that mean he doesn't trust me? That this illusion of perfection he's displaying is more important to him than being honest with me?

This fucking sucks.

"I'm going to get changed for the pool," Oliver says, nabbing his bag from the floor. "Can't wait to get drowned by a ghost."

The bathroom door closes behind him with a *click*, and I quickly wipe away the tears that have spilled over.

I wish a ghost was the most of my troubles.

The pool, it turns out, is not haunted. At least, not by ghosts. What we do find is a gaggle of old ladies participating in some sort of underwater yoga class, complete with noodle floaties and an instructor who looks like he was pulled off the cover of one of my Nana's romance novels. He speaks in a soothing, deep tone, and his hair never gets wet, no matter how violently the class splashes.

So, we hang out in the hot tub till the old ladies vacate the area, and by the time we've all gotten pruney and waterlogged, it's time for us to get cleaned up for dinner.

Theo doesn't avoid me, per se, but every time we end up even remotely alone, he makes an excuse to leave or calls Harrison over to ask a question about tonight's camera setup or breaks away to do a cannonball in the deep end of the pool.

I'm fuming by dinnertime as we enter the hotel restaurant. My frustration has built to volcanic levels, and I could blow at any second, turning my friend group into the new Pompeii.

I hang back from the group as Ashley speaks to the guy at the host stand.

"What is your deal?"

Wren appears beside me, their arms folded across their chest. Their black hair is swept to the side in a messy taper, and their outfit of a black button-down on black jeans is just so perfectly Wren.

"I don't have a deal," I say, tugging at the cuffs of my sweater. Even with Wren, there's an edge in my voice. The threat of eruption is nearing cataclysmic.

"Bullshit," Wren breathes. "Now out with it because I'm not going to sit through an entire dinner of you moping around like you're the lone survivor of *Slumber Party Massacre 3*."

"I'm not moping," I say, and even I can hear the petulance in my voice.

"Caleb, seriously, I'm starting to get worried. You're in a haunted hotel with your amazing friends, Oliver's try-hard stepmom, and your adorable boyfriend. What could possibly be the problem?"

"It's nothing," I say through an exhale, dragging a hand through my chlorine-stiff hair. "I'm sorry. I'll try and pep myself up."

Elise waves from the host stand, the sleeve of her lavender dress billowing. "Wren, Caleb, our table's ready!"

"Are you sure you don't want to talk about it?" Wren asks, making it a point to stare me down. "Because dinner can wait a few minutes."

"No, I'll be fine. Let's go."

Wren wraps an arm through mine as we follow the others into the dining room, and I'd be lying if I said it didn't help. At least a little.

Much like the pool, the dining room is also free of any ghosts or ghouls. Unless you count the guy with the shock of white hair who serves us dinner, but let's be fair, he's got at least a couple of years left before he's haunting anyone.

I do my best not to sour the mood, and every time Wren makes eye contact with me from across the table, I slap on a smile, if only to prove I'm trying. But I haven't forgotten my conversation with Oliver from earlier, and even though Theo is sitting right next to me, laughing along with his friends, I've never felt further away from him.

That sentiment isn't helped when Theo pulls out his phone in the middle of dinner to answer a text. I can't help myself but look over his shoulder and spot the name "Jake" at the top of the conversation. I also can't help but notice the slight twist of a smile on his lips as he types his reply, and I have to make myself look down at my plate of alfredo pasta to avoid a complete spiral.

So what if he's talking to another guy? The guy that he didn't want to talk about this morning in the car. The guy who, apparently, he's been hanging out with and not telling me about. It's not like he's *into* him.

Right?

The idea worms its way deeper into my head, and I spend the rest of dinner pushing my pasta around my plate and trying not to puke.

After dinner, it's time for us to head up to the suite. We go back to our rooms first for a quick change and to grab all of the gear we need. Theo is in high spirits, and Harrison and Oliver seem just as excited as they test the devices that Ashley ordered from some site her friends run. There's a lot of beeping and white noise, so I assume they work as intended.

I get changed in the bathroom, trading my sweater and slacks for a hoodie and my comfort jeans. My hair is still a mess of curls from the pool, but there's no helping that now. I finish getting dressed, but I linger, staring past my reflection in the mirror.

Maybe I should skip out on the activities tonight. Theo is so stoked, and I don't want to be a wet blanket with my moodiness. Then again, if I don't go, he'll probably spend the whole night worried that he did something wrong, and I'll have ruined his night either way.

Come on, Caleb. Get it together.

A soft knock on the door, and Theo's face appears in the crack.

"Hey, are you ready to go?"

He's practically beaming with excitement, and his mischievous grin melts my insides till they pool in my stomach. Stupid Theo and his stupid smile.

I can't let this go. I have to talk to him before I explode.

"Theo, can we please talk for a second?"

His grin fades a bit as he straightens, pulling the door open and stepping inside. "What's wrong?"

How do I even begin? I have so many thoughts buzzing around my head I can't even manage a coherent question. But they're all racing to the surface and before I can stop myself, I'm saying, "You're avoiding me. And I know you said you're fine and that I didn't do anything wrong, but I don't believe you."

Theo bristles, closing the door behind him. "Wh–what are you talking about?"

"I messed up–crossed some kind of line, and you won't tell me what it is. I can't keep pretending like there's nothing going on because you want this–" I gesture between us, "to be perfect. It's killing me."

"Caleb, slow down, you're not–"

"I get it, you know if you're having second thoughts about me. I know that you're still working through things, so if you're regretting rushing into a relationship, you can just tell me."

There it was. The unspoken anxiety that's been clawing at my mind since he ran away from me. I push down my encroaching thoughts of whoever "Jake" is, waiting for Theo to answer.

He looks like he wants to throw up. I *do* want to throw up.

"That's not–I'm not regretting you, Caleb. I love you."

"Then why won't you talk to me? Why won't you tell me why you ran away that night?"

Another soft knock on the door and Oliver's voice comes through. "Guys, Ashley's here, and we're ready to head up to the suite."

"Be out in a second," Theo calls through the door. He takes a step closer to me, but I back away, bracing myself against the counter because, at this point, I really do feel like I'm going to be sick. "Caleb, please, I just need a little more time. I promise I'll have everything figured out soon. You don't have to worry about this—"

"But I'm right here, Theo. If I'm not the problem, then let me help you. Talk to me!"

Theo digs his fingers into the back of his neck, letting out a sigh. The voices of the others drift under the door as Harrison and Oliver join the group out in the hallway.

"I'm sorry." My voice is a whisper. I close my eyes, wishing I had stayed quiet. "I know this isn't fair. I'm putting you on the spot. It's just... I love you, Theo. And I can't stand the thought of being the reason you're hurting."

He doesn't respond, his hands clenched tightly at his side, the line of his jaw taut. A banging on the wall outside the bathroom makes us both jump. Elise's muffled voice streams through, "Come on, lovebirds, get a move on!"

At last, Theo looks at me. His eyes wide, and his breathing erratic. And his lips part, finally ready to let those walls crumble down and let me in. But then he turns his back, opens the door and leaves without a word.

Again. He's running away from me for a second time. I would be lying if I said it didn't hurt. But there's something more than just hurt bubbling in my gut. It's anger, billowing like sails catching a newfound wind as it swells within me.

How can Theo say he loves me, then walk away from me?

Propelled by it, I follow him out of the bathroom and through the heavy door to the hallway. The gang's all here, including Ashley, who herds us towards the elevator, checking the time on her phone. Theo keeps his distance from me, Harrison and Elise serving as a buffer between us. Wren falls to the back of the group as we wait for the elevator at the end of the hall, positioning themselves at my side.

"Are you okay?" they whisper, "your face looks like a tomato."

"Fine," I manage through clenched teeth.

The elevator doors open, and there are already two people waiting inside as the crew piles in.

"We'll catch the next one," Wren announces, holding onto my elbow. "Save some ghosts for us."

Theo watches me till the doors close, his expression somewhere between pained and annoyed. I know the feeling.

"Now do you want to tell me what's going on?"

I press the "up" button, watching the arrow light up.

"Not really, no."

Wren snorts a laugh. "Too bad, do it anyway."

"Leave it alone, Wren."

They cross their arms, brow furrowing. "Fine. Suffer in silence. See if I care."

Great, now I feel guilt on top of all of this anger. What else could go wrong?

The elevator arrives, and Wren and I ride in silence up to the thirteenth floor, where we find the rest of our group getting a rundown by one of the staff members outside of Suite 1313.

"--screaming to a minimum if possible. At the end of your allotted time slot, a member of our concierge staff will alert you and we'll kindly ask that any activities be wrapped within a timely fashion to make way for the next group. Now, are there any questions before you go inside?"

Ashley raises her hand, bouncing on the balls of her feet. The exasperated staffer gives her a nod. "What apparitions do people usually see in this suite?"

"We've had reports of the original owners, Charles and Clara Kendling, appearing in the boudoir–"

"The boo-what?" Elise asks loudly.

"The bedroom," the staffer explains through a sigh. "And, of course, there's also been recent sightings of the Newport Newlyweds."

"Who?" Elise questions.

"A young couple who died in this suite back in the sixties. Suite 1313 was the honeymoon suite for a number of years after they rebuilt from the fire, but after the Newport Newlyweds were found murdered in their wedding bed, no one has been allowed to stay here overnight."

"Murdered?" Ashley squeaks, although it sounds like more of an excited noise than scared. "Oh! I think I heard about them on the *Murders and Muffins* podcast!"

The staffer does their best to hide the roll of their eyes. They step aside, flinging the door to the suite open. "Please enjoy yourselves, and don't hesitate to reach out if you need anything during your stay."

I follow Wren in after everyone else, the door shutting with a creak behind us.

The suite has been restored to its original 1930s glory, complete with crystal light fixtures, elegant wallpaper from corner to corner, plush carpets, and even an old-school rotary phone on the table by the couch. From the sitting room, a pair of glass doors leads into the bedroom, where a king-size bed is made up with a dozen throw pillows. In the opposite direction, a small kitchenette with marble counters and one of those retro refrigerators with rounded edges. Across from the entrance, huge windows overlook the city of Atlanta–a more spectacular view here than the sixth floor–alight with life.

A thrill shoots through me, tamping down the heat of my anger like a cool breeze. No matter what's going on between Theo and me, I can't deny that this is so fucking cool.

"Does anyone else feel that?" Elise asks, wrapping her arms around herself. "It's freezing in here."

Ashley steps over to the thermostat, pressing a button to make it light up. "That's because they have the AC cranked down to sixty. It's like someone invited Elsa to live here, am I right?"

Oliver shoots her a look, and she immediately cringes.

"Sorry, Bella is obsessed with that movie. I could probably quote it front to back."

"Please don't," Oliver adds, pulling out one of the devices from his pocket and switching it on. "Okay, Theo, Harry. Where do we want to set up?"

"The bedroom has the most activity," Harrison says, and Elise giggles at his side. "So, maybe we start there and work our way through the place?" He sets his camera bag down on the long table that runs behind the couch, unzipping it.

"Yeah," Theo agrees, his voice soft. He clears his throat then continues, "That sounds good. At Saint Catherine's, it was kind of a lucky thing, so let's just start recording, and we'll see what we can find."

Oliver starts to distribute the instruments among the group, taking his role as tech support very seriously. He hands a small black box–an ambient temperature sensor, he explains–to Elise. Then, another similarly shaped instrument to Ashley.

"Sweet! The spirit box! I've been wanting to play around with it." She switches it on, and radio static emanates from it.

Next, he hands me two rods, bent at a ninety-degree angle, but Wren quickly snatches them from me.

"I already called the dowsing rods," they say plainly, brandishing them like it was any other day. Something tells me they've had previous experience with these.

"That just leaves the EMF meters," Oliver says, holding up the two identical black devices. He hands one to me, and I study the row of red lights that run along the top. "The on switch is at the bottom," Oliver adds, giving me a wink.

"Thanks, I couldn't have figured that out myself."

Oliver's smile fades a bit, and I immediately add, "Sorry. Thanks, Oliver."

"Sure thing," he replies, a little less pep in his voice.

Damn, I'm like a walking time bomb. Who knows who I'm going to end up exploding on?

Everyone powers on their devices, a cacophony of beeps filling the space to the point that I plug one of my ears.

"Spread out!" Harrison calls over the noises, pulling on the neck strap of his camera. He holds it up, peering through the lens before snapping a shot of the sitting room.

Theo heads towards the bedroom, so I move in the opposite direction, moving over to the tiled floor of the kitchen. I shiver, which isn't weird seeing as it's only slightly warmer than the winter weather outside. This side of the suite quiets down once the others have spread out, and I hold up my EMF meter, watching for any of the lights to come on. When Hudson does this on Triple H, the lights always seem to go on at the perfect moment in the video, but I assume that's just a trick of good editing. Who knows how long he has to stumble around a place before he gets anything interesting?

Curiosity ends up getting the better of me, and I set the EMF meter on the counter as I explore the small kitchen. The tiled floor is a checkered black and white pattern, and a bowl of wax fruit sits on the countertop, a layer of dust clinging to the faux grapes and apples.

These ghosts need to get better housekeeping.

I wonder if they even care about that kind of thing once they're no longer among the living. It must be kind of peaceful, not having to worry about the mundanity of cleaning or eating or any of the annoying things that it takes to stay alive. Or relationships, for that matter. A ghost doesn't get angry when their boyfriend ignores them or keeps secrets. A ghost doesn't have to tiptoe around a problem, waiting for their ghoul-friend to decide whether or not to let them in. And a ghost definitely doesn't have to worry about their significant other texting other boys who they don't want to talk about.

Ghosts have it so easy.

A crackling noise pulls my focus, sending a wave of goosebumps across my arms. On the counter, the small black box emits the crackling sound again, the first of the lights flashing for a moment, then going dark. I rush over to the EMF meter, my heart pounding as I scoop it up. As soon as my hand touches it, the light comes on again, the crackling noise returning.

Holy shit, does this mean there's actually something here with me?

I scan my surroundings, looking for anything that might confirm my suspicions. I hold the device out in front of me, slowly sweeping it through the air. I take a step further into the kitchen and the light flashes again, another round of the noise. Glancing over my shoulder, I spot Wren closest by, standing by the window.

"Wren!" I whisper loudly. "Over here!"

"Did you get something?" they ask, crossing into the kitchen. As soon as Wren makes it over to me, the second light illuminates as well, the crackling noise getting louder. "Oh fuck! What do we do?"

"I don't know!" I say, still whisper-yelling.

"I could try and ask it a question?" Wren suggests, holding up the dowsing rods. They point away from them, towards a small breakfast nook in the corner of the kitchen. "Maybe they'll answer?"

"It doesn't hurt," I agree, moving a step closer to the table. The third light on my device lights up, the noise getting louder still.

Wren clears their throat, holding their arms out straight. "I'm going to ask you some questions if that's okay?" they pause, as if waiting for a response. "Oh, shit. Sorry. Um, cross the rods for yes and spread them apart for no. Do you understand?"

We both hold our breath as the lights on the EMF meter flash for a moment, then the rods tip towards one another, crossing.

"Oh my god," Wren breathes, their face paler than I've ever seen as they straighten the rods back to face away. "Okay, um. Shit. I can do this. Uh, are you one of the owners? The Kendlings, I mean?"

The rods remain motionless for a long moment, then slowly spread apart.

"I can't believe this is happening–oh fuck!" I realize that neither of us are filming this. I tiptoe over to the counter, trying not to move my arm too much and keep the device pointed at the table. "Harrison! Theo!"

Theo is the first to pop his head through the double doors leading to the bedroom.

"We've got something over here," I say, still afraid of raising my voice over a whisper.

"Harry, Oliver, come on," Theo says, moving quickly across the suite, his phone in hand.

Wren stands perfectly still, their nostrils flared as they take careful, steadying breaths. "What should I ask next?"

"Have you been getting clear responses?" Theo asks, holding his phone up to eye level.

"So far," Wren says.

"Can't imagine what that's like," I say, cutting a look over at Theo. It's petty, I know, but I'm still so mad at him, ghosts or no ghosts.

Theo ignores my jab and Harrison joins us in the small kitchen, hovering behind because there's not enough room for us to stand side-by-side.

"Ask if they died here," Theo says.

Wren nods, repeating the question. The rods slowly drift inwards, crossing.

"That means yes."

"Shit," breathes Harrison behind me.

"God," mutters Theo at the same time.

"We should try and find out who they are," I say, taking another careful step towards the table. The fourth light illuminates on the EMF meter, and the speaker pops loudly.

"Are you one of the newlyweds?" Wren asks after straightening the rods again.

The four of us hold a collective breath till the rods cross once more.

"Are you both here?"

Again, the rods cross.

"What's going on in there?" Oliver calls from the sitting room.

"Shhh!" we all shush him.

"Whoa, whoa, what did I do?"

"Don't scare away the spirit, man!"

It's Harrison's turn to whisper-yell.

Wren looks back to Theo, "What else should I ask?"

"Ask if they were murdered," he says after a moment. "Harrison, quick, get some shots of the table."

The shutter sound on Harrison's camera sounds under Wren's question, and the rods separate.

"No?" Theo questions, looking back at Harrison. "That tour guide is going to get an earful later."

"How did they die then?" Harrison asks.

"Maybe it was a lover's spat," Oliver suggests, leaning over from the other side of the counter.

"That can't be right," Theo disagrees.

"One way to find out," Wren says, turning back to the table. "Did you two fight before you died?"

The rods cross.

"That doesn't mean they killed each other," Theo argues, his voice louder.

"I don't know, man," Oliver chimes in. "I've heard enough of Ashley's podcasts to know a crime of passion when I hear one."

"Yeah," I agree, not so much because I believe Oliver, but mostly because I want to disagree with Theo. "Maybe one of them was keeping a secret from the other."

Theo's eyes are on me, and the corner of his mouth twitches. More camera shutter sounds.

"Did one of you keep a secret from the other?" Wren asks. The rods cross again.

"This is getting juicy," Oliver murmurs. Harrison stands on his tiptoes to shoot over our heads.

"I'm sure there was a good reason," Theo says, voice still too loud. "Ask if they had a good reason."

"Uh, did you have a good reason?"

The rods don't move.

"It doesn't matter the reason," I say, moving towards Theo. Harrison steps back out of my way. "They shouldn't keep things from each other if they love one another."

"And why is that?" Theo replies, his phone lowering to his side as he steps to meet me. "Maybe they kept it to themselves because they were afraid of hurting each other!"

"They're already hurting each other!" I exclaim, matching his volume. "So they might as well hurt each other with the truth!"

"But what if it blows up their relationship?" Theo retorts, moving another step closer. "It's not worth it if they love each other!"

I let out a grunt of frustration. "Wren, ask them if they think it's worth it."

Wren lowers the rods. "Um, we're not talking about the ghosts anymore, are we?"

Harrison and Oliver exchange a look and step out of the kitchen. Theo stands almost toe-to-toe with me, his chest heaving with quick breaths. I'm panting too, I realize, the embarrassment of the moment sinking in as we stand in awkward silence.

I slam the EMF meter on the counter. "Forget it then. I'm done."

Pushing past Theo, I head for the door, not pausing to see if he follows. Out in the hall, I follow the sign to the staircase, maneuvering through the heavy door and starting my descent from the thirteenth floor.

TEN
THEO

The force of Caleb slamming the hotel door sends a tremor across the hotel room, rattling furniture and dishes in its wake. The silence that follows Caleb's abrupt exit, however, is far louder.

"What the hell just happened?" Elise asks loudly from the bedroom, joining the rest of us in the kitchen.

"Do you mean with the ghosts or with Caleb?" Oliver asks after a beat.

"Not the time, Oliver," Harrison mutters.

"It's called 'comic relief,' Harry," Oliver replies, retrieving the discarded EMF meter from the counter and examining it for damage.

"Theo, what did you do?" Elise demands, punching me in the shoulder a bit more aggressively than usual, but I can't help but feel like I deserve it.

"I...I think I fucked up," I choke out, my throat suddenly tight.

"Oh, you think?" Wren snaps coldly.

Guilt twists in my stomach while tears quickly start stinging at the back of my eyes. This is all my fault. I fucked up. I've fucked everything up. Everything—the trip, this night, my entire relationship—is ruined, and it's all my fault.

"Is everything okay?" Ashley asks, suddenly appearing behind Elise.

"Something tells me that wasn't a ghost that just slammed the heck out of that door."

All eyes are on me to provide an explanation, but I'm frozen. If I open my mouth, I'm certain a sob will escape, so I drop my gaze to the floor and shrug.

"Where's Caleb?" Ashley asks when no one answers.

Caleb. My chest aches. I want to go after him—I want to wrap my arms around him, hold him close, bury my face into his neck, and tell him everything—but I can't move. I'm paralyzed under the intense stare of my friends and our chaperone, with every ounce of energy I can muster focused solely on not bursting into tears in the middle of a haunted kitchenette.

"Okay, fine, *I'll* go check on him, then," Wren hisses, angrily shoving past me toward the door.

"Thank you, Wren," Ashley says warily. "Text me if y'all need anything, okay?"

"Yep," Wren barks back, immediately followed by the *thunk* of the door.

After another beat of tense silence, Ashley clears her throat. "So, we still have just over an hour of time left in this room. Do y'all still want to do this, or are we done for the night?"

I swallow the lump in my throat and blink away my tears. "Let's keep going," I croak, desperate for a distraction and eager to no longer be the center of attention. "I think there's still enough time to get something, right?"

No one says a word for several seconds, and my heart sinks. I deserve this. Not only does Caleb hate me, but now everyone else does, too. I deserve it.

"Definitely," Oliver finally declares, retrieving the dowsing rods that Wren must have abandoned on the kitchen counter. "We might as well get our money's worth, right?"

Harrison looks to Elise, who is still trying to stare me down, but I carefully avoid eye contact. "Yeah, I'm down to keep looking if you guys are."

Ashley offers us a smile. "That's the spirit!"

"Where?!" Oliver asks, dramatically holding out the dowsing rods close to

Ashley, and everyone collectively rolls their eyes.

The last hour of our paranormal investigation is completely uneventful. The EMF meter gets a few random hits, and of course, we have some audio recordings that we'll have to playback and review later, but otherwise, the only unseen forces I experience are guilt, embarrassment, and anxiety about what the rest of this trip will bring.

"Okay, idiot, start talking."

I glance up from packing the equipment to see Elise glaring down at me, arms crossed over her chest. I've felt her furious eyes on me ever since Caleb left, so I knew it was only a matter of time before she confronted me. I was just hoping it would wait until after we left the haunted room.

"What did you do to Caleb?"

I sigh. "I don't want to talk about it right now."

"That sure is a shame," she scoffs. "Now, spill."

"Babe, come on," Harrison says, gently placing his hand on Elise's shoulder. "Let them sort it out. It's their first fight, and it's not our place to butt in."

Elise opens her mouth to argue with him but turns back to me. "Fine. But you're *going* to sort it out, right?"

"I would hope so," Oliver chimes in from beside me, zipping up one of the bags. "Considering that you and Caleb are sharing a bed tonight."

Shit. I completely forgot about that.

Well, not completely. I've just been very intentionally trying to avoid thinking about it. Does that count as forgetting?

"Yeah," I finally say. "I'm going to try to talk to him. If he still wants to listen to me, that is."

Elise's expression softens. "I'm sure he does. Caleb loves you. You'll get through this."

My shoulders slump. Caleb *did* love me. Maybe he doesn't anymore. I wouldn't blame him. I'm a shitty boyfriend.

"Okay, gang," Ashley announces from the front door. "Our time's up! Let's head back downstairs to our rooms and get settled in for the night."

"Coming," Harrison calls back, carefully slinging his camera bag over his shoulder. "Is that everything?"

"Think so," Oliver replies as he stands up, towering over me as I'm still on my knees over the bags of equipment on the floor. He extends a hand to me, lifting me to my feet effortlessly. "You want us to give you and Caleb some space to talk it out?"

I swallow. "Yeah, I think that might be good."

Oliver nods, giving me a hearty pat on the back before gathering the rest of the equipment.

The four of us make our way out into the hallway with Ashley and to the elevator in relative silence. I keep my gaze fixed on the floor as we awkwardly board the fancy mirrored elevator, and I can feel Ashley's eyes watching the shame burning my cheeks in my reflection. She may not be my parent, but she definitely has that mom radar, and I imagine that she's debating whether or not she should try to intervene. I just really hope she doesn't. I've had enough confrontation for one day—I certainly don't need more.

As the elevator makes its slow descent, my stomach is in knots. What do I even say to Caleb? Obviously, he knows I'm hiding something from him, so there's no point in lying about it anymore. I have to come clean about how much the stuff about my dad is weighing on me. But what if it makes Caleb want to break up with me? That's a very Caleb thing to do—if he thinks he's the problem, he'd rather just cut himself out of the equation to try to "protect me" than stick it out if he thinks it's only going to make me miserable. I need him to understand that I'd rather be miserable with Caleb than be miserable alone.

Maybe that's it. Maybe that's all I need to say.

Unless of course, this entire relationship is no longer something Caleb wants. Maybe having a (mostly) closeted bisexual boyfriend with a close-minded dad is in and of itself unbearable for Caleb. Maybe Caleb is actually sick of being with someone like me—someone who forces him to hide who he is and hide how he feels about his own boyfriend.

Maybe Caleb finally realized that I'm not worth the trouble after all.

My head is spinning by the time we reach our rooms on the sixth floor. I don't think I can do this. I can't do this. I can't lose Caleb. I can't.

"So, do you guys want to start reviewing some of the audio recordings tonight?" Harrison asks as he digs the key card to the room from his wallet.

"Yeah, that's a good idea," Oliver agrees. "Ashley, can we use y'all's room? Theo's not feeling too great and might want to go to sleep early." He raises his eyebrows at me, a signal to play along.

"I don't see why not," Ashley replies as she opens the door to the adjoining room. "I might slip down to the lobby to Facetime your dad and the girls for a few minutes anyway." She gives Oliver a pointed look. "Don't do anything stupid while I'm gone, though, okay? If y'all are ever interested in doing stuff like this again in the future, it would be wise not to make things unpleasant for me. Capiche?"

"Capiche," Oliver echoes.

Ashley clicks her tongue, shooting Oliver finger guns. I have to look away to stop myself from visibly cringing.

"Did you just shoot me finger guns?" Oliver asks incredulously.

"Sure did!" She smiles. "Got a problem with it?"

Oliver opens his mouth to answer, then thinks better of it. "Nope."

"That's what I thought."

With that, we enter our respective rooms to find that the connecting doors between the rooms have both been left open. The boys' room is mostly dark, only lit by the television. Stepping in further, my stomach drops as I spot Caleb sound asleep in our bed, his head in Wren's lap as they bury their fingers in his russet curls. Wren gives me an icy glare from where they are seated, propped up on my side of the bed.

"Oh shit," Oliver whispers as he enters, and Wren momentarily shifts their hostility to him instead. "Is he out for the night?"

Wren nods, gently untangling their digits from Caleb's hair. "Let him sleep," they whisper. "He needs it."

"We were heading into y'all's room anyway," Harrison chimes in from behind me. "To review the footage and recordings, see if we got anything."

"We can all join in the other room, then," Oliver whispers to me, a sympathetic smile on his lips. "So he can sleep."

I turn my attention back to Caleb, my chest aching at the sight of him. There's a tissue box on the nightstand and a trashcan full of used tissues on the floor beside Wren. I distinctly remember that trashcan being empty when we left.

Caleb's been crying. He cried himself to sleep. Because of me.

I feel like an absolute monster.

Wren slowly and carefully slides out of the bed, cradling Caleb's head as they replace their lap with a pillow. Once he's settled, Wren turns to me with a scowl. "You're going to fix this."

I nod weakly, staring at the floor.

"Tomorrow," Wren continues. "Tonight, you're going to leave him alone and let him sleep."

I nod again.

Without another word, Wren steps around me and through the connecting doors to their own room. Footsteps follow behind them until Harrison puts a hand on my shoulder.

"You coming?"

I shake my head. "I'm going to bed," I whisper. "I just—I just want to sleep."

Harrison gives my shoulder a gentle squeeze before turning to join the others in the adjoining room.

As quietly as possible, I retrieve my overnight bag, retreat to the bathroom, and start up the shower. The bathroom fan and water pressure from the shower are enough to muffle my sniffling, and I'm finally safe to open the floodgates. Tears flow freely down my cheeks, mixing with the scalding water that fills the room with steam.

I should've followed Caleb downstairs.

I should've left room 1313 to talk things out with Caleb, to fix what I broke, to undo the pain I caused him.

Better yet, I never should've given him a reason to cry in the first place.

I'm such a fucking monster.

When I've finally finished crying and showering, I toss on a T-shirt and gym shorts, brush my teeth, and slip out of the bathroom. I find Caleb exactly where Wren left him, his breaths still deep and even with sleep. My fingers itch to touch him—just a gentle kiss on the forehead or a stroke of his cheek—but I remember Wren's warning about letting him sleep, and I know they're right.

Before I do something I'll regret, I delicately slide under the covers beside Caleb, careful not to pull the blankets or disturb the bed too much. As I settle in the sheets, Caleb stirs, and I freeze. His eyes flutter open, and before he can focus on me, I quickly shut my eyes and pretend to be asleep. I listen as Caleb stills, shuffles, and then goes quiet again. A moment or two passes, so I peek one eye open, only for my heart to sink into my stomach. Apparently, upon seeing me next to him, Caleb turned to face away from me and scooted his body as far away from me as possible. He's practically dangling off the edge of the double bed, clearly preferring to fall onto the dingy, century-old hotel carpet than be close to me.

I squeeze my eyes closed, willing myself not to cry again.

"It doesn't matter the reason. They shouldn't keep things from each other if they love one another."

"Maybe they kept it to themselves because they were afraid of hurting each other."

"They're already hurting each other! So they might as well hurt each other with

the truth!"

Caleb's words echo in my head as I blink away more tears.

I have to fix this. If I don't fix this, I'll lose him forever.

Sunday, January 21

"Caleb!"

I'm running—sprinting down an endless wallpapered corridor, racing to escape the billowing smoke rising from the elevator shaft.

I'm running, but I'm also looking for Caleb—panicking, screaming his name. Where is he? Why isn't he with me?

Mom and Dad are calling for me from outside the burning building. Sienna is at the top of the stairwell with an outstretched arm, ushering me to come with her.

"Theo, we have to go! Now!"

"Where's Caleb? I have to find Caleb!"

"There's not enough time, come on!"

"*Not without Caleb!*"

I burst through another door, desperately searching for my boyfriend. Where did he go? Why can't I find him?

"Come on, brother, it's time to go!" Chase yells from the stairwell. "Maybe he's already downstairs!"

No. I know he's not out of the building yet because Caleb wouldn't have gone without me, so I can't leave without him. "Caleb!" I scream, but no sound escapes my throat.

"Theo, over here!"

It's Jake Buchanon, pointing out a broken window in the hallway. "I found him! Down there!"

I dash to the window with Jake and look down. Sure enough, Caleb is on the ground, safe and sound with the rest of the crew—Harrison, Elise, Oliver, Wren, Freddy, and Andrew.

Oh, thank God. Caleb is safe. They're all safe.

Just as I go to sigh with relief, I feel an intense heat surround me, pressure building on my chest. Shit. I have to get out of here.

"Come on, let's jump!"

An unfamiliar female voice giggles behind me. I spin around to find a strange woman in a flapper dress with a wide smile. Her eyes are milky white, glazed over as she approaches the window.

I gawk at her. "We can't jump," I exclaim. "That fall would kill us!"

The woman shrugs. "Might as well hurt each other with the truth!" And with that, she flings herself over the ledge and out the window, and I shove myself away from the edge so I don't see her hit the ground.

The heat on my chest intensifies, and I feel myself start to panic. "No, no, no—"

"As long as you're under my roof, I can't put up with blatant immoral behavior."

I freeze. "Dad?"

Sure enough, Dad is standing in the stairwell. He shakes his head, watching me in disgust.

"Dad, we have to get out of here–"

"French kissing a boy at a public event *and* declaring your sexuality on an internet show? That's blatant immoral behavior. It's unacceptable, and you know it."

Unacceptable. Unacceptable. "Dad, I–I'm sorry. Please, you have to—"

"Do the right thing, Theo."

I stare at him, trying to take a breath, but I can't breathe. The pressure on my chest—hot, heavy, solid pressure—I can't breathe, I can't breathe—

"Do the right thing."

I wake up with a yelp, covered in sweat and struggling to breathe. I frantically look down at my chest to find the source of the pressure—

"Theo?"

Caleb's eyes flutter open above me, his curls even wilder than usual from sleep.

I blink several times, reality slowly coming back to me as I get my bearings straight.

I'm in an unfamiliar bed—a hotel bed. The Kendling Hotel.

Memories immediately flood back into my mind—room 1313, the dowsing rods, Caleb storming out, Wren's icy glare, Caleb scooting away from me in the bed.

Our bed. We're sharing a bed. The heat and the pressure from my dream was just Caleb's weight concentrated on my chest and stomach as he lays on top of me, our legs entangled under the sheets, our waists pressed together, and—

Oh. *Oh.*

"Hey, are you okay?"

Caleb is on top of me.

In a matter of moments, the terror from what must have been a nightmare morphs into unmistakable arousal as I feel every burning point of contact between us. Blood travels south at lightning speed, and I'm suddenly very aware of a rapidly growing problem.

Oh, oh *no*. Oh no, no, no.

"I got, um—" I grunt. "I gotta pee. Right now."

"Hm?" Caleb blinks, then begins to understand. "Oh. Oh, shit, I'm sorry, I don't know how I got here—"

"It's fine, it's okay, I just—I just need to—"

"Yep, sorry, I'll just—"

There's no way Caleb doesn't notice my *problem* while I scramble away, despite my valiant effort to hide it. I whisper a quick prayer, thanking God that the bathroom isn't occupied as I rush in, locking the door behind me. I turn the sink on, splash cold water on my face and forearms, and then sit on the toilet lid, burying my head in my hands.

That was a fucking disaster. How did Caleb end up on top of me? When I fell asleep, he was at least two full feet away from me. And what was up with that dream? The details are already fading fast, like sand slipping through my fingers. It was definitely a nightmare, though. I haven't had a nightmare in ages.

"Hey, Theo, you okay in there?"

I sigh. It's just Harrison. "Y-Yeah, I'm fine."

"Okay, good," Harrison mumbles groggily. "I've gotta pee when you're done."

I squeeze my eyes shut. Fortunately, trying to recall specific elements of my dream has helped distract me from my other problem, so maybe now I can play this off like a normal visit to the bathroom.

Once I am finally able to regain my composure, I open the door, almost slamming into Harrison. "Morning," I say as cheerfully as possible.

Harrison simply grunts in response, then retreats to the bathroom. Even after all these years as best friends, it always surprises me that he's not a morning person.

I take a deep breath, bracing myself for whatever is around the corner.

The lights in the hotel room are still out, but rays of sunlight have crept in through the edges of the curtains. I can faintly see one of Oliver's gangly legs dangling off the side of his bed, but otherwise, he must still be asleep.

And then, propped up on his side of our bed, there's Caleb. His face is dimly lit by the light of his phone, and my stomach flutters with a conflicting mix of anxiety and affection.

God, what is wrong with me?

I make my way over to our bed, awkwardly crawling in. "Hey," I whisper.

Caleb locks his phone and puts it face down in his lap but doesn't look at me. "Hey."

We sit in agonizing silence for several moments until I can't stand it anymore. "Caleb, I'm so sorry. Can we talk?"

Caleb doesn't move or speak. He eventually sighs.

A lump is already forming in my throat. "Please?"

Caleb looks over at Oliver's bed, then at his phone. "The hotel tour is in an hour."

"We don't have to go," I say without hesitation. "This is way more important."

Caleb runs his fingers through his hair. "You shouldn't have to miss it. I've already ruined this trip for you, and any chance of you capturing any footage—"

"I don't care about that stuff."

He scoffs. "Yes, you do, don't—"

"Not as much as I care about you. About us. I want to fix this, please."

Caleb pulls his knees to his chest and turns away, sending a new wave of agony through my chest.

"Please, Caleb. I love you."

Before Caleb can respond, Harrison opens the bathroom door and rounds the corner. "Who's showering first? We've got about an hour before we're supposed to meet downstairs."

Oliver groans.

"I showered last night," I answer.

"I'd like to go first if that's cool," Caleb says, and my heart sinks again. "I'll be quick."

"Sure," Harrison replies. "Oliver?"

Oliver lets out another groan.

Harrison makes his way over to the bed, picks up his pillow, and gives Oliver a gentle whack, eliciting a louder groan. "Come on, dude. Do you need to shower?"

"Don't wanna," Oliver grumbles, his voice muffled by the pillow.

"There's free breakfast downstairs."

Oliver perks up immediately. "Oh shit, why didn't you open with that?"

Harrison snorts. "Do you ever listen to your stepmom at all? She told us last night."

Oliver sits up, stretching his long limbs and yawning. "I forgot! A lot happened last night."

While Harry and Oliver bicker, Caleb slips out of bed, grabs his overnight bag, and disappears into the bathroom. As soon as I hear the shower running, I collapse back onto my pillow, pulling the covers over my face.

"Uh oh," Oliver mutters. "Everything okay, man?"

I don't answer. What is there to say?

The mattress dips slightly with the weight of someone sitting on Caleb's side. "Did you guys talk last night?" Harrison asks.

"Nope."

There's a pause. "Do you guys need us to clear out so you can talk once Caleb is out of the shower?" Oliver asks.

"We both have to shower, too," Harrison counters.

"I can go get breakfast while you shower and then they'll be alone in here," Oliver replies. "Perfect opportunity."

My eyebrows shoot up in surprise. Oliver is being shockingly helpful. "Maybe," I croak. "I was thinking about skipping the tour to talk to Caleb, but I don't want him to have to miss it if he doesn't want to."

"Well," Harrison starts hesitantly. "I don't think Caleb cares about the tour anymore. Wren said he was considering calling his sister to come pick him up."

I shoot upward, knocking the covers off. "What?"

Harrison raises his hands. "I'm just saying I wouldn't worry about whether or not Caleb wants to see the tour. I think you guys should both skip the tour and talk."

I rub the back of my neck. "How? Ashley's not going to let us do that."

"Pretend you're sick," Oliver suggests. "Y'all were both acting weird last night anyway. It's believable enough."

"Do you really think that'll work?" Harrison asks, cocking an eyebrow at him. "I mean, she's not stupid. She knows Theo and Caleb are dating, right?"

"Let me handle Ashley," Oliver says, waving his hand dismissively. "As long as you guys don't have make-up sex after, I don't think it'll be a problem."

My stomach swoops at that, instantly sending heat to my cheeks, and I bark out a dry laugh. "Yeah, no, that's not going to be a problem."

"Then it's settled," Harrison continues. "You guys ate something funny last night that didn't agree with your stomachs, and you're not feeling up for the tour."

"You both got the shits," Oliver says with a grin. "You'll need both bathrooms available. We should go ahead and initiate the ruse. Theo, go bang on the door and tell them you've got to use their toilet—it's urgent."

My face twists with disgust.

Harrison rolls his eyes. "Oliver—"

"What? It's got to be believable!"

From our bathroom, I hear the shower cut off. "Come up with something better," I say, lowering my voice. "You know the girls and Wren are going to be using their bathroom to get ready. Plus, that's disgusting."

"Ugh, fine," Oliver whines. "We'll figure it out. You just stay here with Caleb and do whatever you guys need to do. Preferably something that involves you two staying together. I've already dealt with my parents' divorce, and I'd rather not go through it again with y'all."

I manage a weak laugh. "I'll try my best."

Harrison puts a hand on my knee above the covers. "Good luck."

"Thank you."

As soon as Caleb leaves the bathroom, Harrison immediately claims the shower, and Oliver loudly announces his departure to breakfast through the adjoining door that connects our two rooms and disappears. Caleb settles in the chair in the corner—seriously, why is there always just one random chair in hotel rooms? That's weird, right? —so I stare aimlessly at my phone until I hear Harrison's shower start.

"So, Oliver says he's going to cover for us so we can talk. If you still want to."

Caleb doesn't look up from his phone. "The tour starts in like twenty minutes."

"I'm not going."

Caleb finally glances up at me, studying me curiously. "Really?"

I nod. "You were right. I shouldn't keep things from you, regardless of my intentions. I don't want to lose you, Caleb."

Caleb's expression softens. "I don't want to lose you, either."

My heart thuds in my chest. "So, can we talk?"

He nods. "Yeah."

My face cracks into a smile as relief washes over me. I can fix this. Everything is going to be okay.

ELEVEN
CALEB

"We're heading out for the tour. You two feel better," Ashley says, poking her head through the adjoining door. "I'll grab you both some electrolyte drinks from the gift shop on our way back."

"Thanks, Ashley," I say, not hiding the hoarseness in my voice. Crying yourself to sleep has its perks, at least if you're faking sick.

She shuts the door, and Theo and I sit in silence till the footsteps in the other room fade, and we're truly alone. For the first time since my blow-up in the suite, I allow myself to look at Theo. He's sitting on the bed, his legs folded under him as he leans back against the headboard. His dark curls have gotten longer over the winter, and they hang down low enough they almost obscure his eyes. He's still in his sleep clothes, tattered shorts that hit him at the knee, and a green t-shirt that nearly matches the forest color I painted my nails.

And when he raises his gaze to meet mine, I suck in a breath because he's never looked more miserable. And that's my fault.

"I'm so sorry, Caleb." He buries his face in his hands, letting out a sigh.

"I know," I say, not sure what else to add.

He drags his fingers down his face, his head falling back against the board once more. "That night," he starts, his eyes drifting to the window. "The reason I left—it really didn't have anything to do with you. My dad texted me, and it sort of started a spiral. He... he isn't getting any better, Caleb. About the two of us, I mean. Mom keeps talking to him, and Grace is doing what she can, but he won't listen. He's just so stubborn. Rigid. It doesn't matter what I do. He won't bend. And the worst part is, I still care–so *fucking* much–about what he thinks of me. It kills me that he sees me as this immoral, corrupted person." Theo's nose scrunches, and he takes a shuddered breath before continuing, "He used to call me his 'perfect son.' Now, he thinks I'm rebelling against him by saying I'm bisexual. Like it's just something I decided one day. He's fully convinced that if he prays hard enough and keeps me on a short enough leash, I'll 'straighten out' one day, and this whole thing," he motions between the two of us, "will be a distant memory."

Theo sniffles, wiping the end of his nose with the back of his hand.

"Why didn't you tell me?"

He looks up at me, eyes shining. "I was afraid. I still am, actually. That you'll think I'm not worth the trouble. Or you'll convince yourself that breaking things off with me would hurt me less. And I don't want that, Caleb. I don't want you to leave me. You make my life better."

I cross over to the bed, sinking onto the corner opposite Theo. "I'm not going anywhere, dummy. So, put that out of your mind. But you've got to talk to me, Theo. At least to tell me what's going on. I'm not, like, a therapist or whatever, but I can listen. I can hold you when you're feeling down. I can tell you how much you mean to me. I can bombard you with silly memes till those tears are from laughter, not heartache."

Theo lets out a broken chuckle.

"You don't have to be perfect for me, Theo. I never expected you to be anything other than the goofball I fell in love with."

Theo nods, curls falling into his eyes once more.

"You deserve more," he mutters, hands clenched on his knees.

Any remnants of my anger or frustration melt away, dissolved by the pain in his voice. He doesn't understand how much he means to me. How long I've waited to feel this way about someone and for those feelings to be returned.

Moving closer, I rest my hand on his. "You make me happy, Theo Briggs. I think that's all anyone can ask for. And yes, I know we're sort of in the middle of our first fight, but I'm not ready to give that up. So, please. Keep talking to me. Don't shut me out again."

He shifts his hand, wrapping fingers around mine and stroking it with his thumb. "I don't know how I'm supposed to feel about my dad. I love him, of course, but every time I'm around him, I just want to scream. He won't listen. He's convinced that I'm rebelling, that I'm doing this as a way to punish him. How am I supposed to make him see it's got nothing to do with him?"

It's not fair. Theo shouldn't have to deal with this bullshit from someone who's supposed to be on his side through everything. My parents have never once tried to change who I was. They only celebrated me at every turn, every moment of self-discovery. Sure, there have been times when I wish they took more time away from work, and the whole sex-talk ambush thing was wild, but I can't help feeling lucky to have them.

I need to give them an extra hug when I get home.

"What happens if you can't change his mind?"

Theo looks up at me again, his eyes wide. "What?"

"You said it yourself, he's not going to bend. So, what happens if he doesn't change his mind? What does that mean for us?"

"I-I don't know."

It's not exactly the answer I was hoping for. It would be great for him to make some grand gesture, telling me that he'd cut ties with his parents if that's what it took for us to be together, but this isn't some rom-com that wraps neatly in ninety minutes. This is real life, and it's far more complex than the movies ever make it out to be.

"I'm not trying to put you on the spot or anything," I say, suddenly feeling very selfish for bringing up the topic.

"No, you're right to ask it. The truth is, I have no idea what I'm going to do if my dad doesn't have a change of heart. And that scares me. But so does the thought of losing you, and I feel paralyzed waiting for one of them to happen."

I squeeze his hand, drawing his attention back from the edge of the spiral he's teetering on. "Hey, you're not losing me, Theo. I'm right here."

He nods, taking a deep, shuddered breath.

"This is something that a lot of queer people have to deal with, unfortunately. And it doesn't always have a happy ending. But you've got friends and family who love you, Theo. Who celebrate all of who you are, not just the pieces they like. If your dad chooses not to see the incredible, sincere, hard-working person that you are, then that's *his* loss."

Theo's eyes go wide like he's afraid of what I'm saying.

"That's his loss," I say again, taking his free hand and tethering him to me. "You're a good person. Nothing he says can change that. His morals don't mean a damn thing."

"But what if he's right about me?" Theo says, his voice so quiet I can barely make out the words.

"Then you'd better get used to being a degenerate because I'm not letting you go that easily."

A ghost of a smile plays across Theo's lips.

"Plus, Wren has already offered to fight your dad, so there's always that."

Another laugh, and some light returns to Theo's eyes. He's slowly coming back to me.

"I'm going to struggle with this for a while," he says, looking down at our intertwined hands. "But as long as you're with me, I think I'll make it out on the other side."

I embrace him, pulling him into my chest and wrapping my arms around his shoulders. "Just keep talking to me. Together, we'll figure it out."

He clings to me, head buried in my chest, and we stay like that for a while. Until finally, he shows his face, and I fall over onto the bed, suddenly overwhelmed by the emotional drain of the last twelve hours. Theo lays next to me, the two of us staring up at the ceiling.

I don't know how long it takes us to doze off, but when Theo stirs against me, and I open my eyes again, the sunlight is shining from a different angle through the window.

"Hey," he mutters sleepily, letting out a yawn that tugs at my heartstrings.

"Hi," I say back, running my fingers through his bedhead. "So, can I ask you another clarifying question?"

Theo looks up at me with his big brown eyes, nodding slightly.

"When you left the other night, did it have anything to do with you not liking the way I looked with my shirt off?"

Theo chokes on a laugh. "Are you insane? Is that why you thought I left?"

I shrug. "It may have crossed my mind."

"Caleb, that's ridiculous. You're, like, the hottest person I know."

Warmth blooms under my cheeks, spreading across my face. "Shut up."

Theo rolls onto his side, grinning at me. "I'm serious. You are so hot, I can't even stand it sometimes."

My face is on fire, and I cover it with my hands. "Oh my god, stop talking."

There's shifting on the bed and when I pull my hands away from my face, Theo's is hovering above me, head inverted and a goofy smile spreading his lips. "No talking, huh? What do you propose we do instead?"

I reach up, wrapping my fingers around the back of his neck, and pull him down till the ends of his curls tickle my cheeks. "I've got a few ideas."

Theo's lips hit mine, and my heart skips a beat as he melts into the kiss. It's an odd experience, kissing him upside down, but not unpleasant. The novelty doesn't wear off as his hands cup the side of my face.

But soon, I want more of Theo, and I can't reach him at this awkward angle, so I push him away only long enough for me to roll on my side and get my legs under me. He grins as I grip the front of his shirt, pulling him close.

"See? That was hot."

"Shut up," I say through a laugh, then kiss him again. His hands wrap around my waist, then slide under my t-shirt, and I shiver as his fingertips sink into my skin.

"Can I take it off?" he asks, lips moving against mine.

I nod, but a little too eagerly, and end up bumping noses with Theo. "Shit, sorry," I apologize, my eyes watering.

"I'm good," he laughs. "You?"

I swipe the end of my nose just to make sure there's no blood. "I'm fine. Where were we?"

Theo grabs the hem of my shirt, lifting it slowly. I raise my arms above my head, and he pulls the shirt off, tossing it on the floor by the foot of the bed. He sits back on his ankles, his dark eyes trailing down my newly exposed body.

"You're so beautiful, Caleb."

Heat floods my face, dripping down the nape of my neck and trailing down my spine. And it's like my body moves on its own, my hand pushing into Theo's chest till he falls backward toward the headboard. I crawl on top of him, placing a knee on either side of his thighs as I bend down to kiss him again, my hands finding the fabric of his shirt as I pull it off of him so we're finally skin-to-skin–

The sound of the door unlocking derails the action, and I roll off Theo, scrambling to get under the sheets.

"--imagine what the sound would have been? Like a bag of meat hitting the ground at a hundred miles an hour."

Oliver freezes at the corner of the bathroom, Harrison just a step behind.

"What are you–oh." Harrison throws a hand in front of his eyes. "Sorry, we'll give you two a second." He grabs Oliver by the elbow, dragging him back out into the hallway.

As soon as the door closes, I grab my shirt from the floor and pull it over my head. "Well, shit. I think we broke Oliver."

Theo snorts a laugh, retrieving his own shirt. "He'll be okay. In hindsight, we should have locked the door."

My skin is still hot where Theo's hands were just a moment ago, and I'm pretty sure both of us are going to need a minute to calm things down.

"Maybe it was for the best," I say, reaching for Theo's hand. "I don't think either of us is in the best headspace to make decisions right now."

His fingers interlock with mine. "You're probably right. But that doesn't mean I didn't want to keep going."

"Same," I exhale, letting my head fall back onto the pillow. "So, maybe we can talk about it when we get back? Just to make sure we're on the same page?"

Theo nods, giving my hand a squeeze. "We shouldn't make the guys wait out there much longer."

"Yeah, you're right." I pause, taking stock of my current situation. "Um… give me another minute? I need to do some long division or something."

Theo smirks. "Practice your multiplication tables. That always works for me."

I throw a pillow at him.

The ride back to Specter is a swirl of chatter. Elise takes on the role of the narrator, filling Theo and me in on everything we missed during the tour, which apparently, got cut way short. Wren and the tour guide got into a disagreement over some historical inaccuracies in the guide's materials, which evolved into a full-blown shouting match in the lobby. Most of the tour group was on Wren's side by the end of it, and the manager had to get involved to keep the peace.

"It's like the guide hadn't read a single pamphlet. I did get us free tickets to the haunted hor d'oeuvres event next month," Wren says, capping off the story. "Ashley, maybe you can hawk them online."

"I'll try and convince your dad to take me down for a little getaway," Ashley says, leaning over to Oliver. "It'll give me a chance to cash in that babysitting coupon you got me for Christmas."

"Wait, you're actually going to use that?" Oliver questions, crossing his arms. "It was supposed to be more of a symbolic gesture."

"Then you'll watch the girls symbolically," Ashley replies, elbowing him.

We hit a bump in the road, and Theo lets out a murmur in his sleep. I can't be certain, but I'm pretty sure he said my name. He fell asleep on my shoulder about ten minutes into the ride. I'm honestly surprised he hasn't woken from Elise's shrieking laughter or the incessant buzzing of the phone in his pocket. I think for a moment about waking him up, but he looks so peaceful, and we're only a few minutes away from Oliver's house now. He can finish his nap.

"How are things?" Wren asks in a low voice while Elise continues to dominate the conversation in the front half of the van. "Did that knucklehead apologize to you?"

"Yes, and I apologized, too, for my part. We talked, and I think we're at a good place now. At least, better than we were before."

Wren nods, pulling out their phone and snapping a quick picture of Theo and me. "Cute. You two are good together. I'm glad that you figured it out."

"Me too. Sorry for all the drama."

"Oh, honey. Between you and Freddy, drama is what I've come to expect."

"I haven't heard from Freddy today. How do you think his weekend with Andrew went?"

"I'm sure the two of them will be as lovey-dovey as ever tomorrow. If Freddy falls any harder for that boy, I wouldn't be surprised if he ends up with a ring on his finger by senior year."

Wren cracks a smile, and I can't help but laugh at the ridiculous idea. Freddy may be making small steps in his relationship with Andrew, but he's still Freddy. If they last through the summer, then I'll be impressed.

"Are you free after school tomorrow?" Wren asks, still looking at their phone. "Even through all the bullshit, I managed to come up with a look I want to try out. The whole newlywed thing got my brain churning."

"Yeah, for sure."

"Bring Theo with you if he can make it. It's about time I got to paint him again."

"You can say that he's your favorite canvas. You don't have to be coy."

Wren gives me a sly smile. "I'm not saying anything."

The van pulls into Oliver's neighborhood, and everyone goes quiet, the excitement of the trip finally sputtering out as we pull into the driveway.

I gently shake Theo, and his eyes flutter open. "Huh?"

"We're back at Oliver's," I say, holding back a laugh at the dent my shoulder has left in his curls. "You nodded off and were too cute, so I let you sleep."

Theo massages his neck. "Gee, thanks. I've always wanted to have a crooked spine."

"It'll match that crooked nose," Elise quips before sliding out of the side door.

"Don't listen to her," I say, still riding the wave of affection. "I love your nose."

"I love yours too," Theo says, eyes still heavy-lidded.

"And I'd love to get out of here," Wren says, banging on the seat in front of them. "Someone let me out!"

Harrison pulls the lever to fold the seat forward, and Wren escapes into the bright afternoon sun.

"Everyone, get your stuff!" Ashley yells, lifting the back gate.

"Theo, Caleb, your stuff is on top, so I'm going to toss it on Eileen," Oliver says, helping Ashley unload.

"No worries," Theo mumbles, stretching.

"Did you want to hang out for a bit before you go home?" I ask Theo, in no hurry to end our time together. "We can go back to my place."

"Yeah, that sounds good," Theo says, wiping the sleep from his eyes. "I should probably check in with my parents and let them know we made it back." He pulls out his phone and his expression goes slack.

"Hey, Theo?"

Harrison's head pokes through the open side door. "Your dad is here."

"I guess that's a no on the hanging out, then?" I ask, turning to Theo.

"Uh, Harry, can you stall my dad for a second?"

Harrison quirks an eyebrow but eventually nods. "Okay, sure." After a second, his booming voice echoes through, "Mr. Briggs! Good to see you!"

"What's wrong?"

"Don't be mad," he says, stashing his phone back in his pocket. "But I told my parents that you weren't coming on this trip."

"What?"

"They would never have let me come!" Theo exclaims, looking over his shoulder. "What else was I supposed to say?"

"You should have told me, at least." I bury my face in my hands. No. No way. This is starting all over again.

"You're right, I'm sorry." Theo's voice is tight like he's struggling to hold it together. "I'm going to make this up to you, Caleb. But right now, I have to go face my dad." His hand is on my back one moment, and the next, it's gone.

Slowly, I make my way out of the van. Wren is standing by their car, watching as Theo makes his way down the driveway to meet his dad. Harrison has done a good job keeping him occupied, so maybe I can run over and jump into Wren's car before he sees me. Before I can take a step, Mr. Briggs' voice calls out, "Caleb, would you mind joining us?"

Theo stops in his tracks, turning to look at me, his eyes wide. I try to give him a reassuring smile, willing my stiff legs forward till I've caught up to him, and we continue down the driveway to where Mr. Briggs and Harrison wait.

"I'm so sorry," Theo whispers just out of earshot of his dad. I take his hand, giving a silent acknowledgment.

Theo's Dad watches as we approach, his lips pulled tight. "Harrison, I'm going to need a moment with these two. Tell your folks they're missed in my Sunday school class."

"Uh, yeah. Sure thing, Mr. Briggs." Harrison gives us a concerned look, then heads back up the driveway to where Elise, Wren, and Oliver have gathered by Wren's car.

"Hey, Dad," Theo greets his father, slapping on a smile. "Sorry I didn't reply to your messages. I fell asleep on the way back."

Mr. Briggs doesn't respond, his attention focused squarely on me. I don't think he's ever looked at me for so long. I've gotten used to him pretending I don't exist, and to be honest, I prefer it that way.

His expression shifts, morphing into a polite smile. "Caleb, I wasn't aware that you were attending this little field trip. In fact, I'm certain that Kora told me that you had a family engagement."

"I told her that," Theo cuts in, taking a half-step in front of me. "I knew that you wouldn't allow me to go if you knew Caleb would be there."

Mr. Briggs' pleasant expression doesn't change. "And was this your idea, Caleb?"

"No," I answer flatly. "I didn't know about it until Theo told me just now."

He gives a curt nod. "It strikes me as odd that Theo has always been truthful with us until you came into the picture, Caleb. Forgive my bluntness, but I have to assume it's your influence on him."

Theo opens his mouth, but I cut him off. "Maybe he wouldn't feel the need to lie if you were more open and accepting."

I can feel the tension radiating off of Theo as I square up with his dad.

"I accept my son for who God made him to be," Mr. Briggs replies, a crack appearing in the pleasant facade. "And I will be here for him once he realizes that this little infatuation is nothing but a lie built on societal pressures."

"Dad, stop. Don't talk to him like that–"

"At least society didn't shame him for being himself! That was all you."

A vein appears on Mr. Briggs' forehead, and Theo steps fully between the two of us. "Caleb, please stop. This isn't helping."

I know he's right, but the anger in my gut is still roiling. His dad takes a deep breath, his faux smile returning as he speaks in a low voice. "Theo, you are to come straight home. Do you understand?"

Theo nods. "Yes, after I take Caleb home."

"No, *now,* young man."

"I'm taking my boyfriend home," Theo argues, his tone taking on confidence. "Then I'll be home, and we can talk."

Mr. Briggs squares his jaw, giving another curt nod. He eyes me one last time before turning and getting into his car.

Once his dad pulls away, Theo deflates with an exhale, running a hand through his curls. "God, that was so bad."

"I'm not sorry," I say, my face still hot.

"You shouldn't be," Theo agrees. "He was out of line to talk to you like that. You didn't have to defend me, though. This was all my fault."

"I can't help it. He just makes me so mad when he treats us like that. Yeah, you shouldn't have lied to him, but it was only because your parents are unreasonable."

"Are y'all okay?" Oliver calls from the porch. The others are there, too, minus Ashley, watching us with a mixture of concern and curiosity.

Theo gives them a thumbs up, then turns back to me. "Come on, let's get you home."

"I can have Wren take me if you need to go."

He shakes his head. "No, he needs time to cool off anyway. Besides, I get the feeling that the hammer's about to come down pretty hard on me, so I want to enjoy the time I have with you."

"Fair enough."

Theo gives me a weak smile, and we walk up the driveway, collecting our bags from where Oliver tossed them onto the hood of Eileen. My bag is upside down, so when Theo grabs it, a small box falls from the outside pocket, and I nearly choke as Theo picks up the box of condoms I had all but forgotten about.

"Don't look at those!" I say, snatching the box from Theo's hand and stuffing it into my hoodie pocket. A different heat flickers under my cheeks, spreading across my face. "I didn't even know those were in there, I swear."

"Then where did they come from?" Theo asks, a certain amusement in his voice that tells me he's trying not to laugh.

"My parents," I mutter, aware of our friends making their way down from Oliver's porch. "We can talk about it in the car, but please don't make this worse than it already is for me."

"Everything okay?" Harrison's voice announces their arrival, he and Elise hand-in-hand while Oliver and Wren look like they're ready to pounce on someone at our order.

"Just my dad being my dad," Theo says with a weak chuckle. "I've got to get home so he can yell at me. But this was really dope, guys. Sorry if I ruined the vibes last night."

"S'okay," Oliver replies, stepping forward to wrap Theo into a headlock. "As long as you two figured your shit out, then I'd say it wasn't a complete bust."

"You can make it up to me by letting me paint your face," Wren adds, eyes narrowing at Theo. "Then maybe I'll call it even."

"Yeah, I can do that."

"Why is your face all red?" Elise asks, stepping in front of me and poking at the pocket of my hoodie.

"Nothing!" I half-shout, dodging a second poke and opening Eileen's passenger door. "Come on, Theo. We don't want to keep your dad waiting."

Theo detaches himself from Oliver, giving Harrison a fist bump and waving to Wren and Elise before tossing our bags into the backseat. Once we're both in the car and the engine is cranked, I let out the world's longest sigh, kicking the seat back till I'm almost completely flat.

Theo laughs as he backs out of the driveway.

"What's so funny?"

"Oh, nothing. It's just that my dad is happy pretending that we're not dating while your parents assume we're banging. It's funny, right?"

Yeah. I guess it is.

But there's an ache in my chest that the laughter doesn't alleviate.

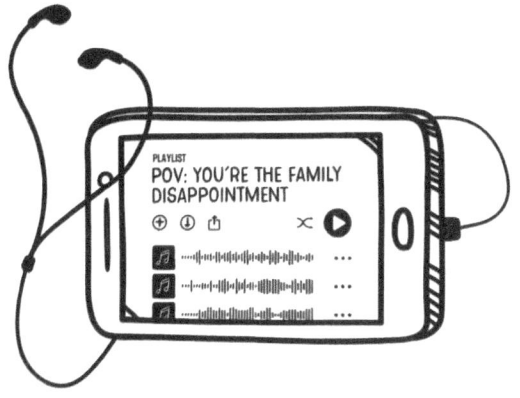

TWELVE
THEO

If Dad weren't such a strong Christian, I'd be fully convinced that I'm driving to my execution right about now. Fortunately for me, filicide is generally frowned upon by the church at large. Well, at least since the New Testament. You'd be surprised by how many times God told fathers to kill their kids in the Old Testament. It's actually kind of disturbing to think about.

After dropping Caleb off at his house, I make the agonizing drive home. I try to listen to music, but for once, it doesn't help.

Instead, I decide to try something a little different.

I clear my throat. "God?" I pray aloud.

Unsurprisingly, I don't hear any kind of response—only the ambient driving sounds as Eileen and I travel just under the speed limit to stall the inevitable. Nevertheless, I persist.

"I know I haven't talked to You much lately," I continue. "And, honestly, I don't even know if You're listening ever since I started liking Caleb."

Again, no response.

"And, well, I know I messed up by lying to Mom. That was definitely stupid of me, so I am sorry for that."

No answer.

"But," I press on. "I just—I don't know what to do. About Dad. I don't know what to say. He thinks that my relationship with Caleb is a sin, but—" my voice cracks, and I take a shuddering breath. "You wouldn't make me like this if it was a sin, right?"

Nothing.

"I've always been taught that You are a loving God. And I believe that. At least, I want to believe that. And from what I've seen, and from what Grace has taught me, I see no reason not to believe that You love me and made me just the way I am." I grip the steering wheel tighter. "But, is Dad right? Is what I'm doing immoral? Is it a sin to love Caleb?"

Silence.

"Because if it is," I rasp, my voice breaking again. "Then—then why? Why would You put this love in my heart—and in Caleb's heart, and in so many queer people's hearts—only to tell us we aren't allowed to feel it?"

Once more, I am met with nothing.

I sigh. I don't know what I expected.

I pull into my driveway and park Eileen in her usual spot. Only Dad's car is in the driveway, which sends a fresh wave of dread through my chest as I realize Mom won't be there to mediate.

With a groan, I run my hand through my unruly curls and squeeze my eyes shut. "Please, God. If You're listening at all, just—just give me something. Anything. And if You're not, well…" I hesitate before inhaling sharply. "Then, I guess it doesn't matter, does it?"

Instead of focusing on the silence that follows, I think of Caleb. I picture his honey-brown eyes and sweet, loving smile. I imagine the constellations of freckles that decorate his skin. I recall the sound of his laugh and the way his arms feel wrapped around me. I remember the sparks that dance between us when we touch and the bubbling joy he brings me whenever we're together.

No matter what Dad says or how he punishes me today, I know that everything is going to be okay. Dad can take away my phone, my car, my money, and my freedom, but he can't take my love for Caleb away from me. And for right now, that's enough to get me out of the car and through the front door.

"Theo, is that you?"

I follow Dad's voice to find him in the dining room. Dad sits at the head of the table, hands wrapped around a cup of tea that smells faintly of cinnamon. He watches as I seat myself at the other end of the table, keeping as much distance from him as possible.

We sit for several horribly uncomfortable seconds before Dad finally speaks. "Theo, I'm going to be very honest with you."

I swallow. Here we go.

"I've been praying about this a lot. About you and about this ongoing…" he hesitates, twisting his lips. "…situation. And quite frankly, I'm at a loss."

I sit silently, waiting for him to continue.

"Over the past six months, I feel like I've been watching my oldest son drift away from me. Away from this family, away from the church, and away from God. And while I can't know what's going on in your heart, I have definitely noticed quite a change in your behavior. And it's not good."

My jaw clenches, and I have to bite my tongue not to speak.

"It feels like you're becoming someone else, transforming right before our eyes. And this new person you've become, Theo, it's…it's not who you are. Lying to your mother, sneaking around behind our backs, deliberately disobeying me when I tell you to come straight home? The Theo I raised never would have done any of that." He pauses, eyeing me sternly. "And I can't help but notice that none of these changes started happening until after you started spending time with Caleb."

I shake my head. "Dad, don't bring Caleb into this—"

"How could I not?" he counters with a scoff. "He has everything to do with this. Clearly, he has much more of an influence on you than I thought."

"No," I argue. "I already told you, Caleb had nothing to do with me lying to Mom. That was completely my idea. He didn't even know that I—"

"So you said, but how am I supposed to believe you?"

I hesitate. "Look, Dad, I get it. I'm sorry I lied. I shouldn't have lied. I only did it because I knew y'all would never have said yes if you knew Caleb was coming—"

"And why is that?" Dad asks, leaning back in his chair. "Why do you think that would be a deterrent?"

It's my turn to scoff. "Well, obviously, because you think we would have been doing something we shouldn't have."

"And *did* you do something you shouldn't have?"

"No!" I shout.

Dad shakes his head. "Does Mrs. Hammond know that the two of you are…romantically involved?"

I gulp. "I'm…I'm not sure."

Dad runs a hand down his face. "That sure seems convenient. So does that mean you shared a hotel room with Caleb overnight with no adult supervision?"

"Dad, it's not like—"

"It's a 'yes' or 'no' question, Theodore."

I shove my hands into my pocket to stop myself from throwing my hands in the air. "Okay, fine, yes, we did, but we didn't *do* anything. Besides, Harrison and Oliver were in the room with us, too, so it's not like we were alone."

"Oh, so am I supposed to believe that would have stopped you two from doing anything sexual? Just because your friends were there?"

I twist my face in disgust. "Uh, yeah, Dad. That's gross."

Dad barks a laugh. "Oh, well. It's good to know you have at least a little shame left."

My jaw nearly drops as I process his words. "Wh–what is that supposed to mean?"

He opens his mouth to answer, but he's interrupted by a loud buzzing on the table that startles us both. Dad sighs as he peeks at his phone, then turns his eyes back to me as he answers the call. "Hello, Kora."

"Michael, don't do anything until I get home," Mom's voice pierces the air over Dad's speakerphone. "I'm five minutes away. Is Theo home yet?"

"He only just got home a few moments ago," Dad replies calmly. "We're chatting in the dining room."

"Mike, I'm serious," Mom urges. "You and I need to talk before we confront Theo about this. You've been really emotional about this whole thing, and I'm worried you might not be in the right headspace—"

"We'll see you when you get home, dear," Dad cuts in. "Drive safe." And with that, he ends the call.

I stare at him in shock. Did he really just hang up on Mom?

Dad huffs a humorless laugh as he puts his phone in his pocket. "You know, son," he continues. "Your mother and I used to be on the same page about these kinds of things. We've always been a united front, parenting as a team, as God calls us to do. But ever since you and Grace decided to convince your mother that having traditional values makes us bigots…" he trails off.

"Dad—"

"Don't interrupt me," Dad snaps, a flicker of something frightening flashing in his eyes, but then he pinches the bridge of his nose with a sigh. "Look, Theo, I just want what's best for you. You're my son, and I love you. In Proverbs, we are instructed to 'train up a child in the way he should go, and even when he grows older, he will not abandon it.' It's my job as your father to set you on the right path, and up until six months ago, that was never something I worried about with you. You've never challenged or questioned us, or the church, or your sexuality or gender, but now, all of a sudden, out of *nowhere*—" he squeezes his eyes shut and his fists tight. "You make one gay friend at school, and, *poof,* now you're gay, too? Just like that?"

Frustration boils in my chest, bubbling out in the form of defiance. "No, Dad, that's not how it–"

"Next thing I know, you're lying to us and sneaking off to do God-only-knows-what in a hotel room? It's like I don't even recognize you anymore."

Tears begin to form in my eyes, and I desperately try to blink them away. *Unacceptable. Unacceptable.* "I'm—I'm sorry. I said I was sorry for lying—"

"Nevertheless, if Caleb is the problem, then the solution seems fairly simple."

No, no, no. "Dad, please, would you just—"

"Give me your car keys."

My blood runs cold. "But–"

"Now, Theo," Dad commands, holding out his hand. "Don't make me take your phone, too."

I snap out of my paralysis and hand over my keys. I can live with that—as long as he doesn't take my phone again, I can survive without my car for a bit.

Dad pockets my keys, then turns away. "Now, go to your room until it's time for dinner. Your mom and I will need to figure out where to go from here."

I don't need to be told twice. I quickly make my way upstairs, gently shutting the door behind me. With trembling fingers, I reach for the closest Sufjan Stevens vinyl to put on my turntable and press play. The music calms me—just barely, but it's enough—and I release a shaky breath as I finally allow myself to cry alone.

Instead of crawling under the covers as I usually do for times like this, I'm pulled to my closet. While it's less of a "walk-in" closet and more of a "barely-step-one-foot-in" closet, there's plenty of space for my basic wardrobe and other random knick-knacks. However, after Christmas, I moved a lot of my crap out of the way so that I could store something far more valuable—the single most important object I've ever owned.

There, tucked safely behind my single suit, various blazers, and button-down shirts, sits Caleb's Christmas gift to me—the photo collage that nearly brought me to tears in front of him. A beautiful paper tapestry made with more love and care than any gift I've ever received in my life.

It's here where I crumble to my knees and weep, my teary eyes traveling across every inch of Caleb's masterpiece. For perhaps the hundredth time, I marvel at the way each image perfectly captures the joy of its subjects. All the photos of the two of us, of all our friends, of Grace and Nathaniel, flawlessly arranged to make a giant empty heart—the only blank spot of the composition.

"I left the center empty. I figured we could put a really special picture there."

I choke out a sob and squeeze my eyes shut. We still haven't taken a photo deserving of such an honor. At least, not a photo that I've deemed worthy. Caleb has made dozens of suggestions, but I've been stubbornly turning them all down. For as hard as Caleb worked on it, the centerpiece has to be perfect.

But is that even possible? Will it ever be?

We'll never be perfect, will we?

Of course we won't. "We" includes me, after all. I'm so astronomically far from perfect that it's almost laughable. Throughout our relationship, my imperfections have always been the root of all our problems. My fear of what people think, my obsessive people-pleasing, my absolute terror of losing Caleb—my anxieties have been at the heart of every obstacle we've faced, and I hate myself for it. The harder I try to be perfect, the farther I seem to get from it.

Caleb, on the other hand, *is* perfect. I mean, he's as close as a person can get to being perfect. He's patient, compassionate, and strong. He's sincere and honest in everything he does, and he's never afraid to be himself. He's thoughtful, generous, and kind. Caleb is perfect, and he deserves perfect.

He deserves better. So, so much better.

"Theo?"

I'm jolted awake by three knocks on the door and the sound of my mother's voice on the other side. Shit, did I fall asleep in my closet? My body protests as I abruptly prop myself upright against the doorframe. "Yeah?"

"Can I come in, *aroha*?"

I sigh, too tired to pretend I've been in bed this whole time. "Sure."

Mom opens the door, her expression morphing from alarm to confusion as her gaze darts around the room until they find me. "Oh," she says aloud.

"Wha—what are you doing on the floor?"

I shrug, not really interested in explaining myself to her, especially if she's just here to dole out more of a punishment.

Warily, Mom steps further into my room, sitting on the corner of my bed to face me. "I think we need to talk."

I nod. "I'm sorry for lying to you, Mom," I blurt out. "It was really stupid and selfish of me."

Mom studies me silently for a few moments. "It was very unlike you."

"I know," I agree. "I'm really sorry."

Mom's lip twitches into a small smile. "I know, sweetie. And I forgive you."

I manage a weak smile in return, then drop my gaze to the ground and wrap my arms around my knees, unsure of what to say at this point. Nothing I could say would change anything, anyway. It doesn't matter how sorry I am—I have to face whatever consequences my parents have deemed appropriate for my crimes. All I can do now is wait.

"What's that?"

I blink, glancing back up to see what Mom's referring to. She's looking past me into the closet. "What's what?" I ask.

She squints, frowns, then stands and takes a few steps towards me. "Are those pictures back there?"

My stomach drops. *Shit, shit, shit,* Caleb's collage. "Oh, um—" I can't say it's nothing. I just apologized for lying. *Shit.* "Yeah, it's, uh, it was just a gift, thing. From, um—"

Mom crouches down beside me and pushes aside the suit I wore to Granny's funeral last spring, fully revealing the collage. Her breath catches in her throat as she takes it in. I watch as her eyes bounce between the faces of each photo, widening with wonder and recognition. "Oh, Theo, this is beautiful. Did you make this?"

I gulp. I might as well come clean about it. "No. Caleb did. He made it for me for Christmas."

Her brows shoot up in surprise, her mouth still agape. She slowly outstretches a hand, pointing at the blank spot in the middle. "Is this bit empty on purpose?"

"Kind of," I admit. "We're waiting to put the perfect picture there. Of… of us."

Mom turns to look at me, eyes glistening as she considers my words. Her gaze is a bit too much for me at the moment, so I turn away. None of this matters. I'm still getting punished. Why doesn't she just give me my punishment already? Why prolong the inevitable?

"Caleb really loves you, doesn't he?"

My heart nearly stops. I swivel my head to look at her once again, and she's studying me. Without any further hesitation, I nod. "Yeah, he really does. And I love him, too."

Mom nods, inspects the collage for a few more seconds, then stands up straight with a soft huff. "That's such a thoughtful gift. Caleb did an incredible job."

I follow her lead, forcing myself up from the floor and moving to my desk chair. "Yeah. He really did."

Mom sighs. "Theo, your father and I…" she starts, hesitating. "We have very different feelings about Caleb. Your father sees Caleb as a negative influence on you, and I, well—I just don't see that at all."

I try my best to mask my surprise, but it's probably a lost cause. "Really?"

"Unfortunately, however," she continues. "Things aren't looking great in Caleb's favor when you decide to lie and go behind our back to spend more time with him."

"Mom, I already told Dad, but I swear, Caleb really didn't—"

"I know he didn't," Mom cuts in. "It was your idea to lie. I know that."

I stare at her, my mouth gaping.

"That said," she proceeds. "You still lied, and therefore, you need to face some consequences."

Here we go, I think, bracing myself for the blow. What will it be? Another lockdown? Caleb won't be allowed to visit ever again? I mean, what more could they take away from me?

"This Saturday, I'm co-hosting the quarterly luncheon for the On Our Knees Women's Ministry. We are actually in need of a few more volunteers to help set up and serve the meals. We can use all the help we can get, so I'm volunteering you to do both."

I blink, waiting for the rest of the punishment, but Mom says nothing else. "That's…that's it?" I hear myself ask aloud.

Mom chuckles. "Oh, is that not enough? Did you want more?"

"No, no," I blurt quickly, my cheeks burning with embarrassment. "I mean—okay, that seems fair."

"That's what I thought," she replies with a grin. She takes a few steps towards the door but hesitates in the door frame. "And, like I said, we could use all the help we can get, so—" she pauses, meeting my eyes. "If Caleb wants to earn some extra brownie points with us, that might be a good opportunity. But only if he wants to, of course. After all, you're the one who lied, so you're the one who has to give up a Saturday to serve, not him."

I nod. "Okay, yeah. Totally. That's more than fair." I manage a smile. "Thanks, Mom."

Mom hums a response. "Oh, and Theo?"

"Yeah?"

"You shouldn't have to hide that collage in your closet," she says softly, her eyes boring into mine. "It's far too sweet to stay hidden away."

Without thinking, I let out a dry, humorless laugh. "I think Dad might disagree," I mutter.

Mom's smile fades, and she lingers wordlessly at the door while I silently chastise myself for saying anything at all. God, why am I like this? Why did I say that? Why couldn't I have just let Mom have the last word and kept my mouth shut?

Before I can take it back, Mom is gone, and I'm left alone on the floor of my room.

From somewhere on my bed, I recognize the incessant vibrations coming from my phone, and I finally force myself up to retrieve it. I have dozens of notifications, but the persistent buzzing can only be from one place: the group chat.

OLIVER: ok gang, harrison and I just finished going through all our footage and recordings from the hotel...
and here we go...
I hope you're hungry...
for ~Nothing~

ELISE: *eyeroll emoji*

WREN: Seriously?

OLIVER: we got NOTHING

HARRISON: That's not exactly true, but it's definitely not anything to get excited about.

WREN: Not even with the weird stuff happening in the kitchen?

OLIVER: dude, it's nothing
the kitchen footage was just yelling (sorry Theo/Caleb)

CALEB: No worries. It wasn't my proudest moment.

HARRISON: By TikTok standards, yeah, it's probably nothing.

OLIVER: LIKE I SAID
> NOTHING

ELISE: I'm so sorry, guys :(
> we'll get something next time! <3

OLIVER: theo, are you still alive?
> your dad didn't burn you at the stake did he?
> or whatever it is the church does the gay people

WREN: Bro??

ELISE: not funny, Oliver. WTF.

HARRISON: Not funny, dude.

THEO: I'm okay guys. thanks for checking in.
> I'm sorry we didn't get anything at the hotel :(

OLIVER: AYYY

ELISE: Theo!! we love you! how are you holding up?

OLIVER: you still have your phone??
> God is real!!

HARRISON: Glad you're okay, man. We're here for you.

THEO: thanks guys. yeah, my dad only took away my car for a while but he's letting me keep my phone

THEO: also I have to volunteer at church on saturday morning

OLIVER: ughhhhhhh boooo

CALEB: *crying emoji* <3 <3 <3

HARRISON: Oof.

ELISE: ugh, that sucks. I'm so sorry!

THEO: all things considered, it's really not that bad though
 I think my mom convinced my dad to go easier on me

ELISE: niiiice!

OLIVER: what a queen *crown emoji*

FREDDY: Did someone say queen? *nails emoji*

WREN: *eye roll emoji* put us back on mute, Freddy.

THIRTEEN
CALEB

Monday, January 22

"It's just like old times."

I grunt an acknowledgment as I climb into the passenger seat of Wren's navy blue sedan, letting out a yawn. It's been months since I've had to ask Wren for a ride to school, but with Eileen being held hostage by Theo's archaic dad, I'm just grateful that they're still willing to drive out of their way to get me.

"Theo must be in pretty deep shit," Wren continues, shifting the car in reverse and resting an arm on the back of my seat as they turn to look behind. "How bad is it?"

"Not as bad as last time, I think. At least he still has a phone. He wasn't exactly in the mood to talk last night, so I'll get the details at lunch, I'm sure."

"What did his dad say to you yesterday? I swear, you looked like you were about to explode when you got into Theo's car to leave."

"Oh, just the usual nonsense. He thinks that I've corrupted his perfect son and pressured him into thinking he's bi so that I can turn him away from the love of God or whatever. I popped off at him, and it probably just made things worse."

"Good for you," Wren congratulates me, but it doesn't help the pit in my stomach. "Let me know the next time you're going toe-to-toe with the guy, and I'll come back you up."

"I don't think Theo's going to let me anywhere near him for a while, which is fine by me. The way he speaks to Theo… I've never seen someone with such disdain for their child. It just makes me so mad."

"We can't all hit the jackpot when it comes to parents, Caleb. My moms may yell sometimes, but it's only about stupid shit, never an attack against who I am. My dad, on the other hand, is a mixed bag, but that's only because he's an emotionally stunted man-child who never wanted to have kids in the first place."

"Shit, Wren. You make my parents sound like saints."

"Nora and Bert are great, but I'm sure they've got their own hang-ups. The point is, no parent is perfect, but at least ours accept us for who we are."

"True. I shouldn't take that for granted. I don't know what I'd do if I were in Theo's shoes."

Wren nods, their attention drifting over to me after we come to a stop at a red light. "How are you two? I know that you patched things up after the bullshit that happened in the newlywed suite, but it still seems like something's off."

"We're okay for now," I say, fidgeting in my seat. The heat from the vents is starting to make me sweat, so I crack the window to get a breath of cool air. "He pretty much said the stuff with his dad is the reason he's been acting so weird. But he's promised to do better at talking to me, so that's all I can really ask right now."

The light changes and we're moving again, Wren's attention back on the road. "Still think it's worth all the fuss?"

I look at them, my questioning expression making them elaborate.

"Having a boyfriend, I mean. A few months ago, you'd have done almost anything to have someone like Theo. Now that you do, I'm curious if you've changed your opinion at all."

It's a legit question. If I had a time machine and could go back to warn past Caleb of the trials ahead, would it have made a difference? If I hadn't taken the time to get to know Theo, to fall for his awkward charms and adorable optimism, maybe I would have thought twice about getting involved.

But I *had* fallen for him. And the feelings I still have for him throw all the hypotheticals out the window. The truth of the matter is that I love Theo Briggs. And no amount of religious drama or disapproving parental glares is going to change that anytime soon.

"Theo is worth it all," I say finally, and it's both a resolution to myself and an answer for Wren. "I can't say I'd feel the same about anyone else. But for him, yes. A thousand times, yes."

Wren's nose scrunches. "Oh my god, that was so sweet I might cry."

I snort a laugh. "Don't start, or I'll do it too."

Wren nods, then puts on their blinker, turning a few blocks earlier than usual.

"Where are we going?"

"It's a Monday, people suck, and I'm cramping like a motherfucker, so we're getting coffee. Mr. Reynolds can eat my shorts."

"Wren, have I ever told you you're my favorite person?"

They crack a sly smile. "It never hurts to hear it again."

The first half of the school day drags by, not helped by the gloomy weather outside. Even though Wren and I stopped at Spookies for a caffeine fix, we still made it in time for first period. From the classroom windows, I watch the low clouds drift overhead and worry about Theo.

I think back to last year, after Sienna went and outed Theo to his parents, and we could only see each other at school. Even if that happens again, they can't keep us away from one another. We'd find a way to make it work.

By lunch time, the anticipation of seeing him has grown to the point that I can't sit still as I scan the cafeteria for a head of familiar dark curls.

"Caleb, you're about to shake my lunch onto the floor." Freddy shoots me an annoyed look from across the table.

"Sorry." I press a fist into my thigh to keep my leg from bouncing.

"Did you guys have fun on your little ghost adventure?"

Wren slides into the seat next to me, and I'm thankful they're here to field Freddy's questions while I search for Theo.

"There were fun moments," Wren says, unzipping their lunch bag. "And some that were not so fun."

Harrison and Elise arrive next to the lunch table, already engrossed in a conversation of their own.

"Don't you think it's strange that we've never seen them in the same place? It's weird, that's all I'm saying." Elise gives me a smile as she sits next to Freddy.

"There's plenty of people that we've never seen in the same place. That doesn't mean that they're leading some secret double life." Harrison pops open a can of soda with a *hiss*.

"What are you two going on about?" Freddy asks, getting pulled into the discussion.

"Elise thinks that Principal Miller is moonlighting as the new janitor."

"They look the same!" Elise argues, her volume shooting up.

"Wait, are you talking about the janitor with the ponytail down to his butt?" Wren asks.

Elise nods emphatically, and even though I'm still on high alert for Theo, I can't help but be pulled into this ridiculous conversation. "But Principal Miller is bald."

Harrison points in my direction. "Thank you."

"He could be wearing a wig, obviously," Elise rebuts, crossing her arms. "It's not impossible. That's all I'm saying."

"You can't argue with that," Wren concludes, unwrapping their sandwich.

"Stranger things have happened."

"Are we talking about *Stranger Things*?" Oliver pipes up, sliding into the seat at the end of the table. "Because I've got a theory about how they're going to keep putting off the last season till everyone just forgets about it."

"I wouldn't doubt it," Harrison says, leaning closer to Oliver. "I keep seeing this stuff online about how they're filming the finale…"

"Psst."

Freddy tosses a baby carrot at me. It bounces off my chest and lands on top of my salad.

"You two haven't asked me about *my* weekend yet."

Wren and I both lean forward over the table. "Sorry," I apologize, tearing my attention away from the search for Theo. "How did things go with Andrew?"

Freddy grins, his tanned cheeks turning ruddy. "Good. Like, really good. Like, I can't stop thinking about him, good."

"Does that mean the two of you—" Wren makes an obscene hand gesture that goes on a bit too long.

Freddy nods. "Twice. It was incredible. He was so sweet and nervous, but when things got going, the boy was a natural."

"That's amazing, Freddy," Wren says, reaching a hand across the table. "And kind of gross. See? You had nothing to worry about."

Heat builds in my gut, and it takes me a second to realize that I'm *jealous* of Freddy in this moment. Jealous of the ease that seems to surround his relationship with Andrew. Everything comes so easily to them, while I have to fight tooth-and-nail for Theo on a daily basis.

It's not fair. It shouldn't have to be this hard.

And, of course, there's the sex thing. It's hard not to be jealous of that.

"Hey, Theo."

Harrison's greeting pulls me away from my thoughts. Theo has finally made it to the lunch table, an apologetic grin on his face as he looks at me, and me alone. The heat in my stomach flickers, morphing into something completely different than the jealousy I was wrestling with. Fuck, I missed him. How stupid is that? I saw him literally yesterday.

Wren slides down, and Theo takes the spot next to me, bumping his shoulder into mine as he sits. "Hey, babe," he mutters in my ear, and electricity surges from one side of my body to the other.

"Hey yourself," I reply, the cafeteria around me going quiet as my world narrows to include only the two of us. His hand finds mine under the table.

"Sorry I couldn't pick you up this morning."

"Don't be. I totally get it."

"Dad insisted on driving me and Nate to school himself. If you think I took it hard, you should have seen Nate when we pulled up. I've never seen him run away so fast."

I laugh, which in the grand scheme of things feels silly, but I won't deny myself the little joys of being with Theo, even if our situation is less than ideal.

"How long do you think he'll hold Eileen hostage?"

Theo shrugs. "I guess that depends on how well I behave."

I cringe. "That's so fucked up, Theo. Eileen is your car! You paid for her with your own money. He shouldn't be able to take her away."

"Yeah, I thought about that argument too, but I know it wouldn't get me anywhere. Dad would just spout off some 'under my roof you live by my rules' bullshit, and we'd be back at square one."

"Did he take anything else away from you?" I ask, already feeling guilty for my part in his punishment.

"No, not yet. Mom did rope me into helping out with a church thing this weekend as 'punishment,' so she kinda came to my rescue. She even wanted me to invite you to come along to help out, which I totally don't expect you to do–"

"She wants me to come along?"

"Yeah. She's trying, Caleb. I honestly think she's doing her best to understand me."

A spark of hope kindles in my chest. "Okay, sure. I'd love to come along."

"Really? Are you sure?"

"Of course! I'll be there to keep you sane," I say, resting my head on his shoulder. "I love you, Theo."

He sets his head against mine. "I love you too."

"Ew, you guys are so gross." Wren elbows Theo in the side, breaking our bubble and thrusting us back into the real world. "Are you still able to come over this afternoon, Theo? I've got inspiration coming out of my ass, and I need as many victims—I mean *models*—as possible."

Theo shakes his head, giving Wren an apologetic smile. "My dad is picking me up right after school. I may not be able to come over for a while."

"Boo," Wren pouts, turning to the rest of the table. "Any other takers?" "I'll do it!" Oliver calls from the opposite end. "I want to be in your catalog!"

"You'll regret those words," Freddy warns, frowning.

Wren shoots him a look that could curdle milk, then turns to Oliver. "You'll be immortal, Oliver Hammond."

He strikes a dramatic pose. "That's all I've ever wanted."

"I'll miss you," I say to Theo, trying not to sound as bummed as I feel.

"Ditto, babe."

"Are you going to shave my face? I've been working on this mustache for, like, three months."

Oliver spins in Wren's makeup chair, his long legs reaching the ground where the rest of us have to brace against the footrest. Wren digs through their drawers, assembling the components needed for their latest masterpiece. Freddy and I have taken over the bean bag chairs surrounding Oliver, ready to offer moral support if he should start to regret his decision to allow Wren anywhere near his face.

"What mustache?" Freddy asks, squinting as he leans forward.

"Rude!" Oliver quips, hand moving to cover his top lip. "Caleb, tell Freddy that my mustache is beautiful."

I wrinkle my nose. "Is the alleged mustache in the room with us right now?"

"Double rude. You two are just threatened by my innate masculinity. It's understandable. I'm the epitome of the male form."

Freddy grins, knocking his knee into mine. "If we figured out a way to bottle some of Oliver's delusion, do you think we could sell it?"

"Sell it? If I had a fraction of that self-confidence, I'd be unstoppable."

"Wren," Oliver pouts, sticking out his bottom lip, "they're being mean to me."

Wren lets out a sigh, fastening their apron around themselves before pointing a brush at the two of us in a threatening gesture. "No bullying my canvas, boys. If he leaves, one of you has to take his place."

Oliver sticks his tongue out at us, and Freddy rolls his eyes. "Snitches get stitches, Oliver. Remember that."

"Are you ready?" Wren asks, squeezing a huge glob of white goo onto the back of their hand and dabbing their brush into it.

Oliver retracts his tongue, giving Wren a nod, then flinches as the brush smears the first bit of white paint onto his skin. "That's freaking cold."

"Sorry," mutters Wren. "It'll warm up as we go. Now stop talking." They brush against Oliver's lips, and with the contrast of the white paint, I can just barely make out the line of thin hairs that runs under his nose.

"Oh, hey, there it is. You're right, Oliver. Your mustache is beautiful."

"Thank you–*blegh*!" Oliver spits and sputters, having gotten a taste of the white paint.

"I told you to stop talking," Wren chastises him, dabbing their brush before attacking Oliver's mouth once more.

"You ask for the impossible," Freddy chimes in. "Asking sweet Oliver to be quiet is like asking the sun not to shine. The birds not to sing. Caleb not to chew with his mouth open."

I kick Freddy's shin. Oliver cracks up, and Wren shoots us both a dirty look.

"That was pure poetry," Oliver says, trying his best not to move his lips.

"It was pure something," mutters Wren, squeezing more paint onto their hand.

I snap a picture of Oliver in the chair, sending it to Theo.

> CALEB: Oliver has already had a mouthful of face paint, and Wren's only just getting started. His tongue is going to be eight different colors by the time they're done.
>
> THEO: oh my gosh, he looks like a ghost. What is Wren making him into?
>
> Caleb: They haven't said yet. But if he keeps talking so much, it may be something with its lips sewn shut.
>
> THEO: that would be sick as hell.
>   I miss your face.
>
> CALEB: I miss you too. How's the no-car life?
>
> THEO: my dad drives like, five miles under the speed limit and puts his blinker on half a mile away from his turn. I'm about ready to tuck and roll.
>
> CALEB: Yikes. Does he at least let you play music?
>
> THEO: nope. It's nothing but sermons and sports radio. what a day to forget my headphones at home.
>
> CALEB: Oh my god, you poor thing. Is there anything I can do to help?

THEO: keep sending me updates on Oliver. I need to know someone else is having a worse time.

CALEB: I don't think that's possible.

THEO: yeah, me either. but we gotta try, right? Dad roped me into coming to his small group tonight, so I may not be able to talk till later.

CALEB: Stay strong. I love you <3 <3 <3

THEO: love you too. <3

Oliver looks like a mime at this point, any color of his face bleached out with white as Wren grabs a small glass bottle of liquid rubber, uncapping it with practiced dexterity, and slathering a layer onto the side of Oliver's face.

"That smells like gasoline," Oliver says, a bit of concern creeping into his features.

"You'll get used to it," I tell him. "Or you'll pass out. Either way, it gets better."

"He's kidding," Wren adds quickly. "The only time someone has passed out is when Freddy huffed all of my spirit gum remover."

Freddy pops out of his beanbag seat. "Whoa, whoa, huffing is a strong word. I was simply enjoying the intoxicating aroma, and then I got really sleepy."

"You're not inspiring a lot of confidence," Oliver says, wincing as Wren lathers on a second coat.

"Just think of the catalog," Wren mutters, using their clean hand to pat the top of Oliver's head. "That's got to dry for a little bit, so you get a break." A buzzing noise from their pocket, and Wren pulls out their phone, a frown spreading across their face. They swipe the screen, setting down their supplies and stepping quickly past Freddy and me. "Dad? What's up?"

Freddy shoots me a concerned look, and I just shrug. Wren hasn't mentioned anything about their dad since his surprise visit over the Christmas holiday. For all I know, I thought he was back in Australia.

"Yeah, I have a second. Hold on." Wren looks back at us, pointing a finger upstairs, then disappears around the corner.

"What do you think that was about?" Freddy asks.

"Who knows? Knowing him, it can't be anything good."

Oliver leans forward in the makeup chair. "Who are we talking about?"

"Wren's dad," I explain, keeping my voice low. "He's not exactly the best guy."

"Yeah, that's an understatement," Freddy says with a huff. "Let's just say he makes Theo's dad look like the father of the freaking year."

"Whoa, what's his deal? I don't think I've ever heard Wren talk about him before."

"For good reason. He was—well, I guess he still is—an alcoholic, so he hasn't been around for much of Wren's life. He fucked off a few months before they were born, leaving their mom to fend for herself. But a few years ago, he started reaching out to them, saying he wanted to connect with his child—"

"He says daughter," Freddy interjects. "Because the piece of shit refuses to call Wren anything but their dead name."

"That's so shitty," Oliver breathes, folding his arms across his chest.

"Yeah," I agree. "Wren's moms put up with it because Wren asks them to, but I know it bothers them. Wren wants to keep that door open for some reason."

"He's their family," Oliver says, frowning. "I get it. It can be a hard thing to let go of."

"Not for me," Freddy scoffs, flopping back down in his bean bag chair. "My dad was a homophobic asshole till the day he died. Mom was smart to leave him when she did. I never wanted anything to do with him."

And once again, I'm reminded that I need to hug my parents tonight, because in the parental lottery, I'm a winner through and through.

Oliver's frown deepens and it's weird seeing him without a smile.

"We're all a little fucked up," I say, trying to lighten the mood. "But I trust Wren to do what's best for them. And let's be honest, their moms will absolutely go scorched earth before they'd let anything hurt Wren."

"Truth," Freddy adds. "You should have been here when they broke up with their middle school boyfriend. I thought Patricia was going to murder the kid and bury him in the backyard. She's got the power tools to make it happen."

"She would have done it too." Wren stands at the base of the stairs, stowing their phone in their back pocket. "Mom has always wanted an excuse to dig up Mama's rose bushes. She was just waiting for a good reason."

"Everything okay?" I ask as they cross the room, immediately busying themselves with brushes and bottles.

"Super." They keep their back turned to us, pulling open a drawer and digging through it. A soft sniffle carries over the silence.

Freddy and I exchange looks, but before I can even get out of my beanbag, Oliver is out of his chair. He places a hand on Wren's shoulder, and as they turn to face him, Oliver wraps them up in a tight hug.

Wren doesn't move, the top of their head barely visible over Oliver's shoulder.

"I'm sorry people suck sometimes," Oliver says, his tone uncharacteristically serious.

Freddy's eyes are wide as he looks back at me, and honestly, I'm just as shocked as he is. Wren eventually wraps their arms around Oliver's waist, and the two of them stay like that for a little while, neither saying anything else.

When they do break apart, Wren sniffles again and wipes the end of their nose on their sleeve, clearing their throat. They reach out, brushing a hand against Oliver's cheek. "You're ready for another layer."

Oliver nods, settling back into the makeup chair.

"I'm in your hands."

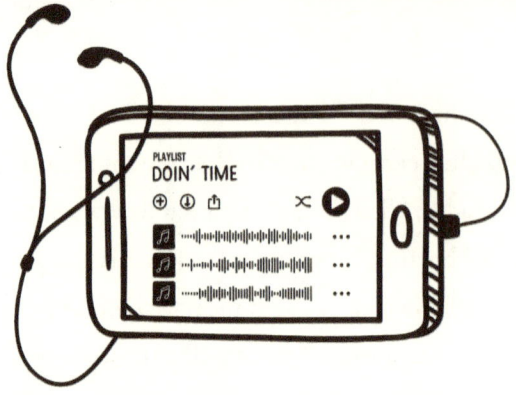

FOURTEEN
THEO

Saturday, January 27

"Rise and shine, Theo! We need to leave in about an hour, okay?"

I let out a groan as Mom raps her knuckles against my door. I barely have to open my eyes to see that no sunlight shines through my curtains, so it can't possibly be time to wake up yet.

Just five more minutes…

"You up, *taku tama*?" Mom calls out from the other side of my door again. "You haven't answered my calls, so I'm about to come in there!"

Shit, I must have dozed off again. Through the grogginess, I manage to peek at my phone for the time. 6:04 AM. Ugh, it's so early. And it's Saturday? Why is Mom waking me up so—

Oh shit, the church luncheon thing. My punishment. Caleb.

"Theo?"

"Yeah, I'm up, I'm up," I grumble, voice thick with sleep.

"We're leaving in forty minutes."

With effort, I lift myself upright. "Okay, I'll be ready."

One thing that my mother failed to mention about my "punishment" until yesterday was just how early I needed to be awake and ready to head to the church. I'm never up this early. Not even for school.

Fortunately, I told Caleb he doesn't have to show up until 8:00 AM, but I still feel guilty that he has to wake up early on a Saturday. I mean, he doesn't *have* to, but he said he wants to. For me.

I really don't deserve him.

The morning moves fairly quickly from there. Mom and I leave the house to arrive at the church at 7 AM. Apparently, there was some type of children's ministry event last night, so now we have to set up the chairs in the sanctuary in preparation for Mom's thing. One of the church custodians is supposed to be here soon to guide the volunteers on where and how the rows should be arranged, but until he arrives, I follow Mom into the kitchen for some mediocre church coffee.

"Oh, praise God," I hear Mom exclaim as we round the corner. "Megan, you're a lifesaver."

At that moment, the smell hits me, and I nearly start salivating on the spot. A modest spread of breakfast sandwiches and pastries from Cathy's has been set up along the stainless-steel countertop, complete with several cartons of Cathy's coffee. My eyes are immediately drawn to the individually wrapped fried chicken biscuits—at least twenty of them. Suddenly, I feel like I haven't eaten in days.

"Oh, it's my pleasure," Megan says from the end of the table, sipping on a steaming styrofoam cup. She smiles at me. "We really appreciate you volunteering your Saturday morning for us, Theo. Help yourself!"

I look to Mom for permission, which she grants with a nod. "Thank you, Mrs. Megan," I declare before snatching up a warm sandwich, tearing through the silver foil, and shoving the chicken biscuit into my mouth with a sigh.

"Sup, Theo?"

I spin around to find the source of the familiar voice and offer him a smile and a wave. "Mm, hi, Jake," I manage to mumble through a mouth full of buttery biscuit and juicy chicken.

"Theo!" Mom reprimands.

Jake laughs. "Don't choke, dude," he says, giving me a friendly pat on the back. "We've got work to do!"

I nod, fully chewing and swallowing my bite before speaking again. "I didn't know you'd be here today, man." I step closer and lower my voice. "Did you get in trouble, too?"

Jake furrows his brow incredulously. "Nah, dude. I'm here most Saturdays."

I stare at him. "What? Really?"

He shrugs. "Yeah."

"Why?"

Jake hesitates, glances behind me at Mom and the other ladies chatting by the coffee cartons, then gestures for me to follow him out of the kitchen. I join him out into the main corridor, mirroring him as he leans against the opposite wall from the kitchen. "So yeah," he continues. "Whenever there's an event on a Saturday morning, I almost always volunteer to help with the set-up. They almost always give me free breakfast and lunch, and once the event starts, I can just fuck off and do whatever I want until it's over."

I can't stop myself from flinching at Jake's casual dropping of "fuck" within the church walls. Even if no adults can hear us, I can't help but wonder if God might frown on us cursing in His house. But then again, all things considered, that seems like a pretty minor offense, especially when Jake and I are here for volunteer work. It feels like that might balance it out a bit, right? Does it count if my presence here is a punishment? But Jake is here by choice, so maybe only I can't curse.

As if reading my mind, Jake chuckles. "Dude, you can say 'fuck' at church on a Saturday. I've been saying it for years and God hasn't struck me down so far, so I think it's safe."

I huff a small laugh. "If you say so." I take another bite of my biscuit, chewing slowly and savoring it for a bit before swallowing. God, it's been so long since I've had Cathy's for breakfast. They stop serving it at 10:30 AM every morning, and I'm rarely out of the house earlier than that for any reason other than school or church, and there's definitely not enough time for a Cathy's breakfast run on those days. A heavy, satisfied sigh escapes my lungs before I can stop it.

"Jeez, Theo," Jake says with a laugh that almost sounds nervous. "Do I need to give you and your biscuit some privacy?"

My cheeks start burning immediately. "S-Sorry."

"I'm just messing with you," Jake says, bumping into my shoulder with his. "Although, I'm surprised you like the food at Cathy's at all. You still work there, right? Don't you get sick of it?"

I shrug. "I get sick of the place, but never the food. I swear they put something addictive in the chicken."

Jake snorts. "Crack, maybe?"

"Nah, probably just an insane amount of MSG."

"Eh, '*to-may-toe, to-mah-toe.*'"

I burst into giggles, almost dropping the biscuit completely, which makes Jake laugh, too.

"All right, boys, it's time to get started with the chairs," booms a familiar voice from down the hall. Jake straightens up immediately, and I turn to see Jim Buchanon, Jake's dad, waving us into the sanctuary.

"Yes, sir," Jake replies robotically before marching ahead. I pop the rest of my biscuit into my mouth and follow Jake's lead, tossing the foil in a nearby trashcan and wiping my hands down my pants as we enter the sanctuary together.

With all eight volunteers and the church custodian, the set-up takes about forty minutes. The church custodian is a soft-spoken, curly-haired guy around Grace's age with a thick southern drawl and a warm smile. He does most of the heavy lifting and seems very appreciative of our help. To think that he has to do this stuff by himself most weekends before church each Sunday is appalling. No matter what he's getting paid, it definitely doesn't seem like enough.

Just as we're wrapping up, my phone buzzes in my pocket, and my stomach flips with excitement.

CALEB: Just got dropped off by the big building...where should I go?

THEO: cool, just stay put, I'm on my way to let you in <3

"I'll be right back," I blurt out before jogging to the entrance. Sure enough, there's Caleb, standing rather awkwardly under the awning, hands tucked in his hoodie pocket. His face lights up as soon as his eyes meet mine, and my heart swells.

I press on the push bar and hold the door open for him. "Hey, you."

"Hey, yourself," he replies, stepping inside.

After a quick glance around the room, I wrap him into a quick hug. "Thank you so much for coming. I'm sorry it's so early."

As he pulls away, Caleb peeks at his phone. "It's no problem. It's not even that early. How long have you been here?"

"Eh, not too long," I reply. "Are you hungry? There's some breakfast from Cathy's in the kitchen for the volunteers."

"That sounds amazing."

I guide him past the entrance to the sanctuary and into the kitchen, where Mom, Megan, and several other church women I recognize are hard at work on various platters and desserts.

"Oh, hi, Caleb!" Mom calls out, elbow-deep in what appears to be dough. "So good to see you!"

"Good to see you, too, Ms. Kora," Caleb says politely.

"Help yourself to some breakfast," Megan chimes in. "We appreciate you giving up a Saturday to help us out!"

Caleb thanks her, picks out a chicken biscuit, and the two of us make our way into the hallway. Before Caleb even manages to get his biscuit unwrapped,

Jake suddenly appears next to me, and I jump.

"I was wondering where you ran off to," Jake says, then curiously glances between Caleb and me. "Who's your friend?"

"Jake, this is Caleb," I say slowly, raising my eyebrows in hopes that he remembers to stay discreet. "Caleb, this is Jake. He's in my small group."

Jake nods knowingly. "Ah, so *you're* Caleb. Glad to finally put a face to the name!"

"Likewise," Caleb replies curtly before shoving a bite of biscuit into his mouth.

There's a moment of uncomfortable silence before Jake clears his throat. "So I think the chairs are done. Now we're just waiting for the next task." He turns to Caleb. "Are you here to volunteer, too?"

Caleb nods.

"Cool, cool." Jake looks back at me. "With this many guys, I imagine we'll get this stuff done pretty fast."

"Yeah, probably," I agree.

"Once the luncheon starts and they don't need us, I'll show you guys where I usually hang out until we have to come back to break stuff down," Jake continues. "Y'all in?"

"Sure!" I exclaim, then look to Caleb. "I mean, if you want to stay that long, that is. You really don't have to."

Caleb shrugs. "I'm down for whatever you want to do."

"Cool," Jake says with a smile. "I'll let you finish your breakfast, Caleb. See you guys in a bit!" He extends out a fist, which I instinctually bump with my own fist, and Jake turns and jogs away.

I watch Jake disappear back into the sanctuary, and I can't shake the feeling that there's suddenly a tension between Caleb and me that wasn't there before. Am I being paranoid?

"So," Caleb says abruptly. "Is that the same Jake that your dad mentioned when he called you on Saturday morning?"

I frown, then I remember. "Oh, yeah, I forgot about that." I try to calm the random nerves in my stomach. "Our dads are both elders, and I think they both like the idea of us hanging out so we can be good influences on each other or whatever."

Caleb considers this as he chews another bite of biscuit. "I guess that makes sense. I'm sure he's a much better influence than I am, huh?"

I wince. "Caleb–"

"Sorry," he backtracks. "That wasn't fair."

I sigh. "I mean, you're not wrong." I glance around the room for anyone who might be listening in but still lower my voice to continue. "But my dad doesn't have any idea how wrong he is."

Caleb quirks a brow, but I quickly regret saying anything. Jake came out to me in confidence, and I don't know if he's out to anyone else. As someone who has been outed before, I refuse to even come close to doing the same to someone else.

Instead of elaborating, I clear my own throat. "Anyway, you ready to do some annoying manual labor for no pay?"

Caleb tosses the last bit of his biscuit into his mouth, crumples up his foil wrapper, and gives me a thumbs up. And with that, I lead the way back into the sanctuary to join the other volunteers.

Once we start getting specific tasks assigned to us, the morning moves much faster. We set up tables, arrange signage, assist with decorating, and eventually are given some type of kitchen duty. I try to keep an eye on Caleb at every turn, ensuring he isn't cornered by any nosy elders or left alone with any overly observant church ladies. Caleb isn't exactly subtle about who he is—which is something I love about him, but I can also recognize the danger that it poses in a place like this. If I think about it too hard, it'll make me sick.

Jake, on the other hand, is a lot more like me when it comes to appearances. He doesn't give off "gay vibes," at least not as far as I can tell. I do wonder if Caleb will sense it, though. I kind of hope so.

Before we know it, it's already 11 AM, and guests begin trickling in. Some of the volunteers have already disappeared, but Jake, Caleb, and I linger in the kitchen and await our next instructions.

"Well, I think that's everything for the time being," Megan declares to the handful of others in the kitchen, then turns to us. "Boys, thank you again for all your help so far!"

"You're welcome, Ms. Megan," Jake replies, peeling off his serving gloves. He looks at his mom. "We're going to hang out upstairs in the loft until you need us again. Is that okay, Mom?"

Nina Buchanon gives her son a nod. "Fine by me. We'll call you when it's time for clean-up. Be smart, don't get into any trouble up there."

"And stay together," Mom chimes in, looking directly at me. "Don't you two wander off without Jake and get lost, okay?"

I try not to roll my eyes at the heavy implication in her voice. "We won't. Thanks, Mom!"

Following Jake's lead, the three of us manage to sneak outside the back door, avoiding the luncheon completely by circling to the opposite side of the building. Jake retrieves a massive keyring from his pocket, covered in dozens of keys of varying colors and sizes. Somehow he knows exactly which key to use, unlocking the door on the first try.

"Wow, you really *are* here all the time," I mumble as we cross back over the threshold.

Jake laughs sarcastically as he relocks the door. "Man, you have no idea. As often as I have to help out with all the different stuff going on, it's no wonder my parents haven't been reported to CPS for breaking child labor laws."

I frown at him. "Wait, I thought you said you volunteer most Saturdays because of the free food and free reign you get when it's over?"

Jake leads us through another door, this one with a staircase. "Okay, I may have lied to make you feel better."

"Are you saying your parents force you to volunteer every Saturday?" Caleb asks from behind us. "Or is it more like Theo, and this is a punishment?"

Jake pauses mid-step, turning around slightly to face us. "'Force' might not be the right word. 'Punishment' might be a little closer." He resumes his trek up the stairs, and we continue to follow him.

"Punishment for what?" Caleb asks.

Jake doesn't answer. He picks up the pace a bit so he can switch on the lights at the top of the stairs, illuminating our destination. What I was expecting to be a dusty, mostly abandoned attic turns out to be a strange combination of a storage room and a tech room. The walls are lined with a half-dozen racks full of costumes, baptism robes, and other random clothing. At the far end of the room is a window overlooking the sanctuary, as well as a massive switchboard. The rest of the space is full of random stacks of chairs, boxes, folding tables, and several bizarrely shaped pieces of furniture.

"Where are we?" I finally manage to ask.

"Oh shit," Jake replies. "You've never been up here before?"

I shake my head.

"That's crazy!" Jake says with a chuckle. "I've been coming up here for years! Dude, do you remember those fasting lock-ins we used to do in middle school?"

"Nah, man, my parents never let me go to those things!" I answer, rolling my eyes. "Apparently, they didn't like the idea of starving their kid for thirty hours or whatever it was."

Jake laughs. "Ooh, fancy-pants, little golden boy over here with parents that actually care about their kid's well-being? Couldn't be me!"

I scoff. "Are you kidding? I always wanted to go to one! Lock-ins sounded so much fun!"

"Yeah, they actually were pretty fun," Jake admits. "It's actually how I found this place, like two years ago. They don't use it for anything more than a storage room nowadays, but it used to be where they controlled the lights, sound, and technology shit for service before we got too fancy for it. Now they control everything from the booth downstairs."

"Hang on, going back to the fasting thing—are you saying adults just let middle schoolers roam free in the building during the lock-ins?" I ask incredulously. "That's insane!"

"Right?" Jake shakes his head. "Most kids just made out in storage closets or drew dicks on the dry-erase boards in the classrooms. I know because I was one of the lucky elders' kids who had to go in and erase all those dicks before Sunday school the next day."

"That sucks, dude," I lament. "Damn, that makes me really miss Keith sometimes."

"Ugh," Jake sighs. "Keith was something else, man. He was way more fun than Chase, but boy, he was fuckin' crazy. I'm surprised he didn't end up getting fired for all the shenanigans we got into back in—"

"So, Jake, you never answered my question," Caleb interrupts, and I immediately feel a swell of guilt for leaving him out of the conversation for so long.

"Sorry, man," Jake replies casually. "What question was that?"

Caleb rolls his eyes. "About why you're here every Saturday? If it's a punishment, what is it a punishment for?"

Jake furrows his brow and then looks at me. "You didn't tell him yet?"

I shake my head. "That's your business, not mine."

"Aww, Theo," Jake coos, clutching a hand to his chest and batting his eyes at me. "You really are a sweetheart." He winks at Caleb. "Caleb, you better hold him tight and never let go."

"Cool, so are either of you planning to clue me in on anything?" Caleb asks, an unexpected sharpness to his tone. "Or is making me feel like a third wheel more entertaining?"

My jaw drops. Oh shit, I've messed up again.

But before I can answer, Jake laughs. "Here, let me clear this up. I'm gay."

Caleb inhales sharply, and it looks like he's about to continue, but he hesitates. "Okay, yeah, I kind of gathered—"

"And Theo's one of the very few people I've come out to so far," Jake adds. "Since you guys are boyfriends, I was sure he had told you, but I think it's really sweet that he didn't. Makes sense, given that shit Little Miss Christian pulled last fall. God, I can't even fucking imagine."

"Hang on," I interrupt, shaking my head. "Caleb, you just said you 'gathered' when Jake said he was gay. What does that mean?"

Caleb rolls his eyes again. "My gaydar might not be perfect, but I picked up on these vibes right away." He gestures between Jake and me, which confuses me even more.

Jake frowns, then puts his hands up defensively and takes a step back. "Whoa, no, dude, it's not like that."

"And what *is* it like, then?" Caleb asks, a challenging tone in his voice I've only heard once before with Dad last week.

Jake turns to me for help, and the pieces finally fall into place in my brain.

"Oh, Caleb, no," I say quickly, closing the gap between Caleb and myself and taking his hands in mine. "Jake and I are just friends. Always have been, always will be."

"Yeah," Jake agrees. "I mean, don't get me wrong, Theo's a catch, but I respect him and his boundaries." Jake smiles at me. "Plus, I consider Theo to be one of my closest friends, and I would never do anything to jeopardize that."

I blink, slightly taken aback at Jake's abrupt sincerity. He considers me one of his closest friends? Since when? I hadn't really considered that until this moment, but it makes sense. We're both mostly-closeted queer guys with homophobic dads in conservative Christian households. I share more in common with Jake than I even do with Caleb.

Caleb's eyes are locked on me, and I'm suddenly aware that Jake's confession feels like it could be misinterpreted as romantic. It could just be my imagination, but I can't shake the feeling that I need to say something to set the record straight with Caleb—and fast.

"And we're basically like brothers," I add quickly, glancing back at Jake for confirmation.

Jake says nothing. His smile falters, and he looks away completely. My stomach sinks.

Ugh. No. Surely, this is just in my head. *Not every gay guy has a crush on you, Theo. Snap out of it and focus on what matters.*

I turn my full attention back to Caleb and grip his hands tighter. "I'm sorry I didn't tell you about this stuff sooner. But this time, I actually had a good reason."

After a tense moment, Caleb sighs. "Yeah, okay, you're right." He leans in closer and begins to relax his posture. "Sorry, I don't know what came over me."

"I get it, man," Jake calls back to us from deeper into the room—I apparently had been so concerned about Caleb that I didn't notice Jake had meandered away. "Jealousy is one hell of a drug."

Caleb stiffens. "I'm not jealous."

I bite my tongue before I wind up digging myself deeper into a hole.

Jake snorts. "Sure, babe." Before Caleb can respond, Jake reappears from whatever corner of the room he'd escaped to with a wide, mischievous grin. "Have y'all ever heard of carpetball?"

"Carpetball?" Caleb repeats skeptically.

Curious, I interlock my fingers with Caleb's and make my way to Jake, gently leading Caleb behind me. "Is that supposed to be a euphemism for something?"

Jake snickers. "Oh, my sweet, innocent boys. Y'all are in for such a treat."

FIFTEEN
CALEB

I am *not* jealous. I'm annoyed.

Annoyed at how Jake keeps looking at Theo. Annoyed at the way they joke back and forth so easily like they've got their own secret language I'm not allowed to know. Annoyed at all of the little ways Jake keeps popping into Theo and my conversations and how he talks like he knows the first thing about me.

I pull my hands out of Theo's–pretending not to see his disappointed look–shoving them into my pockets as Jake leads us further into the dusty storage room to a long rectangular wooden table with pale orange paint peeling off the sides. It's about waist-height, with dull, gray carpet lining the interior and a recessed pocket on either side of the long table. In the pockets are billiard balls, seven on each side, and a cue ball sitting in the middle of the table.

"What is this supposed to be?" I ask, not doing a good job of hiding the disdain in my voice.

Jake props himself against the sturdy frame, throwing a cocky look my way. "This, dear Caleb, is carpetball. A game of our parents' youth, by the looks of it. I found it last year and asked my dad about it, and he said it was in the youth center when he was in high school, so it's like ancient now. But he was able to tell me the rules, and I have to say, it's much more fun than it looks."

Yeah, I'm sure he says that about a lot of things.

"What are the rules?" Theo asks, moving to one end of the table.

Jake sets himself up opposite Theo, collecting the billiard balls from the recess on his end and setting them on top of the table. "We each set up the balls on our side of the table. You'd be stripes. I'm solids. Then, we take turns rolling the cue ball down the table and trying to knock each other's balls into the pocket. Easy enough, right?"

Theo snickers. "That's a lot of ball talk."

"Get your mind out of the gutter, Briggs. What would your dad say?"

"Screw you," Theo claps back, setting up the striped balls in a line along the wall of the table. He hesitates, then looks at me, waving me over to his side. "Come help me set up my balls."

"You just like saying balls," I tease him, approaching the orange construct. I reach into the table, rolling the yellow "eleven" ball closer. There's a chip in the side of the smooth surface, probably from the decades of abuse it suffered at the hands of teenagers. "I don't know if I'm going to be any help here."

Theo finishes setting up the rest of his striped set, taking the "eleven" from me and placing it at the front of his formation. "You'll be my good luck charm," he says, giving me a wink that makes my face burn before addressing Jake again. "Okay, now what do we do?"

"Now we play! I'll go first. Everybody watch your fingers."

Jake takes the white cue ball, stands at the opposite end of the table, then rears back and launches it down the carpeted runway. It collides with Theo's formation, knocking two of the seven balls into the pocket. The clacking noise of the collision echoes against the slanted roof.

"That's how it's done," Jake calls, pumping a fist in the air.

Theo rolls up his sleeve, grabbing the cue ball and taking the time to line up his shot. His brow is furrowed with concentration, the tip of his tongue sticking out over his bottom lip. With a quick flick of his wrist, the cue ball sails down to the opposite end of the table, completely missing Jake's formation.

"Big yikes," Jake taunts, grabbing the cue ball and firing off another shot. Another two of Theo's balls go into the pocket, leaving three on the board.

Theo lines up again, testing the weight of the cue ball a couple of times before he finally tosses it. It makes contact this time, Jake's formation clinking together, but none of them are pushed far enough to make it into the pocket.

"I don't think your good luck charm is working," Jake says, retrieving the cue ball. "Maybe you should come stand by me, Caleb. It'll even the odds out."

"I'd rather eat one of those dead cockroaches in the corner, thanks."

"So prickly," Jake says through a laugh. "Theo, you must have to wear gloves around this one." He throws the cue ball again, sinking another of Theo's balls into the pocket.

"I'll show you prickly," I mutter, and Theo shoots me a concerned look.

"Are you okay?" he whispers.

"I'm fine. Kick his ass."

Theo doesn't smile like I expect him to, but he does manage to sink two of Jake's balls in the next throw. They continue on, trading blows back and forth till they're each down to their last ball. Theo's teeters on the edge of the pocket, and a strong exhale could send it over the edge. He takes the cue ball, banking it off the wall to try and hit Jake's last remaining solid ball, resting in the center of the table, but it misses, and Jake quickly recovers the cue ball, a victorious smile already creeping across his face.

"Sorry, Theo, I didn't mean to embarrass you in front of your *boyfriend*."

"That's a lot of smack talk for someone who still has to make the shot," Theo replies, obviously not ready to admit defeat.

"Aw, if you only knew that I've been going easy on you."

"I call bullshit," Theo says, bracing himself against the table so he can lean in. "Just make your shot."

Jake shrugs. "Don't say I didn't warn you."

He rolls the cue ball down the table, striking Theo's last remaining ball dead center, and just like that, the game is over.

Theo groans a noise of defeat, shuffling over to me with his head hung low.

"You did great," I say, wrapping him up in a hug.

"Thanks," he mutters, stretching to rest his chin on my shoulder.

"That was a great game," Jake says, making his way down the table. "You had me on the ropes there at the end." He extends a hand to Theo.

Theo releases his hold on me, and I pull away. He takes Jake's hand, giving it a quick shake. I swear Jake cuts a smug look at me for a second, but then they break apart, and Theo is at my side again.

"I think it's your turn, Caleb," Jake says, motioning towards the game table. "You've got the chance to earn redemption for your boo."

"I'm good," I retort, folding my arms across my chest. I've had about enough interaction with Jake to last me a lifetime.

"It's actually really fun," Theo adds, nudging me with his shoulder. "Even if you lose. You should give it a try."

And Theo is looking at me with those big, doe eyes, and I just can't bring myself to deny him. "Okay, fine," I say through a sigh. "One game. Then maybe we can go outside? This place smells like mildew and repressed trauma."

Theo snorts a laugh as I gather the collection of billiard balls, haphazardly arranging them in a pattern that I find appealing. Jake raises an eyebrow from the other end of the table, but I ignore him, setting the last of my balls in place.

"How about we make this game more interesting?" Jake suggests, setting his side of the table up the same way he had for Theo's game.

"And how would we do that?" I asked, not even trying to keep the irritation out of my voice now. He's worn out my good graces.

"For every ball sunk, you get to ask a question. And the other person has to answer truthfully. We are in a church, after all, so no lying." His eyes drift over to Theo again, then back to me in a way that makes my stomach churn.

What is he playing at? Is he trying to make me think something is going on between the two of them? I won't deny I've already had a similar intrusive thought, but that doesn't mean I gave in to it. I trust Theo, and even though Jake has been acting sketchy as hell, I know that nothing has happened.

Okay, I'm ninety-nine percent sure nothing happened.

Theo takes a step toward Jake. "I don't know, man. That seems kinda weird–"

"Let's do it," I cut him off.

Jake's smile widens. "Sweet, let's get this show on the road. You can throw first, Caleb."

I grab the cue ball, tossing it back and forth between my hands to get a feel for the weight.

Okay, Caleb. You've got this. Right down the center.

I rear back and toss my first shot, somewhat surprised when it collides with one of Jake's balls, pushing it back a good bit but not far enough to sink it into the pocket.

Not bad! I just need to give it a little more *oomph*!

"Alright, Caleb!" Theo cheers from the sidelines.

"Good shot, man," Jake says, retrieving the cue ball.

"Thanks, *bro*."

Jake's smile falters for a moment, and he lines up his shot, making quick work of sinking one of my balls.

"That's one," he says, marking an invisible scoreboard with his index finger. "We'll keep the first question easy." He pauses for a moment, making a big scene out of pondering the question. "What do you think about mine and Theo's religion?"

I pause, straightening. "What?"

That wasn't what I was expecting.

"What do you think about Christianity?" Jake clarifies. "As someone who doesn't practice, how do you feel about it?"

"What the hell, man," Theo interjects. "You don't have to answer that, Caleb."

"No, it's okay," I say, reassuring him. "I don't mind answering."

I've been preparing for this for a while, anyway, just in case Theo asked me about it directly. I don't want to lie to him and say that I'm cool with everything that his religion entails, but I also don't want to condemn him for believing in something if that's what makes him happy.

"I think that a lot of people get something good out of it. A community. Something to believe in. But I also think it's used like a weapon too often, and I hate that it makes Theo think he needs to feel guilty about being with me. He's a good person, and he shouldn't have to feel like shit because of something that he can't change."

Theo swallows hard and Jake remains silent on his side of the table.

I grab the cue ball, tossing it across the table and actually sinking one of Jake's balls this time with a satisfying *clunk*.

"One for me," I say, reveling in the moment of distress that flashes across Jake's features. "Have you come out to anyone besides Theo and me?"

Jake's shoulders relax as he nods. "Yeah, Harrison knows. I've also told a friend of mine at school, Shauna. She's, like, my ride-or-die." He grabs the cue ball, holding it out. "My turn."

With a loud *clunk!* another of my balls sinks into the pocket.

"When did you come out?"

"I was ten when I first voiced it to my mom. She said that she'd known since I was four and wouldn't stop watching *How to Train Your Dragon* on repeat because I had a thing for Hiccup."

"Are you shitting me?" Jake laughs through the words. "Hiccup was my first crush too!"

"Well, I guess you've got good taste. But yeah, I've technically been out since ten."

"And your family is cool with it?"

"Yeah, completely. My dad actually told me that he was glad to have someone who wasn't straight in the family because, growing up, his favorite uncle was gay, and he passed away when my dad was a kid in the nineties. Dad says that he was like me in a lot of ways."

Theo moves beside me, resting a hand on my shoulder. "Oh, babe. I didn't know that."

"It doesn't really come up," I say, though I think there's more to it than that. Even though Theo and I have grown so close over the last few months, there are still plenty of things I haven't told him. Parts of my life that I'm excited to share when the time comes.

We're both startled by another throw from Jake, and two more of my balls sink into the pocket. He gives us a sheepish grin, scratching the back of his head. "Uh, sorry. Didn't mean to throw it that hard."

"Guess you get two questions," I say, grabbing the cue ball again. "Let's hear them."

"Why did you agree to come help out today? You're obviously not being punished like Theo and me, so what's the deal?"

"Because Theo asked me, and I thought it would be a good chance to find out more about this part of his life." I look over to Theo, and he's watching me with wide eyes. "I want to understand what he's going through, so it just makes sense to be here for it."

"Like you ever could," mutters Jake.

A twinge in my chest tells me that I can't argue the fact. He's right. I can't know for certain what Theo is going through, especially if he's hiding it from me. But we've talked about it, and he's promised to do better. This is me supporting him in that effort.

"Caleb," Theo says, his voice a whisper. He stops and swallows again. "You don't have to worry about me so much."

"For fuck's sake, Theo. You're my boyfriend. Of course I'm going to worry about you. That's part of the deal."

"Second question," Jake raises his voice before Theo can argue further. "How did you know Theo was into you?"

My attention returns to Jake, but I can feel Theo's eyes on me as I speak. "It was a gut feeling, mostly. I don't know. He made me feel warm. Wanted.

There was this spark between the two of us that I couldn't ignore. I had really bad luck before him in thinking that guys were flirting with me, so I almost ignored it. But I'm so glad I didn't."

Jake nods slowly, his expression somewhere between pensive and confused. I grab the cue ball, tossing it across the table and managing to sink another of his balls into the pocket.

"Why are you so interested in mine and Theo's relationship?"

Jake snorts another laugh, shaking his head. "Because he's the only other queer person I know in real life. And he was raised in the church, like me. There's no one else I know who's going through the same thing, the same questions, that I am."

The heat of my animosity cools a bit as Jake retrieves the cue ball. It makes sense why he'd be drawn to Theo. Why he'd want to talk to him. Maybe it was good for them both? Theo needs someone who understands the balance between his faith and queerness. And try as I might, Jake's right. I'll never be able to relate on the same level.

Jake throws his next shot, sinking another ball. There's only two left now.

"What was your first kiss like?"

Heat builds under my cheeks as the memory of Theo's car and that night in my driveway. Theo looks down at his feet, his hands sinking into his pockets.

"It wasn't great," I say, leaning into the awkwardness because I have Theo beside me. "I misread a situation and kissed Theo before he was even ready to admit he had feelings for me. It ended up working out for the best, but I kinda regret that it was our first."

"I don't regret it," Theo mutters, giving a small smile. Then he looks up and says louder, "The second was much better."

And I'm suddenly distracted by those moments when it was just me and Theo, his fingers twisted in my hair and mine gliding along the contours of his chest–

The cue ball skips along the carpet, jumping over one of Jake's balls and sailing into the pocket alone.

Well, shit. I blame Theo for distracting me.

Jake wastes no time sinking another of my balls, and there's only one left on my side of the table now.

"This one's for Theo. What do your parents think about Caleb?"

I turn to Theo as well, watching as he decides how much information he wants to share.

"My mom is cool with him. She's really putting in an effort to get to know him. Dad, on the other hand, is ignoring our relationship and thinks that I'm just going through a phase. I've tried to argue with him, but it's no use."

"Sounds familiar," Jake replies, downcast.

They really do have a lot in common. I can't deny that. But the glaring difference I can spot is that Theo isn't alone. He has supportive friends in Harrison, Oliver, and Elise, who will be there for him no matter what. He has Wren and Freddy, too, who can be there for him when it comes to questions or emotions that accompany a queer identity.

And he has me. Someone who will love him through it all.

I toss the cue ball, careful to take better aim and manage to sink another ball into the pocket.

"Theo's mentioned how guilty he feels sometimes, not just about being bisexual, but a ton of other stuff as well. Things that shouldn't matter. Is that guilt something that you experience, too?"

Jake doesn't say anything, but after a moment, he nods, his hands clenched into fists on top of the table. He doesn't move or reach for the cue ball. He just stands there, staring down at his hands.

"Jake?" Theo's voice echoes against the high ceiling.

I move without really thinking, crossing to the other side of the table and placing a hand on Jake's shoulder. He flinches away from my touch, blinking a few times before his eyes lock on me.

"It's okay," I tell him, holding my hands out in front of me. "You're okay.

I'm sorry if that was too much. I just… I wanted to understand."

Jake nods, wiping the end of his nose.

"I know you didn't ask for my opinion, but I'm going to tell you the same thing I told Theo. You are not a bad person, Jake. Having these feelings doesn't make you some irredeemable deviant. I don't care what the church says. You're exactly who you are supposed to be. And I'm sorry if they made you feel guilty for that."

Theo is by my side now. "I'm still working through it myself," he says, taking my hand in his. "But Caleb has been helping me. And we can help you, too, if you want."

Jake lets out a shuddered breath. "Yeah, I think that would be nice."

"I'm sorry," I add. "If I came off like a jerk to you earlier."

"Don't sweat it," Jake says, his smile returning. "I'm about to kick your ass in this game, anyways, so we'll call it even."

"Once again," Theo interjects, "that's a lot of confidence for someone who still has to sink the last ball."

Jake picks up the cue ball, aiming quickly, and perfectly sinks the last ball on my side of the table. "You were saying?"

Theo snorts a laugh, looking over at me. "Yeah, sorry, Caleb, but he really did kick your ass."

"I think I'll add carpetball to the long list of sports I'll never be great at. Somehow, I don't think I'll lose any sleep over it."

All three of us laugh, and the heaviness from before melts away.

"Oh, you've got one more question," I say to Jake.

"And I've got the perfect one. Who's ready for some fresh air?"

SIXTEEN
THEO

So carpetball is…interesting. To be fair to the sport—if we can even call it that—I'm sure that not all games consist of the same level of tension and interrogation that ours did today, but it's still not one that I'm eager to play again any time soon.

Fortunately, after that final round, the animosity lingering between Caleb and Jake is finally starting to dissipate. Maybe Caleb was on to something about the air in the loft being full of repressed trauma or something.

The three of us spend the next hour or so meandering around the outer perimeter of the church grounds until Jake receives a call from his mom summoning us back to the sanctuary. Clean-up doesn't take as long as the set-up did—or at least, it doesn't feel like it. It could be because Caleb, Jake, and I are able to continue chit-chatting and goofing around while we work this time, and before we know it, the afternoon is over, and we're free to go.

"Thank you again, boys, for your hard work today," Mom says to us as we loiter just outside the kitchen. "Especially you, Caleb. It really means a lot."

Caleb smiles. "No problem."

Mom glances between the two of us and then focuses on me. "Your father is in Athens today with Chase and a few other elders, helping out with the college ministry there. He probably won't be home until late this evening, around eight or nine."

I furrow my brow. It feels like a random piece of news, but Mom must feel like it's important to tell me. "Okay."

Mom then turns to Caleb. "Caleb, you're welcome to come to the house for the rest of the afternoon if you'd like. The usual rules apply—no closed doors, no excessive PDA—but otherwise, I'd love to have you over for dinner. I'll be ordering takeout because I've done enough work in the kitchen for one day."

Caleb and I share an excited grin, and Caleb nods. "Sure, thank you, Ms. Kora. I'll text my sister and let her know."

I beam at Mom. "Thanks, Mom!"

"You're welcome, *aroha*," she says softly. "Just don't make me regret it, okay?"

"I won't. We'll be on our best behavior, I promise."

"Good. Let me say my goodbyes, and then we can head home."

As Mom disappears back into the kitchen and Caleb texts Lola, I peek into the sanctuary to find Jake and give him a wave.

"Heading home?" Jake calls out, already making his way over to Caleb and me.

"Just about. You?"

"Nah, I've got to help Dad out with a few things before I'm released," Jake replies, rolling his eyes. "But soon, I hope."

"Man," I lament, shaking my head. "Well, see you tomorrow?"

"Yep, see you tomorrow." He steps in to wrap me in a hug, which I reciprocate. "Always good to see you, Theo."

"You, too, Jake."

As we pull apart, Jake extends a hand out to Caleb. "I'm really glad you joined us today, Caleb."

Caleb steps forward to shake his hand, only for Jake to pull him in for a brief hug. Caleb accepts it, albeit with a nervous smile. "I'm glad, too. It was a lot more fun than I thought it would be."

"Agreed. I especially enjoyed kicking both your asses at carpetball," Jake adds with a wink.

"Enjoy it while it lasts," I say with a smirk. "I just need a little more practice, then we'll see whose ass gets kicked."

Jake laughs. "Oh, yeah, we'll definitely see."

"Whose car is that?" Caleb asks as we pull into the driveway.

I follow his gaze to Grace's gold Toyota Prius, and I grin widely. "That's Grace. She must have just gotten home from work."

"She might be napping," Mom adds. "Last I heard, she was up late studying and then had to open this morning. She was out of the house before you were even awake, Theo."

"Yikes," I mutter. "Poor thing."

Mom parks the family car in the garage, and we make our way inside. I glance at my phone to see that it's just after four.

"What time is dinner?" I ask Mom.

Mom sighs as she collapses on the couch. "Maybe 6:30 or 7? Honestly, whenever you guys are hungry."

I look to Caleb, who shrugs. "We're fine with whatever," I reply.

"Well, look who it is," a female voice calls out from the stairs. "Is the prisoner allowed visiting hours now?"

"Watch it, Grace," Mom warns, but with no real threat behind it.

"Hi, Grace." Caleb politely waves as she descends the stairs.

"Hiya, Caleb!" Her hair is damp, and she's wearing an old t-shirt and sweats, which tells me she must have just showered after a long shift. The scent of her lavender shampoo travels down with her. "What are you guys up to?"

"They helped with setting up for the women's luncheon today," Mom answers, propping her feet on the coffee table. "Caleb was nice enough to volunteer his services, so I'm treating them to some pizza for dinner. Should I order an extra cheese, or do you have plans for the evening?"

"I'll be around," Grace replies, walking over to rustle my hair. "I've got more studying to do, but I also haven't seen this guy in forever, so we need to catch up. Oh! Caleb, are you any good with a dye bottle? I need to recolor my roots, and I don't always do a good job on the back."

Caleb grins, nodding. "Yeah, I've done it a couple of times before for my sister. I'd be happy to help."

Grace gives Caleb's shoulder a squeeze. "Bless you. You guys can come chill in my room if you want. I'll get all the dye stuff set up in a minute."

"Okay," I say, grabbing Caleb's hand and leading him to the stairs. "We'll be upstairs, Mom."

"Door open," she calls after us, and Caleb chuckles under his breath.

Grace follows us up to her room, opening the door for us and sliding her desk chair out of the way. Her Bluetooth speaker is playing some lo-fi track that Caleb must recognize because he starts humming along to it quietly in the most adorable way.

"Excuse the mess," Grace says, even though her room is nearly spotless. She pushes a stack of notebooks out of her way as she unpacks a plastic shopping bag onto her desk, three different boxes of hair color, and an assortment of bottles. "I had to leave at the ass crack of dawn to get to work—well, actually, I left before the sun was even up. How fucked is that?"

"Opening at Cathy's is the worst," I explain to Caleb. "Especially on the weekends. You have set everything up and then work the busiest breakfast shift, followed by a crazy lunch. It's insane."

"The tips are usually pretty good," Grace adds, crumpling the bag and tossing it into the small trash can under her desk. "As long as I don't get stuck in section D. Those tables suck, and all the old people sit there for three hours sipping on coffee and tip you, like, a quarter."

"Sounds like hard work," Caleb says, his attention drifting to the wall of artwork that Grace has collected. He hovers at one of the dreamcatchers, taking in the intricate design.

"It's grueling sometimes," Grace agrees, tearing into one of the boxes and dumping out the contents onto the desk. "But it pays the bills, so I can't complain that much. That's enough about work. How was the day of punishment, bud?"

"Surprisingly good," I answer, pulling Caleb over to the edge of Grace's bed. "We got to hang out in the loft after we set up, and Jake taught us how to play this old game called carpetball."

"Is that a euphemism?" Grace asks, raising an eyebrow.

"That's what I said!"

"It's hella sus." Grace snorts a laugh, turning her attention to Caleb. "How was it for you? Nobody tried to indoctrinate you, did they?"

Caleb shakes his head, lowering himself onto the bed next to me. "Not at all. Everyone was very nice. Alarmingly so. I did catch an old lady staring at my nails, but she kept her mouth shut. Or at least she didn't say anything to me directly."

"Nah, that's not their game," Grace says, squeezing a bottle of blue dye into a small black bowl. "The old church ladies are always sweet to your face, and then they go back to their little Sunday school class and talk shit when the door is closed."

"They're not all like that," I argue, shooting Grace a look. "Some of them are really nice."

"And some of them are evil old bats without an empathetic bone in their body," Grace adds, moving on to the next color of dye. "You should have seen the looks when I dyed my hair after graduation. You would have thought I rode in topless on a motorcycle."

I grimace, shaking my head. "Thanks for the mental image, Grace."

"You're welcome, bud. Anyways, I'm glad you survived, Caleb. You're very brave to put yourself through the judgment of strangers just to hang out with Theo."

"I don't know about all that," Caleb says, then he turns to me and adds. "It really wasn't that bad. I'm glad I got to come!"

"Me too," I tell him, a bit of guilt still worming its way into my stomach. Was I being selfish, exposing Caleb to judgmental people just to spend time with him? Sure, it's not like I made him say yes, but he's too nice to have turned me down. Did he think he didn't have another choice?

"I think we're about ready," Grace announces, setting down the third bowl and pulling the chair back over to the desk. "If you'll just match the colors, Caleb."

"Sure thing," he says, releasing his hold on my hand and moving over to the desk. He pulls on the disposable gloves from one of the boxes and picks up the pink dye first. He hesitates for a moment, then looks at Grace. "Do you think you'll have leftovers of the pink?"

Grace raises an eyebrow. "Yeah, probably. What are you thinking?"

"Can I use some? I've always wanted to put a streak in my hair."

"I don't see why not. We might have to lighten the streak first to make sure it takes, but that won't take long."

Caleb's face lights up. "Awesome! Thanks, Grace."

"What about you, bud? You want to get in on the hair coloring scheme?"

All I can think about is Dad walking in and seeing me with pink hair and spontaneously combusting on the spot.

"I think I'll pass this time," I say, my voice uneven.

Caleb shoots me a concerned look, but I smile through the anxiety in my gut, hoping it's convincing enough.

Caleb sets to work, painting the bleached roots of Grace's hair. She's got three different colors running through her normally dark locks. Pink, purple, and a deep blue. I make myself comfortable on Grace's bed, watching Caleb work. Grace starts him down the path of shows that he watches, and Caleb chatters excitedly about the new reality show that he and Lola have started binging. By the time he's swapped over to purple, my heavy eyelids droop, the early morning wake up call catching up with me, and before I can do anything about it, I nod off.

I don't know how long I doze, slipping in and out of slumber as Caleb's voice lulls me back and forth from the edge of sleep. My name rouses me back to consciousness.

"Theo has always been like that," Grace says, her voice low enough that I have to strain to hear her. "He tries so hard to make everyone else happy, and I just worry that he's making himself miserable in the process."

That's not fair. I don't try to make *everyone* happy. Just my parents. And Caleb. And my friends. And my teachers. And—shit, okay, maybe she has a point.

"I just hope I'm not making things harder on him. I kinda got into it with your dad the other day, and I know he came down hard on him for it."

No, Caleb. Don't say that. It was my own stupid fault for lying to them. You did nothing wrong.

"Trust me, Caleb. Dad was going to lose his shit whether you were there or not. He's gone full nuclear lately. I think he's scared that Theo is going to end up like me if things continue in the same way."

"What do you mean by that?"

"Like, Theo is going to leave the church. Renounce his faith. It's our father's biggest fear. So, we keep on filtering ourselves around him. Hell, I haven't even told him that I'm agnostic because I know it could give the guy an aneurysm."

"But that's not fair to you," Caleb says, his voice a little louder. "Either of you. You shouldn't have to hide who you really are. Especially to your family."

Grace huffs a quiet laugh. "Yeah, kid, you're right. But we do if we want to keep the peace. I don't know. Maybe one day that will change. Maybe once I'm out on my own, it won't seem like such a big deal. But until then, I don't want to be the one who blows up the family."

Does she really think telling Dad her truth would blow up the family? I can't imagine it would be a pleasant conversation, but would he really do anything rash? Would he stop paying for her tuition? Would he kick her out of the house?

I want to say no. But....

"I'm glad that he has you, Caleb. I know that this can't be easy, walking him through this season of self-discovery, but he's a good kid. And he really loves you."

"I love him too," Caleb says. "He's one of the kindest people I've ever met. I just hope that he stays that way if the worst should happen."

The worst? I don't like the sound of that.

"I think you're ready to rinse," Grace says, followed by the sound of her rolling chair moving across the floor. "Come on, we'll wash it off in the bathroom sink."

The room goes quiet for a bit, and I'm about to drift off again when they return.

"It should lighten up more once it dries. It's going to be so cute!"

"Thanks again," Caleb says, his voice closer than before. "Wren and Freddy are going to freak out when they see it."

"You're so welcome. It's the least I can do to pay you back for being so good to my little bro. Look at him, just snoozing the day away. I should jump on him."

"No!" Caleb exclaims, quickly lowering his voice again. "I mean, let him sleep. We'll wake him when the pizza gets here."

"Aw, you're no fun. Fine, I'll let him keep spooning my pillows for a little longer. But I do need to get back to studying at some point."

"I'll be quiet," Caleb says, and I feel him sink onto the edge of the bed, keeping a polite distance from me.

I want nothing more than to roll over and wrap my arms around him. He places a hand on my ankle, his fingers dragging lightly across the exposed skin before settling on top. I should probably rouse myself, but now that Caleb is touching me again, the comforting embrace of sleep takes me once more.

Caleb runs through my disjointed dreams, chased by a giant white billiard ball like he's in that old Indiana Jones movie. Then we're both running from it, Caleb's hand in mine as we narrowly escape with our lives. And in true dream fashion, we somehow end up tumbling into the bed at the Kendling Hotel, tangling in the sheets as skin touches skin, and Caleb's lips find mine…

"Theo? Hey, Theo. The pizza's here."

My eyes shoot open, and I blink away the blur of sleep to find Caleb leaning over the edge of Grace's bed.

"Good morning, sleepyhead."

I quickly take stock of my situation, the residual memory of my dream causing a rising panic, but thankfully, I've clutched one of Grace's pillows against me, and it's hiding any of the evidence of my lingering *excitement.*

"Sorry," I mumble, my voice gruff. "I didn't mean to sleep so long."

"Don't be," Caleb replies, brushing a curl of hair out of my eyes. "I like watching you sleep." He pauses, face contorting with a cringe. "That sounded a lot less creepy in my head. Forget I said that."

"Nope, I'm definitely going to remember it now."

He gives me a playful shove, looking over his shoulder before he leans down further and gives me a peck on the lips. "Come on, your mom is going to send a search party if we don't make it downstairs."

"Okay, okay, I'm coming." I rouse myself from the bed, swinging my legs over the edge and stretching both arms over my head.

Caleb waits by the door, a goofy grin plastered over his lips.

"What?" I ask, suddenly worried that I'm still pitching a tent.

"Your hair is amazing."

"Shut up. Your hair is–" I stop, taking in the streak of bubblegum pink that swoops off his forehead. "Oh my god, your hair is so cute!"

Caleb's cheeks flush as he leans against the door frame, and I've never wanted to kiss him so badly.

"Pizza, Theo. P-I-Z-Z-A. Come on!"

I launch myself off the bed, wrapping Caleb up in a hug and hoisting him off the ground.

"Put me down!" he shouts through his laughter. "Theo! God, don't drop me!"

"I'm getting some mixed signals here," I say, holding tight and moving him into the hallway.

"Down!" Caleb shouts again, and I drop him at the top of the stairs, leaning in to steal a quick kiss. A groan vibrates his lips as I do, and it only makes me want him more.

"Your mom is going to see," Caleb whispers, pulling away.

"Ugh, fine. You're right." I reach up, running my fingers through the slightly damp patch of pink hair. "You're just too cute now. I can't help myself."

Caleb rolls his eyes, but his face gets a shade redder. "I'm hungry. I'm going down now."

And I follow the boy I love down the stairs.

After we've eaten our fill, Grace heads back upstairs to continue her studies while Caleb and I stretch out on the couch, watching TikToks on his phone. At some point, Mom looks up from her laptop across the living room, and for a split second, I think she's going to tell me that we're sitting too close or something, but then she says, "It's getting late, *aroha*. Your father will be coming home soon."

"I can call Lola," Caleb says, swiping the video off his phone.

"How about Theo give you a ride?" Mom suggests, looking over at me.

"Really?" I ask, a bit dumbfounded.

"Straight there and straight back," Mom clarifies. "And if your father asks, it never happened. Capiche?"

"Capiche," I agree quickly.

"I'll grab your keys." Mom sets her laptop on the coffee table, then disappears down the hall into her bedroom.

"Wow," Caleb whispers with a grin. "Maybe I should volunteer at your church more often."

"I don't know who that woman is, but she's not my mother."

We both laugh, and Caleb sits up, stretching.

"So, maybe we'll get to have a couple of minutes of alone time tonight?" he asks, suddenly averting his gaze.

"I mean, she did say straight there and back," I say, joining him on the edge of the couch. "But that doesn't mean we can't sit in your driveway."

Caleb nods, still looking down at his feet.

Mom returns, tossing me Eileen's fob. "Thank you again for all your help, Caleb."

"Glad to do it," Caleb replies, standing.

"Thank you, Mom," I say, waving the keys.

She nods, her smile tight. "Of course, *aroha*. Be safe."

"We will," I say, already ushering Caleb towards the hallway. "Caleb's leaving, Grace!" I call up the stairs.

"Bye, Caleb! Thanks for your help! Sorry you have to date my lame brother!"

"Very funny!" I shout from the door, and Caleb giggles all the way out to Eileen. Now that the sun is down, the late January chill is in full force, and I hurry to crank the engine so we can get the heat running. Once I've selected a playlist–God, I've missed this–I shift into reverse.

"Brr." Caleb shivers in the passenger seat. When we're out of the driveway, I reach for his hand, wrapping it in mine. He pulls it closer to him, resting our hands on his thigh.

It gets a little more difficult to focus on the road.

We don't really talk on the way to Caleb's house, my playlist filling in the silence, but there's an electricity that builds the closer we get to his neighborhood, like the pressure change of a thunderstorm looming overhead.

"Pull over here for a second," Caleb says, a street away from his house.

I do as he asks, parking Eileen in front of the empty lot and switching the headlights off.

"Everything okay?" I ask, a nervous curiosity causing my voice to crack.

Caleb's eyes catch the light from my dashboard. "Yeah, I know you're supposed to get right back, but maybe we can spend a few minutes together?"

My mouth is suddenly very dry. "Uh, sure. I mean, I'd like that."

He unfastens his seat belt, and then, without further explanation, he climbs into the darkness of the back seat.

My heart hammers in my ears. I reach over and adjust the volume of the stereo, then take a steadying breath before I join Caleb.

His lips are on mine as soon as I crash into the seat, his fingers digging into the front of my shirt. A surprised gasp escapes my lips as he drifts down my neck, planting kisses along my collarbone. Heat surges under my skin, dulling my other senses as it burns.

"Is this okay?" he asks, his hands at the buttons of my shirt, waiting to undo them.

I nod, a trill of electricity shooting down my spine as his fingertips graze my skin while he works. My shirt comes off, disappearing into the floorboard. Caleb's hands trail down my exposed chest, and I shudder at the sensation.

"You're so hot," he whispers before our lips collide again. And there's a new urgency in his movement, a feverish intensity as his hands wrap around the nape of my neck, and he pulls me closer than we've ever been.

I tug at the bottom of his hoodie, and he breaks away long enough to pull it off. Caleb swings a leg over me, straddling my hips. The warmth of his skin against mine is enough to drive me crazy, and the friction as he leans closer, pulling me in for another kiss, robs me of any hesitations.

When Caleb pulls away again, we're both panting, the electricity in the air reaching maximum saturation. "Sorry, I need a second."

"It's okay," I assure him as he rolls over into the space next to me, propping his head against the door. The windows have all fogged up, blocking my view of the street outside and offering us privacy that I appreciate as I suddenly feel very exposed.

"I didn't want to stop," Caleb says after a moment.

"Me neither," I agree.

"But I also don't want to get you into any more trouble," he adds. "And there will always be time for… *more*. We don't have to rush."

I exhale, letting my head fall back against the seat. "You're right."

"Are you okay?" he asks, voice brimming with concern.

How do I answer that? It feels like every vein in my body is filled with fire. I can hardly think straight. It's taking every ounce of restraint I have not to dive across the seat and into Caleb's arms.

"I'm finding it difficult not to jump you right now, to be honest."

Caleb laughs, knocking his shoe against my knee. "Same."

"Are we—" I stop, trying to organize my thoughts. "Are you ready, I mean, to, um, take things further? Not now, obviously. Like, later. Whenever. In the near distant future. I'm going to stop talking now."

"I think I am," Caleb says, still grinning in the dark. "But like I said, we don't have to rush anything. I'm happy just being with you, Theo. I don't want you to feel any pressure to do something you're not ready to do."

I want to tell him I'm ready. I want to say that I don't feel any hesitation. But that wouldn't be the truth. So, instead, I have to do the impossibly hard thing of saying, "I don't think I am. At least, not right now. I'm sorry."

Caleb is beside me in a second, running his fingers through my hair. "Hey, you don't have to apologize for that, Theo. Never. Do you hear me?"

I nod, embarrassment swelling my vocal cords shut.

"I'm not interested in pushing you into anything. We'll take it at your speed, and if I ever make you uncomfortable, you tell me right away. Deal?"

"Deal," I manage through the tightness of my throat. "I love you, Caleb."

"I love you, too. Now, we should probably get dressed before we pull up to my house. I don't want to catch pneumonia."

I snort a laugh, and Caleb plants a kiss on my forehead.

We gather ourselves back into Eileen's front seats and finish the trip to Caleb's house. And after he's gone, I spend the rest of the drive replaying those moments when his lips were on mine, and nothing else mattered.

SEVENTEEN
CALEB

SIX WEEKS LATER

Saturday, March 9

"Caleb! Over here!"

Elise stands on top of her chair, waving both arms over her head. The patio at Spookies coffee shop is packed. The early spring warmth arrived last week, and everyone seems more than eager to shed their winter wardrobes and spend some time in the fresh air.

"Do you think Elise ever has the thought, 'Maybe I shouldn't yell at the top of my lungs?'" Wren asks as we make our way down the sideway to the outdoor seating area.

"I think there's a better chance of Freddy swearing celibacy."

The gang has pulled two of the metal tables together to make enough room. Harrison and Elise are on one end of the table, while Freddy and Andrew anchor the opposite end. Oliver sits in the middle, an open book face-down on the table in front of him as he scrolls on his phone. Theo isn't here yet, but that's only because he needed to shower after his early morning shift at Cathy's.

It's amazing how the smell of fried chicken and syrup can stick to a person.

"About time you showed up," Freddy quips as I take the seat opposite Oliver. He checks an invisible watch on his wrist, then cracks a smile.

Wren rolls their eyes, patting me on the shoulder. "Caleb needs his beauty sleep. And I was up late working on my submission."

"Submission?" Andrew repeats, his fair brow twisting with confusion.

"Wren's submitting their work to a special effects contest down in Atlanta," Freddy explains, his left hand wrapped up in Andrew's right. "They can win scholarship money for one of the institute's certificate programs over the summer."

"That's awesome!" Elise chimes in, leaning forward on her elbows. "What are you designing?"

"It's not done yet," Wren says, waving a hand like they are swatting away the question. "I'll show y'all when it's ready."

Elise sticks out her bottom lip in a pout. "Come on, not even a little hint?"

"Relax, babe," Harrison tries to console her, running a hand up her arm.

"Don't tell me to relax," Elise snips, pulling away from him. "You know that drives me up the freaking wall."

"Okay, I'm sorry," Harrison says quickly, an undertone of frustration in his voice.

"Mom, Dad, stop fighting in front of the kids," Oliver says, not bothering to look up from his phone.

Elise flicks a straw wrapper at Oliver, but it goes wide and lands in Andrew's lap, who calmly sets it on top of the empty plate in front of him.

"I'm going to order," Wren announces. "Caleb, you want the usual?"

"Yes, please."

Wren gives me a thumbs-up before heading into the cafe.

"I need another drink, too," Harrison says, grabbing his empty cup and following after Wren. Elise watches him go, a frown setting in deeper and deeper.

"I'm going to the bathroom," Elise says, making her exit as well.

"What's up with them?" I ask Oliver once she's out of earshot.

He shrugs. "Who knows, man. I can't keep up with those two. If they're not fighting about one thing, it's another."

"The straights are not okay," Freddy jokes and Andrew chuckles.

"Where's Theo?" Andrew asks, nodding to the empty chair beside me.

"He should be on his way," I say, checking my last message from him again. This is the first weekend since he's had his driving privileges reinstated. For the last month-and-a-half, we've been constrained to hanging out at Theo's place (not the best place for making out), so everyone is eagerly awaiting his arrival. "He had to work this morning."

"That sucks," Andrew replies, scrunching his nose. "Thank God I don't have to work the weekends at the floral shop. Mom says that she doesn't want to steal all of my free time."

"Your mom is the best," Freddy says, grabbing his cup and taking a swig. "Mine keeps saying that she wants me to start looking for summer jobs, but I think I can get away with helping at one of the youth soccer leagues instead."

Oliver looks up from his phone. "I wish I could get a job. Dad already has the whole summer planned out with camping trips and our semi-annual drive out to Yosemite. I'm going to be stuck in a car for three days with my little sisters fighting over the iPad."

Freddy grimaces. "That's brutal, buddy."

"What about you, Caleb?" Andrew asks. "Any cool summer plans?"

"I'm supposed to be traveling with my dad for a few weeks, shadowing him on set. He said they've technically got it set up as an internship through his company. That way, I can earn some college credit for the time I'm there. The schedule is kinda wonky, so we don't know exactly where we're going to be quite yet, but it'll still be exciting wherever we end up–"

A pair of arms wrap around my neck, and the weight of someone's head rests on my crown. "Sorry I'm late, guys."

Oliver looks up from his phone. "Oh, I guess he is alive."

Theo pulls away from me, sinking into the chair beside me, his still damp hair clinging to his forehead, and the pleasant, clean smell of his shampoo drifts through the air.

"What did I miss?" Theo asks, scooting his chair closer to me so his knee knocks against mine.

"Wren's inside ordering and stayed up too late working on their submission for the scholarship contest," Freddy starts, working through the recap. "Elise and Harrison are mad at each other for who knows what reason. Oliver is dreading a summer road trip with his family. Andrew's mom is the coolest for not making him work weekends. I'm going to spend the summer bossing little kids around, and Caleb is going to be on set somewhere having a summer romance with Timothée Chalamet."

Theo gives me a concerned look, and I snort a laugh. "Very funny, Freddy. That's some imagination you have."

"A boy can dream," Freddy replies, wistfully staring into the middle distance.

"We're talking about summer plans," Andrew explains to Theo. "You know, the first warm week of the year, and everyone wants to skip right to the fun stuff."

"Ah." Theo lets out a sigh, slumping into his chair. "My family is going on our usual beach trip to Destin. Other than that, I'm stuck working at Cathy's. Mom will probably volunteer me to work at Vacation Bible School again, too. Me and Harrison always get stuck running the soundboard for them."

"Vacation what now?" Freddy asks, coming back to reality.

"It's a church thing," Andrew says, patting Freddy's hand. "Don't worry about it."

"Bet," Freddy replies, giving a thumbs up.

"I get roped into those, too," Andrew continues. "I have to learn all those annoying songs that get stuck in your head for weeks. If I have to sing about Jonah and the whale one more time, I'm going to lose it."

"Oh my god," Theo groans. "Same. Last year was all about Joshua and marching around Jericho, and that marching song they sang still pops into my head at the worst times."

I look over at Freddy, who returns my confused expression. "Are you getting any of this?"

"It's like they're speaking a different language," Freddy replies, rolling his eyes. "Here, let's show them how it feels. *Nuestros novios son tan latosos.*"

I snicker as Theo and Andrew continue their conversation over shared trauma. Brushing off my three years of Spanish electives, I reply, "*Sí, pero son lindos.*"

"Who are you calling cute?" Wren asks, setting my drink down before settling into the seat beside Oliver, who has picked up his book again.

"Don't worry about it," Freddy says quickly, craning his head to talk over Andrew. Theo and his conversation has moved on to ranking which puppet mascot they found the creepiest, which honestly sounds like a nightmare. "The church bros are having a moment."

I cringe. "Can we chill with that nickname?"

"Agreed," Wren chimes in. "It conjures images of frat boys with giant crucifix necklaces and a 'hanging with Jesus' tank top that even *I'd* find in poor taste."

Elise returns to the table next, setting her bag down before sliding into her chair. "They're not talking about VBS, are they?"

Freddy nods. "Unfortunately."

"Gross. Harrison tricked me into helping last year, and there were just children running around everywhere with sticky fingers and runny noses. Never again."

Harrison returns as Theo and Andrew reach a consensus on which mascot haunts their dreams. He sets a cup in front of Elise and then a plate with a gigantic chocolate chip cookie. "I'm sorry about before," he says in a low voice, then kisses the top of her head. "Would you please forgive me?"

Elise eyes him for a moment, then scoops up the cookie, taking a bite. "Schorgiven," she mumbles through the crumbs.

"Now that everyone is here," I say, addressing the group. "My mom keeps asking me to solidify my birthday plans, but I have no idea what I want to do. Anyone have an idea?"

"Bouncy house!" Oliver suggests, straddling the edge of his seat.

"Uh, that's certainly an idea. Anyone else?"

"I vote bowling," Harrison adds, and Elise rolls her eyes.

"You always want to go bowling," she nags.

"Goth party," Wren says, their black nails drumming against the tabletop like rain on a tin roof. "I can paint everyone up to look extra spooky, and we can thrash around to death metal in your basement."

"Okay, I'm starting to regret asking."

Freddy props himself on an elbow, leveling a look at me. "It's your party, Caleb. What kind of vibes are you going for?"

"Something a little more low-key? I kind of like the idea of having a party in the basement, just maybe not with death metal."

"Your loss," Wren says with a shrug.

"I've got a projector," Andrew chimes in. "We could set up a movie thing?"

"Ooo! What if we did a good old-fashioned sleepover?" Elise suggests. "PJ's, pizza, movies, the works!"

"I kind of like the sound of that," I admit. "Is that okay with everyone?"

A murmur of agreement spreads across the table.

"What about you?" I ask Theo, giving his hand a squeeze.

"I don't think my parents will go for the sleepover part," he says, his lips pulled tight into a frown. "But I can hang out till my curfew."

"I'll take it. Maybe you could still wear some cute PJs even though you're not sleeping over?"

"I don't really have any pajamas," he says, keeping his voice low while the others chatter excitedly about the party. "I'm usually a shorts and t-shirt kind of guy."

"My birthday is still a few weeks away. We can go shopping for some. I'll help you pick out something perfect."

That gets a smile out of him.

"Deal."

"Caleb," Freddy interrupts, "tell Wren they can't fill a piñata with fake blood. This isn't going to be *Slumber Party Massacre 5*."

Wren snorts a laugh. "I should hope not. Too many tiddies."

Theo pulls into my driveway, leaving the engine on.

"Can't you come in for a few minutes?" I ask, checking the clock. There's still half an hour before his curfew. "Both of my parents are home."

Theo gives me a sly grin. "Wouldn't you rather hop in the backseat for a little bit?"

My cheeks flush. "I'd like that very much, but I also know that Mom would come looking for me, so it's better if I go ahead inside."

"Fair," Theo concedes, shutting off Eileen.

The warmth of the day left with the sun and I shiver as we get out of the car, making our way up the sidewalk to the front door.

"I'm home," I announce, shedding my shoes and jacket by the door. Theo does the same, staying close to me. He's been over enough times to have a place where his shoes stay, right beside mine.

A pleasant narrator's voice from the living room tells me that Mom and Dad must be watching another documentary, so I take Theo's hand and lead him down the hall, poking my head around the opening to find them sprawled out on the couch.

"Hey, honey," Mom says, pressing pause on the remote. She's got her laptop open in her lap and a heap of files stacked neatly on the coffee table. Dad snores softly on the other end of the couch, his arm tossed over his head in a way that seems like it should be painful. "Theo, good to see you. What are you two up to this evening?"

Theo and I take a spot behind the loveseat, and he's trying to hide the fact we're holding hands, but I place our clasped hands on top of the cushion in a way that I hope communicates that he doesn't have to hide here.

"I think I've finally reached a decision on the birthday thing."

Mom sets her laptop aside, giving me her undivided attention. "I'm all ears."

"I want to have a slumber party with my friends in the basement. Freddy's boyfriend Andrew is going to bring his projector over so we can watch movies down there and I figured maybe we can order pizza?"

"Sounds simple enough," Mom says with a smile. "Theo, are your parents okay with you sleeping over?"

Theo stiffens beside me. "Probably not, ma'am. I'll be leaving before midnight."

Mom's face scrunches. "I'll mention it again, you can just call me Nora."

"R-Right," Theo stutters, "sorry, Nora."

"No worries," Mom replies, then snaps her fingers, causing Dad's snoring to sputter. "That reminds me, Caleb. Your Nana is going to be in town for your birthday weekend. She wants to come over and have dinner on that Sunday. Theo, I was going to see if your family wanted to come and join us to celebrate?"

I look at Theo, and there's panic in his eyes. "You don't have to invite the whole family," I add. "If you just want to come, that's fine too."

"I'll ask them," Theo answers. "Thank you, Mrs. Ray–*Nora*."

"Of course," Mom says, grabbing her laptop again. "Caleb, I'll take care of the food for the slumber party, and I'll make sure that your dad doesn't try and crash the party with his karaoke machine. We don't want a repeat of your thirteenth birthday."

I cringe at the memory of Dad with a microphone in his hand and some horrible nineties hip-hop song blasting through the tiny speaker.

"You're the best," I say, pulling Theo back towards the hallway. "We're going upstairs for a few minutes."

"If you see your sister, tell her I need the Henderson file back."

"Will do," I call from the bottom of the stairs. Theo follows me up to my bedroom, and I tell him to have a seat while I poke my head into Lola's room.

She's at her desk, headphones on and fingers flying across the keyboard. I tap her on the shoulder, and she jumps, letting out the tiniest yelp.

"Jesus, Caleb. Thanks for making me piss myself."

"My apologies to your chair, but Mom said something about needing the Henderson file back."

Lola grunts, shuffling through a pile of paperwork beside her laptop. "Yeah, yeah, I'll find it. What are you doing home so early on a Saturday night?"

"Theo's got an early curfew," I answer, motioning back toward my room. "We're working on wrapping up my birthday plans before he has to head out."

"Did Mom tell you Nana is coming over?"

"Yeah, she also shared the bright idea of asking Theo's family to join us. Is that as crazy as I think it sounds?"

Lola purses her lips. "Do you think they'll actually do it?"

"I don't know," I answer truthfully, keeping my voice low. "I'd be okay with Kora and Nate coming, of course. But what if his dad shows up? I don't know if I'll be able to make it through the night without screaming at him. Or worse, Nana will get ahold of him. Can't imagine that would go over well."

Lola snorts a laugh. "I think I'd actually pay money to see that."

"It's the stuff of my nightmares, Lola."

"And you'll be just fine," she says, pulling a file from the stack she's been rifling through. "Mom and Dad aren't going to tolerate some homophobic asshole in their house. If he acts up, let them handle it. There's no need for you to play mediator. It's putting way too much pressure on yourself, Cal."

I nod, letting out a sigh. "I just wish this were easier. That Theo didn't have to come with all of these strings attached. I love him so much, but more and more, I find myself getting angry. Not at him, but the whole system that's convinced him that loving me is a moral failing."

"And you've got every right to be angry," Lola agrees. "But maybe you should talk to Theo about how this is making you feel. Not to place blame or anything, but just so he knows what's going on in your head if you happen to lash out at his dad over the dinner table."

I grimace. "Sometimes I think I'll scare him away if I told him what I really thought."

Lola offers a sympathetic smile. "The same goes for all of us, Cal. Trust me, I've seen plenty of Mom's clients speak what's on their minds. Brutal honesty is just that. Brutal. But sometimes, it's what's needed."

"I just don't want to hurt him." My voice cracks at the last word.

"I know, honey. But if you keep all of this anger bottled up, you'll only end up hurting yourself. Or worse, hurting Theo in a way you can't control."

I wrap my arms around Lola, pulling her into my chest. "You really excel at this sisterly advice thing," I say, resting my chin on top of her head. "You should be a shrink."

She snorts another laugh, pulling her face from my shirt. "Let me take down at least one oil baron, Cal. Then we can talk about a career change."

"Fair."

"Now get out of my room. Your boyfriend is waiting for you, and I have to deliver a really gross file to Mom."

"Do I even want to know?"

"I wouldn't tell you if I could, kiddo."

Lola ushers me out of her room, disappearing downstairs with the file tucked under her arm. I find Theo sitting where I left him, looking down at his phone and tapping his sock-covered foot on the floor in an aimless rhythm.

"Stop being adorable," I tell him, crossing the room and sinking into the chair by my desk.

"Sorry, it's my natural state," Theo says with a grin, stashing his phone in his pocket. "We've got about five minutes before I need to be on the road."

"Five minutes, huh?" I say, glancing over at the door. Pushing off, I roll my chair over and shut it, then hop out. "What could we ever do to fill the time?"

Theo's hands are on me before I can finish the teasing sentence, his lips finding mine in a flurry of motion that leaves me breathless.

EIGHTEEN
THEO

Sunday, March 10

"So, I've been thinking about coming out to my mom."

I nearly drop my thermos full of steaming coffee at Jake's words. My head instinctively swivels, scanning the narrow tech storeroom to see who from the church's AV team now knows Jake's grave secret—only to find it empty.

"Dude, you gotta chill," Jake says with a laugh. "I'm not an idiot."

I let out a relieved sigh. "Sorry, man." I hold up my dark green thermos. "It's the espresso."

One of the perks of volunteering for the AV team is unlimited access to their surprisingly fancy espresso machine, hidden away in the tech storeroom. Since I have to get here so early every Sunday, I've been putting it to good use. It's only 9:20 A.M., but I've already downed two almond milk lattes, and I can hear my heartbeat in my ears as the caffeine flows through my bloodstream. I probably shouldn't have a third at this rate, but, as I said, it's only 9:20 A.M., and I'm not free to go until at least 12:45.

"Lightweight," Jake replies, giving me a playful shove. "Anyway. As I was saying… I'm thinking about coming out to my mom."

"Yeah?"

Jake fidgets with the lid of his yellow thermos, his expression uncharacteristically serious. "Yeah. Do you think it's a bad idea?"

I frown. "That's not something I can answer, man."

"I know, but, like—I don't know. I don't want to risk them finding out before I can tell them myself, you know?"

I huff a dry laugh. "Yeah, I can't imagine what that would be like."

"But at the same time," he continues. "I'm not seeing anyone, and the only people that know about me don't talk to my parents. So, I'd say my risk of getting outed is pretty low."

"That's true."

"Because what if—" he hesitates for a few seconds before continuing. "What if she ends up hating me for it? What if she and Dad try to ship me off to some conversation therapy camp? Or kick me out of the house? I mean, would it be smarter to just stay in the closet for one more year just until I can get the fuck out of there?"

"Do you really think that's how your mom would react?" I ask softly.

Jake blinks. "I—I don't know." He sniffs, then clears his throat. "That's the thing, I just—I don't know, and that fucking sucks."

My heart aches for him, so I put a hand on his shoulder. "I'm sorry, Jake. It does fucking suck."

"S'okay," he replies quietly. "I just hate it. The whole thing. The pretending, the hiding, the guilt, the anxiety, the not knowing who I can trust... It's all shit."

"I know."

We stand together silently for a few moments before Jake clears his throat again. "Anyway, enough about my shit. How's your shit? Anything new?"

I take another sip of my latte and check the room again to make sure we're still alone. "Caleb's parents want to have my family over for dinner for Caleb's birthday."

Jake barks a laugh. "Oh, shit, for real? That sounds like a horrible idea."

"Right?" I scoff. "That's what I said."

"So, what are you going to do?"

It's my turn to fidget with my mug. "I told Caleb that I would ask my parents, but I haven't yet. It's two weeks away, so I have time, but…" I rub the back of my neck. "I don't know, man. I don't know what to do."

Jake presses his lips together thoughtfully. "Yeah, I don't see that dinner going well."

"I mean, Dad's usually really good around strangers," I continue. "Like he's generally a friendly guy, so I don't think he'd instigate anything. But, then again, he kind of went off on Caleb that one time." I shudder at the memory. "That was pretty out of character for him, so maybe it was just a one-off thing."

"Maybe," Jake says. "If he's anything like my dad, he probably just views Caleb as a child, and he's an adult, so he'd probably be less antagonistic around other adults."

"Yeah, that's true," I agree. "And he wouldn't dare talk down to Caleb in front of his parents."

Jake taps on his thermos. "Probably not."

"In some ways, I think it might make Dad feel better about letting me go to Caleb's house more often, having talked to his parents," I add.

"Or, it could make him feel worse," Jake counters. "Because Caleb's parents are probably pretty progressive and chill, considering they have an openly gay son with a boyfriend. And your dad won't want his son hanging around parents with such 'loose morals.'"

I wince. That's exactly how Dad will feel about it. "That's what I'm afraid of," I admit, leaning back against the wall. "But I also think it'll hurt Caleb's feelings if I don't at least try."

"That's not fair to you," Jake says, his brows furrowed. "Caleb knows what he got himself into when he started dating you. He should know how this stuff works by now."

I shake my head. "It's not that simple."

"Seems pretty simple to me," Jake retorts flatly. "But, then again, I'm still mostly in the closet, and I've never had a boyfriend at all, so…what do I know, right?"

I want to argue with him, but the tech storeroom door swings open, and Frankie saunters in. He's a tall, balding man in his mid-to-late fifties with thick-rimmed glasses and a surprising proficiency in AV technology. "Service is about to start, boys," he grumbles. "All hands on deck."

"Yes, sir," Jake and I say in unison.

"And seal up those cups," Frankie adds gruffly. "No open containers in the booth."

"All clear, boss," Jake says as we dutifully show Frankie our securely sealed thermoses.

With a pleased grunt, Frankie leads us back to the tech booth at the rear of the sanctuary, where the first of two services is about to begin.

As I settle in at my stool in front of the audio switchboard, I catch a glimpse of Dad, completely in his element, greeting church members and guests at the door. He's all smiles, hugs, and handshakes—outgoing and sociable with every person in his path. It's here where my father has always thrived. Growing up, I remember watching him engage with people and wondering what was wrong with me. Why couldn't I be as friendly and approachable as my dad was? It wasn't until fairly recently that I learned I was something called an "introvert" and that being introverted wasn't a character flaw.

But now, as I watch my father on his home turf, I don't find myself envying his good-naturedness. Instead, I remember the version of him I saw in the Hammonds' driveway in January. I recall how he spoke to Caleb and how demeaning and hostile he was. I think back to how he blew off Grace's earnest attempts to open his mind and how he continues to push back on anything Grace says or does. It really starts to dawn on me just how belligerent he's become over the past few months. Or maybe he's always been this way, and I'm only just now seeing it because who I am goes against his sacred beliefs.

Does he only love me because I follow the rules?

Our eyes meet across the sanctuary, and he flashes me the widest grin. I manage to smile back at him, but something deep in my gut churns sickeningly.

"Hey, you good?" Jake whispers next to me.

"Yeah," I reply, focusing back on the setlist. "All good."

It's going to be a long morning.

Sunday, March 17

It isn't until a week before Caleb's birthday weekend that I finally summon the courage to ask my parents about the Sunday dinner.

It's a bit of a special dinner already because the whole family is here tonight—even Grace—so Mom's in high spirits, and Dad's on his best behavior. Grace is pretty exhausted from a ten-hour shift at Cathy's, but the fact that she's here gives me the extra boost of courage I need.

"Hey, Mom, Dad," I say after clearing my throat. "Are y'all busy on Sunday night next week?"

Mom perks up at the question while Dad casually glances up from his plate, peering over his reading glasses at me with brows furrowed.

"I'll check our calendar, but I think we're free," Mom says, looking to Dad for confirmation. "Why do you ask?"

Grace and Nate watch silently on with wide eyes.

I take a steadying breath. "So, Caleb's birthday is on Sunday, and he's having a birthday party at his house on Saturday night, but on Sunday, he and his family have invited us over for dinner."

"Us?" Dad echoes.

"Yeah, like, the whole family?" I answer hesitantly. Glancing briefly at my siblings, I continue. "Nate and Grace, y'all are both invited, too, but I told them Grace probably won't be able to because of school."

Grace continues staring at me, brows raised in surprise, while Nathaniel simply shrugs before scooping another spoonful of peas into his mouth.

Mom and Dad exchange cryptic glances, and my anxiety prickles against my nerves. *Please say no, please say no, please—*

"That's so sweet of them to invite us," Mom says with a smile. "We would love to!"

My heart sinks in my chest, but I conjure a smile. "Great!" I manage to croak. "Cool."

Grace clears her throat. "I think I'm technically scheduled to work on Sunday, but I should be able to make it to dinner." She smiles at me. "I wouldn't want to miss it."

"Don't you need to drive up to campus after work?" Dad asks Grace with a raised brow.

"My first Monday class isn't until eleven," Grace replies. "I can make time for Caleb."

Relief washes over me. Having Grace in my corner is exactly what I need.

"Well, it sounds like it's settled!" Mom says, patting Dad's forearm excitedly. "Right, honey?"

Dad takes an extra few seconds to chew on his chicken. "Do Caleb's parents know about…" he gestures vaguely towards me. "You two?"

I have to force myself not to roll my eyes. "Yes, Dad. They know."

"Michael," Mom says, a warning tone in her voice.

Dad keeps his eyes on me. "And they don't have any issue with it?"

"Not everyone shares your delightfully antiquated worldview, Dad," Grace mumbles before I can answer.

"Grace, don't start," Dad snaps, his gaze still fixed on me, waiting for an answer.

"No, they don't have an issue with us being a couple," I reply, keeping my voice steady. I'd love to join Grace in her sarcasm at Dad's expense, but not if I want to stay on Dad's good side.

"Hm." Dad takes another bite of chicken, and the table goes quiet. After a moment, he continues. "Do they have a church family?"

"There it is," Grace mocks.

"All right, that's enough—" Mom starts.

"I think the better question, Theo," Grace says, ignoring Mom. "—is, do Caleb's parents know what they're getting themselves into by inviting Michael Briggs into their home?"

"I've had just about enough of your nasty attitude, Sarah Grace," Dad snarls.

Grace barks a laugh. "Oh, the feeling is quite mutual, I assure you."

"I said, that's *enough*!" Mom shouts, and the room immediately falls silent. She furiously locks eyes with Dad. "We're not doing this at the dinner table. Not here, and especially not in front of Caleb's family." Her hold on Dad finally releases, and her gaze bounces between him and Grace. "If you two can't find a way to get along, at least learn to hold your tongues at the dinner table. Do you understand?"

Grace and Dad continue staring daggers into one another until Grace breaks first. "I understand, Mom, but I can't promise to hold my tongue if Dad says anything shitty next week. You know I can't."

"That's not going to happen," Mom says, casting another glare at Dad. "Is it, Michael?"

Dad stares at her, his face reddening. "Kora, come on, we shouldn't play into her—"

"It's not going to happen, is it, Michael?" she repeats.

Dad's eye twitches. "No," he says through gritted teeth.

"Good. So, we're all going to be on our best behavior and make sure Caleb has a nice birthday dinner with his family. Right?"

Grace, Nate, and I nod. Dad doesn't say anything, but his lack of response must be enough for Mom.

"Good." Mom's smile returns, and her posture relaxes. "Now, Theo, can you ask them if they'd like us to bring anything? You know I can't come empty-handed!"

"Sure, I'll ask."

"Excellent! I can't wait!"

Almost immediately after dinner, I find myself lingering by Grace's closed door, silently debating whether I should knock or just retreat to my own bedroom for the night. Grace is probably packing up to drive to campus for the week, and I don't want to slow her down. But at the same time, it's been a while since I talked to her, and I could really use some of her older-sibling wisdom right about now. Especially if—

"That you, Theo?" Grace calls from the other side of the door.

Oops. "Uh, yeah. Yep."

The door swings open, revealing a slightly more disheveled Grace. She studies me with a hand on her hip and an amused grin. "Get in here, dummy," she says after a beat, beckoning me in with a nod.

"Thanks," I mutter sheepishly, shoving my hands into my pockets and stepping inside.

"How are you holding up, bud?" Grace asks as she closes the door behind me.

"I was just coming to ask you the same question," I answer, plopping down next to Grace's overnight bag on her bed.

Grace runs a hand through her multi-colored curls. "Eh, I'm here. For now. But soon I'll be heading back to campus, where I have five full days of classes, studying, and papers to write. Then, on Friday, I'll make the drive back up here, where I'll work a full weekend at Cathy's and try my best to avoid Dad until Sunday night. And then I'll rinse and repeat until May when I'll hopefully start my internship at The Carter Center, and then…" She trails off, her gaze slowly coming back to me. "But hey, that's the crazy life I signed up for. What's going on with you, little bro?"

I blink. "Wow. That's a lot."

Grace shrugs. "It is, but I like staying busy. I'll slow down once I start working at a real job in my field."

"Yeah, I guess that makes sense," I say, watching her as she zooms about the room, packing various items. "I guess that means you're too busy to date, then, right?"

Grace hesitates and throws me a wary look. "I thought you were here to talk about your problems."

"We can talk about yours first."

She laughs. "Hard pass."

"Oh, come on," I press. "You help me with my stuff all the time. I feel like you always know everything going on in my life, but I never know what's going on in yours."

Grace narrows her eyes, studying me for several seconds before she relents. "Okay, fine. You remember Chloe?"

I nod. Chloe and Grace have been roommates for nearly two years now. They were randomly assigned as roommates the first time, but they quickly became best friends and stayed together the following year. They're both pursuing the same major, so they have at least one class in common every semester. As far as I know, Grace and Chloe are inseparable outside of Grace's weekends spent at home.

"Chloe and I…we sort of tried dating. Back in January."

My mouth drops open. "Holy shit, Grace! Really?"

"Yep."

"That's dope!"

Grace's lips curl into a smile, but it doesn't reach her eyes. "Yeah. Maybe I was inspired by how you've been so brave with everything lately, or maybe I was excited to see how happy you've been with Caleb, but either way, I figured maybe it was time I put myself out there, too. Try something new."

"And?"

"And…it didn't work out." Grace shrugs. "It was a disaster. *We* were a disaster. She had just left a pretty serious relationship, and I think I was too eager to have my first girlfriend. I think part of me was trying to prove to myself and the world that I was actually bi, and that's a horrible reason to be in a relationship with someone. Especially someone as important as her."

I wince. "I'm so sorry, Grace."

"It's okay now," Grace continues. "It was rough there for a while, but I think we're going to get through it."

"Well, that's good," I say earnestly. "I hope you do."

Grace absentmindedly fidgets with a ring on her index finger. "Me too." A moment later, she straightens and turns her attention back to me. "Okay, now it's your turn. How are you feeling about Dad interacting with Caleb's family next week?"

"Ugh," I groan, burying my face in my hands. "It's going to be a disaster, isn't it?"

Grace chuckles. "It's possible." She pulls over her computer chair, swiveling it around so that she faces me as she sits. "What's Caleb's family like?"

"Oh, they're great," I answer. "His parents are super nice. His older sister, Lola, reminds me a lot of you. And his Nana is kind of crazy but in a fun way."

"Good," Grace says with a smile. "It sounds like you'll be surrounded by support then. Dad will be outnumbered."

I try to return her smile, but it's hard. "You don't think he'd actually, like… say something homophobic, do you?"

Grace takes a deep breath. "You know, if you had asked me that two years ago, I would have said something like, 'Oh, no way! He's way too concerned about making a good impression and befriending people. He just wants to spread the love of Christ by example. He'd never intentionally say something to make anyone uncomfortable!' But now…"

"Now it's different," I mutter.

"Now it's different," she echoes sadly. She shakes her head. "Shit, dude, when you told me how Dad talked to Caleb after that hotel trip y'all went on? Ooh, boy, it's a *real* good thing I wasn't there. You know I would have thrown hands for Caleb."

I snort. "I know you would have."

"That still blows my mind," Grace continues. "I can't believe Mom stays with him sometimes."

I bristle at that. The thought of my parents splitting up over this has crossed my mind before, but I don't like to dwell on it. Grace's words to Caleb all those weeks ago still haunt me. *"I don't want to be the one who blows up the family."*

"But I feel like I have to ask," Grace says, her hazel eyes piercing mine. "What if Dad does say something shitty next week? What will you do?"

My gaze drops to the floor. "I don't know," I admit.

"Well, let's talk it through." Grace clasps her hands together thoughtfully. "When you picture the worst-case scenario, what does it look like?"

I shudder. "Okay, sure. Worst-case scenario: Dad gets into an argument with Caleb's parents about how their son is a bad influence on me. Or Dad lectures them about how being gay is a sin, and Caleb is going to hell if he doesn't change his ways. And if I try to step in at any point, Dad will take my phone and Eileen away again." I can feel the backs of my eyes burning and my throat swelling as my deepest fears pour out, one after another. "As a result of Dad's outburst, Caleb's parents won't want him spending time around me anymore because they don't want him around that kind of homophobia. Then Caleb—" I choke on a sob but press on. "Caleb ends up agreeing with them and finally decides that I'm not worth all the trouble after all, so we break up. I only see him at school from then on, but now the whole friend group has to choose who to stay friends with, and obviously, they should pick Caleb because—"

"Whoa, whoa, whoa," Grace's hands wrap firmly around my forearms, halting my spiral. "Holy shit, Theo, honey, that's so much."

At this point, I can't stop the sobs as they tear through me. Grace yanks me into a hug, cradling my head against her shoulder and running gentle fingers through my hair. She holds me tightly against her, grounding me back to reality, and I do my best to regain control of my breathing.

"It's okay," Grace whispers over and over. "I've got you. You're safe. It's okay."

"I'm sorry, I'm so sorry," I manage to chant through the tears, not even sure she can hear me.

"Shh, don't be sorry. I'm the one who's sorry." Grace pulls back to look at me, tears streaking down her cheeks, too, but I'm too embarrassed to look directly at her. "That was dumb on my part. Of course there's a lot at stake, and you have every right to be afraid. But, Theo, look at me."

I warily meet her gaze

"Caleb adores you, Theo. He's not giving up on you, especially not over this. He knows that none of this hate is coming from you."

My breath catches in my throat, and more tears blur my vision.

"Not only do you have Caleb in your corner, but you've got such a good group of friends that I know are sticking by your side through this. Harrison, Elise…even Oliver and his goofy little ass. All those new kids, too. They're good people, Theo. They love you so much."

I sniffle and wipe my face with my sleeve. "Yeah. They're pretty great," I blubber.

"And I hope it goes without saying, but you know you've got me, too. I've got your back. Even if Dad ends up showing his ass and I have to take him out back and wear him out. You know I'd do that for you."

"I know," I say with a weak chuckle. "I know you would."

"You are so loved. Theo. Even if Dad's love is conditional, ours is not."

Warmth radiates in my chest at her words, chasing away the lingering pressure that squeezes my lungs.

"Thank you," I say, wiping my face. "Honestly, you being there next week makes me feel so much better. You have no idea how much I appreciate it."

"I think I do, bud. And you're so welcome. Now, my eyeliner is fucked, so I'm going to go wash my face before Mom accuses me of being a raccoon on my way out the door."

"I love you, Grace," I say, pulling her in for one more hug.

"Love you too, bud."

Back in my room, I reach for a vinyl—The Band CAMINO feels right—throw it on the turntable, then collapse onto my bed face-first. My anxiety revolving around Dad has eased, at least enough that I can breathe normally again. Grace is right. Even if the worst should happen, I'll be okay.

My phone buzzes in my pocket, and I pull it out, swiping to open the message:

CALEB: Thought any more about what kind of PJs you're going to wear next weekend?

I grin, tapping out my response.

THEO: i've got something in mind...

CALEB: *eyes emoji* Do I get a hint?

THEO: don't want to ruin the surprise

CALEB: Fine. Keep your mysterious booty shorts a secret.

THEO: How'd you know??

CALEB: What?? Seriously??

THEO: Nice try. :P

CALEB: I hate you. (I love you.)

THEO: love you too, babe. <3

NINETEEN
CALEB

Sunday, March 23

"Caleb, how does this look?"

Dad steps back from his work–two old twin bed sheets clipped together and fastened to the basement wall with a pair of bungee cords–with a look of satisfaction.

It looks like a hot mess, but I tell him, "Looks great, Dad. Can you help me move the table? I think Wren wants to have their set up over here in the corner."

He grabs the other end of the folding table, helping me carry it to the opposite end of the basement. I've spent all week transforming the usually dark, dank space into a scene right out of a nineties movie. Neon streamers hang from the ceiling, bean bags (borrowed from Wren's basement) form a circle in the center around a coffee table stacked with old board games Mom pulled down from the attic, and I've gathered every pillow, blanket, and cushion in the house to form what I'm calling the 'pillow pit' by the projector.

All we're missing is a Ouija board, and we'd be the opening scene of *Slumber Party Massacre 2*.

"I think that'll do it," I say, wiping my brow. "Thanks for all your help, Dad."

"No problem, kiddo. There's still room over there if you want to break out the karaoke machine. I've got it all charged up and–"

"I think we're good," I interrupt, then cross and wrap my arms around him, pulling him into a hug. "You're the best."

Dad embraces me, resting his chin on top of my head. "Happy birthday, son. I love you to pieces, no matter how old you get. I mean, you're seventeen now, so I guess that makes you an old man."

I pull away from him, giving a sly grin. "What does that make you, then?"

"Ancient." Dad braces his hands on his back, grimacing, "And I feel every bit of time passing through me. I need to lie down for about twelve hours now."

The doorbell rings upstairs, and I leave Dad to his dramatic groaning as I race up the stairs, skidding on the tile floor in the kitchen on my way to the front door.

"Happy birthday!" Freddy shouts, thrusting a box into my arms before the door even finishes swinging open. He pushes past me, letting himself in and kicking off his sneakers. His pajamas–if you want to call them that–are an old soccer jersey that he's cut into a crop top, a pair of striped knit shorts that ruffle at the bottom, and a small backpack slung across one shoulder.

Some much skin on display. I wish I had half the confidence Freddy has.

"Happy birthday," Wren adds, appearing from around the door like a pale, Victorian ghost child. Their black hair is slicked back off their face, a frilly white nightgown draping down to their knees, and a pair of black leggings hiding the rest of their legs. "Here," they say, handing me a stack of clear plastic bins, then ducking outside to wheel in a utility cart behind them stacked with more supplies.

"You can't make him carry all that shit, Wren." Freddy cocks his hip to the side, giving Wren a withering look. "It's the man's birthday."

"I don't see you helping," Wren replies, already halfway down the hall to the kitchen.

I level a look at Freddy who simply gives me a shrug, then follows after them.

"Don't worry, I got it." I close the front door with my foot, the top container shifting dangerously, and I have to dip to the side to keep it from tumbling over as I follow after them.

"Papa Bert!"

Freddy's voice echoes up the stairs as I start my careful descent.

"Hey, Freddy! Hey, Wren! You two look comfy cozy."

"Are you going to be setting up the karaoke machine?" Freddy asks as I round the foot of the stairs. "It's not a party until I hear you sing 'Baby Got Back.'"

"You know, I was just telling Caleb that I could fit it in the corner over there—"

"No karaoke," I cut him off, hefting the stack of containers onto the table. "Dad, I love you, but no."

Dad's karaoke obsession is borderline criminal. If I give him an inch, he'll take a thousand miles (by singing *A Thousand Miles*.)

Freddy pats Dad on the shoulder. "It'll be alright, Papa Bert. We can do karaoke for my birthday, and your party pooper of a son will have no say in the matter."

"That's why you're my favorite," Dad says to Freddy, giving him a wink. He glances at me, and I guess he gets the hint because he follows up with, "Okay, I know when I've overstayed my welcome. Caleb, do you need anything else before I go upstairs and pretend not to exist?"

I snort a laugh, giving him another hug. "I've got it from here, Dad. Go rest your old bones."

Dad gives me his best salute. "Roger that. Hey, Wren, you're in charge tonight. Please make sure no one dies while they're under my roof."

"I make no promises," Wren replies, already unpacking their cart onto the table.

"No one is going to die," I say, ushering Dad towards the stairs. "And if they do, we'll take them off property before the time of death is called like they do at Disney World."

"That's my boy," Dad calls behind as he hurries up the stairs. "Let me know if you change your mind about the karaoke machine!"

"I won't!"

"Bert is the best," Freddy says, flopping into one of the bean bags. "You really lucked out with the Dad Distribution system, Caleb."

"He's pretty great most of the time," I conceded, joining Wren by the table where they've laid out a few rows of nail polish. "But the karaoke obsession definitely takes some points off."

"Still a ten in my book," Wren chimes in. And there's something under their words, a sadness that clings on, weighing them down. But before I can press them, they stop what they're doing to look me up and down. "Is that what you're wearing tonight?"

I look down at my ripped shorts and hoodie. "No, I just finished getting everything set up! I haven't had time to change yet."

"Well, go! Freddy can man the door if anyone else shows up, and I'll finish getting everything set up down here. It's almost party time, and we can't kick things off without the birthday boy."

"Okay, okay, I'm going."

"And maybe run a comb through your hair while you're at it!" Freddy yells after me as I trudge up to the main floor. The television is on in the living room–where I assume Mom and Dad will be hanging out all night, trying not to hover–and I hustle up the stairs to my bedroom, where I've already got my outfit laid out on the bed.

Peeling off my hoodie, I realize just how much of a sweat I've worked up setting everything up, and I decide that a quick shower is the best option. I grab the towel from the back of my door, making my way across the hall to the bathroom. Setting my phone by the sink, the screen lights up with Theo's "on the way" message.

Once steam billows up from the shower, I peel back the curtain and dive in, hurrying through the motions. Freddy was right about my hair, and I make the quick decision to condition it so maybe the curls won't be so crazy.

The doorbell rings while I'm lathering, signaling another arrival.

After I've rinsed all of the conditioner out and scrubbed my pits twice, I shut off the water, pulling the curtain back and shivering as a blast of cold air hits me. I wrap myself in the towel, swiping a hand across the foggy mirror to clear a path for my face. My cheeks are red from the heat of the shower, and the patch of soft pink hair plastered to my forehead looks especially sad in its current state.

Okay, it won't take that long to do my hair.

Over the blow dryer, I hear the doorbell again, and more voices as the next round of partygoers arrive. I check my phone, counting the minutes between when Theo texted me and the normal time it takes him to drive to my house. I should still have time.

Once my curls are under control, I pull the towel around myself tighter, open the bathroom door, and dash back into the safety of my bedroom. I stop short of the bed as I realize someone is waiting for me.

"Oh!"

Theo's hands fly up to cover his eyes. "God! I'm so sorry, I didn't–Freddy said you were getting ready but I didn't think that meant–never mind. I'm going to go now–"

"It's okay," I manage through a fit of laughter, pulling the towel tighter around my waist. "Just keep your eyes closed for a second."

Theo nods, the parts of his cheeks I can see under his hands turning deep red.

I hurry over to my dresser, grabbing the first pair of boxers I can get my hands on. I glance over my shoulder to make sure Theo's still covering his eyes, then drop my towel and pull them on. "One more second," I say, moving over to the bed to retrieve the pajamas I laid out earlier. Once I've got the bottoms on, I tap Theo on the shoulder. "All clear."

He sheepishly spreads his fingers, peering through the opening. "Happy birthday," he says in a diminished sing-song voice.

"Thank you!" I land on the bed beside him, knocking my shoulder into his. It's only now I realize he's wearing a normal T-shirt and jeans. "You're kinda overdressed for the party, aren't you?"

Theo's eyes drift down my exposed torso, then snap back to attention. "Oh, yeah, I brought my pj's to change into once I got here. Figured my parents didn't need to know *all* the details about the party. No need to give them extra reasons to say no."

"Okay, bet. Well, sorry to keep you waiting. We can head downstairs now if you want."

"Actually, there was a reason I came looking for you. I wanted to give you something before we join the others." He reaches behind him, grabbing a brightly wrapped object from the bed, and offers it to me.

"You didn't have to get me anything," I say, already hooking a finger under the seam of paper to pop it loose. The sparkly paper peels back, revealing a purple leather-bound notebook engraved with blooming lavender. I run a finger over the smooth surface. "It's beautiful, Theo. Thank you."

"There's more," he says, looking down at his hands now. "Um, if you look at the first couple of pages, I wrote something for you. Well, there's several of them, actually."

Flipping open the journal, I find the first page scrawled with Theo's familiar handwriting. It takes me a second to recognize the structure of the paragraphs. "Are these lyrics?"

Theo nods, his cheeks now fully flushed with color. "I was listening to that playlist you sent me a few weeks ago, the one with the lofi beats, and they just started coming to me. I wanted you to have them, you know, since you inspired them. You don't have to read them right now or anything. I just wanted to make sure you saw them."

A swelling in my chest swallows up any words I try to squeeze out.

"Sorry, I know it's sort of a lame gift, but I couldn't think of anything else–"

I shake my head frantically, clearing my throat. "No! No, Theo. That's not–I love it. Really. I just, I don't know what to say. This is the most thoughtful thing anyone has ever done for me. Thank you."

"You're welcome," he says with a chuckle, his gaze finding mine once more. He smiles, and it's enough to make the swelling in my chest surge till I think my heart is going to pop right out.

"I want to read them now, but I'll wait till later tonight," I say, stretching to tuck the journal under my pillow.

Theo nods, and his eyes are lingering on me again. "Are you ready to go down to the party?"

"You should get dressed first," I say, elbowing him gently. "Freddy will make fun of you if you show up to a slumber party dressed like that."

Theo leans over, picking up his duffle bag from the floor by the foot of the bed. "Yeah, you're right. Is it okay if I change in the bathroom?"

I hesitate, glancing over at the cracked door. We're alone upstairs, which makes me feel brave enough to say, "You can change in here if you want."

"In here?" Theo echoes, his brow drooping. What I said must click a moment later because then he's stumbling over his words again, "Like–you mean in front of–like with you in the room?"

"It's not like you're getting naked," I say with a laugh. "But if you don't want to, I understand. It's just a selfish birthday wish on my part."

Theo smirks, some of the panic melting away from his features. "You want me to undress in front of you as a present? Got to say, I wouldn't have thought of that in a million years."

"You've got to get more creative," I tease him.

"I'll try and remember that next time."

He stands up, taking a second to rifle through his bag and pull out the pajama pants and matching three-quarter sleeve shirt. He tucks them behind his back before I can make out the details of their pattern, then drops them to the floor beside him.

"I feel like there should be music," he says, fiddling with the hem of his shirt like he's still trying to decide whether or not he wants to do it.

"Seriously, Theo. I was mostly joking. You don't have to do anything you're not comfortable with—"

"Oh, this is happening," he cuts me off, a devilish grin spreading across his face. "Whether or not you choose to look, that's up to you."

My heart hammers in my chest. "Will you think any less of me if I watch?"

Theo shakes his head. "If the roles were reversed, I wouldn't be able to help myself."

I snort a laugh. "Says the guy who covered his eyes when I walked in earlier."

Theo paws at the nape of his neck, his gaze falling to the floor. "I may have peeked once or twice."

"Theodore Briggs!" I shout, laughing through the giddy nerves in my stomach.

"I'm being honest with you!" He defends himself, folding his arms across his chest. "I'm only human. You're, like, the most beautiful person I've ever seen."

It feels like my heart is going to explode. Like fireworks are shooting out of my ears. Like lava is dripping down my spine. And as he reaches behind him, pulling off his shirt, I don't look away. I soak in all of the details of Theo, the boy I love.

The contrast of our bodies is what I focus on first: the light olive color of his skin still warmed from a summer of pool parties. The stretch of his broad shoulders as he pulls the shirt over his head, discarding it on the floor. The tuft of dark hair on his chest that's filled in over the last six months.

He's every bit as beautiful as I remember.

"I know you've been dying to see what pajamas I picked out," Theo says, squatting to retrieve the shirt from his set. "I wanted it to be a surprise."

Straightening to full height again, he pulls on the pajama top, pausing only for a moment as it gets caught around his chest. Once he tugs the garment straight, I let out a sharp laugh.

"Oh my god, it's perfect, Theo."

He brushes his hand along the decal in the center of the shirt—a unicorn with a blue, pink, and purple striped mane–pulling off a stray thread. "It's got the bi-flag colors, but it's not like, super obvious enough that my parents will say something."

"It's incredible," I breathe.

"Wait till you see the pants," Theo replies, a new sense of confidence behind his voice.

"Oh, I'm locked in."

Theo unfastens the buttons of his jeans, taking a second to adjust the band of his boxers before sliding them down and kicking them to the side.

Blood thrums in my veins.

He reaches for the pajama pants, carefully stepping one leg in, then the other. From the front, they look simple enough, just black fabric. But once he's pulled the drawstring tight, he turns around, and I burst out laughing.

Across the seat of the pants in glittering font, the words 'Bi As Heck' pop out in full sparkling glory.

"These I will definitely have to hide," he says, turning back to face me. "Mom might laugh, but Dad would have a stroke if he saw them."

I hop off the bed, closing the distance between us. Theo catches me at the sides, his warm fingers sinking into the exposed skin above the waistband of my shorts. "You are so adorable right now," I say, throwing my arms over his shoulders. "Thank you for my presents."

"You're welcome. Thank you for being born."

"You're welcome?" I say with a laugh. "Although I didn't really have much say in the matter."

Theo presses his forehead to mine, his eyes fluttering closed. "You make my life so much better, Caleb. I love you."

Cue another heart implosion.

"I love you too," I whisper, leaning my body against his and planting a gentle kiss on his lips. Theo sucks in a surprised breath through his nose, then surrenders himself, the kiss deepening between us.

As we pull apart, my head swimming, he gives me a mischievous grin.

"We'd better get downstairs, or else I'll want to keep you to myself all night."

"Yeah, I should probably put a shirt on first. Oh my god, I can't wait to see Freddy's face when he sees your outfit."

"I'm never going to hear the end of it, am I?"

"Never."

Theo's outfit earns a squeal out of Freddy, a high-five from Wren, a 'so what?' from Oliver, and a laugh from Harrison–who has no room to judge, seeing as he showed up with Elise in matching kitty cat onesies.

"Is the projector up and running yet?" Freddy asks from his seat on a beanbag chair.

"Almost," Andrew responds, fiddling with a mess of wires connected to his laptop. The projection flickers to life, prompting a group cheer, then flickers out again, the cheer morphing into a collective groan.

Theo and I have claimed a spot next to each other in the pillow pit, watching the madness unfold around us.

"Maybe it's a faulty HDMI?" Harrison suggests, pushing up the sleeves of his furry onesie. "I think I have one in my trunk. I can go grab it. Be right back."

"Wren, oh my god! They are so pretty!" Elise holds her hand up to the light, marveling at her new nail art. "Is there anything you can't do?"

"Parallel park," Wren says, screwing the cap back onto a bottle of polish. "I hit every cone they had during my driver's test. I think the old man felt bad for me, though, because he only counted me off for one."

"Did you want to get your nails painted?" I ask Theo, nodding my head towards Wren's table.

"Maybe later," he replies, leaning his head over onto my shoulder. "I kinda want to just vibe right now."

"Seriously, Wren. You could charge people so much money for this," Elise continues to gush, getting up from their seat. "Harry, you have to see these—where is Harry?"

"He went to grab an HDMI," Andrew answers, not looking up from his laptop.

Elise makes an annoyed face. "Why?"

"He says that's the problem with the projector," Theo explains.

"Who's having a problem projecting?" Oliver asks in a booming voice from the beanbag circle. "Ms. Laugherty says it's all about breath support."

Freddy cracks up, and Wren rolls their eyes.

"Quit yelling, Oliver!" Elise shouts even louder.

"I wasn't yelling. I was projecting! Keep up!"

I raise a hand in the air, adding my voice to the fray. "Birthday boy says it's too loud!"

Elise and Oliver both mutter an apology, the former stalking over to kick Oliver's beanbag, which starts them up into another argument, but at least they've lowered the volume.

Theo shifts, sitting upright to look me in the eye. "Do I need to go break them up?"

"Nah, they're fine. I warned my parents about the friend group's lack of volume control, so hopefully, they won't run down here thinking someone's being murdered."

Harrison returns after a few minutes, and after a few choice words with Andrew's laptop, the projector whirs to life.

"Movie time!" Freddy announces, running and jumping into the pillow pit like a kid doing a cannonball at the neighborhood pool. Elise, Oliver, and Wren join us too, everyone figuring out the seating arrangements in real time.

"What movie did you want to watch, Caleb?" Andrew asks above the din of chatter.

"I don't think I ever decided on one," I admit. "Help me out, people."

"Something from Studio Ghibli!" Elise is the first to shout.

"*Inception* has my vote," Oliver adds.

"Isn't there a new Godzilla movie?" Harrison asks.

"*Aristotle and Dante Discover the Secrets of the Universe,*" Freddy suggests.

"Too sad," Andrew says, to which Freddy responds by sticking out his tongue.

"*Death Note the Musical,*" Wren suggests.

"Please don't make me watch a musical," Harrison groans.

"If we're doing musicals, I vote *Chicago,*" says Freddy. "Pop, six, squish, not-uh, cicero, lipschitz–"

"Hold on, hold on," Theo calms the crowd. "Caleb, we're going to need some direction here, babe."

After a moment of deliberation, I say, "I'm in the mood for something happy, so maybe a Disney movie?"

"Old or new?" Andrew questions.

"Older ones are better," Oliver joins in. "Like *Treasure Planet* or *Atlantis.*"

"I've never seen *Atlantis,*" I admit.

"Seriously?" Oliver questions.

"And that one's not a musical, Harry," Theo adds.

"It's got my vote," Harrison replies.

"Princess Kida was a sexual awakening for me," Wren says with a rare smile. "I'm in."

"Sounds like we're approaching a majority here," I conclude, giving Andrew a thumbs up.

Andrew types away on his laptop. "Got it. Give me just a second to log in, and we'll get it started."

The group settles in, Freddy hopping up to dim the lights before the movie starts. Wren lays their head against my leg, and Theo returns his head to my chest. Andrew takes the spot next to Freddy, leaning back into a pillow and stretching his long legs off to the side. Oliver splays out under the spot on the wall where the projection hits, his head at an angle that shouldn't be humanly possible. Harrison and Elise drag over a couple of bean bags, sinking into them behind us.

The movie begins to play, and I take a second to soak in the moment around me. All of the people most important to me in one place. The boy I love close enough that he can feel my heartbeat. As the title rolls, I sink further into the pillow pit, reveling in the warm, fuzzy feeling that radiates through me.

But like all good things, the peace can only last for so long.

"Harry, put your phone down. You're missing the movie."

Elise's whisper is the same volume as most people's regular speaking voice.

"Hang on, I just have to finish checking–"

"You always do this," Elise says with a huff, sitting up tall enough that her head blocks the bottom corner of the movie. "Why can't you just listen to me for once?"

Harrison mirrors her posture. "Are you being serious right now?"

Elise pulls back the hood of her cat onesie. "When am I not being serious, Harrison?"

"Guys, keep it down," Oliver interjects.

"Why are you yelling at me, Elise?" Harrison continues, ignoring Oliver. "Can we go one day without you bitching at me over every little thing?"

Theo sucks in a breath, lifting his head from my chest. I miss the weight immediately. "Hey, Harry, chill out for a second–"

"Oh, is that what you think I'm doing?" Elise replies, her volume only increasing. "Newsflash, Harrison. A woman voicing her dissatisfaction with something doesn't mean they're being bitchy."

"Well, you sure do voice your dissatisfaction a lot," Harrison argues, standing his ground. There's an edge in his voice I've never heard before, and I can feel Theo's body tense against me.

"Because you never listen to me!" Elise shouts, standing. The upper half of her body is washed in the light from the projector. "And I'm sick of it!" Elise moves for the stairs, stopping halfway there to turn back to me with what I can only imagine is an apologetic glance. "Sorry, Caleb."

Harrison scrambles after her, skidding on the fabric feet of his onesie. Elise is already climbing the stairs, so he bounds after her, their voices growing distant as their footsteps sound over our heads.

"Should I pause the movie?" Andrew asks, looking over at me and Theo.

"No, you guys keep watching," Theo answers, detangling himself from me. "I'm just going to go check on them really quick." His attention turns to me, "Is that okay?"

"Of course," I say, giving him a nod. Theo gets to his feet, and I miss the warmth of his touch immediately. Once he disappears up the stairs, I wrap my arms around my chest in an attempt to self-soothe. Thankfully, Wren picks up on my mood and comes closer, snuggling up against me as the scene shifts in the movie.

Oliver looks back after a few minutes, his brow knitting into a furrow. "Wait, where did everybody go?"

Wren throws a pillow at him, and it's enough to get a smile out of me and lighten the overall mood of the room. When Theo comes back about halfway through the movie, Wren scoots back to their original position but keeps an eye on me.

Theo's face is pulled tight, the sides of his mouth dragged down into the void of his dimples.

"Everything okay?" I whisper as he settles against me once more. Theo takes a second to reply, staring ahead at the movie, but his eyes never move.

"They left," he replies. "Said they needed to cool down before they continued talking. Lola offered to drive Elise home." He falls quiet, his eyes still distant, like they're looking into the space between our world and the next, searching for something.

"Theo?"

He looks at me, finally, shaking the daze from his eyes. "I'm sorry this happened tonight."

"You literally had nothing to do with it," I remind him, patting his chest. "So don't be sorry."

"I should have talked to Harry more about what's going on," Theo continues, his breath catching in his throat. "At the very least, I should have seen that something was off between them. How did I miss it? What kind of best friend am I?"

"Hey." I press my hand harder into the warm skin of his chest. It's supposed to help people who are experiencing anxiety–I've been reading up on the topic ever since last fall. "You're being too hard on yourself. This isn't your fault."

Theo nods, his breathing slowly returning to a normal pace. I hold onto him still, making sure he feels safe. That's all that matters to me at the moment.

About an hour into the movie, Mom comes downstairs with a stack of pizza boxes. We pause the movie, everyone suddenly too preoccupied with the smell of cheese and pepperoni to care about the fates of Kida and Milo.

We dive into the pizza, the conversation drifting from one lazy topic to the next between bites. Oliver and Wren get into a friendly disagreement on which of the *Conjuring* movies is better while Andrew and Freddy whisper to each other in the corner.

Theo and I find ourselves back in the pillow pit, our legs tangled together under a blanket while his latest playlist plays softly from his phone. He's been nodding off for the last few minutes, mumbling through replies as his eyelids droop. His early morning shift at Cathy's must be catching up to him. But I don't mind, as it gives me an excuse to hold onto him. Theo is so beautiful when he's sleeping. When the stresses of existing melt away, smoothing the lines of his face and giving into a serenity that only comes from drifting off.

I reach over, brushing aside a curl that blocks his face, and he stirs, eyelids fluttering open.

"Sorry," he mumbles, letting out a yawn. "I think I dozed off."

"It's okay," I tell him, taking the opportunity to brush the hair from his forehead. "This is a slumber party, after all."

"But it's your birthday," he says, voice becoming more lucid with every word. "And I shouldn't be sleeping it away."

"It's my birthday," I repeat, "and I say it's totally fine."

He smiles, that soft, sweet smile that melts my insides. But then it falters, and he digs in his pocket for his phone. "I should check in with Harry."

"Or you could let them work it out?" I suggest. "You're not always going to be there to keep the peace between them, Theo. If they're going to have a relationship, then they'll have to figure it out together."

He nods an acknowledgment but checks his phone anyway.

"We should play a game," I say, raising my voice so everyone can hear. I sit up from the pillow pit, pulling the blanket off Theo and me.

Freddy perks up at this suggestion, pulling away from his intimate conversation with Andrew. "Game? I love games. And I've got just the thing for it!" He runs over to his backpack, unzips the top, and pulls out a small, clear bottle. "Courtesy of my mother's liquor cabinet."

Wren lets out an exaggerated gasp. "Freddy, you didn't."

"Of course I did. It's a special occasion! Plus, games are ten times more fun when you're a little tipsy. As long as it's cool with the birthday boy?"

"Just don't let me drink as much as Wren's last birthday," I say, shuddering at the memory of hugging Wren's porcelain throne all night.

"We'll take it slow," he promises, going for the stack of cups on the table with the pizza and cans of soda. "Anyone else want to get in on the fun?"

"I will," Oliver says, joining Freddy at the table. "As long as it's not tequila. I've had a bad experience with tequila."

Theo raises an eyebrow, suddenly more alert. "You drink, Oliver?"

"There's a lot you don't know about me, Theo Briggs," he says in his best impersonation of an international man of mystery. "But seriously, only a handful of times."

"You've never drank before?" I ask Theo, even though I shouldn't be surprised.

He shakes his head. "My parents don't keep alcohol in the house."

"Theo, are you in?" Freddy asks.

"You don't have to," I assure him. "I know you have to drive home later."

"Yeah, it's probably not the best night. But don't let me stop you! I'll just have another Coke."

"I'll take Theo's," Wren says, joining Freddy and Oliver. "Are we going to play a drinking game?"

"Ooo!" Freddy exclaims, pouring from the small bottle and then cracking open a soda. "I like the sound of that. Andrew, did you want any?"

"I'll pass," Andrew replies. "But I'm all for playing along."

"Gather round everyone!" Freddy continues, passing out cups to Oliver, Wren, and myself. We take our seats in the circle of bean bags, Theo and Andrew grabbing their drinks before joining us as well. "We'll have a game of Never Have I Ever, I think."

"Remind me how that works again," Oliver says, crossing one long leg over the other.

Freddy launches into the rules without hesitation. "We go in a circle and make a statement like, 'Never have I ever shoplifted.' And then whoever has done the thing the person says they've never done has to take a drink."

"Are there any rules on the statements?" Andrew asks, settling into the seat beside Freddy. "Like, topics to avoid?"

"Nope! Nothing is off limits," Freddy answers.

"But don't worry, Andrew," Wren says, lifting their cup in a 'cheers' motion. "There's only a handful of things that Freddy hasn't done by this point, so he'll have to keep it obscure."

"I'll start off," I say, lifting my cup into the air over me. "Never have I ever driven on the highway."

Everyone but Freddy takes a sip from their cups. Oliver coughs, and Wren makes a face. "Jesus, Freddy. Is there any soda in here?"

Freddy swallows with a wince. "I may have been a little heavy-handed. My bad. Just take smaller sips."

"You're next, Theo," I say, knocking my knee into his.

"Uh, never have I ever been out of the country."

Wren and Andrew both take a drink.

"Where did you two go?" I ask, curious.

"Australia when I was seven, to see my dad," Wren answers.

"Guatemala. For a church trip," Andrew explains.

"My missionary man," Freddy jokes, patting Andrew's hand. Andrew's cheeks flush red, even though he's not had a drop of alcohol. "Oliver, you're up."

"Never have I ever gotten a hickey," Oliver says.

Wren, Freddy, and I take a drink. It burns all the way down.

Theo raises an eyebrow at me, and I have to look away. "It was you, dummy. When we were making out in the dark in Eileen's backseat. You left one right here." I point to my collarbone.

"I didn't realize I did that," Theo says sheepishly, then clears his throat.

"I'm not complaining."

Wren raises their cup next. "Never have I ever touched a dick."

"No fair," Oliver says, taking a sip. Everyone else follows suit. "That's AFAB privilege."

Wren sticks out their tongue. "Suck it, loser."

Andrew's turn now. "Never have I ever gotten an F in a class."

Freddy and Oliver both take another sip, their cheeks tinted red.

"Your turn, Freddy," Wren says.

"Oh, god. This is the hard part…never have I ever had sex in a car–shit, no, I can't say that. Never have I ever had sex in a church–wait, that's not exactly true either anymore, is it, Andrew?"

Andrew coughs, his face flushing as all eyes turn to him.

"Never have I ever had sex on a park bench."

Wren is the only one to take a sip here, and Andrew sighs with relief as the attention shifts to them.

"Don't give me that look," Wren huffs at Freddy. "My ex lived by the park and shared a room with her little sister. Sue me."

"Back to me," I say, my tongue loosened and my brain a little fuzzy by this point. "Never have I ever punched someone in the face."

Wren and Andrew take a sip.

"Babe, what the hell?" Freddy asks, looking at Andrew.

He shrugs, not matching Freddy's gaze. "I used to fight a lot in middle school. It's not a big deal. Go on, Theo."

"Right, uh, never have I ever skipped school."

Freddy, Wren, Oliver, and I take a drink. This one burns less, or maybe I'm just getting used to it by this point. My throat is pleasantly numb.

"Never have I ever had a wet dream," Oliver says, holding up his cup.

"Aw, come on," Wren huffs, taking another drink. Freddy, Andrew, Theo, and I follow them. And suddenly, my hazy mind is filled with thoughts of Theo in bed, under the sheets, and the kinds of things he would dream of— would he dream of me that way?

"You okay?" Theo asks. "You're staring at me."

"I'm good," I say quickly, adjusting my shorts as inconspicuously as I can manage. It's harder to rein in my wild thoughts, but I somehow manage that, too.

"Never have I ever had a crush on a teacher."

Freddy and Theo take a sip.

"You have to tell us which ones," Wren says, giggling.

"Mr. Harris, eighth-grade social studies," Freddy answers. "He was a smoke show, for sure."

"And yours?" I ask Theo, enjoying the color spreading over his face.

"Ms. Livingstone. Sophomore Social Studies."

"Oh my god, good choice," Wren says, giving Theo a thumbs up. "Andrew, you're next."

The game continues for a couple of rounds, and after Freddy has to refill our cups, I'm even more lightheaded. Am I drunk already? I can't seem to organize my thoughts. It's like there's a disconnect between my brain and my tongue.

Theo looks so cute in his pajamas. I wish he was closer to me. I want to hold him again. A round of laughter spreads through the group, and I join in, even though I didn't catch the joke. Theo's looking at me now, an expectant expression on his face. Is he waiting for me to say something?

"Caleb?" he says gently. "It's your turn."

My turn? Right, the game. I remember now. We're playing a game. A game where I'm supposed to say something I've never done. What's something I haven't done? God, Theo is so fucking adorable. I just want to kiss him.

"Never, I have never," I say, the words slurring. "I mean, have I ever had sex with Theo. Never. But I want to. Shit, I don't think I'm supposed to say that."

No one lifts their cup, but there is more laughter. Theo is looking at me now, a mixture of shock and something else I can't really interpret on his face.

"Maybe we should take a break for a bit," Wren says, staggering out of their bean bag chair. "Andrew, I can paint your nails now if you still want."

"Yes, please," he replies, standing as well and helping Freddy to his feet. Freddy sways a bit but follows them over to the table. A soft snore from Oliver's bean bag tells me that Theo and I are the only ones still conscious in the circle.

"Sorry," I say, my tongue still weirdly thick in my mouth. "I don't know why I said that. I mean, I think it was the vodka, but I don't–I'm sorry."

"It's okay," Theo says, that weird expression still twisting the edges of his mouth. "You don't have to apologize."

Unfortunately, I've lost the ability to hold back the words. "But I think I made you upset, didn't I? God, that was so stupid of me. I shouldn't have said anything–"

"Caleb," Theo cuts me off, the unreadable expression morphing into a smile. He clears his throat before adding in a hushed voice, "I want the same thing."

It takes me a moment to realize what he's saying. He wants the same thing.

Me. He wants me. He wants to have sex with me. The tips of my ears smolder like hot coals.

"You do?"

He nods, reaching out his hand to take mine. "Yes, dummy. Of course, I do. You are my boyfriend, after all."

"When?" I ask, still emboldened by the fog in my brain.

"I don't know," Theo admits, scratching the back of his head. "When the time is right, I guess. And when we're both sober, for one thing."

I nod, feeling a little foolish for being in this state to begin with.

"We don't have to rush it," Theo continues. "But I just wanted to let you know I want it, too."

"Oh my god, I love you so much," I blurt out, pulling on his arm till he rolls over onto my bean bag, his head landing beside mine. He kisses me, slow and sweet, and I know the alcohol isn't the only thing I'm drunk on. His lips are a vice in and of themselves.

"I love you too, Caleb. Happy birthday."

TWENTY
THEO

I've never wanted to drink before. Not even once.

My parents, teachers, youth leaders, and pastors have spent years convincing me of the dangers of drugs and alcohol, and therefore, the inclination to indulge has literally never crossed my mind. It helps that my friend group, up until this point, hasn't been interested in experimenting, either, but even if they had, I'm fairly certain I still would have declined their offers. Drinking never felt worth the consequences. And not just the illegal part, but it doesn't even seem like it would be fun to do. For one thing, alcohol tastes gross—a fact that I discovered after my grandfather snuck me a sip of wine one Thanksgiving. For another, it makes you lose control of your own body, which makes my stomach flip just thinking about it. And worst of all, drinking makes people sick. My parents have plenty of horror stories from their youth—apparently, my dad drank a lot in college and spent far too many weekends getting drunk, passing out, waking up in an unfamiliar place, and puking his guts out the next morning. And quite frankly, that sounds like a nightmare. Why would anyone *want* to do that?

Tonight, however, I think I finally see the appeal. Watching Caleb's cheeks flush and his lips fumble over his words with every sip of booze has been both enlightening and entertaining. Everyone is clearly having fun. Maybe losing control every once in a while isn't as scary as I imagine. The key must be moderation, I suppose. If I didn't have to drive home to my strict conservative parents in just forty-seven minutes, I might even be tempted.

Maybe next time.

For now, I want nothing more than to revel in the pure bliss of being cradled in Caleb's arms. Everything is perfect here—tucked away from my father's critical gaze, hidden from the world of expectations and the gnawing guilt that trails me at church. It's freeing, being in his arms, letting the coil of anxious energy in my gut ease.

I could stay like this forever. Or at least for another thirty minutes.

My phone buzzes in my pocket, startling Caleb and prompting an annoyed groan from me.

"Shit, what time is it?" Caleb asks, shifting his legs to allow me to access my pocket.

I don't even have to look to know the answer because I've been subtly checking the clock every few minutes. "It's almost 11:20. I need to go soon, but not yet." I pull out my phone to see a text from Harrison, and my heart sinks.

> **HARRISON:** Hey. Elise and I are home safe. Hope you guys are still having fun. Sorry if we spoiled the evening.

> **THEO:** hey, glad you're both safe...you didn't spoil anything, man. I just hope everything's okay...
> do you want to talk about it?

> **HARRISON:** No.

"Is it Harry?" Caleb asks, gently rubbing my back.

"Yeah."

"Are they okay?"

I swallow. "I don't think so."

Caleb presses his head to my shoulder. "I'm sorry."

I sigh. "Me, too."

>   **THEO:** everything is gonna be okay, dude, just give it time :) you guys are solid. you'll get through this.

I watch anxiously as the three dots appear and disappear a number of times. Harrison has never been a long-winded texter—he'd sooner just call if he has a lot to say or wait until we're in person. Finally, his reply appears, and my heart plummets down to my gut.

>   **HARRISON:** I guess we'll see.

I squeeze my eyes shut. The fight must have been worse than I thought. Does this mean Harry and Elise are going to break up? No. Not a chance. I can't even fathom it. They're the strongest couple I know. Their relationship has always been the relationship golden standard—the epitome of true love, the ultimate example of what soulmates are supposed to look like. If a relationship like Harrison and Elise's fails, then what hope is left for the rest of us?

>   **HARRISON:** I'm going to bed. Go enjoy the rest of your time with Caleb while you still can.

>   **THEO:** okay…but I'm here if you need to talk, okay? you're my best friend and I hate that you're going through this.

>   **HARRISON:** Thanks Theo. It means a lot. Goodnight.

"Theo?"

"Sorry," I mutter, typing out a quick "goodnight" and sending it before stowing my phone back in my pocket. "I just...just wanted to make sure he was okay."

Caleb doesn't respond. Instead, he takes my hand in his, gently rubbing his thumb across my knuckles. I bury my face into his neck and inhale deeply, reminding myself of how little time I have left with Caleb like this. The moment I'm back home, I'll have to hide this Theo. I'll have to put up the perfect façade again.

I'm so tired.

"This party's been quite the shitshow," Caleb says with a sigh. "Everything is kind of falling apart."

I shake my head. "No, no, it's not," I argue, pushing away so I can meet his eyes. "I've been having a blast. And so has everyone else. The Harry and Elise thing has nothing to do with—"

Before I can finish, we're all startled by a door slamming shut.

"I'm awake," Oliver blurts abruptly from his beanbag after very obviously being asleep.

"Was that Freddy?" Caleb asks as he struggles to his feet. I quickly pull myself up and extend an arm to help him.

"I'm on it," Wren announces, stumbling over to the stairs and starting up them. Caleb isn't far behind, giving me an apologetic glance before disappearing with Wren.

"What happened?" Oliver asks groggily, rubbing his eyes with his fists. "Who's slamming doors?"

"Hey, Theo?"

I turn to find Andrew standing behind me with his overnight bag slung over his shoulder. His blue eyes are bloodshot and puffy, and a spike of anxiety shoots up my spine. "Yeah, what's up?"

"Do you mind giving me a ride home?"

I blink, dumbfounded for a moment before answering. "Um, well—" I glance at my watch. 11:28. "I have to be home by midnight, or my parents will kill me. Where do you live?"

"I'm right off of Pineview," Andrew replies softly. "If it's too far out of the way, it's cool. I just…" he trails off, his gaze dropping to the floor. "I just want to go home."

After a beat, I cast a glance at Oliver, who appears just as confused and surprised as I feel. I look back to Andrew and nod once. "Okay. Let me grab my things and let Caleb know."

"Thank you," Andrew whispers, gripping his bag tighter but relaxing his shoulders a bit with relief.

With that, I step away to find my own duffel bag, grab the jeans I arrived in, and quickly change upstairs in the half-bathroom. I check my watch again—11:33—and make my way down the hallway to find Caleb. Before long, I hear muffled voices from behind Caleb's bedroom door and pause before knocking.

"—so stupid. Why would I say that? Who says something like that? What the fuck was I thinking? I'm such an idiot!"

"No, you're not, Freddy," Wren interrupts Freddy's broken cries. "He just wasn't ready, that's all."

"You don't know that," Freddy counters.

"You're right, we don't," Caleb chimes in. "But neither do you. He's a good guy, Freddy. I'm sure there must be a reason why he didn't say it back. You just need to give him some time."

"Maybe he'll never be ready," Freddy's choked voice continues. "What if I ruined everything tonight? How will I ever forgive myself for chasing off the one good relationship I'll ever have?"

"Freddy–"

"See, this is exactly why I don't do this shit," Freddy continues. "I'm not built for relationships."

There's a pause, so I take the opportunity to give the door a quick knock. A moment later, Caleb cracks open the door and slips outside. His eyes land on my duffel bag, and his shoulders slump. "Shit, you have to leave now, don't you?"

"Yeah, and, um…Andrew asked me for a ride home," I add, rubbing the back of my neck.

Caleb's eyes flash with surprise. "Do you have time?"

"Yeah, if we leave now, I can make it."

Caleb sighs, then nods. "Okay." He leans forward and wraps his arms around me, and I melt into him. "I'll tell Freddy," he adds quietly.

"Thank you," I whisper. "I'm so sorry all of this is happening, babe."

"Not your fault," he mumbles, then pulls away. "You should go so you don't get in trouble."

I nod and try to smile. "I'll see you tomorrow, right?"

"Yeah. Tomorrow."

Caleb holds my gaze for another moment or two, and before I can overthink it, I grip his shoulder and pull him in for a kiss. It barely lasts more than a second, but it's enough to prompt a soft moan from Caleb's throat, which fans the flames of desire in my gut. Chill bumps prickle up and down my arms, and I want nothing more than to slip my tongue into his mouth, run my fingers through his soft curls, press our bodies together up against the wall until—

Focus, Theo. Focus.

"Love you," I mumble against his lips, forcing myself to step away.

Caleb releases a shaky breath but quickly recovers. "Love you, too. Drive safe."

I finally peel away, returning to the pillow pit downstairs to find Andrew and Oliver right where I left them. I turn to Andrew with determination. "Ready to go?"

Andrew gives me a short nod but says nothing.

"Should I be worried?" Oliver asks, expression tight and uncharacteristically serious.

I drop my gaze and fumble with my keys in my pocket. "About what?"

Oliver scoffs. "Oh, I don't know. Maybe about our friend group literally falling apart in real-time?"

Shit. "I sure hope not," I answer honestly. When Oliver doesn't respond after a beat, I sigh. "I'll see you on Monday."

Oliver doesn't answer. He simply watches Andrew and I leave without another word.

The short drive to Andrew's house is mostly silent other than Semler's soft vocals playing over Eileen's stereo. But the silence is anything but comfortable. I'm not sure if I should ask about his and Freddy's fight or just mind my own business. Andrew and I have barely spoken at all outside of just hanging out as a group—wouldn't it be weird to start now? Or should I speak up because I might know what he's going through? He's also a queer Christian guy dating a non-religious boy that doesn't understand what it's like to feel guilty about everything. Maybe we can help each other. Maybe—

"Can I ask you something, Theo?"

Okay, that works, too, I guess. "Yeah, shoot."

Andrew doesn't hesitate. "Have you and Caleb started saying 'I love you' to each other yet?"

I smile, grateful that it's an easy question. "Oh, yeah," I reply. "Ages ago."

He bristles, looking at me. "How many ages ago?"

"I think it was like a month into our relationship," I answer casually, despite the fact that I can name the exact date, time, and place we first said the words aloud to each other.

"Seriously?" Andrew asks incredulously. "That soon?"

I shrug. "Yeah, but I mean, every relationship is different. It's okay if it took you guys a little longer. Caleb and I had a bit of a dramatic start to our relationship." I glance at him to gauge his reaction, but it's too dark to read his expression. "Why? How long did it take you guys?"

Andrew doesn't answer. He stares straight ahead for several moments, and it's just enough time for me to finally catch on.

"Oh. Oh, shit, I'm—I'm sorry, that was dumb of me to assume—I shouldn't have—"

"It's chill," Andrew says with a weak chuckle. "It's just further proof that I'm a heartless jerk, and Freddy deserves better."

Taken aback, I shake my head. "What are you talking about?"

"Forget it," Andrew mutters. "I don't want to drag you into our mess." Before I can protest, he points at a modest brick house up ahead. "This is me, up here on the right."

Sure enough, we've arrived. As I pull into Andrew's driveway, I check the clock on the dashboard—11:49 P.M. I'm only about five minutes from home, so in theory, I still have time to offer some advice or at least hear him out. "Hey, if you want to talk—"

"I appreciate it, bro," Andrew interrupts. "But honestly, it's probably over between Freddy and me, anyway, so you might not be seeing me around after tonight."

Shit. I try to think of something to say, but I'm too stunned to speak. What the fuck happened tonight?

"Thanks again for the ride," Andrew says, unbuckling his seatbelt and lifting his bag up from the floorboard.

I manage a weak smile. "Of course, man. Anytime."

"For what it's worth," he continues, finally meeting my eyes. "I've always thought you're a really good friend and boyfriend. I hope Freddy finds someone who can love him like you love Caleb someday."

I stare blankly at him. "Oh. Well—"

"See you around, Theo."

Before I have the chance to respond, Andrew opens the car door, stands, slings his bag over his shoulder, and shuts the door behind him, leaving me even more unnerved than I already was.

Sunday, March 24

"Are you absolutely sure we're not going to get in trouble for this?"

I roll my eyes. "Yes, Harry, I'm sure. Jake's covering for me for at least the next thirty minutes. Now, spill."

It took far more convincing than I expected to get Harrison into the loft. Initially, he didn't believe the room existed—which is fair, given I only just learned of it from Jake a few weeks ago, and Harrison and I have been going to this church for most of our lives. Then, Harrison was insistent that we were falling for some elaborate trap set by my and Jake's fathers to catch us skipping church. Now that I finally have Harry here alone, I can only assume he's stalling because he just doesn't want to talk about what happened last night.

I can't say I blame him, but he has to talk about it sooner or later. Right?

Harrison sighs. "Okay, fine." His shoulders slump. "Elise and I decided we're taking a break."

There it is. My worst fears are all coming true. "Taking a break? But why? What does that even mean?" I run a frustrated hand through my hair. "What the hell happened last night?"

"I don't know, Theo," Harrison admits, burying his face in his hands. "You've met her. You know how she gets when she's upset. She doesn't make any sense and absolutely refuses to listen to logic. She won't even try, and I–I can't take it anymore, man. So, instead of talking her down or biting my tongue like I usually do when we fight, I just agreed that we should spend some time apart for a while." He shrugs. "And that was that. She didn't even try to argue."

The room goes quiet, and it's only then that I realize that my leg is bouncing rather audibly, so I stand and pace the floor. I blame the fancy espresso machine.

"So that's it?" I blurt. "You and Elise are over, just like that?"

Harrison shrugs.

"After, what, four years?"

"Almost five, actually."

"Jesus."

Harrison sighs. "Maybe it's for the best. We've been fighting a lot lately. Like, way more than usual."

I glance back at him. His shoulders are slumped in defeat, but he definitely doesn't seem as distraught as I'm sure I'd be in his shoes. "But that's...kind of what you guys have always done. Like an old married couple, right?"

He shakes his head. "Not lately. We used to just bicker over silly, stupid stuff. But now...it's different."

"How?"

"Just *different*, Theo."

I fold my arms across my chest. "Well, have y'all tried talking about it?"

Harrison's eyes roll to the back of his head. "Oh, wow, Theo, what a novel idea! We haven't tried talking about it before! Gee, maybe we should try it!"

Ouch. "Okay, sorry, that was—"

"Boy, we sure are lucky to have you and your expert relationship advice!"

"Dude, come on—"

"Of course we've fucking talked about it, Theo," Harrison growls, his tone no longer dripping with sarcasm. "She says I don't listen to her, but I know I do. I say she's too critical of me and always complains about everything I do, but she claims that's not true. Every fight—big or small, silly or serious—everything boils down to that stuff. And neither one of us is willing to budge, so I guess we're at an impasse."

The reality of the situation begins to set in, and I return to my spot next to Harrison.

"I'm sorry, man. I'm not trying to beat you up about this. I just want to make sure you're okay. If this is what you want right now, then I'm behind you."

Harrison lets out another deep sigh. "I don't really have another option. I still love her, I think. But everything is different now. It's like we've been holding onto the cracked pieces of this relationship for so long, and now that we've let them go, they're shattered all over the ground. I don't know if it's something that can be put back together, you know?"

"It's gonna be okay, Harry."

"I haven't been by myself in a really long time," he continues, a sad laugh breaking through his scowl. "I don't really know who I am apart from her."

"Maybe it's a good time to figure it out?" I suggest.

"Yeah. Maybe."

TWENTY-ONE
CALEB

Freddy doesn't pack his things till Nana shows up around three. Mom and Dad told me they'd take care of cleaning up the basement, so Freddy and I spent the day curled up in my bed, watching his favorite musicals and abandoning our phones across the room. Wren and Oliver left earlier in the morning after we each chugged a sports drink to combat the collective headache from the night before. Then, there was a lunch of leftover pizza to help soak up any of the remaining alcohol.

I'm sort of glad Theo didn't stay the night, if only because he dodged the hangover horrors. We need at least another year under our belt before I let him see me like that.

Freddy seems better after a while. At least he's not crying anymore. It's weird seeing him like this. Over all the boys that he's dated, I've never seen him shed a single tear. But with Andrew… there's something different going on.

"Thanks for today," Freddy says, zipping up his duffle. "I'm sorry my relationship drama ruined the party."

"You didn't ruin anything," I tell him, pulling him in for another hug. "Everything is going to be okay. I promise."

Freddy hugs me back, sniffling in my ear before he breaks away, his eyes shining. "I'll see you at school tomorrow," he says, heading for the hall. "Good luck tonight. Let me know how it goes. Especially if Nana Lynn punches Mr. Briggs."

"We can only hope," I call after him, running a hand through my hair as the reality of what lies ahead of me starts to sink in. Theo's family will be here in just a few hours.

Why did I ever think this was a good idea?

"Where's the birthday boy?" Nana's boisterous voice drifts up from downstairs. "Caleb, are you hiding from your grandmother?"

"Be right down, Nana!"

I change into some jeans, not even bothering to comb through my bedhead. When I make it downstairs, Nana has already taken over the coffee table in the living room with a stack of boxes, wrapped hastily in brown butcher paper and tied with string.

"There he is!"

Nana launches herself off the couch, wrapping me up in a hug that nearly squeezes the air from my lungs. The bedazzled embellishments on her blouse dig into my chest as I hug her back, breathing in the familiar perfume of lilac and spice.

"I swear you get taller every time I visit," she says, holding me at arm's length. "My god, Caleb, those bags under your eyes. Did someone have a long night?"

"You could say that," I agree, stifling a yawn. "I had some friends here for a sleepover."

"Mother, is that you?" Mom's muffled voice comes from the kitchen.

Nana releases her hold on me, moving to stick her head around the corner. "In here, Nora."

Mom shows up, her hair pulled back off her shiny face. "When did you get in? I wasn't expecting you for another hour at least."

"Got an early start this morning," Nana answers. "I woke up at four, bright-eyed and bushy-tailed, ready to hit the road. I'm telling you what, those hot springs out in Wyoming are just what the doctor ordered. My joints haven't felt this good since the Bush administration." Nana turns to give me a quick wink, "The first one."

"Bert and I are just finishing up in the basement," Mom explains, eyeing the stack of boxes on the table. "Can I come help you in the kitchen when we're finished?"

"That's not necessary," Nana says, grabbing the stack of boxes that are nearly tall enough to block her vision. "I'll go ahead and get the oven preheating. Caleb, sweetheart, I left a basket of heavy veggies in the Nana wagon. Can you grab those for me?"

"I'm on it," I say, moving past Mom and heading out the front door. Nana's RV is backed into the driveway, taking up nearly half of the available space. Poor Lola is going to have to park on the street tonight, but that's the norm when Nana's in town. It's honestly impressive how well she is able to maneuver this monstrosity, as I can hardly stay between the lines in a normal-size car. Then again, maybe I'm just a bad driver.

Inside, the RV is tidy as always, sunlight streaming through the windows and a large digital photo frame on the counter, displaying Nana's adventures. A wire basket filled with vegetables is sitting beside the sink, so I grab it and start to head out when something catches my eye. The picture on the frame has changed again, this time showing Nana hooked into a hang glider, thousands of feet in the air. My stomach lurches just looking at it.

Nana is fearless. She's handled more in her lifetime than most people can dream, and she shows zero signs of slowing. Maybe I need to take a page from her book. If Nana can jump off a mountain, then I can make it through one dinner with Theo's dad.

What's the worst that could happen?

Theo texts me when they're on the way. I stare at my reflection for a moment longer, making sure I've tamed the last remnants of my bedhead. I've ditched the normal hoodie in favor of a button-down that Nana got me for my birthday—my favorite shade of soft pink. The streak in my hair has faded over the weeks to almost total blond, and I sort of wish I had thought to redye it before tonight.

A knock on the door pulls me out of my head.

"Come in."

Lola pokes her head through the door, showing a small polka-dotted bag. "Happy birthday, little bro."

"I was wondering when you were going to show up," I say, opening the door all the way. She's still wearing her work clothes, which are far nicer than anything I ever put on, and she's even wearing mascara, which means she must have been face-to-face with clients today. "Now I feel like I'm underdressed."

"I'm changing," Lola says quickly, setting the bag down at the foot of my bed and pulling me into a hug. "Sorry I've been MIA today, but I had to take care of this emergency thing at the office involving livestock–it's not important. I'm just glad I made it."

"Me too," I say, hugging her back. "I have no idea how tonight is going to go, and I'll need you there to help run defense if Nana decides she wants to pick a fight."

"Aw, it's cute you think that I have any chance of stopping Nana. She's a force of nature, Caleb. Sometimes, you've just got to hunker down and hope for the best." She reaches over and grabs the gift bag, offering it to me. "Here, you're not supposed to open it until after dinner. Those were Mom and Dad's specific instructions."

"Then why are you giving it to me now?" I ask, taking the lightweight bag and sizing it up.

"Because I'm tired of being responsible for it, and I figured it would be like a little prize for making it through the night. Like a 'I survived dinner with my boyfriend's intolerant parents' prize."

"Yeah, I don't think those will really catch on." I set the present back on my desk, tucking it behind my laptop, next to the journal from Theo that I still haven't had time to sit down and read. A pang of guilt flares in my gut, but with everything that's happened since last night, he'll understand.

"Okay, I'm going to go peel some of this makeup off. I don't want the conservatives thinking that your sister's a drag queen or anything like that."

"At this point, I don't think Theo's dad can have a lower opinion of me, so knock yourself out. I'll throw on a wig and join you."

Lola snickers, giving my shoulder a gentle squeeze. "Any parents should be over the moon that their child is loved like you love Theo. I'm sorry that his don't see it."

"His mom is coming around, I think," I offer, shrugging away from her touch. "So, it's not all bad. I'll take the small victories where I can."

"That's the spirit, little bro."

The doorbell sounds, and my heart rate spikes.

Lola gives me a lazy salute. "I'll see you on the battlefield."

"You're so cringe," I say, even though I'm laughing. She moves across the hall to her room, and I head for the stairs, calling, "I've got it!"

Theo is all smiles when I open the door, and the nervous tension in my gut disappears when he wraps me up in a hug.

"Happy birthday," he whispers in my ear, sending shivers down my spine that spread out like ripples on a pond.

"You already told me that," I tease him, cautiously glancing over his shoulder, expecting to see his family coming up the driveway. But it's only Eileen I spot.

"They'll be here any second," he explains, as if reading my mind. "Dad had a thing at church this afternoon, so we had to drive separately." He takes a step back, eyeing my outfit as his grin widens even further. "You look so good, babe."

Heat sears my cheeks. "Shut up."

"No, really. I mean, I always think you're freaking hot, but pink is definitely your color–"

"There he is!"

Nana is a blur of sequins as she streaks past me, nearly tackling Theo with a hug. His eyes widen for a moment before he realizes what's happening and clings to her to keep from toppling over.

"Long time no see, cutie pie," Nana says, releasing Theo from the embrace but holding him at the elbows. "Where's the rest of the family?"

"They're right behind me," Theo replies with a nervous chuckle. "It's good to see you, Ms. Murphy."

"Please, call me Lynn. Or Nana. Or whatever you want, honey, I'm not fussy." Nana's attention shifts to me, "Caleb, sweetheart. That shirt looks fabulous on you. I knew it would. I saw it at this roadside stand in Nebraska, and I just thought to myself–this shirt screams Caleb."

"It fits great, Nana. Thank you again."

"Anything for the birthday boy." She spins back to Theo, wrapping an arm around his shoulder and steering him into the hallway. "Now, I'm going to borrow your boyfriend for a few minutes because I need a pair of strong arms to help me set the table."

Theo throws me a concerned look over his shoulder, and all I can do is wave as he's swept up in the storm that is my grandmother.

Before I can follow after them, the doorbell rings again, and I find myself alone in the foyer to receive the rest of the Briggs family.

Pulling the door open, Nate's voice carries in before I can greet them.

"--is messed up, Mom. Even I know that."

Kora glances up at me, a cake in her hands and an apologetic smile on her face. "Sorry we're late," she says, waiting for Nate to step through the door first. "Nathaniel, we will finish this conversation later."

"Whatever," Nate says, pulling his Switch out of his jacket pocket. "Sup, Caleb. You got a charger I can use?"

"Yeah, there's one in my room upstairs. It's the second door on the left."

"Sweet." Nate heads up the stairs and Kora looks like she's about to say something, but then she deflates a bit, letting it go.

"I can take that," I say, grabbing the cake container from her. "Is this strawberry?"

"Yes, it's a family recipe. Theo said strawberry was your favorite."

"He's right. Thank you so much. I can't wait to try it!"

"I just hope it's good. The frosting came out a little funny, and I tried to remake it, but Nathaniel had already used the rest of my butter for his–sorry, I don't mean to bore you, Caleb."

"It's okay," I tell her. "I'm sure it'll be amazing. Here, you can follow me, and I'll introduce you to everyone."

Kora straightens out the lines on her floral dress then gives a slight nod. We move down the hallway, ducking into the living room where Mom is lighting one of her three-wick candles on the coffee table.

"Oh! Sorry, I didn't hear the doorbell ring." She pulls out her earbuds, tucking them into her pocket with an apologetic smile. She crosses over to us, extending her hand with the confidence that comes with nearly twenty years of intimidating other lawyers. "You must be Kora. I'm Nora. Oh dear, that rhymes. Well, I guess I won't have to worry about forgetting it. It's so nice to finally meet face-to-face."

"Likewise," Kora replies. "Michael is running a bit late. He had an elders' meeting that ran over at the church, but he promised me he's on the way."

"No worries at all," Mom says, motioning for her to take a seat on the couch. "My husband Bert can't make it to something on time to save his life. I had to tell him we were getting married at noon just to make sure he showed up to the ceremony. Please, make yourself at home."

"Kora made a cake," I tell Mom, holding up the container. "I'm going to take it into the kitchen and make sure Nana isn't cross-examining Theo."

"That was so nice of you," Mom says to Kora as she settles into the chair across from her. "I'm afraid I'm not very much of a baker. I remember when I tried to make a cake for Caleb's first birthday–"

I move down the hall, Mom's voice fading as I pass through the swinging door to the kitchen and into Nana's domain. The stovetop is seeing more action than it has all year, all five burners engaged and steam rising from each of the pots. The smell is heavenly, and it makes me that much hungrier. Theo is standing at the island bar, a knife in one hand and a lemon in the other, as he silently deliberates which angle to slice it.

"Figuring out the best plan of attack?" I ask, setting the cake container on an empty patch of counter space.

Theo looks over to me, a bit of panic in his dark eyes. "Lynn told me to slice some lemons, but she didn't tell me which way, and I have no idea where she went."

"Deep breaths," I say, moving beside him and taking the knife from his hand. I grab another lemon, and cut it in half, then quarters, then again to make a pile of wedges. "There, just like that."

"You look like you've done this before."

"Nana always likes to cook when she visits, so I've picked up a thing or two. Are you telling me that you've never cut a lemon before?"

"I can't say I have. I'm a busboy, Caleb. They don't let me touch the food. Besides, I've seen the servers do it at Cathy's, and they have this weird lemon guillotine that does all the work for them."

"Lemon guillotine?" I repeat with a laugh. "That sounds like the coolest band that no one's ever heard of."

"You're right. Think of the T-shirts. The merch would be epic."

We're both laughing now, standing in the middle of the kitchen. It's easy to let myself get caught up in the moment–this touch of domesticity–and imagine what it might be like for Theo and I to share a space one day. I know it's crazy, seeing as I literally just turned seventeen, but I can't help myself. It's intoxicating picturing the possibilities that lay in front of us.

I'll probably do the majority of the cooking.

Then, Theo's hands are on my waist. I set the knife down as he pulls me closer, planting the softest whisper of a kiss on my lips. A disappointed noise escapes my throat when he pulls away, quickly dropping his hands.

"We're almost ready, Caleb." Nana's voice shocks me back to reality, her short-cropped gray and blonde curls entering the periphery. "But I can't have you distracting my help."

My cheeks are flushed when I turn to speak to her, Theo sliding the lemon wedges into a bowl to make himself look busy. "Maybe we can find him something to do that doesn't involve a knife, Nana. I'd like for him to stay in one piece."

"I won't hold the lack of knife skills against you, Theo." Nana grabs a spoon, lifting the lid off one of the pots and giving it a stir. "Nora–Caleb's mom–is one hell of an attorney, but still can't dice an onion to save her life. Some people just weren't cut out–" she snorts a laugh at her own joke, "for this type of thing."

The swinging door opens again, and Dad steps through, sporting one of his nice polos and a freshly shaven face. "There you are, Lynn. I'm reporting for duty."

"Thank heavens," Nana says, pointing back to the cutting board where Theo and I stand. "Take over for Theo before he maims himself. Theo, it's been swell, but you are relieved of your duties."

"Jeez, it's my first time getting fired," Theo says, a playful smile spreading across his face. "Guess I'm not putting this on any future applications."

"We're just moving in a different direction," Nana says with a knowing smile, ushering us both to the door. "Dinner will be ready in fifteen if you want to spread the word."

"That was harsh," says Theo once the door swings shut behind us.

"Nana only picks on the people she likes," I reassure him, grabbing his hand and leading him down the hall back towards the living room. I poke my head in, Mom and Kora sharing a laugh over something I didn't hear. "Dinner will be ready in fifteen minutes. Theo and I are going to go upstairs for a bit."

Kora checks her phone. "Perfect. Michael should be here by then, and Grace just let me know she got off late, but she's coming straight from work." She smiles up at me and adds, "She didn't want to miss your birthday, Caleb."

A new heat burns behind my cheeks. "Um, that's cool. I'm glad she can make it."

"I'll give a shout when the food's ready," Mom says, giving me a nod.

"Maybe try and get your brother to put down his game for a minute, Theo?" Kora says.

"I make no promises," Theo replies, holding up his free hand.

I drag Theo away from the living room and up the stairs just as the doorbell rings again and he freezes halfway up.

"I got it!" Mom calls from down the hall, and I glance back at Theo, his grip on my hand tightening. It's like every muscle in his body went rigid, locking us down. Is this how he reacts every time his father shows up? I can't imagine being that tense around my parents, except maybe when Dad is trying to put condoms on fruit.

"Hey, you okay?" I ask him, turning around and sitting on the stairs.

"Yeah," he replies, voice just a murmur. "Sorry, I'm just nervous. I don't want him saying something stupid to you again. Or your parents."

"Don't worry about us," I say, rubbing the back of his hand with my thumb. "We can take care of ourselves. And my mom is a master of tiptoeing around topics. She won't let the conversation drift into anything crazy."

Theo nods as Mom moves to the door, not noticing us only halfway up the stairs. The front door opens with a burst of sunlight. "You must be Michael. Please, come in."

Theo's dad steps into the foyer, pulling off his windbreaker and hanging it by the door. "I apologize for my tardiness," he says, voice cordial enough to sweeten the air around him. "I'm sure Kora told you that I had a meeting run long."

"No worries at all," Mom replies, mirroring Mr. Briggs' friendly energy. "You're just in time, really. Dinner will be ready in just a few minutes, and your wife and I were just getting acquainted in the living room."

"Wonderful," Mr. Briggs says, moving to join her but stopping short as he notices the two of us on the stairs. "Theodore, where are you two headed?"

Theo's posture straightens, and he drops his hand from mine as he turns around on the step. "Hey Dad, me and Caleb were just going to get Nate from Caleb's room."

Something flashes in Mr. Briggs' expression and he steps forward, placing a well-shined shoe on the bottom stair. "Why don't you come with me? There's something that I wanted to discuss with you."

"Uh, can it wait for a minute? We'll be right back down."

"No, it can't, actually," Mr. Briggs counters, his voice taking on an edge. "Now come here."

I bite the inside of my cheek to keep from speaking up. Mom flashes me a look of surprise, but I'm focused on Theo again and his body language. His hands clench into fists at his side. He doesn't move from the stairs.

"Is there a problem, Theodore?"

His father's voice is a warning. A promise of something I don't understand. Theo finally moves, descending the stairs to join Mr. Briggs.

"Let's step outside for a moment," Mr. Briggs says, motioning to the door.

"Michael," Mom intervenes, approaching the two of them. "Is everything all right?"

Mr. Briggs' smile is wide but insincere. "Just need a moment alone with my son," he says in a placating tone.

Mom's eye twitches. "Of course. Well, don't be too long. I'd hate for you two to miss out on any of the fun."

She gives me a final look of disbelief before heading back toward the living room. Mr. Briggs doesn't even acknowledge my presence as he crosses to the door, opening it for Theo to exit out onto the front porch. Once the door shuts behind them, I dash for the frosted window, pressing my ear against the cool glass.

"—right now, Dad? It's Caleb's birthday. We can talk when we get home."

Theo sounds frustrated, which is no surprise. I'm actually impressed by the controlled tone he uses.

"No, it can't wait, Theodore. In fact, I've been neglecting my duty for too long as it is. Do you want to know why the elders' meeting ran so long today?"

Theo exhales loudly. "I don't know. They couldn't decide on which brand of grape juice they want to switch communion to?"

I have to press my lips together to keep from laughing.

"Jim Buchanon brought up the fact that you and Jake have been spending a lot of time together at church, and he had some very interesting accusations he decided to air out in front of the entire board of elders. He claims that you've been encouraging Jake in his *perversions* and that Jake has been talking about openly discussing these ideas in the church."

My heart hammers in my ears, and I press harder against the glass.

"Dad, what are you even talking about? Perversions? Is this because Jake is gay–"

"Do not say that," Mr. Briggs cuts him off. "This is the problem, Theodore. You've become so inundated with the worldly ways that you don't even see the sinful behavior you encourage by giving it legitimacy."

"Giving it legitimacy?" Theo echoes. "Do you mean acknowledging the fact that Jake likes guys? I know how you feel about this stuff, Dad, but–"

"It's not just how *I* feel about it. It's the church's stance on the matter. It's God's stance."

"Well, I'm sorry, but I don't agree. And Mr. Buchanon can come and talk to me himself if he has such an issue with Jake and me hanging out. Or, God forbid, he can have an actual conversation with his son."

"It wasn't just Jim who voiced concern," Mr. Briggs continued, his voice a growl. "Apparently, your galivanting around town with Caleb has drawn the attention of several members who have lodged their own concerns. And as you can imagine, it doesn't look good for an elder's son to be the target of such rumors."

"I'm not galivanting. Caleb is my boyfriend, Dad. I don't know how many times I have to tell you that."

"Not anymore, he isn't."

Theo goes quiet.

I hold my breath.

What is that supposed to mean?

"What?" Theo's voice is barely audible.

"You have to stop this nonsense, Theo. I've entertained it this long, hoping that you would work through it on your own, but enough is enough. You are not bisexual. You're just confused. One of the elders has agreed to meet with you one-on-one to help you overcome this behavior, but starting today, you need to tell Caleb that he is no longer to associate with you or our family."

"You can't be serious."

"This is not a joking matter. Either you will tell him, or I will. You are my son, Theodore, and I cannot allow you to continue to embarrass myself and your mother–"

"Embarrass you?" Theo says through a barking laugh. "So that's what this is really about. You can't stand the fact that you have a son who is any kind of *queer*, and now you're trying to save face with your bigoted friends."

"You are not *queer*," Mr. Briggs starts, but Theo cuts him off again.

"You don't get to tell me what I am, Dad! That's not up to you. And I'm sorry if that doesn't fall into the narrow definition of your perfect family, but that's the reality."

Fuck yeah! I want to wrap my arms around Theo's neck.

"This isn't an open discussion, Theodore. You may not see it now, but I'm doing what's best for you, like a father should."

"Keep telling yourself that," Theo says, his voice strong. "But what you're actually doing is driving me away, Dad. Can't you see that? I love Caleb, and I'm not going to throw that away just so you can be comfortable around your friends!"

Mr. Briggs lets out an exasperated sigh. "I've already told you, there's no other choice. You are to end this nonsense with Caleb immediately, do you understand?"

"And if I don't?"

Mr. Briggs hesitates, his voice wavering. "Then we will have a different conversation. One that revolves around whether or not you will be allowed to continue living in my house."

My stomach drops. He can't be serious. Is he really making Theo choose between me and having a home?

"Are you fucking serious?"

A third voice draws my attention, another shadow joining the other two on the porch.

"Watch your mouth, young lady."

"It's fine, Grace. I'm handling this."

"Well, too bad, bud, because I'm pretty sure I just heard Dad threaten to kick you out of the house. That was what I heard, right?"

"I was simply informing your brother of the consequences of his selfish actions."

"Why don't we go get Mom and see how she weighs in on this decision of yours," Grace says, her footsteps up the stairs drawing her voice closer. "I think she might have a few thoughts."

"I have the final say in the matter," Mr. Briggs concludes. "And I would ask that you keep your thoughts to yourself, Grace. Now go inside."

"Not a fucking chance."

"*Language.*"

"I have a better idea," Grace suggests. "Theo, go inside and be with your boyfriend. I need to have a very frank and possibly colorful-language-filled conversation with our father."

"Are you sure?" Theo asks after a moment.

"Positive. Don't let this asshole ruin Caleb's birthday."

"Thank you."

"Theodore, we are not finished here, young man."

"I am. And I don't know what I'm more upset about, Dad. The fact that you're asking me to do this, or the fact that I'm not surprised."

The door opens beside me, and I step back in a rush as Theo, red-faced and wide-eyed, walks into the foyer, shutting the door as Grace starts in on her father.

"What the hell is wrong with you—"

"Caleb?"

Theo's expression softens when he sees me, the anger in his brow melting away. I grab him before he can say anything else, pulling him into me. I wrap my arms around him, pressing him against me with all of my might.

"How much of that did you hear?" he asks through a grunt.

I just squeeze him tighter.

"That much, huh?"

I don't know what to say, so I just hold onto him, hoping my touch can communicate all of the things I need him to know.

"I wasn't going to do it," he says, rubbing the small of my back. "I didn't consider it, even for a second."

He's comforting me?

"But what if he's not bluffing?" I ask, my voice catching in my throat at the thought.

"Then I'll figure it out. I can crash on Oliver's couch if I have to or Harrison's. Yeah, it would suck for a bit, but it's not the end of the world. Plus, I'd still have you, so either way, I'm ahead."

"I'm not worth all that trouble, Theo." I squeeze out the words, the back of my eyes prickling with tears.

Theo's hands drift to my hips, pushing back gently so he can look into my eyes. "Don't say that. I'm crazy about you, Caleb. You know that, right?"

I nod, blinking away the moisture. "I feel the same way about you."

"Good. Because this would be really awkward if you didn't."

I choke out a laugh, and Theo pulls me in again. "Me and Dad were going to have this stand-off sooner or later. I'm just sorry it happened on your birthday."

"It's not too late for me to tell Nana to put dirt in his food."

"Let me get back to you on that."

As if on cue, Nana pokes her head out of the hallway. "Time to eat, kiddos."

Theo and I break away from each other.

"Be there in a second."

"I should probably make sure Grace hasn't drawn blood out there," Theo says, swiveling to glance out of the frosted window. "Something tells me that Dad isn't going to want to stick around for dinner."

"Maybe we should just start making out until he leaves."

Theo smirks. "Is making out your solution to all of our problems?"

"Damn, you caught me."

Another wave of shouting sounds through the door, and Theo flinches. "I'd better get out there."

"I'll get Lola and Nate," I say, motioning towards the stairs. "Promise me you'll come back?"

Theo hits me with those big, brown eyes. "You couldn't keep me away."

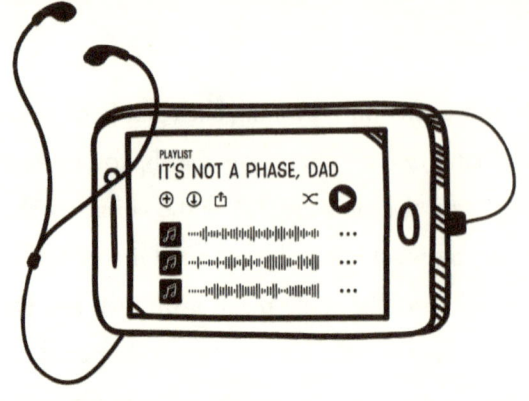

TWENTY-TWO
THEO

Caleb disappears up the stairs, and I stand with my hand on the door handle, frozen in the Raynards' foyer. Grace and Dad's voices seep through the door, clashing against one another, but I can't seem to focus hard enough to understand their words.

This feels like a bad dream. My worst nightmare, really. Dad showing up, demanding that I break things off with Caleb—it's what I've been dreading. But I didn't think it would be today. Not here. This is the kind of stuff that happens in the movies, not in *my* life. The Raynards are practically strangers to Dad, which, in any other circumstance, would mean he should be at his most charismatic and friendly. He's always been eager to befriend others, especially when he knows they're not believers.

But this? This overtly hostile and confrontational behavior completely contradicts the man my father represents himself as. It goes against everything he's *supposed* to believe in. If we were at home, that would be one thing. It's not like what he's saying is coming completely out of nowhere. I've been preparing for this outburst for months but never imagined it occurring anywhere outside of our living room.

The handle turns, and the door cracks open, letting Grace's voice carry,

"—might as well know that *I'm* bisexual, too! Should I go home and pack my things?"

"So, that's where he learned it from. I knew sending you to that school was a mistake," Dad retorts, his voice razor-sharp and biting. "You came home with all of that liberal nonsense and *poisoned* our home!"

I open the door, Dad and Grace both turning toward me, their faces different shades of red.

"Now it's Grace's fault?" I question, my words tinted with the anger building in my gut. "Why does it have to be someone's fault, Dad? Why is this so difficult for you to understand? Nobody *made* me bisexual. That's not how any of this works. And before you start down another tirade, it's not your fault either. Grace and I accepting who we are doesn't reflect poorly on you or Mom. Most people would say that means you're a good parent."

Grace wraps an arm around my shoulder. "Well said, little bro."

Dad exhales a long breath, pinching the bridge of his nose. "Give me strength, Father."

"Is everything all right?"

We all three turn to find Mom in the doorway now, her arms folded across her chest. Behind her, standing on the staircase, Nathaniel watches too. The whole Briggs family is here for the show.

"Dinner is ready," Mom continues, her eyes trailing from Dad to Grace and finally landing on me. "What is everyone doing out here?"

"Having a discussion," Dad says, lowering his voice as if he just realized where we are. "We'll be done in a moment."

Mom steps out onto the porch, her brow furrowed. "What kind of discussion?"

"About Theo's behavior, Kora. I'm putting my foot down. We cannot allow this to go on any longer."

"He's telling me that I'm not allowed to date Caleb anymore," I explain, earning a shocked look from Mom and a "What the fuck?" from Nate inside.

"*Language!*" Dad shouts, his hand clenched into a fist by his side.

Mom moves to Dad's side, placing a hand on his shoulder. "Michael, this isn't what we agreed on."

"I've been patient long enough," Dad says. "The time has come for action to be taken, and I will *not* allow my children to continue straying from the path. It is my duty as their father—"

"Your duty is to *love* them, Michael." Mom squares her shoulders, straightening her posture to full height. "The Word asks us to show compassion and understanding, or they will become discouraged."

Grace snorts a laugh. "I think we're a little past 'discouraged,' Mom. Dad is threatening to kick Theo out of the house if he doesn't break things off with Caleb."

Mom reels around, her eyes wide. I give her a small nod and she redirects herself towards Dad.

"*Michael.*" Her voice trembles with rage. "What are you thinking?!"

"This isn't open for debate," Dad says, injecting as much sternness into his voice as he can muster. "I've only told Theodore what I am willing to do if he keeps ignoring our rules. If he keeps going down this road of sinful behavior–"

"You need to leave," Mom cuts him off, stepping between us and Dad.

He blinks like he doesn't believe his eyes, his mouth hanging slightly open. "Kora?"

"I mean it, Michael. Get out of here. We will continue this discussion at home. I will not let you ruin Caleb's birthday like this."

Dad peers through the door where Nora and Bert are now standing in the foyer, and Caleb watches from the stairs with Nate. It must finally click that he's making a scene because he reaches up to straighten his tie–a nervous habit–and clears his throat. "Fine. Theodore, say your goodbyes, and we'll continue this at home."

"Theo isn't leaving," Mom says, her voice taking on an edge I've rarely heard. "The rest of us are going to go inside and celebrate Theo's boyfriend. I suggest you take that time to pray and seek wisdom because right now, you are seriously lacking."

Grace snorts, covering her mouth.

"Kora," Dad starts, reaching for her, but Mom smacks his hand away.

"I will be home after dinner, Michael. We can pick up this discussion then."

Dad's frown deepens as he looks over to me, a twist of pain in his expression. My chest squeezes, my pulse spiking, but then he's walking away, and I allow myself a few steadying breaths.

Mom watches him get into his car and drive away, propping herself up on the railing. Grace goes to her side, whispering something in her ear. Mom's lip begins to tremble as she nods, releasing a shuddered breath.

Nathaniel steps out onto the porch, turning to address the Raynards in the foyer. "We're gonna need just a minute. Sorry."

"Take your time," Caleb's voice trails through as Nate shuts the door.

Mom turns to look at me, tears brimming in her eyes, and I close the distance between us, wrapping her up in a hug. She embraces me, head resting on my shoulder as she lets out a choked noise.

"Thank you," I tell her because I don't know what else to say. I've never seen her stand up to my father like that. Not so directly. Sure, they'd have disagreements, but to assert herself like that? I know it took a lot of courage on her part.

She pushes me to arms' length, her dark eyes locking onto mine. "I will *never* let him force you out, *aroha*. You will always be safe with me, do you understand?"

And I'm crying now too. Big, heavy tears roll down my cheeks as I cling to my mother. Nathaniel is on one side of me, a hand on my back, and Grace is on the opposite side, dabbing at the streaks of mascara running down her face with her sleeve. And it's an incredible feeling, having (most of) my family surrounding me.

"Sorry Dad is such a dick," Nate says, resting his forehead against my shoulder.

"Me too," I say, a laugh breaking through the lump in my throat.

"Me three," Grace chimes in.

"Thanks for sticking up for me, Grace. I don't know what I would have done if you didn't swoop in to save me."

"Any time, bud. You know I'll always go to bat for you."

"Me too," Nate adds. "Though, I'm not really great at talking. But I can stare at people and make them uncomfortable."

"I'll keep that in mind," I say, chuckling.

Mom releases her hold on me, letting me drift between my siblings. She wipes at her face, sniffling. "Poor Caleb, I feel awful about all of this. What he must be thinking of us."

"I'm thinking about dinner," Nate says, seemingly over the family bonding moment.

Grace, Mom, and I share another laugh, and it lessens that squeezing in my chest, allowing me to breathe a little easier.

"Come on," I say, herding my family towards the door. "We've got a birthday to celebrate."

Caleb's family are probably the chillest people in all of Specter. They don't ask questions when we come back inside, eyes bloodshot and noses running. Nana Lynn serves us a mouth-watering dinner of Caleb's favorite foods—creamy pasta with vegetables and garlic bread—while entertaining us with stories of her many trips across the country, and the colorful characters that she's met along the way. Nate ends up enamored by the older woman, hanging on each story like Caleb and I do with Triple H episodes. He doesn't touch his Switch once during dinner.

Mom agrees to a glass of wine when it's offered, which makes me and Grace exchange looks. Grace also accepts a glass, and Lola and her end up talking about recent school drama between their two campuses. Apparently, they each have a class with the same professor who got caught pulling pranks on his students from one school while dressed as the mascot from the other. It's hard to imagine a sixty-year-old man wearing a panther costume while plastic-wrapping a toilet, but hey, to each their own.

And the best part is Caleb's hand doesn't leave mine for the entirety of the meal.

When Bert dims the lights, and Nana Lynn brings out the cake, with seventeen little candles blazing on top, I watch the flames dance in Caleb's eyes as he leans over them, making an unspoken wish, and we all sing happy birthday in different keys.

And when the dishes are washed, and the adults have adjourned to the living room for more wine, Caleb, Nate, and I retreat to his room for Mario Kart. I laugh when Nate schools us both, and Caleb immediately demands a rematch, blaming an ill-timed blue shell for his defeat.

It's almost enough to forget everything that happened with Dad.

Almost.

Mom comes upstairs after a while, knocking gently on the doorframe to announce her presence. "I'm heading home, *aroha*. Nate, Grace is going to take you over to Dante's before she heads back to school. Come grab your stuff from the car."

"Later, Caleb," Nate says, sliding off the edge of the bed. "Let's race again soon. Beating Theo over and over again gets boring."

"You're on," Caleb says, waving as Nate ducks around his mother, disappearing down the hallway.

"Don't worry about curfew tonight, Theo, but let me know when you're headed home, please. I'm sure your father and I will just be getting started by then."

"Thank you for coming, Kora," Caleb says, giving one of those smiles that makes my stomach flip. "The cake was amazing."

"You're most welcome, honey. I'm sure it goes without saying, but I'm very sorry for my husband's behavior. It breaks my heart that he refuses to see the love the two of you share."

I get up from my spot on the floor, crossing the room to wrap her up in a hug. "That means so much, Mom. Really."

She sniffles when she pulls away, ducking her chin to try and hide the tear she wipes away. "Have a good night, and I'll see you in the morning, *aroha*."

"Good night, Mom. I love you."

"I love you too, Theo."

"We'll be back later, Mom!"

Caleb shuts the front door behind him, skipping down the porch stairs to join me on the sidewalk, taking my hand in his.

We walk past Nana Lynn's RV, climbing into Eileen and I crank up the engine, plugging in my phone and picking the perfect playlist.

"Where do you want to go?" I ask Caleb, one hand on the wheel, the other planted on his knee.

His wicked smile shines in the dim light. "Somewhere dark, preferably."

We settle on the park not too far from Caleb's neighborhood. The parking lot is empty this time of night, and I pull into the last row, shutting off the lights but leaving the music playing.

"How are you doing?" Caleb asks me, his hand covering mine on the gear shift. "I know that stuff with your dad was a lot."

"Is it weird to say that I'm surprisingly okay? It's like I've been dreading this moment for so long that now it's finally happened, there's this sense of relief to go along with all the anxiety. I'm just glad the rest of my family was there. I'm so lucky to have them."

"I'm glad they were, too," Caleb says, stroking the back of my hand with his thumb. "Because Nana would totally have fought your dad if Kora hadn't stepped in. Freddy and I had a bet going."

"That would have been epic. I would totally have put money on Nana Lynn. Dad's too proper to hit a lady."

It feels weird talking about Dad after everything that happened. I wonder how his and Mom's *discussion* is going. Something tells me that he may be sleeping on the couch by the time I get home.

"I brought something," Caleb says, rustling through the messenger bag by his feet.

And my heart is suddenly racing because I'm worried that he's about to pull out that square little box, and I don't know if I'm ready for what all that entails–

"I haven't had a chance to read any of them yet, so I figured I'd do it while you're here with me. You know, for maximum cringe."

He shows me the journal I gave him yesterday, and a different heat starts to build under my skin. "You really don't have to read that–"

Caleb raises an eyebrow. "Oh, you think I'm going to let you get away with writing a *song* for me without a little bit of teasing? It's like you don't know me at all."

"Kill me," I mutter under my breath.

After turning on the overhead light, he flips open the book, stopping at the first song, and I watch him as his eyes drift along the lyrics. He smiles, one of those soft, understated smiles that are my favorite because they make his eyes crinkle at the edges.

"Fuck, Theo, this is actually really good."

"Wow, don't sound so surprised."

"T-That's not what I meant," Caleb stutters, backpedaling.

And I'm laughing, because teasing him is another of my favorite things. He shifts in his seat, the skin along his cheekbones brightening to match the color of his shirt.

"You've never shown me any of your writing before," he continues, eyes still locked on the page.

"I haven't really shared them with anyone," I admit, unfastening my seat belt. "So, I honestly have no idea if they're any good. But it felt like the right thing to do since you're the reason behind those songs."

Caleb nods slowly, flipping the page as he dives into the next one. And I'm happy just watching, taking in the little changes in his expression as he makes it through the half a dozen songs I penned over the last few months. I resist the urge to ask him what he thinks of each one as he moves through them, anxious energy building till he hits a blank page and turns to look at me finally.

My heart sinks as he hands me the notebook, and for a split second, I wonder how I messed up badly enough that he doesn't even want to hold onto–

"I want more."

"What?"

"I want you to fill it," he says, pushing the notebook closer. "Every page. And not just songs about me. I want all of it. All of your experiences, all of your troubles, every bit that makes you the boy that I love more than anything, Theo. I want you."

I take the notebook with a trembling hand. "It may take me a while."

Caleb grins. "We've got time."

My heart swells, my breath catching in my throat. I can't believe that he's here. That he's real. My boyfriend. My Caleb.

And his hands are on me before I can say anything else, cupping the side of my face as he leans over the armrest and kisses me. My anxiety dulls, the buzzing in my stomach melting with the heat of his kiss. The notebook falls onto the floorboard as my fingers grasp at his shirt, hooking between the buttons and grazing the warm skin underneath.

He groans into my mouth, and it's like lightning strikes the base of my spine, spreading fire through my veins.

"Back seat?" I ask, my hand drifting up to extinguish the light overhead.

Caleb nods emphatically, stepping up onto the seat in a crouch, then falling back onto the bench seat. His legs spread wide as he lands, arms outstretched to me, calling me to him. And I'm there in a flash, my knees sinking into the space between his legs as I brace myself against the back headrests before leaning down to kiss him again.

I shudder as his hands run along my thighs, curling around my waist and anchoring me there. His lips drift from mine, trailing down my jawline till they reach my neck, drawing out a gasp as teeth scrape against my flesh.

"Caleb," I whisper because his name is the only thing that makes sense right now, and my brain is on fire as he moves down toward my collarbone. I pull away long enough to remove my shirt, and Caleb wastes no time kissing his way down to my chest, hot breath sending chill bumps across my skin.

He pulls me closer, fingers sinking into my waist. His legs squeeze together, pressing into mine, and it only takes a second for me to understand what he wants. I lift myself off of him, positioning my knees on either side as I straddle his lap. When I lower myself back down, his eyes roll back, and I let out a sigh at the friction between us.

"Theo." My name on his lips is sweet honey, and I eat it up, kissing him again and again till my head is spinning and there's sweat on my brow, and all I want to do is remove any barrier between him and me.

"Hang on," Caleb huffs, pulling away from me with an exhale. His chest is heaving as he stares up at me with half-lidded eyes, the lights from the dashboard reflected in them. "I need a second."

We detangle ourselves, retreating to our respective sides of the car, lucidity slowly sinking back in with each ragged breath.

"You're too hot," Caleb says, knocking his knee against my shoe.

"Shut up, you are."

He snorts a laugh, pulling at his jeans to relieve what I assume is discomfort. I do the same, neither of us willing to acknowledge it.

"Do you think it'll always be like this?" I ask after we've had a second to catch our breath. "I can't imagine ever *not* wanting to make out with you."

Caleb shrugs, a sly grin spreading across his lips. "Maybe once we have post-nut clarity to thank, it'll get easier."

My breath catches, and we're both laughing, if only to keep the tension from ripping through us like a knife.

"Do you…" I stop, trying to organize the words before I say something I will regret. "Want to keep going? It is your birthday, after all."

Caleb watches me, his teeth sinking into his bottom lip. But then he shakes his head, curls bouncing. "Maybe not tonight."

"Oh, okay." Embarrassment scorches my already burning face.

"Not that I don't want to!" Caleb says quickly, a hand on my knee. "It's just—today was a lot, and I don't want us to rush into anything because emotions are high." He looks down at his hands. "Sorry, I know this is difficult for you. I didn't mean to ruin the moment."

"Hey, don't do that." My hand wraps around his, pulling him forward till our foreheads are pressed together. "Don't say you're sorry for being the most considerate boyfriend anyone could ask for."

Caleb snorts a laugh, his free hand cupping the side of my face as he plants a gentle kiss on my lips. "I love you so much, Theo."

"I love you, too."

"Will you text me when you get home?"

Caleb doesn't seem to be in a hurry to get out of the car, even though it's well past midnight and we've been sitting in his driveway for half an hour. My playlist has started over at this point, and I hum along to the song as I twist my fingers through Caleb's curls.

"Yeah, of course."

"I wish you didn't have to go," he says, his voice almost a whisper. "I wish you could just stay with me tonight instead of going back to your dad."

A twinge squeezes in my chest. "Me too."

"That wasn't what I wished for on my cake, though," Caleb continues, eyes heavy-lidded and words slurring together with drowsiness.

"What did you wish for?"

"Jus' you." He blinks slowly, his breathing steady like he's just on the edge of nodding off. "I wished for you to still be here for my next birthday."

The squeeze in my chest blooms with heat. "I'm not going anywhere," I tell him, leaning in to kiss the top of his head, burying my nose in his copper curls. "I promise."

The downstairs lights are on when I pull up to my house. It's a little after one, and I'm already dreading my alarm going off tomorrow for school, but that worry quickly fades as the reality of the last few hours settles in.

Dad threatened to kick me out. Everyone else in the family rallied around me. Mom stood up to Dad in a way I've never seen before. But what was I about to walk into? What kind of compromise would Mom be able to convince Dad of? It's not like he's going to change his mind in a matter of hours.

I pull out my phone opening the group message. It's been quiet since Caleb's party Saturday, the fractures of our friend group evident in the silence. I switch over to Caleb's number, typing out the message—

THEO: made it home. Here's hoping I still have a place to sleep. (Just kidding)

i'll update you in the morning. Goodnight, babe.

Caleb doesn't reply after a few minutes, and I assume he's long asleep by this time. I shut off the engine, and there's nothing left to do but face the music, so I make my way to the front door, finding it unlocked.

It's quiet inside. Mom's purse hangs on the rack by the door, but I notice Dad's keys are missing.

Weird.

"Theo?"

Mom's voice drifts in from the kitchen, and I hold my breath, waiting for Dad to call out next, but it stays quiet.

I kick off my shoes and then move down the hall into the warm light of the kitchen. Mom sits at the breakfast table, still in the floral dress from before, her hair piled on top of her head in a messy bun. A cup of coffee sits in front of her, still full, another half pot waiting on the counter. It looks cold. Like she's been sitting there for a while.

"Hey, Mom."

She looks up, shadows exaggerating the dark circles under her eyes.

"I'm glad you're home, *aroha*."

"Where is Dad?" I ask, looking over my shoulder as if I expect him to pop out from around the corner at any moment.

"We decided it was best that he spend the night elsewhere," she answers, her voice gruff.

"You kicked him out?"

"Something like that," she says with the hint of a smile. "You know how stubborn he can be. It'll take some time for him to come around."

"W-What if he never does?" I ask, voicing the question I've been harboring for the last eight months. My voice trembles. "What happens then?"

"Come here," Mom says, standing up and reaching for me. She pulls me into a tight hug, resting her chin on my shoulder. "You are loved, *aroha*. You are safe here. Okay?"

I nod, my throat too thick to speak.

"I'm sorry, Theo. I'm sorry for how long I let your father intimidate you. I'm... working through a lot of things myself when it comes to my relationship with him. He's not in a place to talk about what needs to change right now, so he's going to spend some time away till he can show me that he's ready.

"And, if he decides that he can't… then we'll cross that bridge when we get to it."

There's a fear laced between her words that sinks into my gut, an uncertainty that takes root and fuels the buzzing anxiety that thrums in my veins.

"It's my fault," I say, squeaking the words out around the restriction in my throat. "God, I'm going to break the whole family apart, Mom."

She takes me by the shoulders, a sudden intensity in her demeanor. "*Aroha, no*. Don't say that. Your father may be doing what he thinks is right, but don't for a second believe that places the blame on you. He is the only one responsible for his actions, just as the rest of us are. And I hope, and I pray every day that his heart will change as you and Caleb have changed mine, but if that doesn't happen, if he comes back unchanged, then I will do what I have to keep this family safe."

I dab at the tears that leak from the corner of my eyes. "Are you–are you saying that you're okay with me being bi?"

"I love every bit and piece of you, Theo. And what you feel for Caleb is just as much a part of you as the hair on your head. Who am I to condemn what God has so clearly given you?"

More tears come because this is all I've wanted to hear from my parents since I first realized what was happening between Caleb and me.

"Thank you," I whisper, pulling her close again. "Thank you, thank you, thank you." It's both a prayer and a statement of gratitude.

"I am so proud of you, Theo. No matter what happens, I hope you'll know that."

And the tears keep coming till we're both exhausted, and the night grows thin, and there's nothing left to do but go to sleep.

TWENTY-THREE
CALEB

Sunday, May 4

"A toast to all that made it through Junior year testing without suffering a nervous breakdown!"

"Freddy, weren't you sobbing into a Lunchable between finals last week?" Oliver asks, looking up from his phone.

"Shut up, Oliver. That totally doesn't count."

The patio of Spookies is packed to the limit as the May sun shines down overhead, locking in the warmth and promise of summer. Freddy and Oliver continue to bicker–a normal pastime for the two of them, especially since Freddy has been single again–and the rest of the table returns to their usual business as the two of them carry on.

"Did anyone else think Mr. Thornton's World History final was weirdly pro-colonialism?" Harrison asks between bites of a chocolate chip cookie.

"Right?" Elise replies from across the table. "That last essay question was wild. Like, was he trying to get us to defend the British empire? Like, my dude, they've had enough people on their side for the majority of history. Let's maybe start talking about the damage they've caused."

Theo watches the two of them as they trade topics from their essays, a small smile playing across his lips. There's no arguing. Elise doesn't even raise her voice above her normal decibel range.

"Seems like they're getting along well," I mutter to him, leaning in close.

"For real," Theo agrees. "Their breakup was honestly the best thing to happen to their friendship."

Things were a little tense the week after my birthday in the friend group. Elise was avoiding most of us, and Harrison went full on obsessive mode with his photography, getting absorbed into his camera. But Elise was at our lunch table the following week, a little quieter than before, but no one complained. When Harrison came and sat beside her, I thought for sure we were in for trouble, but they just talked about a new anime that Harrison saw, and they've been civil ever since.

"Over here, Wren!" Oliver stands up, the top of his head grazing the umbrella above us when he does.

Wren spots us from the parking lot, stowing their keys in their crossbody bag. Oliver pulls out the chair next to him, signaling for Wren to sit there.

"You got my drink?" Wren asks him as they sit, eyeing the paper cup in front of them.

Oliver waves them off. "Yeah, you paid for mine last time, remember?"

"Caleb, are you still going to Arizona with your dad this summer?" Freddy asks. Now that Wren is here, he's lost the attention of Oliver completely.

"That's the plan," I confirm. "It's an indie film, so he said we should be wrapped in about three weeks."

"I'm going to miss you like crazy," Theo says, squeezing my hand under the table. "I should ask Bert if the interns need assistants. I can fetch you coffee for the people you're fetching coffee for."

"Coffee-ception," I conclude, snorting a laugh. "I love the redundancy."

Freddy sets his elbows on the edge of the table, propping his chin. "Am I the only one who's stuck in Specter all summer?"

"What happened to the soccer camp?" Wren asks as they dig through their bag.

"They have too many counselors already. I got backlisted."

"I'll be around this summer," Theo chimes in. "Our family vacation is on indefinite hold at the moment, so all I have to look forward to is full-time hours at Cathy's. They're always looking for more busboys if you need something to keep you busy."

"I'll think about it," Freddy grumbles.

"I got something in the mail today," Wren says, loud enough that the table goes quiet. They pull an envelope out of their bag setting it down in front of them. "It's from the Effects Institute. So, I guess this will determine what my summer looks like."

"Holy shit," Oliver breathes, snatching the envelope and checking the sealed back. "Wait, why didn't you open it yet?"

"I can't do it," Wren says, their voice uncharacteristically shaky. "I know the scholarship doesn't determine whether or not I have talent or anything like that, but this is the first time my work is being judged by someone other than myself."

"Your work is incredible, Wren," Oliver says, handing them back the envelope. "Especially when it's modeled by yours truly. What's inside this thing has zero effect on that fact."

"They'd be crazy not to pick you," I say. "Your work is the stuff of nightmares. And I mean that in the best way possible."

"For real," Theo adds on. "I still can't get that image of Freddy as a radioactive killer clown out of my head."

"I couldn't get the paint out of my hair, either," Freddy says, his frown twitching at the edges. "I nearly gave my mom a heart attack when I showed up looking like that."

Wren cracks a smile. They take a deep breath, flipping the envelope over and running a fingernail along the seal. The table holds a collective breath as they unfold the paper, their lips forming soundless words as they read.

"Well?" asks Oliver as Wren lowers the letter. "Don't leave us hanging!"

"I got in."

A cheer ripples through the group, drawing the attention of the other tables on the crowded patio, but no one seems to care. Freddy is up from his chair, hugging Wren's neck. Oliver holds one of their hands while I reach for the other across the table. Harrison is snapping pictures of us as Elise jumps up and down, shrieking.

"Okay! Okay! Knock it off!" Wren tries to calm everyone down, but we're all too excited to listen, so Wren just has to sit there and bear the brunt of our love for them.

"So, does this mean you'll be going down to Atlanta for the summer?" Elise asks once the fervor has died down.

"Looks like it," Wren replies, looking over the paper again. "Mama and I were up late last night talking about the logistics if I got in, and she's got some time to take off work, so we'll look at renting a place in the city."

"Does that mean we can come visit you one weekend?" Theo asks. "You can paint us all up to look like zombies, and we'll shuffle down the sidewalk."

"Maybe we can just go to the aquarium instead," Wren suggests. "I think I'll have my hands full with the coursework."

"Ooo!" Elise exclaims, "I love the aquarium! The dolphin show is so good!"

"I want to hang out with the penguins," Harrison adds.

"The belugas are my favorite," Oliver says, then launches into a rendition of "Baby Beluga" that has all of us groaning by the second verse.

"I've got to go call my parents," Wren says, excusing themselves from the table.

Freddy wraps Oliver into a headlock in an effort to end his singing, but that just makes him sing louder in this weird, garbled voice that has all of us laughing.

"Hey, um, Freddy?"

Andrew stands at the corner of the table, looking at Freddy with a nervous smile. The group falls silent, and Freddy releases his hold on Oliver.

"Hey." He stares at Andrew, color draining from his face like he's looking at a ghost. And I guess, in some ways, he is. Freddy has been haunted by his love for this boy for weeks.

"Can I talk to you for a minute?"

Freddy looks at me, eyes wide, then back to Andrew, but he doesn't say anything.

Andrew takes a step towards him, then pauses, looking down at his feet. "I've been trying to call you, message you, I even stopped by the soccer field when y'all had a scrimmage last week, but you darted out before I could catch you."

"I thought you'd get the hint," Freddy says quietly.

"I know I messed up," Andrew says, looking up again. "I know that I didn't react like you wanted me to, but you have to understand. It's not easy for me to say something like that."

"You think it was easy for me?" Freddy asks, voice stronger as it takes on an edge. "You're the only guy I've ever said that to, Andrew. The only one. And I know I ghosted you, and that was shitty of me, but I just didn't want to get hurt any worse than I already was. Then I already *am*."

"I didn't mean to hurt you, Freddy. I didn't even know what to say that night. I–I never thought that anyone would feel that way about me. Especially you."

"What's that supposed to mean?"

Andrew wrings his hands together. "You sort of had a reputation. So, when you asked me out, I thought you'd be someone who wouldn't want anything serious."

"Oh, so you just thought I'd put out?"

"That's not what I meant!"

The entire patio is fixated on the two of them now, conversations paused as the argument plays out, drawing everyone's attention. Theo squeezes my hand. "Do we need to do something?"

I shake my head. Freddy's strong enough to handle this on his own.

"What do you mean, then?" Freddy asks, his arms folding across his chest. "Why did you agree to go out in the first place if you didn't think it would go anywhere?"

"Because I had a crush on you," Andrew confesses. "And I never in a million years thought it would last longer than a couple dates. But then, it did, and you were so great, and I was worried that I was leading you on. And sometime around Christmas, things started to change for me. We became so much more than I ever imagined we'd be."

"Obviously, it wasn't enough," Freddy says, voice wavering. "It wasn't enough to keep us together. It wasn't enough for you to love me."

"But that's just it," Andrew says, taking another step closer, his hands reaching for Freddy but stopping short. "I do love you. I just didn't know what it felt like. I didn't know how to put it into words. My family—we don't talk about this kind of thing. I can count on one hand the number of times my parents have said, 'I love you.' My older brothers, they're the same way. So, when you told me that you loved me, I freaked out. I did everything I could to walk away, to keep from going any further because I wasn't going to be able to say it back, and I wanted you to have someone who could return those feelings with no hesitation. You deserve that, Freddy.

"But then you were gone, and I couldn't talk to you anymore, and the longer you stayed away, the more I realized how much I'd fucked up by not telling you what I know to be true. I love you, Freddy Desoto. And I'm so sorry that I didn't say it sooner."

The patio goes quiet once more, all eyes on Freddy as he stares wide-eyed at Andrew.

And Freddy Desoto, Mr. Stone-Cold-Heart, the most confident guy I know, looks more shaken than I've ever seen him before. His fingers curl around the hem of his shirt, twisting in the fabric. For a second, I think he's going to burst into tears, but then he's speaking, his voice soft and even. "You love me?"

Andrew nods, lifting his glasses to wipe at his eyes. "Yes. Sorry it took so long for me to say it back."

Freddy takes the last step to close the distance between them. Andrew's throat bobs, and I swear, we all lean in as Freddy stands on his tiptoes to kiss him. Thunderous applause breaks out from the tables. Elise sobs into her frappe. The shutter of Harrison's camera goes crazy.

Theo squeezes my hand.

Wren appears from around Andrew with a puzzled expression. "I feel like I missed something."

Djo plays over the speaker in the corner of my room. The sun has just started to set, streaming in golden beams from the window that transfigure Theo's tan skin into patches of warm, glowing hues. His eyelids flutter open, breath catching as he spots me curled around his side, our legs tangled together atop the comforter on my bed.

"Did I fall asleep?" he mumbles, stretching his arms over his head. I stare in wonder at the strip of flesh revealed just above his waistline. I want to run my fingers along that exposed skin, but I resist the urge.

"Yeah, but only for a little bit."

He runs a hand through my hair, nails digging lightly into my scalp, sending waves of electric pulses down my spine. "We didn't get any work done," he says, looking at the stack of homework we promised ourselves we'd work on over the weekend.

"It's the last week of school," I say, wrapping an arm around his waist and pulling him closer. "There should be laws against homework during the last week."

Theo's chest rumbles with laughter. "You're not wrong."

The comfortable silence spreads back over us like a blanket, the playlist continuing on uninterrupted.

"I still can't wrap my head around what happened today with Freddy," I say after a moment, holding my phone above my head as I hit "like" on Freddy's picture of him and Andrew outside of Spookies.

"Were you jealous of Andrew's grand declaration?" Theo asks, knocking his foot against mine. "It was much more romantic than dropping it on you in the back seat of my car."

I snort a laugh, dropping his phone beside me on the bed and wrapping my arms around Theo's trunk. "I think we've both had enough grand gestures for a long, long time. Besides, if I'm being honest, I much prefer the quiet, little ways that you show me your love. Those are my favorite."

A warmth blooms in my chest as I nuzzle my head into Theo's side. He feels safe. He feels like home. And somewhere beyond the quiet conversations that last past the sunset, I find myself wishing that I could give him more. More love. More of myself. More of whatever he wants.

"Caleb, we're heading out!" Dad's voice trails up from the first floor. "We'll be back late."

"Okay!" I yell back. Sitting up, I add, "I forgot it's their date night."

"I guess I should get going," Theo says with a sigh, rising from his prone position. His hair sticks out in the back, and it's enough to make me reach out and smooth it down with my hand. Then his lips are on mine, and my fingers twist into his curls, and he lets out a gasp as I tug on them gently, exposing his neck to me.

With a trail of kisses, I make my way to his collarbone, trailing it lightly with my lips as his chest heaves with ragged breath.

"You… don't have to leave," I say, coming up for air.

He looks at me, eyebrows raised. "Really?"

I nod, and he's kissing me again, hands finding my waist as he pulls me onto his lap.

"Are you sure?" he asks, breathlessly against my lips.

"One hundred percent."

His dark eyes find mine once more.

"I want you."

He whispers it like it's a prayer. Like it's his confession, his deepest secret that he's ready to bring to light. And every word sends fire across my skin till my body burns and smolders with heat.

"We can," I whisper back, "if you want. I still have that box."

"I think I'm ready," Theo says, his hands trailing down my body with newfound excitement. "Are you sure it's okay?"

"More than okay," I breathe, the friction between us already sending me into a fit. "But…"

Theo pumps the brakes, gently pushing me away. "What is it?"

"It's going to be our first time," I say slowly, taking a second to calm down. "I just want to make sure the expectations are realistic. We're going to be far from perfect. Is that okay, Theo?"

He smiles, leaning forward to draw my forehead against his. "As long as it's with you, how can it be anything less than perfect?"

Theo isn't perfect. And neither am I. But as we lay under the sheets, the moonlight coming through the window along with the early crickets, I can't help but marvel at all the ways we fit together perfectly.

He was gentle like I knew he'd be. And I tried to be the same way when the roles were reversed because it was our first time, and Theo said he wanted to try it all.

I loved every second of it. Even the imperfect ones.

Theo stirs beside me, his breath catching. "Again?" he mumbles, rubbing his eyes with the back of his hand. "I swear, I don't mean to keep nodding off on you."

"It's okay," I tell him, planting a soft kiss on top of his head. "You're cute when you're dozing. It's only nine-thirty anyway, so you can keep sleeping. I won't let you miss curfew."

He lets out a sigh, nuzzling his curls into me. "You're the best."

"I love you, Theo," I whisper, hoping those words carry him back to his dreams as I hold the boy I love.

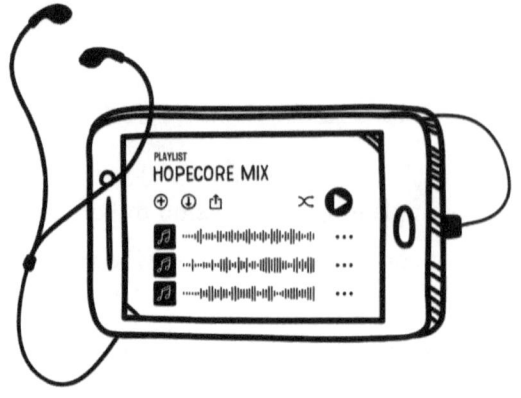

TWENTY-FOUR
THEO

Friday, June 28

The Cathy's dining room is bustling as the lunch rush peaks. A table opens up by the front door, and I hurry over with my bus pan, clearing the cups, dishes, and half-eaten vegetables away before spraying them down with my trusty bottle of sanitizer. Once everything is in order, I heft the pan up onto my shoulder, carrying it back to the bussing station and sliding it onto the cart.

"Did you see the guy on thirty-three?" Jake asks, tossing a cleaning cloth over his shoulder. "I think I'm in love."

"You say that about almost every guy that walks in here," I tease him, making sure the coast is clear before I check my phone. Still no message from Caleb today, but it's still kind of early in Arizona. The regular routine of eight-hour shifts has really kept me from missing him too much while he's been away. That, and the fact that we talk nearly every night.

God, I can't wait till he gets back.

"Ew, you're doing that thing again." Jake scrunches his nose.

"What thing?"

"That thing when you look all doe-eyed while you're thinking about Caleb."

We get it. You're in love. It's kinda nauseating, man."

I shove my phone back in my pocket, then spritz him with my sanitizer bottle.

"Hey!"

"Oops, my bad."

A frazzled server pokes their head around the corner. They've got ketchup smeared across their shirt and desperation in their eyes. "Guys, can I get some help clearing the counter? I just got triple sat."

"We're on it," I say, grabbing my pan again and heading over to the row of stools that line the counter. Jake starts at the opposite end, and we work our way to the middle, emptying drinks and stacking plates.

For only having been working at Cathy's for a few weeks, he's caught on quickly. It was the start of the summer when he called me, from a number I didn't have saved, and let me know that he was leaving his parents' house. They apparently were throwing around the idea to send him off to some conversion camp out in Utah, so he decided it was time to get out of there. His friend from school, Shauna, offered to let him crash at her place for the entire school year if he needs it. He says her parents are super chill, and she's got a little brother that adores him.

I would have offered the same, but he seems happy to be with Shauna's family, so helping him get this job was a way I could still feel supportive of him. There've been some bad days here and there, but he's really taking it all in stride.

It makes me wonder if I would have been as strong if things hadn't panned out for me.

"I'm full up," Jake says, motioning to the overflowing pan beside him.

"Me too," I say, stacking the last few dishes on top. "I'll take these to the back if you want to finish wiping down."

"Do you trust me with your spray bottle?" Jake asks with a sly grin.

I roll my eyes, passing it over the counter. "Be gentle. I've seen how trigger-happy you can get with the window cleaner."

Jake gives me a salute. "I'll treat her well, sir."

I snort a laugh, grabbing the cart from a nearby station to load up the two bus pans of dishes and wheel them into the dish room. The owner's son—Randy, the fifteen-year-old restaurant savant—takes the cart from me, not slowing down for a second as he dumps the dishes onto the wash station. I decide it's best to stay out of Randy's way, lest he accidentally stick me in the dishwasher along with the silverware, and hurry back out into the dining room. Jake's not where I left him at the counter, but the shiny surface tells me that our job is complete, and a clump of customers take the empty seats at the counter.

On my way back to the bus station, I spot Jake in the dining room, talking to someone at a table in the corner. Maybe he's found another love of his life in the two minutes I've been gone? It's almost time for us to go sweep the parking lot, so I make my way over, but then I catch a glimpse of reddish-brown hair and realize too late who he's talking to.

"Look who it is, Theo," Jake says, grabbing me by the elbow before I can sneak away. "Our favorite little missionary, home from her latest trip across the world!"

Sienna bristles at the sight of me, her hand immediately going to her ponytail as she fidgets nervously. "Hi, Theodore. Long time no see. Haven't seen you at church lately."

"Yeah," I say, even though I could have gone the rest of my life without laying eyes on her again and have been happy. "I've been really busy with work this summer."

Better leave it at that than get into the nitty gritty of my choice to stop going to church. Mostly, it's because my dad is there. But if I'm being honest with myself, that's not the only reason.

Jake gives me a knowing look but, thankfully, keeps his mouth shut.

"What about you, Jake? I miss seeing you in worship."

"Oh, yeah, I don't think you'll be seeing me around anymore since I came out and my parents decided it was time for me to be shipped off to some pray the gay away camp out west. I got out of there fast as I could. Told them they can shove that idea right up their—"

"Jake, can I get a hand over here?"

"Sorry, gotta run. Good to see you!"

Jake abandons me. The traitor.

"He moved out?" Sienna says, watching Jake as he leaves.

"It was a better option than what would have happened if he stayed."

"His parents just said he was going through a rough patch," she continues with a confused frown. "They put him on the prayer list like there was nothing more that could be done. Like he was a neighbor with the flu, not their own child who doesn't have a place to live."

"He's staying with friends," I say, not sure why I want to alleviate her guilt. "People who love him completely, no strings attached. But, hey, I'm sure the prayer thing will work out for the best."

"That could have happened to you," she says, her crystal blue eyes finally looking up at me. "It could have happened to you, and it would have been my fault."

A twinge in my stomach and I have to fight the urge to comfort her.

"You're right. I was lucky. I only lost a father, not my whole family."

Sienna's lip trembles, and I find myself holding back anger. What does she have to be upset about? She's the one who blew up my life. She was the one who was so blind in her need to be a good Christian that she destroyed the relationship I had with my father, maybe forever.

And even though I know these things are true, even though the anger roiling in my gut feels more righteous than anything I've ever felt before, I still can't bring myself to come down on her. The heat within me flickers and fades, replaced by a swell of pity. I let out a sigh, sinking into the booth across from Sienna.

She looks up at me, blotting away a tear that trickles down her flushed cheeks.

"I'm so sorry, Theo. I can't—I don't know what else to say. What else I can do."

"There's nothing else to be done, Sienna," I say honestly. "And I can't forgive you. Not right now, at least. Maybe I'll be able to someday. But, in the meantime, there *is* something you can do."

"What is it?" she asks, her voice almost pleading.

"Don't let it happen to anyone else."

Sienna leans forward, her brow furrowed. "What?"

"There's going to be more," I explain. "More people than just me and Jake that question themselves at that church. And if you plan to stay there, if you really want to make up for what you did, then you can help them. There's a good chance they're going to feel alone. Like their community could turn on them at the drop of a hat. They'll need someone who's on their side. Who can advocate for them. That could be you."

"But I don't—how will do that?"

"Do what you do best, Sienna. Just help people. Be kind and empathetic. Listen to them. And if they confide in you, keep that confidence. Let them know they're not alone, and connect them with people who can help. There're some programs over at Specter Methodist that are specifically for queer people of faith. I can send you the info."

Sienna watches me silently, her blue eyes full and cautious, like she's still waiting for me to bring the hammer down.

I slide out of the booth, standing at the edge of the table. "What you did was shitty, Sienna. But what's done is done, and we can't take things back. We can only move forward. If you really want to help, then you'll think about what I asked."

"Okay," she replies, her voice a whisper.

I nod, glancing over my shoulder to where Jake is busy helping clear a large table in the center of the dining room. "I've got to get back to work. But… it was good to see you, Sienna."

"You, too, Theo."

Jake gives me an expectant look when I join him at the table.

"What?" I ask, grabbing a stack of cups and dumping them into the bus pan.

"Nothing. I just expected there to be more shouting."

"I'm not really a shouter," I say.

"That's not what I heard from Caleb."

I fling my towel at him, and he swats it away with a laugh.

The afternoon heat wraps me in a stifling embrace as I leave Cathy's, heading for where Eileen is parked in the gravel lot behind the restaurant. My phone buzzes, and I check the group chat. Harrison is confirming the time that we're going to meet tomorrow to drive down to Atlanta and visit Wren. They've been gone for almost a month now, and other than the daily pictures we get of their grotesque coursework, they've been too busy to do much else.

I tap a "like" to Harrison's message, stowing my phone just in time to catch the shadow of the person moving from behind my car.

"Hello, Theo."

My father stands on the passenger side of my car. He's parked next to me, I realize, his navy sedan looking dirtier than I've seen it in a while.

"What are you doing here?" I ask, not wasting time with pleasantries.

I haven't seen him in a few weeks. The last time he tried to stop by the house, Mom wouldn't even let him inside. Nathaniel was in the kitchen, eating breakfast with his headphones on. They stood out on the porch and talked for an hour, but then he left, and Mom went straight to the guest bathroom downstairs to try and hide her bloodshot eyes. I tried to ask her about it, but she said it was nothing and that he'd be back soon.

But I knew she was lying.

"I wanted to speak with you. Would that be okay?"

I glance around, a few of my coworkers lingering in the lot between their shifts.

"Can we go someplace else?"

"Sure," Dad says, a weak smile spreading across his face. "Anywhere you want."

"Spookies. I'll meet you out on the patio."

"Okay. See you there."

I climb into the driver's seat, my hands shaking as I plug in my phone out of habit. A song starts up, but I don't even register what it is. I text my mom, letting her know that Dad showed up and wants to talk. She responds immediately asking if I want her to be there, too. But I tell her I'll be fine and that I'll let her know when we're done.

I think about texting Caleb, but I don't want to worry him.

The drive over to Spookies takes only a few minutes, and I've already drummed up enough theoretical scenarios to make my head spin. But once I'm in the parking lot, surrounded by the familiarity of the inflatable Halloween décor, there's nothing left to do but face my father.

He's waiting for me on the patio, staring down at his phone. The patch of grey in his beard has doubled in size since the last time I saw him up close. He looks up as I approach, sitting up straight and stowing his phone back into the pocket of his button-down shirt. He must have come from work.

"Thank you for coming," he says, his voice softer than I'm used to hearing. "Did you want something to drink?"

"I'd rather we get right to it," I reply, my stomach clenched tight enough that I might be sick. "What do you want?"

Dad fidgets, moving his hands from the table to his lap and then back to the edge of the table before he speaks. "I wanted to apologize to you, Theo, for the way that I responded to you. It was wrong of me to try and make decisions for you, especially in that manner, so I wanted you to know that I'm sorry."

"Okay." I'm not sure I can manage anything else around the lump in my throat.

"I've been staying with my brother over in Gainesville while your mother and I work some things out. He's been helping me think through how best to move forward as a family, but I needed to make sure that we spoke first, man-to-man. For me to tell you just how much I miss you, son. How much I love you."

I swallow harshly, a tear spilling as I blink, unable to look away from my father's face. He sounds so sincere. And as much as I'd like to deny it, I've missed him, too. So much. But things are different now. I'm different. I need to know that he is, too.

"Do you still think that me loving Caleb is a sin?"

"Theo, we don't have to talk about that right now—"

"Answer the question."

He flinches. I've never seen my father look small before. He's always been an imposing presence. But right now, as he fidgets in his chair, I can't help but think about how small he seems.

"It's complicated," Dad finally says.

"It's really not," I reply.

"Theo, I didn't come here to argue theology with you—"

"How am I supposed to have a relationship with someone who thinks that my love is a sin? Who thinks that my *existence* is enough to damn me forever?"

"Theo, please," Dad pleads, shaking his head. "We're a family."

"You don't get to say that anymore. I have a family, Dad. A family who chose to love all of me, not just the perfect parts. Mom, Grace, Nate—their love was never conditional. My friends never stopped loving me for a second when I came out. This is a 'you' problem, Dad. Your love for archaic rules must outweigh the love you have for me, and if that's the case, then I want nothing to do with you."

I stand, my knees shaking only for a second before I ground myself and square a look at my father. He's slouching again, his back against the chair as he watches me.

"You've grown."

"I miss you, Dad," I say because it's the truth. "I'm also happier than I've ever been."

Dad nods, his face crumpling.

I walk away before he can hear me cry.

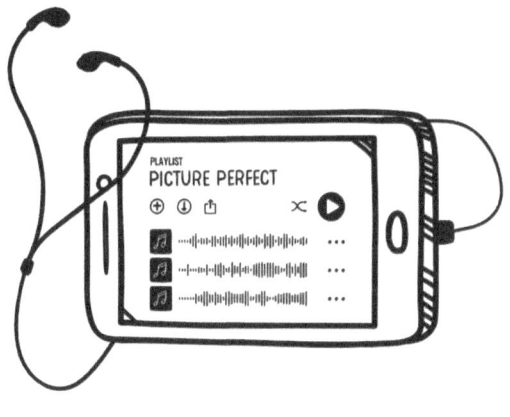

EPILOGUE
THEO

Saturday, July 13

Any minute, Caleb is going to walk through the front door, and I'm trying not to stare a hole into it.

"Dude, you're going to vibrate into the fourth dimension if you don't calm down."

Lola sits on the couch, a neat stack of files beside her laptop on the coffee table and a legal pad in her lap. She was nice enough to let me in when I showed up an hour ago, too excited to sit at home any longer. I've tried to keep myself contained to a recliner, but the nervous energy got to be too much and now I'm pacing the edge of the long rug that runs through the middle of the living room.

"Sorry," I mutter, kneeling down next to the coffee table and folding my legs under me. "I'll try and sit still."

"Best of luck," Lola replies with a grin, scribbling something down on her pad before she moves on to the next file. "You know, it's been so quiet around here without Caleb and Dad. Mom and I end up talking about work all day. It'll be nice to get a break from all of the cutthroat, soul-eating carnage for a while."

"That sounds... unpleasant."

Lola shrugs. "I'm getting kind of into it, actually. I understand why Mom's stuck it out as long as she has. There's just something exciting about taking these two diametrically opposed forces and standing between them while they hurtle toward each other at a thousand miles an hour. Plus, you get to stick to awful rich men every now and then, which is something I could *really* get used to."

"Glad to see you're starting to enjoy your work," I say, leaning my elbows on the table as I glance at the stack of folders. "It's sort of hard to imagine all of these relationships coming to an end. Doesn't it make you sad?"

"It did when I first started," Lola says, shuffling through the next file. "But not so much anymore. People get divorced for a multitude of reasons, not all of them are sad. And to be honest, most divorces are very cut and dry. Just an agreement between two partners to go their separate ways. One could look at it as a new beginning if they were optimistic enough."

She grabs another file, and my eye is drawn to a familiar name on the next folder. *Kora Briggs.* My heart skips a beat, then slams into my chest like a jackhammer. I reach for the file, Lola's head snapping up from her work.

"Hey, you can't—"

"It's my mom," I say flatly, opening the file and scanning over the information.

"Oh, honey." Lola sets aside her work, coming to my side and kneeling next to me. "I didn't know that was in my stack today. I'm so sorry, Theo. This is a terrible way to find out."

"I'm okay," I say, setting the file down face up on the table. My mind races, linking together the evidence I've been ignoring over the last few months. "I had my suspicions that this would happen, but it's still kind of wild to see it for real."

"Are you going to talk to your mom about it?"

I shake my head. "Not till she comes to me, I think. She'll let me know when she's ready."

"You're taking this really well, Theo."

Am I? It feels like this whole situation has been inevitable since Caleb's birthday. Not that I blame him or anything. It's just the day that Dad drew his line in the sand. And now the entire family has crossed over to my side. It sucks that he made us choose to begin with, but I'm not going to lie and say that I'm not happy to have Mom, Grace, and Nate supporting me.

The front door opens, Nora's voice drifting in from the other room.

"We're back!"

Lola takes the folder, adding it back to her stack as I scramble to my feet, skidding into the hall. Nora smiles when she sees me. "I had a feeling you'd be here." She wraps me up in a quick hug, then turns back toward the door. "Caleb's just grabbing his luggage. The boy came back with an extra suitcase because he bought so many souvenirs. Just something to keep in mind if you're thinking about sharing a space with him one day." She winks at me, then moves into the living room.

I rush out onto the porch, meeting Caleb at the top of the stairs. I don't care that he's carrying three suitcases and a duffle bag. I grab him, crushing him against me with enough force that his feet leave the ground for a moment.

"Theo… I need to breathe."

I set him down but don't let go, my body too starved of his touch to allow myself. He's grinning at me, his nose red and his freckles darker than I remember. He sets the suitcases down, shoving the duffle behind him as he returns my hug, resting his head on my shoulder.

"Oh my god, I missed you so much."

He smells like sunscreen and peppermint, and I can't get enough of the relief that washes over me now that he's back in my arms. It's a little frightening how much I missed him. But I'll worry about that later. Right now, I just need to soak up as much Caleb as I can.

"Watch out, Dad coming through." Bert maneuvers around us, every spare inch of him covered in luggage. "I can't feel my fingers, but I'm sure it'll be fine."

"Let me help," I say, my body screaming at me when I release my hold on Caleb. I take two of the outermost bags from Bert, slinging them on my shoulders.

"Isn't he the best?" Caleb asks his dad.

"I've always thought so, no matter what your mother says."

I look at Caleb, but he's laughing. "Don't listen to him. Mom's crazy about you, too. She complained all the way home that with me out of the house, you don't come around, and she's missed you, too."

A warmth swells in my chest as we move through the front door, Bert dropping his bags in the foyer.

"Oh, it's so good to be home," he says, bracing his hands on his back and taking in a deep breath. "I never thought I'd miss the humidity so much. Whoever thought it was a good idea to go to Arizona in the summer should be fired. Out of a cannon, preferably."

Caleb makes eye contact with Bert and they both say in unison, "It's a dry heat," then burst into laughter at their inside joke. They seem closer than ever, and that warmth in my chest twinges a bit as I realize I'm envious of that connection.

"I've got so many stories for you," Caleb says, nodding his head towards the stairs to get me to follow him. We climb up to his room, and he sighs with relief as he unloads the luggage onto the floor.

"Oh my god, your bed is actually made," I tease him.

"Mom must have done it while I was gone," he says, sitting in his desk chair and rolling it over to the first suitcase. "Because I know for a fact I left it a mess."

"That sounds more like it."

He sticks his tongue out at me, unzipping the suitcase and pulling out armfuls of clothing that he tosses into the hamper beside his desk.

There's so much I want to tell him. Too many things that happened over the summer that didn't feel right leaving in a text thread. But for the moment, I'm content settling into the corner of the bed, watching the boy I love dart back and forth as he recounts his time away. He tells me about the strange hotel they stayed at that seemed to be carved out of the red-hued rock from the area. About the early mornings out in the desert before the sun rose over the mountains and the amazing colors that changed by the second there on the sands. About the way his dad's job worked and the race against the clock to capture the lighting their shot required. I was enamored with a place I'd never been, listening to Caleb's stories.

And it strikes me just how much I want to be there with him the next time he goes on an adventure. To witness the ways he interacts with the world. I want be the one with the inside jokes and be a part of the stories that he brings home.

Most of all, I just want Caleb.

"Okay," he says, stowing the last of his clothes and collapsing on the bed next to me. "I've done enough talking. Tell me about your summer."

"Work has been good," I start, shifting till I'm parallel with him on the bed, and I take his hand in mine. "Jake's really got the hang of it now. It's actually fun when we're working the same shifts."

"How is he doing?" Caleb asks, rolling on his side to face me. "Is he still crashing at Shauna's?"

"Yeah, he is. And for the most part, he's okay. Or at least, as okay as he can be. I don't really know how anyone can truly be okay with that situation. But I told him that he's going to love Specter High and that he's totally invited to our table for lunch."

"Tell the rainbow sheep he's found his flock," Caleb says with a laugh.

"Wren's Atlanta apartment is really cool. The group went down a few weeks ago, and it's right off the beltline, so we walked over to Ponce City Market and ate ramen, then checked out this cool boutique artist shop, so Harrison and Elise bought matching Pokémon artwork, and Oliver bought this weird fedora because he's Oliver, and Freddy wouldn't stop making fun of the hat, which only made Oliver more determined to wear it, so you know, just the usual shenanigans."

"Glad to see that things haven't changed all that much."

"And then there's the stuff with my dad…"

Caleb wraps an arm around me. "We don't have to talk about it unless you want to."

"No, it's okay. He met me after work one day, sort of out of the blue, and asked if we could talk. He started off apologizing, and for this split second, I really thought he was going to say that he'd had a change of heart. He told me that he was sorry for how he reacted with the whole situation on your birthday and that he wanted to move forward as a family and come back home. But something didn't feel right, so I asked him if he still felt like me being with you was a sin. And he wasn't able to give me a straight answer, which ended up being the answer."

Caleb scrunches his nose. "Fuck that guy."

I snort a laugh. "Yeah, I pretty much told him the same thing. Except, you know, he's still my dad, so maybe I didn't say fuck."

"You totally should have said fuck."

"I totally should have said fuck. But I did tell him that I can't have a relationship with someone who thinks that who I am is literally evil. So, we left it at that."

Caleb places a hand on the side of my face. "Are you okay?"

"Yeah, I'm fine," I say quickly. But that's not true, and I'm trying to do better about putting on a 'perfect' face in front of Caleb, so I add, "I'm not, actually. I'm pretty messed up about it. It really hurt to walk away from him like that. And I know it's what I should have done, and I know if I let him back into my life, it would only hurt worse, but I wanted to, Caleb. I really, really did."

He pulls me closer. "I know, babe. I know. I am so proud of you for standing up to him like that. It took so much courage. Honestly, you're such a badass, and I just want to make sure you're fully aware of that."

The sound of a camera shutter pulls me away from him.

"What was that?" I ask.

Caleb turns his phone around, showing me the picture of us, tangled up in one another.

"For the collage," he says, tapping on the screen. The printer whirrs to life on his desk, the photo coming into existence before I can argue. He rolls onto his side, snatching it and holding it above the two of us. "Oh yeah, that's the one."

It's not the perfect picture. Caleb's eyes are closed and I have my face pressed into his side. It's off-center, and in the corner, you can see a pair of socks on the floor that slipped out from Caleb's suitcase.

It's not perfect. But it is perfectly us.

"You know, I think you're right," I say, letting out a choked laugh as I bury my face in his chest. His words from earlier sink in as we lay in silence. I'm not brave. Not as brave as I should be. But Caleb makes me want to be. He makes me want to be the guy he's describing, to measure up to his expectations—not out of necessity, but because I know he sees the potential in me. The perfection behind the imperfect.

And when he kisses me, it sets my skin aflame, and my brain buzzes with the electricity that followed me home all those months ago from Saint Catherine's, this beautiful, wonderful spark that caught and burned away all of the facades I had surrounded myself in.

I'll never be perfect. But thanks to him, I'll always be me.

ACKNOWLEDGEMENTS

We are so back! Thank you so much for joining us on another dive into the lives of Theo and Caleb. The response from **THEORETICALLY STRAIGHT** has been overwhelming (in the best way) and absolutely appreciated.

Working alongside my best friend, Amy, to bring another story to life has been such an amazing honor. Amy, thank you for allowing me to funnel your creativity into another piece of incredible art. We make a great team, and I can't wait to see what the future holds for you as you continue your journey as an author. I love you so much!

I would also like to thank my husband, Cecil, for his continuous support and for always being my biggest cheerleader. You are so precious to me, and I look forward to many more years of sappy acknowledgments ahead.

I'd also like to thank the award-winning Molly Phipps at We Got You Covered Book Designs for her incredible work on formatting this book and creating the cover design. I cannot recommend her enough for anyone looking for book services! Also, a big shout out to the artist for our cover art, Sara Pulsifer, who did another fantastic job of bringing Theo and Caleb to life. You're amazing, Sara! And lastly, I'd like to thank the readers who have supported me throughout the years. Whether this is the first of my books you've picked up (Dude, that's weird. This is the sequel! You're missing important context!) or the seventh, I can't explain to you how much it means to me. Thank you, thank you, thank you! If you wish to support me further, you can leave a review for this or any of my other books that you've enjoyed (or didn't enjoy! I love a good 1-star review. Keeps me humble).

With love,
ALEXANDER

I'm so grateful to be writing acknowledgments for a second book! Let's see if I can keep it short this time.

To Jackson—my amazing husband of ten human years! Thank you for continuing to be such an incredible, encouraging, and loving partner. It's hard to believe we've been married a decade and yet, in the words of Daði Freyr, "How does it keep getting better? Everyday our love finds a new way to grow." Here's to many, many more years of love and growth with you, my love.

To Alex—my coauthor, my best friend, my person. You've always been the best, but thank you specifically for your unwavering support and encouragement throughout this entire project. You've never given up on me, even on the days that you probably should have. Thank you for getting our story across the finish line and ensuring our beloved boys got the finale they deserved.

To Mal—the Caleb to my Theo, the Ed to my Stede. I love you and I'm so happy we found each other. Thank you for everything.

To the rest of my extraordinary circle of friends and family—I love and adore every single one of you. Special shout-outs go out to Jess, Patrick, Justin, Leah, Cecil, Jaclene, Chance, Jodi, Steve, Carol, Phillip, Laurel, Matthew, Clarice, Staci, and Robert. Your endless support and love mean the world to me.

To Sara Pulsifer, Molly Phipps, Mark Sanderlin, and Jacob Bell—thank you for helping us bring our boys to life! Sara and Molly, thank you for your amazing work on our cover art. And thank you Mark, Jacob, and everyone on the Podium team for giving our boys their own unique voices.

And finally, to our readers—thank you for picking up these queer stories and sharing them in your communities. And to our fellow queer readers specifically---we see you, we hear you, we love you, and we'll never stop advocating for you.

Until next time,
AMY

ABOUT THE AUTHORS

AMY BAILEY (she/they) and **ALEXANDER EBERHART** (he/him) have been best friends for almost twenty years. They both grew up in the Metro Atlanta Area, bouncing from suburb to suburb until they eventually landed in the same church as preteens, and they've been pretty inseparable ever since.

Alexander has always had a passion for writing, even from a young age. He still lives on the cusp of Atlanta with his husband and their pets. He has penned five Young Adult novels, all revolving around the Atlanta area, and enjoys bringing an underrepresented setting to life in imaginative and (sometimes) hilarious ways. When not crafting quality queer fiction, Alexander works for a local company in the service industry and enjoys running D&D campaigns for his friends. Explore the library of his work at **alexanderceberhart.com**.

Amy (known as Bailey to their online friends) has dabbled with creative writing sporadically over the past two decades, but it wasn't until recently that the creative floodgates truly opened up for them. They've written roughly 250,000 words of fanfiction over the past year and won't stop until they've reached a million! When they aren't hunched over their laptop, Amy can be found playing Dungeons & Dragons, going to the movies with friends, or backseat gaming on the couch with their wonderful husband, Jackson, and their beloved pets, Olive and Ruby.

www.ingramcontent.com/pod-product-compliance
Lightning Source LLC
LaVergne TN
LVHW041746060526
838201LV00046B/921